THE

FAIRNESS

of

BEASTS

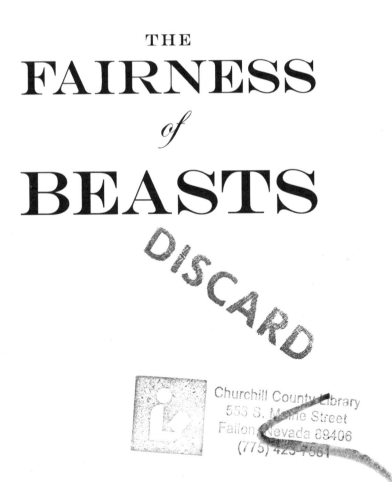

BOOK THREE *of the* WIDOW WALK SAGA

THE

FAIRNESS

of

BEASTS

GAR LaSALLE

ISBN: 978-0-9978436-1-3

Published by Solipsis Publishing Seattle, WA
SolipsisPublishing.com

Copyright 2017 Solipsis Publishing
Editor: John DeDakis

Design: Maps and The Fairness of Beasts Medallion — Randy Mott (MottGraphics.com)

Cover Design: Neil Gonzalez (Greenleaf Book Group - (GreenleafBookgroup.com)

Interior Design: Alex Head (TheDraftLab.com)
Social Media and Web Design: Scott James

Web design: Archana Murthy and Scott James

Audio Book Production: Mike McAuliffe, Tom McGurk, Wendy Wills (Bad Animals.com)

SOLIPSIS PUBLISHING

To the Equanimity

TABLE OF
CONTENTS

DRAMATIS PERSONAE
THE FAMILY

Emmy (O'Malley) Evers – the Widow
Sarah Evers – Emmy's thirteen-year-old daughter
Jacob Evers – Emmy's nine-year-old son
Kathleen (O'Malley) McEmeel – Emmy's older sister
Major Jon Evan McEmeel – Kathleen's husband
*Congressman Kern O'Malley – father of Emmy Evers
and her sister, Kathleen McEmeel*
Na'Pen'Tjo (Jojo) – a Bella Coola Native American

THE COMBATANTS, OPPORTUNISTS
AND BYSTANDERS

Doctor Rory Brett – Emmy's fiancé
*Major Jonah Cross – Dragoon & former special guard for
General Winfield Scott*
*General Benjamin Butler – Commander – Governor of captured
New Orleans, former law partner of Congressman
Kern O'Malley*
Henri Lebo – a contraband smuggler
Pen Basetyr – a contraband smuggler
Otis Loller – Sheriff of Henrico County, Virginia
Reverend Ardy Dabbs – a Methodist preacher
Jedediah – a waif
Clarissa – a waif
Janie James – Proprietress of Noah's Ark
Josie DeMerritt – Proprietress of DeMerritt's "School"
Robby Hoyt – a waif
*Jonny and Falco Scarpello – waifs and friends of Sarah
and Jacob Evers*
Roland Escoffiere – a French diplomat
Doyle "Church" Grimes – a Private investigator

MAPS ONE AND TWO:
THE FIRST BATTLE OF BULL RUN:
MCEMEEL'S MARCH, KATHLEEN'S PICNIC

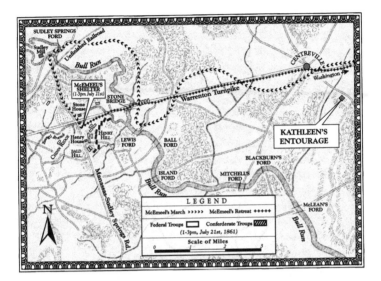

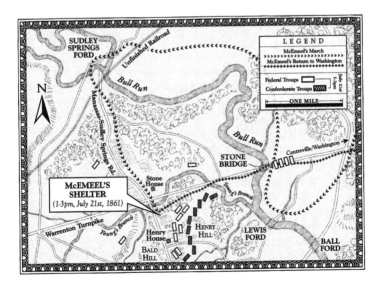

MAP THREE:
THE PENINSULA WAR AND
THE SEVEN DAYS BATTLES

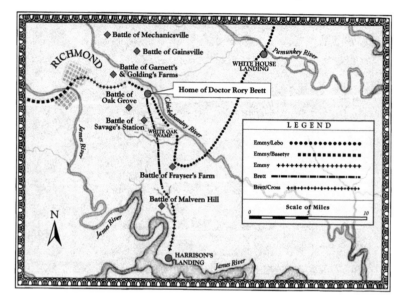

MAP FOUR:
ROUTES TAKEN BY EMMY AND LEBO,
EMMY AND BASETYR

MAP FIVE:
ORPHAN TRAIN ROUTES - 1862

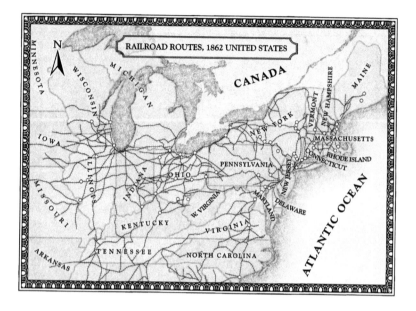

PROLOGUE

◇◇◇◇

Sarah

February 15, 1861 Washington, District of Columbia

Sarah knew how they viewed her and her brother: "Lying bumpkins. "Yarn-spinners," one of the other children had mocked.

"Four steps behind in education and four miles behind in manners" she had heard been said by one of the older girls in the special school created for the children of congressmen and senators.

But they *weren't* tall yarns at all . . . about how a griz killed Marano Levy, bit through his head and jaw, it most certainly did, before he could get off another shot and then she had to help her mother and Jojo bury the poor man with his Spanish Bible in the frozen ground,

– and how she had hit a drunk, naked Russian sea captain in the head with his own whiskey bottle when he was trying to mount her mother,

– and how her step-father had been murdered and the Northerners took his head and showed it off, up and down the coast for weeks, and then her mother lost her baby,

– and how she, because she was old enough while her mother was sick in a coma, had to help her Aunt Cory and Mrs. Crockett with the tiny fetus that would have been another brother if it had lived because she saw it was a boy before they buried him,

– and how her brother Jacob, after he was kidnapped and then got rescued, had told her that he had bitten several of the Northerners who kidnapped him,

– And how he thought the Devil, yes the Devil himself, had taken him,

– and how the Northerners kept him tied up and beat him, and how Jacob thought he saw their father's ghost when he was kept in the Northerner's camp, and how he had started wetting his bed again and was setting fires under their grandfather's desk at his home up in Boston, because he dreamed the devils were coming back again,

– and how she and Jacob and two other kids, little ones, had gotten lost in the Panama jungle during the train robbery when so many passengers had been murdered, and how they had been found by the Panama aborigines and were taken to their huts and kept,

– and how the aborigines put tattoos on her and the other children's faces and chests which kept the flies and mosquitoes away, and how the aborigines had decided to take them back to the railroad and just leave them at the side of the tracks, and how they never heard from their protector, Jojo again after that robbery,

– and how the robber that had taken their mother hostage down there had mailed her brother Jacob a huge diamond that had blood on it. And how their mother had a beau now and both she and Jacob thought he was what their mother needed, to protect them maybe, even if their mother wasn't so sure yet.

They weren't tall yarns. It was *all* true.

But she and Jacob had to fight with the other children, especially the older ones in the school over and over again, every day it seemed, whenever they tried telling any of them about what had happened to them in the Pacific Northwest and down in Panama.

She understood why they thought she was spinning yarns.

She couldn't prove any of it.

Her tattoos had faded away and the rest of the students at the Washington, DC school thought they were a lot smarter than her or Jacob because she and her brother didn't read as well as they all did. Not yet, at least.

She forgave them. She told Jacob he should do the same. Forgive them. Because their classmates were only children, after all. Children. No matter if they were the same age or even older than she was. No matter how the boys behaved, attractive brats that they were. It really didn't matter at all because she was an old soul, after all, and there were more important things she had to worry about.

There was a war going on now.

CHAPTER ONE

◇◇◇◇

Brett

July 2, 1862 Piney Grove, Virginia

He'd never seen roosters run like that, straight in a row-one after another. A brood of roosters, big shiny black ones, bouncing comically, all in a line just over the hill parallel to the ridge, behind a yellow band of low grass and red rocks. They were following each other, spaced neatly six feet apart looking just like some Frisco fancy dancers prancing onto a stage and wearing tiaras with dark, pretty plumes.

So, for a moment it was a wonder, the type he would have marked and then tucked away to be brought out some other time. To reminisce about in a shake of his head, as he remembered his grandfather did from time to time about such things he said he had seen once in his lifetime. And

4

in that moment, he also wondered in his delirium, whether he would live long enough to ever get to do that sort of reminiscing.

But they weren't roosters. They were hats. That's what they were. Felt slouch hats with tall, flounced black cock feathers bobbing up and down. And when he felt the vibration and rumble tumble of hoof beats drumming at the same time, he knew it was cavalry. Union cavalry. Had to be. The rebels riding with J.E.B Stuart didn't wear black hats anymore and Stuart was far away, protecting Lee's far-flung flank from counter attack. And when the riders' heads and shoulders came into full view he saw they had turned at a right angle after cresting the near ridge. Now they were riding right towards him. Down the hill. Fast. Six of them. A brood of fancy-black-hat dragoons, swords clanking in their scabbards.

He hoped no one still left alive, hiding in the burned out wagons would do anything foolish, like take a shot at the oncoming Yankee riders. But no one raised a weapon. They all just waited for yet another cruel, mean attack. He did the same. Waited. They hadn't drawn their swords. So he held his breath, and wondered if he could reason with them. Hoped he could. But then he saw it was Cross who led the troop – Jonah Cross, wearing a white sling around his head and jaw, and he knew he would not be able to get past this one.

After searching through the remnants of the wagons, Cross found him. The Yank reared his mount, then trotted right up to Brett's litter, ignoring all the other wounded men lying around. Cross pushed his hat back on his head with the barrel of his pistol.

"Doctor Rory Brett," said Cross, his jaw thrust forward, his lower lip pulled up on one side into what seemed to be a satisfied smirk. "Been a long time a finding you. Am placing you under arrest for desertion from the United States Army."

Brett wondered if he would be hanged right there on the spot. But they took him away, and left behind all the other wounded in what remained of the destroyed ambulance train, to rot with all the scattered corpses lying around-dead horses and dead men, bloating and popping in the July afternoon's heat.

The Yanks cinched his wrists to the horn on the saddle of a tired mule, hauled him onto the mount, and trailed the animal behind them. As Brett was trotted away, he looked back at the debris left over from the previous day's attack that had left all sixty of the ambulance and supply wagons in ruins and hundreds of seriously wounded, but salvageable men dead.

It hadn't been a fight at all. The rebel ambulances had been caught in the open moving away from the Malvern Hill battle along a trail that some called the Piney Ridge Road. The Union cavalry, at least six or seven hundred of them, charged out of the woods whooping down onto the stumbling, slowly moving defenseless Confederates.

The slaughter was indiscriminate. In one rapid pass through, the cavalry cut down blind men, helpless amputees and debilitated malaria-stricken soldiers like him. They shot the teamsters and all the lorry horses. They set fire to wagons filled with wounded soldiers, barrels of pork and sacks of flour. They shot down anyone attempting to extinguish the flames. Then they rode out, whistling and cursing. With the pork barrels on fire, it smelled like a picnic for a while.

Brett, who somehow had been able to gather enough strength to push himself out and free of the burning wagon in which he was riding, remembered seeing someone wearing a sling around his jaw partially covering a familiar face in the crowd of Blue Bellies that ravaged the train. He thought it might have been Cross, who had paused for a moment, seemed to take note of him, and then had ridden on. But he hoped it wasn't that man, for he knew Jonah Cross all too well.

Two years ago it was Cross who had led the marshals searching for Brett in Panama, after he had abruptly resigned from his commission while part of the entourage of Winfield Scott. Brett's superior officer had refused to accept the resignation and threatened to call the assistant surgeon's departure a desertion.

But Rory Brett had left anyway.

Three weeks later, Brett emerged from Panama's Darién Gap jungle with the famous vigilante, Ran Runnels, and a wounded woman, Emmy Evers, they had rescued from bandits. When the military command learned of this, they sent the only soldier remaining in the isthmus who would have recognized Brett to arrest him. That was Jonah, bringer-of-bad-luck Cross, then a dragoon sergeant who served as a security guard for Winfield Scott.

Cross was a perfect choice for the task, Brett reflected. Always the self righteous one, a fervent follower of Winfield Scott and the general's insistence on order and protocol, he pursued Brett's apprehension with a passionate intensity. He tracked Brett down at the American hospital in Colon-Aspinwall where the love-struck young doctor had encamped himself to attend to the recuperation of the American woman.

Brett narrowly escaped arrest by crawling out onto the ledge of the second floor window of Emmy Evers' hospital room and leaping down into the courtyard below. That evening he made his way by horseback north towards Nicaragua where he later caught a Vanderbilt clipper ship bound for New Orleans and from there took Mississippi riverboats to Vicksburg. From that river port city he rode horseback all the way back home. Six months later, when he arrived at his family estate on the Chickahominy River, he found a personal letter waiting for him from Cross.

It said simply, "We will find you."

CHAPTER TWO

◇◇◇◇

Cross

July 2, 1862-Two miles east of Malvern Hill
Battlefield, Virginia

His toothache had gotten worse over the past two days and it had grown into an almost constant distraction, so that he had trouble concentrating. He hadn't slept or eaten a thing in over a day and a half, water, hot or cold, worsened it and even inhaling through his mouth hurt him.

In the frenzy of the past twenty-four hours, getting someone – anyone – to pull the blasted molar was just not possible. It throbbed so deeply and sharply that for a few moments he actually thought about putting his pistol to his head. He knew that couldn't hurt any more than this. Nothing gave him pleasure right now.

Despite his capture of the deserter, Dr. Rory Brett, Jonah Cross seethed about everything happening around him. So very much was out of his control, and as exciting as it all had been, the utter helplessness he repeatedly felt during the havoc of the fights he had experienced, the barrages that blew apart all semblance of order, caught him in a way he hadn't known before.

It surprised him about himself, for he had always considered himself to be a disciplined man, self-taught in the most rigorous manner that he knew. In many ways it was an awakening. Until this past fortnight, he hadn't really been under fire.

In the week-long series of battles in which he had participated on the peninsula, he had seen desperate acts by men that likely would later be deemed heroic, and for the first time he had witnessed the despair in the voice and eyes of a close friend in his final moments of life. A few days previously, on the fourteenth day of a disastrous campaign led by General George McClellan, Cross had witnessed the loss of several more comrades, and it made him disgusted with the wastefulness of it. Many of the men killed had been his neighbors, or childhood friends from the small township in Pennsylvania he still called home.

He was furious at McClellan, the man who, until the past week's series of disasters, had been heralded by influential publishers like Horace Greeley as the genius leader who would save the Union and its army from the raging rebellion.

Although the Union's desperate stand at a place called Malvern had blunted the effect of sequential victories by the confederated rebel's new commander, Robert E. Lee, "Little Mac" McClellan's battered army was reeling back in disarray. Greeley's "savior" McClellan had abandoned his expensive but overly cautious attempt to take Richmond.

Because of the scale of the operation, it was worse even than the fiasco perpetrated by the inept Ben Butler one year before when that glory seeking, politically-appointed general attempted to take Richmond. McClellan's defeats reinforced the probity that the rebellion would not be quelled any time soon. Indeed, had the Union not secured the high ground plateau in that final battle at Malvern, McClellan's mismanaged, massive assault on the Confederacy's capital almost certainly would have resulted in a catastrophic destruction of Lincoln's army. Washington would have fallen to Lee, easily.

The scuttlebutt and opinions about miscommunication at every level of command ran rampant, and even as a frontline cavalry officer, Cross could sense the verity in those condemnations.

So could his fellow dragoons, all of whom were enlisted men. Emotionally hijacked by their demoralized frustration, whenever and wherever they had the opportunity, they unleashed their wrath with a vicious energy. Cross estimated that he personally had cut down or shot at least twenty-five men in the attack on the rebel supply train the day before. He had lost count by noon. His saber arm and shoulder were aching, and afterwards it took him an hour to clean and re-sharpen the blade. Although he was exhausted from it all, as he honed the instrument he reflected with some satisfaction that at least he had sent many insolent, ungrateful traitors to the hell they deserved.

Now he needed to deliver a deserter, former Union physician Lieutenant Rory Brett, to justice.

He knew he had taken a risk by retracing his route to retrieve Brett, whose face he had recollected only after leaving the scene of the skirmish the day before, unfortunately. He could be reprimanded if he failed in his self-appointed mission, for he had taken his troop behind enemy lines, while the rest of the Union's Army of the Potomac was busy decamping and evacuating south by way of Harrison's Landing to the ships waiting on the James River.

However, although the cavalry's direct orders had been to protect that retreat, he had convinced himself that orders, purportedly given by General Winfield Scott himself two years ago, were still in effect — he was to arrest Rory Brett if given the opportunity. It didn't matter that Scott, his own personal hero, had been quietly retired by Lincoln after the fiasco of Bull Run, and therefore couldn't substantiate the order's continuation. What mattered was that the opportunity to fulfill the orders had presented itself finally.

He had discovered Brett. And the man was not in uniform.

As Cross thought about it, that could also mean that Brett wasn't even protected by the conventions of military exchange. He could be executed as a Confederate spy, if not as a Union deserter.

He looked over at Brett, slumped forward, being pulled along on an old mule by a long leash. He had inspected the man before pulling him off the litter. He wasn't a doctor like his prisoner, but didn't think it likely Brett would die from whatever it was that had sickened him, which was good, because that wouldn't serve anyone's purpose.

He couldn't allow him to die before they got to camp.

Cross thought about what he would tell his colleagues when he delivered Brett to the headquarters. To whom would he turn over Brett? He realized he didn't even know now. Over the course of the previous six days, when the serious fighting had actually started, several of his superior officers in the chain of command had been killed. At the Malvern plateau, two days previously, his immediate commander, a major named Speck, had been blinded in a cannonade from their own batteries as they were charging into rebel troops who were advancing up the slope of the hill where the Union army had entrenched itself. Would Speck still be in camp when Cross and his troop returned to camp?

Perhaps not, he thought, and with the ongoing retreat it would be he himself who would be the senior officer in camp when they arrived. Wouldn't that be interesting! He had been promoted, twice, after all, as the result of his own actions at Malvern. Perhaps he could order the execution himself. But he really didn't know for certain what a "brevet" field promotion meant, what privileges it gave, and in the haste of the battles no one had bothered to explain it to him. In his own mind, he still was a sergeant.

His highest honor at this point in his life had been when he was selected, purportedly by Winfield Scott himself, to be part of the general's personal security guard prior to his trip all the way to the Pacific Northwest's Oregon territory and back, now almost three years ago.

Out of more than two hundred talented men recruited by the United States Army to make up the famous general's honor guard, he had been told that Scott had made Jonah his first choice. Six men, all of the same height, build and with the same shooting and riding skills were ultimately selected and they accompanied the aging general everywhere in public from then on.

Everyone from his home township in Shrewsbury and for miles around had heard about the honor. It was the first time he had ever sensed any form of approval from his father, a square faced blacksmith and part time Lutheran minister who likened the fancy equestrian and bareback shooting skills Jonah had acquired to a squandering of meaningful purpose on this earth.

But General Scott had been impressed! And on one occasion, the general had even spoken to him personally! What Lincoln had done to replace the man was disgraceful, Jonah reflected. An insult.

◇◇◇◇

He estimated they were within a mile of their own picket lines when he saw the gray-clad riders following about five-hundred yards away in the thickets to the right of the cornfield on which he and his troop rode. The rebel riders – it seemed there were at least six or seven of them – rode in a parallel path to their own. He ordered his troop to hasten its pace and started a fast cantor. But the rebel cavalry picked up its pace as well, and as the thickets thinned out, Cross saw that he and his men were being followed by at least twenty riders.

"Move!" he ordered, and spurred his mount.

Cross heard one of the troopers shouting out and when he looked back he saw that the mule on which they had bound Brett braying and digging in its hind legs.

"Damn it b' Jesus, ye bastard son-of-a-bitch-whore!" cursed the trooper as he whipped it and attempted to control the animal. But the mule started bucking wildly. Cross circled back and tried to ride along the other side of Brett's mount, and despite both he and the trooper's efforts, they could not control it. The animal continued bucking, throwing Brett's feet out of the stirrups.

"Jesus will not come at the bidding of those who are profane, Trooper!" Cross shouted across the bucking mule at the soldier, then glanced back and saw that the rebel cavalry had begun to close on their position. He shook his head, drew his sword, stared at Brett who was almost off his saddle, then cut the animal's tow rope. He saw that Brett, with his hands bound to the saddle horn, had not been thrown free, but instead was being slowly dragged along side of the now untethered animal. It had stopped bucking and was meandering away with him towards a shoulder high cluster of milkweed thistles.

"Your godless luck is with you today, Doctor Rory Brett," he shouted through clenched teeth. He spurred his mount again then galloped off to catch up with the rest of his fleeing troops.

CHAPTER THREE

✕✕✕✕

Brett

July 2nd to July 3rd, 1862, Somewhere on the Virginia Peninsula

The Confederate cavalry rode right past him, a few of them close enough that they might have noticed him hanging on to the side of the mule. But they didn't apparently and it didn't matter to him that they didn't stop. He knew that armed men in a frenzy are always a menace, no matter which colors they wear.

He didn't know how long he slept there in the milkweed thistle, but the sun had already passed over the nearby hills when he awakened later that evening. A light slow breeze from the James River a half mile away had started to cool the warm red soil where he lay. A few crickets, the ones that likely had been hiding longer in the shade of the distant thickets, had started a tentative calling out. The mule on which he had been bound was nowhere in sight.

Brett looked at his tied wrists bound to a waist cinch and the long tether that had been severed by Jonah Cross. He didn't know how he had freed himself from the saddle's pommel, but the knot around his wrists was tight and his hands were numb. He could still move his fingers. The thistles all around him pinched into his back and legs, but as long as he didn't move their nuisance was tolerable. He tried to turn over to stand up and walk, but couldn't make it. So he just lay back down and told himself he should wait for full darkness before making another effort. There would be no moon tonight. If he could get the ropes off it would be safe to walk in a short while, he thought.

He drifted in and out of consciousness. When he remembered, he forced himself to move his fingers, as painful as doing it was. That helped him awaken himself and by the time it was completely dark, he was fully alert. To stay that way, he did an inventory of every irritant contributing to his aching discomfort. He needed water. His tongue was parched, he ached all up and down his back, and his head was throbbing.

He heard cannon reports continuing to sporadically boom in the distance all through the night. They were still shooting at each other. Hadn't they fought enough? Lee was not letting McClellan evacuate from the peninsula battles without a final warning, to harass the retreating Yankees so they would remember who had licked 'em. He wondered how many men were lost on both sides for that bitter lesson. The cannons' popping, followed by the reverberating, rumbling thunder, intermittently quieted the songs of the cicadas, until in the darkness, the chirping all around him finally increased to a steady loud din and all but drowned out the periodic reports of the big guns. That was a relief. He was tired of hearing cannons.

As he lay there on his back in the brush looking up at the blackness, he thought about the types of wounds from artillery he had treated over the past week, everything from inevitably deadly, stinking gut wounds to bloody, blown out ear drums.

He wondered if the cannoneers in the Confederate batteries or the gunners in the Union frigates protecting the barges of Union evacuees down on the James knew about the random havoc they created with their work. He imagined there was no way distant killers like them could appreciate the personal, lasting, devastating mayhem they created when they sent each load on its way. Would those men even accept the shamefulness of their acts, in packing the barrel, then lighting the fuse? Or on the contrary, would they be proud of the efficient disorder they leveraged, justified to themselves when overwhelming numbers of straightly arrayed men marched towards them?

But how could the ordnance officers aiming the huge siege mortars rationalize shots lobbed into populated areas that were so far away that they would never see the results? From long distances-the rifled cannons and larger smoothbores now had ranges of over a mile. How could the artillerymen in batteries know whether they were striking enemies or their friends? It was strange that he had not thought about any of that when he had served in the Mexican War, when Winfield Scott had bombarded Veracruz and killed so many civilians.

When the full darkness had finally descended, the cicadas quieted. He could still hear the persistent barrages, miles away, coming from the heights above the river and the stubborn retorts from the flotilla of retreating transport ships.

As painful as his entire situation was, as disturbingly loud as the cannons were, it was the artillery's lighting up of the horizon that irritated him the most, because the fusillades that lit up the sky obscured the stars. From the time he had been a small boy, on hot, dark, cloudless summer nights not unlike this, he would stare up and ponder the heavens, then tell himself that all suffering was ephemeral and thus, simply inconsequential in the grand scheme of things. He surmised that maybe up on Venus there existed an ordered species that had figured it all out.

It had always been the stars above that had given him perspective, but that was lost this evening, when he needed perspective so very much.

It would be hours before the sunrise. Lying there, he thought about the past week. He had tried to stay out of it all, all of this insanity, from the start. After eleven years, the drudgery and even the exciting times as an assistant surgeon in the Mexican War, and then the fighting in the West, he had grown plain weary of military life.

He had decided he didn't like *anything* the military represented any more, so after accepting with extreme reluctance, the mandatory oath of loyalty to Virginia after the war's outbreak, he declined to volunteer for the rebel army, which it seemed so many of the men of his age had embraced as their life-defining adventure. Risking being branded a traitor by his neighbors, hoping that this foolish war would be over quickly and that when the combatants burned their fingers and their women wailed for them they would simply pull themselves back into some form of rational behavior, he tried to stay out of the draft imposed by the Confederate congress.

But it seemed that Lincoln and Stanton were pushing for an aggressive quashing of the rebellion. There just was no reconciliation in sight and every killing simply further entrenched the anger on both sides of the Potomac.

He hadn't seen such a frenzy in all his life. As general worries increased throughout the region with reports of the massive Yankee incursion onto the peninsula, every township on the Chickahominy and James Rivers had slipped into the fever of angry, nervous anticipation. Because of all the depredation and havoc effected by John Pope's Union forces to the towns and farms in the Shenandoah, women began arming themselves too, and their men swelled the ranks of the army of Virginia.

"My sister wrote that the Yankee devils defecated in every room rait before they left. Broke ever dish, knocked out ever window, killed all the livestock they din't steal! Shot a boy dead, they did, an 'e was only twelve, who was jes standing in his doorsill!" he heard one woman say.

He heard more than one female patient declare, "I will shoot myself and my daughters afore we will be raped by those unleashed Yankee animals!" or something of the like.

Although he had heard numerous reports from reliable sources that the attacks on the non-combatant citizenry in Virginia were increasing, Brett kept quiet when he heard such talk. But the sentiment being expressed was understandable. And, having watched how enlisted ruffians behaved when he was in the military himself, he expected that the comments were not exaggerated.

Just what did John Pope think he was doing in his subjugation campaign up north in the Shenandoah? he wondered. He had read that both McClellan and Winfield Scott had vigorously objected to the "Hard War" tactics of Pope and Stanton, the Secretary of War. Did the Union commanders like Nathaniel Banks understand how counterproductive their attempts were to control the people of Virginia? Did Lincoln and Halleck, both of whom he had heard had promoted John Pope, condone a terror strategy like this?

On June 25th, one week before the godawful day he had just experienced, Brett heard the first booming cannon reports coming from up river, at Oak Grove and Beaver Creek, where small skirmishes had turned into a bloody fight with more casualties on both sides than had occurred at Manassas the year before. One of McClellan's generals, Fitz-John Porter, had moved his regiments aggressively to within a few miles of Richmond but ran head-on into determined rebel brigades that had been rushed forward to stop them.

Brett had hoped that the fighting would stay put there, up river, far enough away north so that it would not reach his little township. All day long and well into the night he heard dogs barking at the stream of men and wagons moving up the road in that direction to join the fray. A dirt cloud from the double-time marching of thousands of determined gray and buttercup-clad men hung over his farm and left dust over everything he owned. The more military that moved in that direction, the more he felt that his township would be buffered from the impact of the fighting.

The next morning, however, as he peered out the upstairs window into the distance, the dust cloud was gone and he saw that most of his farm's fences were missing. When he rode out to inspect the damage, he saw what must have been over seven or eight hundred horses grazing in his wheat fields, eating his early crop. The horses belonged to J.E.B. Stuart's cavalry, he found out later that day. The fences had been torn apart for firewood for their camps.

As disturbing as this was, he knew it was futile to protest. No one would sympathize with his financial loss in this intrusion. Stuart, like Stonewall Jackson, was already widely regarded as a hero throughout the South and the needs of an army defending the homeland took precedence over an individual citizen's property rights. Likely his neighbors were missing their fences as well, he reasoned.

And what did the broken fences and fields represent in any case, he asked himself? What had he really lost? Very little was left of his family's estate, after all. Save for a few pigs, he had no livestock, because he had sold all of it to reduce the many debts his father had left after his death. The farm's untilled fields were overgrown with scrub grass, because he had no help left to work it. His overseer and every one of the remaining farmhands had joined the rebel army shortly after Brett had given the estate's slaves their freedom papers. All that remained of the property now were thirty-six fallow acres, a barn with a broken beam, a clinic in his big house, and four acres of fields that he personally had slowly plowed and planted with wheat the previous spring. Looking out at the hungry horses roaming in those wheat fields somehow just underscored the powerlessness he felt, for he knew he really was now completely broke.

"This has not been a good year, he said, as he lay there in the thistles, laughing to the few stars he could see. He barely had started what ultimately might have proven to be a modestly prosperous medical practice when Virginia followed the South Carolina hotheads and joined the secession movement.

As the rebellion continued into the first part of 1862, the Union's tightening blockade of the Southern ports ruined the Virginia economy. Farms, previously self-sustaining even without slave labor, began to falter then failed without a reliable workforce to maintain it, because almost all of the region's men of fighting age, sixteen and up, had been mustered against the invading Yanks. With the demise of the local economy, his prospects for prosperity as a private physician, already severely hampered because of unfounded rumors of his Union sympathies, completely evaporated.

He realized that his destroyed fences, the only visible boundaries of what remained of his modest estate, had been broken apart and taken away overnight by men who were trying to defend it. Somehow that seemed fitting as a final comment to everything in his life that had been torn asunder this past year, swept away by this terrible national conflict.

Staring up at the sky, he laughed again to himself and mused. Slightly more than one year ago, before the firing on Sumter, he had made an offer of marriage to Emmy Evers, a woman he dreamed about constantly. He carried the memory of her image with him. Despite all of the obstacles – the looming conflict between the states, especially – he had risked that proposal based on what had been his reasonable, albeit optimistic hopes for a bright, secure future for them. But now he was no longer certain he could provide for her and her family, or would himself survive at all. Perhaps she had sensed misfortune was what lay ahead and that was why she had decided to wait to commit to him. She certainly had been through enough already in her young life.

He had worried also that perhaps he wasn't handsome or exciting enough for her – that she needed more. He didn't know. She seemed to be slipping away. Perhaps it just wasn't meant to be, and if he did fail or die, his demise might spare Emmy even more pain. But the thought of possibly losing Emmy only worsened the bleakness and despair he felt at that moment in the darkness.

No, it hadn't been a good year at all, he grimly conceded again.

After another hour on his back, he felt that the cinch tying his wrists to the rope around his waist had loosened enough that he tried to get up, but fell back again and couldn't summon the energy for another effort. He still had a fever, and the cool early morning air eased the discomfort very little. He slept for a while. When he awoke he was shaking with chills and coughing with a wet phlegm caught in the back of his throat and upper chest.

Would he survive, he wondered? This was his fifth episode of malarial fever in the past eighteen months. During the other episodes he had been able to remain in bed and nurse himself back to health after all of the symptoms subsided. But he worried that he might be contracting a pneumonia this time.

If he died, would he ever be found out here?

Even before he had become ill three days ago with another recurrence of the malaria he had contracted in Panama, he had exhausted himself by the work into which he, at first reluctantly and then ultimately, had voluntarily thrown himself. Despite the rude comments made about him and willful ostracism by the county's other physicians – everyone knew he had previously been a U.S. Military surgeon, had declined volunteering for military service, and had refrained from participating in the rantings by many of them against Lincoln and the Republicans – he overcame his resolve to stay clear of activities supporting the rebellion. He could not bear to see men suffering the way they did when they started pouring back into the township with their wounds from the first day's fighting.

Three days before, on the second day of what turned out to be several bloody ones, a physician with Lee's army, a Major named Lafayette Guild, arrived on his doorstep.

"I understand, kind Sir, that you were a military assistant surgeon until a few years ago," Guild said, with a distinct and thick Alabama accent. "I do not know where your ultimate loyalties lie in this fight. You may hold back, but respectfully, I need to commandeer this big house and your clinic as my main staging hospital. May I have your permission? We will repair the damage when we win this fight."

Guild then pointed down the gravel lane leading up to the house to a long wagon train that stretched almost a half mile up the road. Brett could see that the nearest open wagons were filled with wounded men.

We will be sending the ones who can travel back into Richmond," Guild told him.

He had no choice but accommodate Guild's request, and within less than an hour every room in his long, two story family home was packed with horribly injured soldiers laid out shoulder to shoulder. By the late morning, he found fresh amputees camped on his porch and in the yard outside.

Someone had ordered the severed limbs to be neatly placed into two large stacks, one for arms and the other for legs, behind the barn and far away from the dogs and his big sow's pen. They were reverently placed, he saw, as if someone had thought they might be used again, easily sorted so they might be claimed again by their owners, if not in this life, then the next. Despite the care someone had taken to keep the bloody extremities in separate piles, however, by three o'clock a soldier was throwing them all indiscriminately into one large pit.

As other county volunteer physicians and township women arrived, Brett's backyard garden had become an operating area where Guild had ordered the kitchen tables carried. Men stricken with dysentery and typhus were laid out on the fields, near whatever shade was provided by the old farm's trees. Every room in his large house was crammed full of men recovering from surgery.

In the garden, Guild and several other physicians, including one of Brett's outspoken detractors, a local homeopathic named Rufus Bolt, performed amputations and extracted projectiles from wounds. Bolt, a brusk, stout fellow was so short that he had to stand on a soapbox to reach the operating table. Brett, who had been attending to minor wounds, stayed back and observed at first, and saw that Bolt, despite the help of a competent assistant, was tentative about everything he did, from cutting through the skin and muscle of the leg with his lancet, to his sawing of the bone. Although Brett detested incompetency in men who were given license to do sacred jobs, he kept his anger contained.

But when Brett saw yet another case in which Bolt was failing to securely ligate the artery, again risking the needless exsanguination of a howling, wounded soldier, Brett could restrain himself no longer. He pushed Bolt aside and off his box, grabbed a clamp and secured the bleeding vessel that was pumping blood all over the screaming soldier and the incompetent surgeon, then proceeded to saw through the shattered bone and completed the amputation in less than thirty seconds. He ligated the remaining bleeding veins and small arteries, then quickly revised and secured the flap over the stump of the amputation.

Ignoring the sputtering of the stunned, furious and embarrassed little country doctor, he handed the severed leg to him.

"Sir, your attention is needed in the parlor for some men with dysentery," Brett told the homeopath. "They may need your herbal remedies."

Brett then handed the bloody saw to the assistant, a young Tennessean named Massingale, and said "Sharpen this, Son, and keep it sharp. Who's next, please?"

Brett's actions were observed by Guild. By the end of the afternoon, at Guild's request, Brett supervised every operation on an almost endless train of men with wounds, including Yankee captives. He had never seen the type of devastating injuries produced by the new *minié ball* projectile from rifled carbines used by the Union's infantry, which caused so much tissue damage that gangrene was almost certain to set in. He personally did over sixty amputations by the time the light had failed.

After the huge day-long battle at the mill owned by his family's physician, Dr. Gaines, Brett treated hundreds more, including a young wounded brigadier general. His name was George Pickett. Brett did not remember Pickett's name from the discussion he had with Emmy Evers in San Francisco two years before, nor did he know that his Emmy had once walked a long beach with Pickett four years ago on San Juan Island.

Two days later, as the fighting swung in the direction of Brett's township, most of the town's civilians moved out of their homes, putting as many of their valued possessions as they could carry with them in wagons, and herding their remaining livestock up onto roads crowded with soldiers. Another huge dust cloud hung over the farm. By ten o'clock in the morning the sounds of cannons were closer and by ten thirty he could hear explosions coming from the township less than a mile away. The Federals were counter attacking and advancing in their direction.

When the shells started hitting the pastures a few hundred yards from his home, he pulled out his pocket watch but he could neither focus on the dial, nor read the time. He finally was able to understand that it was eleven o'clock in the morning and calculated that he had been up operating for almost thirty-six hours.

He looked over at a canvas stretcher close to the table on which he had been operating. A corpse lay there, a soldier who had died while in line for the operation that would have amputated his mangled left lower leg. On the stretcher, in between the body's two brown-shoed feet was another foot wearing a similar shoe. Brett gasped. Then he started to laugh. His exhausted young assistant also saw the three feet sticking out from the blanket and started to laugh too, hysterically. They both sputtered and choked as they laughed louder and louder. Brett became dizzy. He tried to sit down on a blood-covered chair but missed it somehow and fell to the ground. He tried, but couldn't get up.

He felt a cool hand wipe the sweat from his brow.

"You're burning up, Brett," he heard someone say.

Confused and too feeble to protest, he felt himself being carted away, then he was on a wagon, being evacuated from the makeshift hospital that had been his home since childhood.

In the wagon rolling away, looking to the field behind the house, he could see piles of corpses lying in the large flower garden that once had been tended by his mother. He looked down. The pallet on which he lay had once been the solid, ornately carved chestnut door of his parents' bedroom. The last thing he heard before he passed out was the sound of incoming shells, the splintering roof of his barn, and the squealing of the big sow and her small litter penned inside.

◇◇◇◇

The sunrise hurt his eyes, but he had slept well enough in the protection of the thistle thicket that the aching had subsided. He was still warm, but his fever had broken.

He grabbed the front of his pant legs and this time was able to pull himself up into a sitting position and then twist himself onto one knee. He again tried biting the ropes around his wrist to loosen them, but the knots had been expertly done and it hurt his teeth and lips to bite so he gave up. He threw his weight carefully forward and stood upright.

He listened. Except for an occasional faint, far off boom, the cannon noise had stopped.

As he walked out of the shoulder high thistle thicket it came alive with a swarm of monarch butterflies fluttering low to the ground and away from him. A mocking bird called out.

He turned full circle and tried to figure where he was. He estimated that he had to be within a few miles of Harrison's Landing where he had heard the Yankees had been evacuating in their retreat, so he headed away from there, away from the rising sun, south and westward in the direction that would most likely bring him down to the river and then safely back to his home.

He wondered what he would find when he got there.

He had walked for less than a mile when he saw the lone rider coming in his direction from the west.

Cross.
There was nowhere to hide.

CHAPTER FOUR

◇◇◇◇

Jojo

May 1862-New Orleans, Louisiana

S o you want to learn all about sailing, do ya?" the man
in the blue coat said.

Jojo looked for the glint of saliva, a sure sign he
had learned to watch for to see if someone was sizing him
up for a swindle. But the Union recruiter's combed but
bushy boscage hid most of his grin.

"I think we can arrange for that, Boy. Lots of other
Indians signed on, ya know."

Jojo nodded. He had heard about the enlistment sign-
ing bonus and promise of regular, high pay from a sailor
who said he was from a tribe called the *Apalachee*. Both
sides in the big conflict between the *Bostons*, the white

people wearing blue and the ones wearing gray, were hiring on people from the tribes. It didn't matter which side he was on, he thought, as long as he got to be on a big ship where he could watch and learn all about sailing. And the enlistment bonus would finance a trip further north to find Missus Evers.

If he signed on, he wondered if he would be made to wear the same type of stiff wool britches the other sailors were walking around in.

The man asked a few more questions, to which he simply nodded.

"Well then! Put yer mark right here, Mr. Able Body Joe." The man pointed to the paper on the table between them.

Jojo tried to read the paper, but there were too many words. He knew he should have taken his time and forced himself to read carefully, as he had been taught by Missus Evers, but there were other men standing behind him waiting for him to finish, and the recruiter kept pushing the quill into his hand and tapping on the paper.

JoJo wrote his name, "Na'Pen'Jo" on the line.

He was now a naval man for the Union Boston Men! A sailor! Before he left the hotel lobby, the man told him to return for his uniform in a few hours.

"Get yer belongings in order and say goodbye to yer sweeties, Boy," the man said. They would be shipping out that evening.

New Orleans was a smelly, confusing place Jojo had discovered during the three weeks he had been there. It was warm enough that he could sleep outside and he had found different ways to earn a few coins to buy food. He read to people and translated for some passengers from the ships that came in from Europe and South America. He worked as a cook's assistant in a restaurant for rich people for several days. They threw away food and the cook let him and two of the other kitchen helpers have what was not eaten. When he walked the streets, he heard all kinds of languages and accents, especially on the waterfront, where many were unlike those he had heard in Panama City and learned when he had been in Colon.

He was surprised by the energy of everyone in that town, even when it was very hot and moist. Many people selling things on every corner, musicians playing all kinds of instruments he had never seen before, and people laughing — much more than what he had seen in San Francisco and Panama City, it seemed. After the Union had won the battle for the city a few weeks before, he saw military parades marching up and down the streets and afterwards, many staggering drunk Union soldiers.

He wandered onto different streets and found that the further he moved away from the water, the bigger the houses, the taller the gates protecting them, and the less it smelled like sewage. It was like what he had seen in San Francisco where so many of the big houses had been built up on the hills. Whenever he got the chance, he conversed with men and women in the different languages he knew, one of his favorite things to do.

His ankle still hurt from the accident in Panama a few years before. But the recruiter man hadn't really asked him anything about that. He had simply asked him if he was "able bodied," whatever that meant. What a funny saying, "able bodied," he thought. Able to do what?

As he had done in Panama, he had someone write letters for him and send them off to Missus Evers at the city of the *Bostons*. He didn't feel comfortable trying to write very much yet. But he never received a reply in Colon or Nicaragua and was told that was because he didn't put enough information on the post he had sent.

He didn't have any more information. He just knew that he was going with her family to live there and she was going to put him in school. He hoped Missus Evers had survived and Jacob and Sarah or the other two children hadn't been hurt by the *Embera* natives who had taken them away in the jungle. No one had been willing to tell him anything after the accident.

That evening he came back to the hotel after sitting and listening to people talk in the park most of the day. He put himself into the stiff clothing the recruiter man gave him. It itched, just like the clothing he had been given by Missus Evers in San Francisco. He liked the hat with the tassel and pushed it to the side the way he saw the other sailors in the street wear it. A half hour later, the parlor was filled with other men, all now dressed like him in white fatigues, and they walked with the bundles of their possessions down to the wharf along several docks to a group of ships tied next to them. He didn't have a bundle. He had thrown away the tattered clothing he had been wearing for several months.

The recruiter man stopped them in front of a big black structure tied to the dock, with sloping iron sides and open square trap doors with huge cannons peeping out. They looked like resting dogs chained inside of the house they guarded. No masts, unlike most of the other ships in the harbor, just two tall dark smoke stacks pushing up so high that they seemed to be holding up the black clouds above.

The recruiter man who led them down there handed a paper over to a short man completely dressed in blue. Jojo watched the short man doing a count on the paper, then he called out their names. Twenty in all. He counted and listened to each of the names. Many of the men were Irish, a few were Italians, one was a Spaniard and one other was like him. He would find out what tribe he was from. Then the short man gave the recruiter man some money and as Jojo passed by him to board the ship, the recruiter man gave him ten one-dollar bills. It was supposed to be one hundred and fifty dollars.

"Ya gets the rest of yer sign-on dollars when ya leave the service of yer mother here in one year," the man said, pointing to the ugly odd shaped ship, to each man as he passed by.

Jojo watched him roll the rest of the money into a wad and stuff it in his pocket.

"Good luck with yer sailin', Mate," The man called out from the dock as JoJo walked up the plank of the ironclad.

Where were the sails? He wondered.

CHAPTER FIVE

◇◇◇◇

EMMY

July 8, 1862-Washington, District of Columbia

She was tired of this black. It comforted her no longer. In early May, several weeks before the caskets started arriving back in Washington from the late June '62 battles in McClellan's much ballyhooed peninsula campaign, Emmy Evers' father, the Honorable Massachusetts' Congressman Kern O'Malley, informed her about confidential details he had learned of the Army of the Potomac's likely routes in its planned attack on Richmond.

Emmy listened to what her father said to her, conveyed in a quiet, careful, almost conspiratorial whisper. She noticed that he spoke on this occasion with a tone of tenderness that was quite atypical for him. He also seemed a bit confused, she noted. More than once he absentmind-edly called her "Abby," her mother's name.

Emmy surmised that her mother's passing the year before had finally softened him after all the years of his constantly driven self-aggrandizement. And he seemed tired and worn out now, she observed. Emmy, thus listened to him on that occasion much more carefully than she might have otherwise, and that had been fortuitous, she realized later, in retrospect.

The maps of the campaign had been secretly shown to her father by her sister Kathleen's husband, Captain Jonathan Evan McEmeel, who was working for Senator Ben Butler, now the *General* Benjamin Butler, an opportunistic man with a reputation for shrewd, self-serving dealings. Despite the loathing and distaste she had for Butler, a prominent "War Democrat," Emmy understood that the information McEmeel had provided was likely fresh and accurate, because of Butler's significant influence as one of Lincoln's notorious "political generals."

She also realized that her father who, because he was a vocal anti-war "Constitutional Unionist," risked being accused of treason by sharing the information, and did so because he was looking out for her best interests. He knew where Dr. Rory Brett, the young man who had proposed marriage to her right before the outbreak of the war, had set up his general medical practice in Virginia.

Emmy saw that Rory Brett's clinic in the family home he had inherited near a small township on the Chickahominy River, would be directly in the path of this massive Union army invasion now slowly moving up the peninsula. Her father had told Emmy that, although he knew she was still undecided about accepting Brett's proposal, he very much liked the young doctor and said he hoped she would "give that good man's tender heart the honor of graciously answering in the affirmative." He also said that in any case, he wanted to prepare her for the worst "should harm come to your beau."

Emmy had thanked her father for the information, told him she appreciated his concerns, but said she would make up her own mind in good time about whether to marry Rory Brett. She also said that, as worried as she was about the likelihood that he would be in danger, she had confidence he was quite capable of fending for himself.

Privately however, she was worried for she knew she had no reliably safe way to warn Rory of the oncoming peril. Ten Months ago, Jefferson Davis had ordered all "Northern Men" to leave the Confederated States. Rory had been forced to sign an "oath of loyalty" to the Confederacy. Shortly afterwards, all mail had been blocked from that area. Additionally, because of the gossip that had played a part in so many Union defeats, Lincoln also had already declared martial law and had suspended the right to the writ of *Habeus Corpus* in order to allow the federals to arrest suspected spies. The thoroughfares were blocked. The embargo by the Union navy had tightened. She had heard that General Butler, after he had been appointed the governor-general of New Orleans, had imprisoned women there for simply expressing anti-Union opinions.

The anxiety of non-combatants on both sides, especially in the border states, justifiably had reached proportions she hadn't experienced since the Indian wars in the Oregon Territory, not only from the threat of violence by armed combatants, but also because of the measures being taken by the citizens and governments of both sides. As a result of Lincoln's order, in Washington, D.C., men and women she knew had been arrested and imprisoned without representation. And in the South, "Minute Men" and "Vigilance Committees" in Tennessee, Kentucky and Virginia had conducted whippings, mutilations and hangings of suspected spies. Without trials.

Of course, one could still navigate down the western side of the Mississippi, almost as far as Memphis and cross over that way, but that was dangerous as well, particularly for a woman. And it would be likely that anyone traveling without papers to or from that part of Virginia could be detained by one or the other side. The paranoid behavior of everyone she knew on the Union side was so great, she wondered if she or her father could be subject to arrest for even *discussing* this information.

Getting a message to Brett would be close to impossible. What should she do? she wondered. She felt helpless to make any difference.

That, and the conversation with her father caused her to look at her own situation. After a long absence, she hadn't returned to Boston yet, but was still in Washington, obtaining what seemed like reliable counseling and medical help for her son, Jacob. In her circumstances, the limited funds available to her had constrained her wherewithal for helping Jacob recover from a mental disturbance that had grown worse after terrible ordeals he had suffered in the Pacific Northwest, and then again in a horrific series of events that had transpired while attempting to travel through Panama.

Although she felt her son was making some progress in the sessions she had arranged with a competent minister, who, in return for a small contribution to her mission, was willing to listen to Jacob, her son still suffered from occasional night terrors and continued to be withdrawn and uncommunicative. She was relieved that Jacob had immediately responded to Rory Brett on his visit to Boston, clung to him, actually, and then cried when Rory had to return to Virginia.

But that was several months ago and Rory was now unreachable. Jacob had become withdrawn again. If Rory had stayed, might Jacob be recovering, instead? she wondered.

Her sister, Kathleen, who had developed friendships with numerous socially prominent Washington women, had suggested a variety of interventions for Jacob she had heard might be of help, all of which Emmy had rejected because they seemed harsh and backward. Undeterred, Kathleen had told her that one of her friends from New York, a French diplomat, knew of physicians there who specialized in "diseases of the mind," from which she thought Jacob might be suffering. That only made Emmy more angry with her sister who invariably attempted to domineer in every situation. She kept her anger to herself. Perhaps Kathleen would recant, as bull-headed as she let herself be so often.

And what about her decision to not immediately accept Rory's proposal? She wondered about their relationship, and in particular whether her ambivalence had caused him to rethink whether he wanted to commit to her. He had called on her, traveled all the way from Virginia to see her in Boston. They had walked and talked. He had described his hopes in building a profitable medical practice in Virginia, and re-establishing himself as a teacher of medicine and surgical care down there.

She believed, from everything she had witnessed with Rory and his interactions with Sarah and Jacob, that he would be a good father to her children. He had expressed his hope that she would consider raising an even larger family with him. He was handsome and polite. Had a future and was respectable. He was sensible, not wild with ideas the way her first two husbands had been. He never pushed or prodded. He had gently kissed her hands. He had helped save her life in Panama.

But she had told him she was not ready to make a decision yet, was still in mourning after all.

As she reflected on that conversation, quietly exchanged while lying on the grass looking up at the sky, carried on further while sitting on a hill overlooking the small fishing villages north of Boston, the more she thought about it, she knew she had not been truthful with him. She truly *was* ready to make a change in her life.

As much as she owed him, however, and as comfortable and secure he always made her feel, despite what she perceived as a noble, proud bearing, she just wasn't certain yet if he was the right person for her future. Or if any man was. She knew that was also irresponsible, almost capricious, given her financial situation and the recurring problems her son, Jacob was manifesting. Jacob had immediately taken to Rory, who had a calm and reassuring manner when conversing with her son. But she had long ago decided it was always best to not ignore her inner voice. As long as she balanced her feelings with a sound reasoning process to her decisions as well, she seemed to fare well.

Was that right in this situation? Would other women, given similar circumstances, have leaped at the opportunity presented by Rory's proposal? Was she being a fool?

She asked herself: was it his sweet awkwardness when he was with her, almost like that of a tender boy looking up at the schoolmarm he adored, that made her feel as if she might have to be a mother to him? How did that equate with the way Jacob seemed to look up to Rory, the way he had with his own father, Isaac? A boy looking up to an older boy he admired? Were her perceptions, was her intuition, mistaken?

She knew she loved Rory, but also knew she wasn't yet *in love*. Given the issues that had quickly surfaced in her two previous marriages — John Tern had become abusive, Isaac Evers had never appreciated the contributions she made in their partnership — she felt she had to take the time to make a good decision. Not only for her family, but for herself.

◇◇◇◇

That afternoon, when she returned with Jacob and Sarah to the brownstone her father had leased in Washington, she looked over her wardrobe. There was only one piece of clothing that had a wisp of bright color in it. Everything else was somber, cut from dark cloth.

It had become a preponderance, this black, hadn't it? she concluded.

So many women, young and old, were wearing it now, the respectful trappings of grief, ever since the first so very disorganized, so very disappointing, so very surprising and bloody first battle that had occurred in a place they called "Bull Run," where her brother-in-law had fought. Its prevalence, this black, every widow and bereaved mother, so many others who were close to them also wearing it, almost made it seem to fade unnoticeable after a while, because of its familiarity, blending in with the dark blue uniforms of the thousands of soldiers who swarmed the filthy streets of Washington.

Emmy imagined that her counterparts in Charlotte, Knoxville and Richmond must have been similarly attired. It was, this mourning absence of color, perhaps the one thing that bonded them all to each other, the North and South's women, for indeed the losses of their men to bullets and disease were mounting, intolerably, on both sides of this foolish, inevitable conflict.

But she keenly wanted to no longer be affiliated with that aspect of sisterhood. She had always found ways to overcome loneliness, or at least stare it down and then walk past it. She filled up her time with managing countless things, pondering in the interstices about how everything fit together. She had reassured herself often that she didn't need the company of a mate, as much as she more and more frequently found herself longing for the intimacy of an embrace, a gentle touch from a kind, firm hand.

There *had* been a few times, early on in her second marriage, with Isaac, when she had — let herself go, had given herself permission — to unbridle herself, as it were. It was a wild place she visited on those occasions, new rooms in her ordered mind with its tight and ordered compartments. It was wondrous, and she found herself longing for it during their intimate times together. And when they weren't.

Letting go, as it were, had scared her at first and she realized that wandering, like trying new things out, would surely scare Isaac who, as much of a dreamer as he was, always became frightened when he perceived things getting out of control. Had she failed to be patient with him? Had she failed to be aggressive enough with him? Had she waited for his imagination to ignite, respected *his* prerogatives, instead of asserting her own.

Was that one of the reasons he had gone away for eleven months — six months longer than his commission called for — and fought alongsideof the military in their attempts to contain the aboriginal uprisings on the Columbia River? she reflected. If so, that effort — an absence to give him some control over the unpredictability of matters, to stamp down the ready-made terrors and constant fear of night intruders — had failed, certainly personally for her husband, for if it curtailed the aboriginal uprisings in the Northwest, it also had just knocked all of the passion out of him.

He came back deflated and confused.

And after that, she never had the chance again to go back to those places, during their fewer and fewer intimate moments. And she had never let Isaac know what she knew about those places. Never had the chance. The night intruders had visited, afterall.

Months ago, as she began pondering Rory Brett's proposal and everything else she had experienced over the last three years, she had decided it finally would be appropriate to distance herself from the deep mourning and the kinship often found in it — the shared, terrible secret signals that only those who had lost a loved one could truly understand.

She just couldn't summon the empathy any more, she realized. She avoided meeting the eyes of other widows, and the connection sought by those newly grieving in particular, for she had grown so very tired of it all. Her widowhood, the weighty, purposeful widow walk she knew so well, had become a burden she wished to finally put away, and with it the black dresses that were constant reminders of all that had started for her when her husband was — murdered. His death was one that had come by way of a different brand of savage acts than those that now had befallen the rest of the country. And that episode in her life seemed now so very far away, off in the Pacific Northwest, an extreme outpost of this broad and threatened nation.

She had decided she would find a new step, in new attire, nothing gaudy, but something modest that spoke of hope perhaps, to go along with a demure little dance even, like the gavotte she had practiced as a young girl up in Boston, even if she could only dance it in her imagination. She remembered an old dress at home in her armoire, a lighter shade of robin's egg blue with a royal blue sash. She had always loved that dress. It might fit still.

She resolved that she would try it on, in private at her father's house when she returned to Boston. And then maybe she might see how Rory Brett responded to those same colors. Perhaps it might give her a hint of how he might be as a husband and lover?

How *would* he behave? What would he be like if she allowed herself to go beyond the gentle hand-holding and gentle kisses he had given her? Would he change? Would he become frightened and push himself into diversions, as Isaac had done? Or would he not change, continue to be gallant, but restrained, as George Pickett had been? Perhaps those concerns were what had made her hesitate most about accepting Rory Brett's proposal. Would wearing the robin's egg blue dress make a difference?

And then, on May 14th of '62, in the very week she had decided to break out the colors, her father had quietly died — a simple grunt as his final sound was the only utterance he left behind; no wisdom-words to pass on, or strange ambiguities for her to ponder.

Her sister Kathleen's husband, Major Jonathan McEmeel, who had witnessed the event, told her that her father's eyes had seemed to bulge forward, "red" is what she remembered he said, just before he guided her father to the divan. Her father was holding the right side of his head with both hands. He too, had been in the mourning clothing he had worn for months for Emmy's mother. He hadn't recovered at all from his wife's passing the year before, after her long dwindling illness. And just like her mother, he too was gone in the middle of the night, and Emmy found she could not put away the dark veils after all.

What was the mourning dress convention for orphans?, she mused.

◇◇◇◇

May 17th, 1862-Washington, District of Columbia

Just before the funeral, Emmy learned that her father had named her as the executer of his estate.

"You know, Emmy, " Kathleen had declared, "this really is an incredible insult to me personally!"

When Emmy tried to speak, Kathleen turned and walked away, stating without waiting for a response " . . . and it's not about the money. Jonathan and I are doing quite well, thank you!"

But there was nothing to inherit. Her father had again speculated so much during his final years that for the second time he had squandered his family's modest fortune. He had mortgaged his home in Boston beyond recovery and left a number of unpaid, angry creditors.

Although Kathleen and her husband, Jon McEmeel had prospered since his employment with General Butler, Emmy herself had very little saved. She realized she soon would be without the shelter of her family home in Boston.

She wished she could have discussed her dilemma with Rory Brett, because he had dealt with similar circumstances when he had returned to his home in Virginia. But he was beyond reach right now. There was no one she believed she could trust.

On the afternoon after realizing her plight, she sent a telegram to Patrick Dolan, the attorney with whom she had entrusted a package that eighteen months previously had been sent to her son, Jacob. The package, sent without an originating address, was from someone whom she had presumed and hoped was dead — Rafael "Bocamalo" Giannakos, the man who had taken her hostage two years ago in a Panama railroad heist. For whatever reason, Bocamalo had sent her son, Jacob a valuable gift — a large, uncut diamond.

Emmy's message to Dolan was terse: "As much as I regret having to consider this in any way, and in so doing, relive any part of that cursed series of events, I may need to find a buyer for the contents of Jacob's package, after all."

She received a telegram the next day from Dolan's office notifying her that he was away on a trip to England and was not expected to return for a few weeks.

Over the next two weeks, in late May and early June of '62, after the funeral and after the army troops began moving out of Washington onto the Peninsula campaign her father had told her about, she threw as much energy as she could into managing the unfinished business details of her father's estate. Knowing how depressed she might become if she let herself dwell on her troubles, worrying about Rory Brett in particular, Emmy also methodically went about a number of other daily tasks to keep her spirits up.

– She did the laundry for the household, cooked every meal and cleaned the house meticulously.

– She corresponded, sending letters to her deceased husband's brother, Winfield Evers, to whom she had sold her farm in the Oregon territory.

– She wrote to Ari Scarpello in New York, the brave man whose actions had saved her children during the train robbery in Panama. Her letter to Scarpello came back unopened, but was accompanied by another letter from a friend of his, noting that Ari had returned to Panama to search for his wife who still was missing after the tragic events down there. The letter from the friend said Scarpello had left his two small children, Jonny and Falco, in the care of a relative and had told the friend that he hoped Emmy would visit them in New York when he returned from the isthmus.

– She sent additional queries to the Panama Railroad Company and Colombia's New Grenada government offices in Colon and Panama City to see if any information had been found about Jojo, who had been lost during the Panama heist.

– She increased the frequency of her son's visits to the minister who had spent considerable time with both of them to help sort out the causes of Jacob's "emotional disturbance." Her son had finally started giving details about his captivity in the Haida war camp three years previously. Jacob said he missed Jojo, the guardian who had helped save him and had been a surrogate father of sorts. For the first time ever, Jacob said he missed his father, Isaac. More so than in the past, she left those sessions emotionally drained and noticed that Jacob slept for hours afterwards. But he seemed to be much less withdrawn. And, although he still clung closely to his sister, Sarah, he had stopped wetting his bed. And then he again said he missed Rory Brett.

Midweek, she read a new letter from Captain George Pickett. It had no return address but had been posted in New Orleans several months previously. He told her he had left the Pacific Northwest and was somewhere south, headed back to Virginia where he would accept an officer's commission from the Confederate army. He said he needed to defend Virginia, his home. When the conflict was over, he said he hoped to come to Boston to visit. He said he thought of her often. When she re-read the letter, she thought about times they had spent together in the Pacific Northwest, just talking out their loneliness.

After reading Pickett's letter, she read and re-read Rory Brett's long letters and poems to her, and repeatedly the last one she received just before the interdiction of the mail a few months back. He had reiterated his proposal. He used the word "love" five times in the letter. The last few paragraphs she had read so many times that she had almost memorized them:

Em,

> *...I know you have had some reservations about this courtship, about my nascent station, about your starting over with yet another man, one whom you do not know well, about bringing your young family with its own troubles into a troubled land during troubled times.*

> *I know you hesitate because I am younger than you in some ways, and although we both have seen death and savagery, in my case it has been far less personal, far less devastating. In my case, I have been able to displace the pain I witness and experience away from myself, as I must if I am to maintain a competency in what I have chosen to do in my life.*

> *So you must likely believe that I cannot understand. With you, I expect that your competency has come from the opposite direction, in that-as you have attempted to protect yourself and your loved ones, you have experienced and gained by your survival, the pure surety that you will always endure.*

> *You know I admire that confidence you exhibit so very*

well. I saw it the moment we first met, when I watched you closely on that occasion, then later, helplessly from afar, then again as you lay unconscious before me in Panama, and even now, distanced as we are by this war's interdiction.

My love for you has increased with each moment we are away, Emmy, each painful catch of my breath when I even hear in others a gentle round-toned murmur close enough to your gentle voice, or see a brave posture that reminds me of the way you carry yourself always, whether you are in pain or happiness, when I compare others to the way you evenly parry in the patter of conversations, when I visit Richmond but find myself dreaming of being in Boston with you, or when I sit by myself on a tall hill and imagine sitting by your side again in the countryside watching the seaside. Feeling a fresh breeze again. Touching your hand.

I love you. Always will.

Reading those last paragraphs made her come back to the sad helplessness she felt might overwhelm her. He was out of reach. She couldn't talk with him. Reassure him. What could she do?

◇◇◇◇

June 30th-July 15th 1862-Washington, District of Columbia

One week later, as the Union wounded overflowed into every available hospital, church and many private homes in Washington, Emmy read a series of reports in Washington and New York newspapers about two separate battles in a series of seven engagements of the latest massive Virginia campaign which had turned out to be another Union fiasco that already had killed or wounded over fifteen thousand men. She read that the Confederates had suffered a similar number of casualties.

The first report she read on the morning of June 22nd, described a costly battle at a place called Mechanicsville, heralded by the New York Herald correspondent as a narrow Union victory. Rough estimates were that thousands had perished. The Union forces, under the command of General Fitz-Hugh Porter, had valiantly and successfully fought off rebellion forces at a place the Virginians called Beaver Dam. The Washington papers called the Beaver Dam fight, despite the huge number of casualties, an encouraging victory."

The next engagement in the same area had turned out differently, apparently. Reports stated that the Confederated forces had broken through the entrenched Union lines and turned the battle against the Federals. Fitz-Hugh Porter's forces had been forced to retreat. One editorial writer mentioned a rumor that McClellan, dispirited by this and other early setbacks, was considering withdrawing the Union forces and terminating the campaign altogether. Estimating the enormous expense of the campaign, the editor opined that such a retreat would be ruinous to an already ruined army and would encourage the rebels to march on Washington.

All of the news, all of the losses in the ongoing war, was horribly disturbing. However, because of where the battles were occuring, Emmy reviewed the current events and spent at least two hours every morning reviewing several periodicals and papers. She also read through the front pages listing the dead and wounded from the Union armies, looking for familiar names.

When she found no mention of anyone she knew, no matter how long the lists of casualties, she felt some relief. And when she had the opportunity to view on stale newspapers, the lists of Confederate dead and missing, she read and re-read them much more slowly, carefully and with a horrible dread, hoping that she would see neither of the only two names she might recognize — George Pickett and her Rory Brett. And when she could not find their names, that buoyed her as well. Death had taken many others, but had spared her from proximate, personal grief. It was a perverse way of keeping her hopes alive, she conceded.

In the afternoons, she took Sarah to the same hospital on Pennsylvania Avenue where she had found McEmeel, one year previously, after the Bull Run battle. Sarah was old enough and had seen enough in the past few years to help her with the nursing of the wounded soldiers. There was always a lot to do. When it quieted down, both she and Sarah wrote letters for the men.

Two days later, when she read a smuggled copy of the *Richmond Enquirer,* she saw mention that a young Confederated States Brigadier General named George E. Pickett had been severely wounded during an assault at a place called Gaines Mill.

Recalling the maps her father showed her, she realized that both of the fights, at Mechanicsville and at the township near Gaines Mill, were within a few miles of the Brett family estate. She found no further details about Pickett's fate.

She saw a map on the second page of the *Herald,* and realized that Rory — Dr. Rory Brett, irrespective of whether he had declared himself for one side or not — would be right in the thick of it now. She shook her head at the ironic coincidence. The only two living men in which she had any real feelings were now within a few miles of each other, and both were in harm's way — or might be dead.

That night she lay awake until 4 a.m., and less than a half hour later Jacob came to her bed crying. His night terrors had returned.

"Devils. They were there again. They killed my poppa again! I fought them. I killed them," Jacob sobbed.

"There are no devils, Sweetheart," Emmy said, holding him close. "Just people who do bad things that hurt others."

"They hurt me!"

"I know, Sweetheart. I know. But you're safe now. No one is going to take you away again," Emmy said.

Sarah awoke and also tried to console him, but he talked and wept until daybreak when he finally slept.

The next day, she brought Jacob again to the minister, a progressive Unitarian woman who had been working with them on Jacob's troubles. They let Jacob talk for over an hour. Again, he talked about the events on Whidbey and up north while enslaved by the Northerners. He talked about the Embera camp in Panama. Emmy began to understand that Jacob had confused the aborigines — the violent, abusive Northerners, and also the docile Embera — as devils, like the ones they had heard an itinerant fiery preacher-orator describe during a Sunday sermon on Whidbey.

"Jacob, those weren't devils," the minister said. "They were human beings, just like you and me and your mother."

Jacob nodded and seemed to understand. He calmed down after that.

On the next two visits, Jacob was much more talkative and animated, much like the way he had been when he was younger, Emmy noted. Afterwards, the minister told Emmy that she saw real progress with Jacob and thought he was on the road to recovery.

"But I think he needs a father in his life, too," the Minister said. "Any hope of this beau of yours ever joining your family?" she asked.

◇◇◇◇

Later that week, with the military contacts provided by Kern O'Malley's secretary and by Jon McEmeel, her brother-in-law, visiting Washington from New Orleans, Emmy made several pleas to find some way to locate Brett, and if she couldn't find a way to bring him out of harm's way, at least learn about his condition.

She was curtly turned away in every circumstance.

She tried to learn more about George Pickett's fate as well, but could find no further information.

In her queries, the opinion she heard repeatedly was that the disastrous, costly Peninsula campaign and McClellan's retreat from the Virginia had wasted thousands of lives and a fortune in resources. Just as had been the case after Bull Run, military and civilian authorities alike were panicked about the potential for a rebel advance into the capital. She was told over and over again that no one would be allowed a pass over into rebel held territory.

No information, no correspondences would be allowed to pass. One major in McClellan's general staff office told her that other people were in similar situations and such was the consequence of "split loyalties." He said she should not persist in her efforts, lest she be placed on a "list of those suspected."

She grew despondent. In her gut, she sensed she had lost Rory. Pickett was gone too.

◇◇◇◇

At the end of the week, a young soldier who identified himself as Lieutenant Mark Wilford from Boston, part of the Clan Wilford of Springfield, presented his calling card and then visited her home. The lieutenant said he was en route home for recuperation after the Peninsula Campaign, but had made a special detour into Washington to convey information about someone she knew. Doctor Brett.

"It's the least I can do, Ma'am" Wilford said with his hat in his left hand. "I still have this because he stopped one of the butchers down there from sawing it off," he said, nodding down at his heavily bandaged right arm, suspended in a sling.

"When he heard I was from Boston, he told me all about you. About you and your children. Your son and your daughter."

The young man said he had been brought by the Confederates along with a number of other captured, wounded Union soldiers to the makeshift hospital that had been commandeered from Brett's clinic after the Gaines Mill fight. Wilford said he had been left there by the Rebels when they abandoned the place.

He told her that Brett looked haggard and ill.

"They carried him off in a wagon with the wounded. His face was gray, Ma'am." Then Wilford handed her an envelope addressed to her.

It was from Brett.

She waited for the soldier to leave before she fully exhaled and wondered whether the weakness she felt was from hearing the news about Rory or her attempt to contain herself in front of the young Boston-bound lieutenant.

Then she walked up the stairs, entered her room, closed the door and lay down on the bed. She held the tattered envelope next to her face, inhaled to sense any fragrance, and tried to feel the paper's texture on her cheek.

It took her five minutes to marshal the courage to tear its seal.

She opened the envelope and found the start of a letter and a poem dated in late April, written five months after Rory had returned to Virginia from his visit to see her in Boston. She remembered that she hadn't written to him for a few weeks, and as she thought about what she had said or not said in her previous letter to him, just before the mail was cut off, she wondered whether she had conveyed any ambivalence, such that he believed she truly was withdrawing from their relationship.

April 22nd, 1862

My Dearest Em,

> *My last postings to you came back unopened. It appears that the mail may not be going through now, at least I hope that is the reason you have not responded to three previous letters. I am frustrated. We are forbidden here*

to travel north, given the hostilities, and if I do, it most certainly will be misinterpreted here by those so inclined, so that I will likely not be able to practice in my home town ever again. If I were to make a rash decision-to cross over lines — it would certainly destroy whatever semblance of security upon which I have been counting so that I might support you, the children and a future family together. Thus, I will do the prudent thing and stay put here at my clinic, or until I can stand this silence from you no longer. This war cannot last long. I pray that it will not endure or outlast us.

I have tried to not misinterpret what you said in the last letter I received from you, Dear One — to read between the lines. If you are trying to let me down gently — well, I don't know what to say right now, without looking into your eyes again to be certain of my fears or hopes.

I have no idea whether the simple poem below will ever reach you. I am an unpracticed romantic, Em, and a poor poet as I am certain you have decided by now. It is written with some sense of hopelessness, given the circumstances, and the resignation to fate from a separation that results — not from angry words, but rather from simple imposed distance in time and place. Perhaps I am assuming the worst of reasons you are not writing — that it is not from death, which could take any of us at this perilous moment in this young nation's life, which I would sweetly grieve to my own last breath, but rather from that staleness which unfortunately sometimes results when souls are allowed to drift apart, when those we love have an interdiction imposed that is beyond their control.

Please, please let us not forget the fragrant moments that we have shared, Dear Love.

I love you.

Always will.

The letter was unfinished. She could see the impressions of the poem on the front of the second page, written in a hard pencil, was not readable. The script on the back of the second page, apparently scribbled hastily and dated July 1, 1862, was unsteady:

I need you, Em. You, Jacob and Sarah need me.

Please. I need you.

- R.B.

The note on the back had to have been written on the day the soldier told her Brett had been carried off.

By this series of God-given coincidences — with both Rory Brett and George Pickett apparently now missing in the calamitous smoke and bitter haze of war — Emmy realized she would have to find a way to get across the Confederate lines to the Chickahominy. There was no other way than this.

She knew exactly where Brett's township was on the upper fork of that river. With luck, the trip would take only a few days and she could find Brett and find a way to get him out of there. She would have to find the words to help Jacob and Sarah understand that she would be leaving them for a just short while in her sister Kathleen's care. Jacob was doing better. Sarah and the minister would be there. She would be back as quickly as she could. If she found him, she would bring Rory back with her.

Kathleen would have to understand. Could she trust her?

Kathleen's husband, McEmeel would have to help. Could she trust him?

And Emmy reassured herself in a short prayer of supplication to God that she could find a way to get across the lines safely. But she didn't know what she would find when she got there.

CHAPTER SIX

◇◇◇◇

McEmeel

July 15th, 1862-Washington, District of Columbia

H e had to get out of Washington and back to New Orleans before Lincoln and Stanton pushed another offensive. He didn't want to be diverted or be pulled into that fracas. It was inevitable that the Union, with all its might and diverse resources, would win this prolonged conflict, whether by direct victories or by wearing down its enemy. In so doing, its leaders would staunchly promote actions that would result in more carnage and destruction. And he had already done his duty, damn it.

Limping along towards his quarters on Missouri Street, U.S. Army Major Jon Evan McEmeel, a decorated casualty

62

of the First Battle of Bull Run, wondered whether the disguise he wore mattered or was even necessary any more. So many politicians and soldiers were slipping in and out, unnoticed from the "Murder Bay" section of Washington, the four block row of whore houses just a quarter mile away from the half-built Capitol rotunda, that he knew he could easily muster an excuse if someone dared to question his motives for being in that dangerous section of the city. He " . . . had been at a meeting attended by several other officers and congressmen" he found himself saying to himself on more than one occasion. It wasn't lying. He always found a way to tell enough of the truth that he could speak with convincing tone, easily mistaken for earnestness. His wife always seemed to believe him, he thought. The prominent partakers who frequented the dandy houses likely used the same excuse, he reasoned, and it was the scandalous truth.

He took off the plain forage kepi and switched to his Hardee and the uniform officer's coat he carried in his carpetbag. No one saw him.

The capital city bordellos, like "The Blue Goose," "Madame Wilton's Private Residence for Ladies" and his favorite place of covert indulgence "Miss Russell's Bake House" kept by the professional women in Washington were not as colorful as the huge number of leisure houses he had sampled in New Orleans, but they were plentiful and would have to do for now.

McEmeel had exercised every rationalization for his sinful exercise of primal indulgences: his stale marriage was faltering after all, and — he needed so much more — understanding and" diversity" — than what was provided within the bonds and boundaries of a respectable but restrained arrangement. It wasn't that he didn't feel some remorse for these increasingly frequent, quiet little excursions. He did, indeed. But he conveniently confessed these sins as soon as he could after each visit to avert by carelessness, an ignominious passage of his sinful soul directly to Hell. Catholics enjoyed that privilege, didn't they? he mused. It was a fair exchange for putting up with all of the other rules they imposed.

And it wasn't that he was harming anyone. The ladies enjoyed his company. He always paid well — although he resented having to do that. And, knowing of the maladies of the flesh, he had always been careful, for he knew second-hand, from observing what some of his men had to endure, that the cures proffered by every local medical practitioner, including the herbalists and naturopaths, were painful and ineffective. He had no intention of pouring silver nitrate or podophyllin onto his private parts for the syphilitic affliction, or ingesting calomel for "the drip." And it wouldn't do for him to pass on an embarrassing disease to his wife.

While stopping to don the rest of his official identity, he felt his knee throbbing again. That reminded him about how greatly it displeased him to be still detained in here in the north. His presence in this city was really for appearances only now, and was keeping him away from New Orleans, where he was missing one too many excellent opportunities. Ever since his sponsor, Benjamin Butler, had assumed his appointment as *Governor General* of that wretched, interesting port town, McEmeel's own fortunes had expanded fabulously, as had others close enough to Butler's inner circle.

He understood that the death of his father-in-law, Kern O'Malley, had been an unexpected inconvenience, and the aftermath of that certainly had to be endured. Common decency, or at least the appearance of it in this gossip-haven of a town, always dictated one's actions, he knew, and everyone had been told that he himself had been the last one to see O'Malley before the congressman collapsed.

McEmeel had responded similarly in a rehearsed, silken way to each query about the circumstances. To both the sincerely bereaved as well as to the nosey ones who he believed were simply intrigued with morbid details of the moribund, he said, "My father-in-law's entire visage conveyed a peacefulness when I laid him down onto the couch. I am certain he did not suffer."

It was an ingratiating half-truth — old O'Malley had been vehemently arguing with him when the stroke hit the man. "You are a dishonest, smarmy, opportunistic, war-loving, cross-eyed little weasel, Jon! Do you understand that?" O'Malley had bellowed, his face beet red, just before he collapsed onto the marble floor. But O'Malley's face *had* settled into the flat affect ultimately. So half-truths, even telling blatant lies that way at the funeral, somehow made McEmeel feel as if he were relieving the concerns of those lamenting, and disappointing those who had perhaps been hoping for something more lurid. Perhaps, he said to himself, he would win some grace to reduce his time in purgatory for embellishing the details of that burdensome event.

Was he now a complete cynic? he asked himself. That thought gave him pause. What if there were no such thing as purgatory? He would go directly to Hell in the miserable state of grace he knew he had been keeping his soul. Could he find a business there? He laughed. Ben Butler and his brother, Andrew, would help him find some, if there were any.

Crossing over onto Michigan Avenue, two enlisted men, a private and a corporal, walking in the opposite direction, saluted him. Although the novelty of the ritual had worn off, he knew it was better to return their salute than call attention to himself by not doing so. "Soldiers," he called out as he nodded and lifted his right hand to his forehead.

As he thought about it, he realized that the salute was an acknowledgment of the common cause in which they were supposed to be engaged, and the organization to which they had pledged allegiance. Men saluted out of respect, obligation or fear. He could tell by how they did the little exercise of deference just where they were in their feelings for it all. He could tell when men had turned into cynics or never had bought into the practice or game in the first place. When he detected those sentiments, he always flicked a glance at the man's face to see what kind of person he was, if he had been wounded or was a thief or a killer. He could tell a lot by how a man saluted. He thought about how he saluted back now to subordinates and "superiors" and wondered if his own had changed much. It had grown sloppy, he knew, and wondered whether it was due to all of the events that had transpired since arriving here. A cynic's salute. He shook his head.

The dramatic past eighteen months had indeed been propitious, but it had not started out that way, he reflected. Because of his father-in-law's reputation and a letter from the Dorchester bishop, as soon as Lincoln had called for his 75,000 paid volunteers to quell the rebellion, McEmeel had joined and received a commission from the Massachusetts governor as a captain of a 100-man company in a Massachusetts regiment. But he had been a green, a "fresh fish," and he knew it.

Despite his lack of military experience, the officer's appointment seemed not at all inappropriate to him. He certainly was well educated, more than most, and had an extremely amiable disposition. With his easy manner and infectious laugh, he had the ability to put others at ease. Young women always found his company pleasing, and his colleagues envied that. He was well known and well liked by many of the young men in the company, many of them fellow members of the "Wide Awakes," a Republican para-military movement that had demonstrated for Lincoln's election and marched down the streets of many northern cities, as well as Boston. His comrades in the Movement all shared a belief that something — something big and important — was about to happen. His generation, filled with ambitious young men like himself, would provoke and lead profound upheaval that would give them control of the future. Eighteen-sixty-one had been an auspicious, heady and very promising time, he reflected with some satisfaction.

But as he thought more about it on his walk home, as fervent a participant as he had been, and despite his own projections of its purpose, he never truly had known what the Wide Awake Movement truly was all about. He doubted that many others did either. When he subsequently spoke with colleagues who also had dressed themselves in the Movement's black oilcloth capes and silently paraded with long torches to their grand rallies, he realized that there really was *no* unifying credo amongst them at all, other than a poorly articulated hodgepodge of demands insisting on "change" and disruption of the existing social order. Young against "old"? Envy? Have-nots against those who had it made?

It was confusing even now, three years later. Some of his colleagues passionately had espoused abolition, and others were more concerned for parity in incomes. Some demanded the overthrow of the privileges afforded to the practitioners of any religion, and conversely, others seemed to want an expansion of religious freedom. The women they attracted to the Movement's mostly male ranks wanted to have the same privileges in society as their male counterparts. Some of the more liberal men wanted the opportunity to have unbridled promiscuity without the disapprobation of state laws. Within his own company he found several followers of John Humphrey Noys, the founder of the Oneida Colony, who advocated "perfection" within the bounds of "Complex Marriage" doctrine and the communal sharing of sexual partners.

He did remember with great pleasure that the Wide Awakes' marches, attended by thousands of excited young men, followed by many young excited women, seemed to frighten everyone who observed them, particularly those who had achieved security and were ensconced in their own comfort in this thriving American culture. Although the Movement's rallies were always disorganized in so many ways, the very threatening appearance of the silent, non-violent, but nevertheless dramatically-staged throngs of black-clad participants moving down the streets at night, sent shivers up and down the East Coast and provoked angry, irrational, reactionary violence in several southern states.

He marveled a bit how his attitudes had changed so much in such a short time. He hadn't become a cynic yet, back in those heady days. But as one of the marchers himself, and even as one of the "captains" of the movement, he always held back a few steps, staying safe, careful to test the wind.

He knew he had never been an idealist, really. Yes, he had felt an enormous titillating thrill in the power in all of that-watching the startled alarm in the faces of the gray beards. But when he took the time to think about it, he realized that, despite what he had professed early on in the discussions with his colleagues, he really had *no* particular interest in forcing the abolition of slavery. Should he be ashamed of that? he wondered.

He certainly *did* detest wealthy people and their attitudes, however. And because so many of the well-off were also conservative proponents of the status quo in all societal and fiscal matters, he believed that social upheaval was a just process, irrespective of the means taken to attain it. He knew he was young and smart enough to benefit, if only things could be shaken loose a bit. Abolition could be attained in its own good time, and would be hastened by a change in power, he was certain.

Then, for a while, in the immediate months after Lincoln's election, the Movement seemed to lose its edge and momentum, as if the Republican victory had achieved the Wide Awake Movement's primary goals — whatever they were — leaving its members to fend for themselves.

What changed it all was South Carolina's secession and then the firing on Fort Sumter, he reflected. It provoked a quickening of purpose, articulated in an almost pithy way by Lincoln's call to arms. McEmeel, like many of the comrades from his school, had found his next opportunity. He joined the army and changed his garb from that of a black-clad marcher-for-change to that of a soldier who was defending the gains attained by popular election. And then, with a certain easy victory over the upstart rebels, more changes and more opportunities would come.

And now, on top of it all, he shook his head, he was a hero! A very wealthy one at that!

A block away from his deceased Father-in-law's brownstone, McEmeel stopped to admire his newly acquired ruby signet ring adorning his fifth finger. He was a man of means now. He had important business in several states — wherever the business of General Butler sent him.

Where was his excuse to allow him a graceful and understandable exit? Although he couldn't really discuss such business with his wife, Kathleen — as a stubborn woman — she just would never be able to understand the intricacies of such complex business, nor would she likely approve of it if directly confronted with knowledge of where the luxuries she now enjoyed had originated. She would certainly demand to see proof of the cancelation of the furlough he had been granted at her request.

It was a blasted annoying hindrance!

And had O'Malley not imposed his death on the very last day of McEmeel's business in Washington, as he was finishing details of a quiet, four way exchange of quinine, alcohol, rubber and coffee for tons of cotton seized by Butler and his entourage, he would have been back in New Orleans already, closer to the ongoing distributions of confiscated bounty. The small fabric mill in which he had been allowed to invest with Andrew Butler, the General's brother, had already returned tidy profits that had allowed him to purchase four houses close enough to each other that he would soon own an entire block in the upper Common of Boston.

He had to get back to New Orleans before the war was over.

He took a deep breath and paused before his painful struggle up the steps to the brownstone.

Before the first step, a young man walked up and handed him a note.

It was marked "Confidential"

The penmanship told him it was from his widowed sister-in-law, Emmy Evers, who resided in the same building, requesting a meeting in private with him. She had penned a simple direct request

> *Jonathan, a year ago, after you were wounded you promised me that if I ever needed anything you would help me.*
>
> *It is time to call upon that offered favor. As you know and with your help, I have approached every one of the civilian and military contacts you and others have*

provided, but to no avail. No one is willing to help me.

I am aware, however, that in addition to your official contacts, you have connections to persons with special talents.

I would appreciate an introduction.

Please do not mention this request to my sister, Kathleen. She will not understand.

Em

He put the envelope into his carpetbag and tried to recall how that offer had come about. And who *he* was one year ago.

In March of 1861, he had been a very different man, he realized.

◇◇◇◇

Sixteen months earlier, March 14th 1861-Washington, District of Columbia

The captain's gold plated bars on McEmeel's shoulders, — they weren't quite the epaulettes of upper rank yet — added a full twelve inches to his height. At least he *felt* that way, when he wore his parade uniform. Men nodded and women glanced. He could sense them watching after him when he wore them. He read their thoughts. Envy from the men, especially from non-officers. And lust, or something close to it from the women, he hoped. Just what he had wanted, he realized. The perfect response to the figure he had aimed to cut.

He hoped to find the right time to benefit from all of that, sow his seeds, watch for his chances and win his lot. If the luck prevailed, he would keep this commission long enough to leverage it into another fine set of opportunities. He would keep his profile low on that darker side, quietly dally there, perhaps, and maintain a prominent presence on the other, where the epaulettes reflected the light-where it counted, keep the title even if the conflict ended quickly and he mustered out. He had seen it work so well as a stepping-stone for others, a military title without the pain of commitment. On the ascent, he was.

And then, surprising and disappointing him greatly, less than three weeks after McEmeel had received the letter notifying him of his commission as an officer in the Dorchester volunteer regiment, before he had even established a presence, he was told that he would not be assigned to the quartermaster's staff, but rather to the infantry. His uniform had just come back from the tailor. On the same day he received that news, he learned that the entire company would be expected to move out within the next few days from Dorchester to Washington.

Something was afoot. Lincoln and Stanton were intending to accelerate the solution.

He had hoped, like so many others who volunteered their services, that the rebels simply would back down when they understood they were up against a determined and overwhelming Union force. But they hadn't. So now he would be expected to accept this unwanted turn of events.

He thought about it and, as disappointed as he was, he knew he could do the right thing. If real fighting started. Commit, he told himself. There would be benefits if he stayed the course and kept his health, he knew.

Up to that point, he had the privilege of conducting his business within the regiment from the comfort of his home with his wife, Kathleen O'Malley. She, and her younger sister, Emmy, followed him one week later to Washington to set up domicile in a brownstone rented by his father-in-law, the newly elected congressman from Boston's easternmost district.

In the first ten days in Washington, because of all of the activities entailed with establishing a home, he had little time to read about command tactics or sharpen what little martial skill he believed he might possess. Other than being an organizer for some of the Wide Awake marches, McEmeel had never really been in charge of anything in his life, he admitted, but rather, had supported himself as a "strategic advisor" and accountant for the Dorchester Providence diocese. In fact, that had been his only work experience ever. The bishop had vouched for his ledger and writing skills, and apparently that was good enough for the Governor.

This lack of experience bothered McEmeel somewhat, but when he looked around, he realized that very few of his colleagues in the Dorchester regiment had any more than he. However, when orders came three weeks later in June of 1861 to help prepare his troops to cross the Potomac for a march on Richmond, that accelerated his worry regarding his ignorance about fighting matters.

He knew he had some reason to be insecure. He had fired a rifle only once in his life and generally had previously disdained the military. He owned an old single-shot flint smoothbore pistol that had been given to him by a Dublin-born uncle who had served in the Seminole Wars, but he still couldn't hit a stationary target with his military-issued Colt pistol from farther away than fifteen feet!

Like many other Union officers, he carried a sword, an ornate, heavy saber with a gold plated pommel and gilded tassel given to him by Kathleen, but he had taken it out of its scabbard only four times and of that, three were while he marched in parades. On the one episode in which he had attempted to exercise with it against a bag of straw, he realized he had never sharpened it and didn't even know how. He regretted that the chore of keeping hone on the house knives had always been someone else's responsibility.

He did know how to parse Latin and Greek well, could recite from memory Caesar's first chapter about the Gallic Wars and wrote long letters and entered his ledger calculations in a distinctive cursive calligraphy that many admired, and which had made him quite useful to the clerics who ran the parishes around Dorchester. But he still couldn't decipher the communication hieroglyphics and flag movements the Army's signal corps used, despite attempting to read the impenetrably complex manuals more than once.

He knew he looked dashingly handsome in his gray and blue uniform and his long- gaited, dignified strut turned heads of men and women whenever he paraded in it or accompanied his wife on strolls along Pennsylvania

Avenue. But his tight-fitting new boots ached and the stiff wool britches chafed his groin.

That he *looked* like a soldier was at least half of what it took to be a leader, he reassured himself. Tall men always had that natural advantage, he had read somewhere. He also told himself that this insurrection would be over in fewer than one or two months. Like so many of the citizens of the North who pushed Lincoln to move the army southward, he believed that the confederated rabble would easily be discouraged and defeated. He had heard that the majority of soldiers who volunteered likely would see no combat, so the odds of having to prove his mettle in a few confrontations was unlikely.

So, in the end, undeterred by so many glaring assorted deficiencies that seasoned soldiers would have considered an irresponsible naiveté and tender optimism, after a few weeks with his company, Captain Jon Evan McEmeel became modestly confident he was ready to take on the equally green rebels. So were many other young, hubristic, energetic men who marched with him in the early summer of '61. They were brothers in arms! Their collective courage and determination would overcome any obstacles mere men might put forth against them!

As a result of Lincoln's call, which also offered volunteers a guarantee of ninety days of pay, within four weeks, the population of Washington tripled to over 140,000. Two-thirds of that number descended into the capital city after Sumter — the soldiers, the prostitutes, the gamblers, enterprising opportunists, and the camp followers less fortunate than McEmeel and his wife — lived in tents and makeshift shelters inside and on the outskirts of the city.

The open sewer ditches filled quickly and flowed along, a stinking mess, into the Potomac. When it rained, the ditches overflowed into the muddy, unpaved streets. The summer heat worsened the smell of human waste. A minor cholera epidemic began near Pennsylvania Avenue, and the medical corps noted a quadrupling of malaria cases.

McEmeel ignored that and the widespread disorder that would have appeared to even casual observers to be obvious and overwhelming chaos. Several times he commented to his wife, Kathleen, how impressed he was with the apparent ability of the army commanders to control this vast array of brothers in arms, all in units festooned in a wide colorful array of uniforms.

Walking through the encampments on the streets of Washington, he saw a diverse sartorial display of uniforms and banners. In one long row of tents he saw New York Irishmen, followers of the notoriously famous Colonel Michael Corcoran, several sporting about in green jerkins and Tam O'shanters. In another quarter he saw New York "Fire Zuaves," followers of the recently martyred Colonel Ellison, posing for tinted *ambrotypes* in their red turbans, blue blouses, and canvas balloon pants. He met plainspoken Maine men wearing simple blue wool short coats, and Italians from Rhode Island — the "Risorgimento Regiment" — in bright red blouses, worn in honor of Giuseppe Garibaldi, the internationally famous Italian hero.

When the troops made their first parade up Pennsylvania Avenue, accompanied by military brass bands stationed on every corner, the awestruck population witnessed a spectacular grand opera of handsomely dressed men strutting confidently to brass, fife and drum versions of the tunes "Tramp, Tramp, Tramp" and "Drums of War." The differences in uniforms — there were over 240 variations in colors and styles — seemed to reinforce a collective, widespread solidarity, irrespective of the origins of those who donned them, all united as similarly-minded men from all of the communities throughout the North. And, except for those who had joined the army for the pay and the opportunity for mischief, to Jon Evan McEmeel, everyone there had a common purpose, to defeat those who would seek to break up the Union.

The Washington area suffered a terrible heat wave that year, which had a deleterious impact. By not articulating a uniform set of expectations, the high command of the predominantly volunteer army that had encamped in and around Washington lost a valuable opportunity to standardize operations and prepare their troops for combat. Although most of the volunteer commanders dutifully ordered maneuvers and oversaw drilling exercises by their troops, many, especially those without any military experience, did not understand the purpose. Some, like McEmeel, unless they had been ordered to accomplish specific duties such as helping construction projects, abbreviated the drills and allowed their men to relax in camp afterwards and stay out of the sultry Washington early summer heat.

McEmeel wasn't really worried. He learned to expect his lieutenants to keep the men in line. That was what a command structure was all about, wasn't it? He gave crisp orders as they paraded down the corridors of the city, and expected that he would be given the same command respect if the "Dorchester Gray Devils" ever were called into a fight.

He listened to the criticism of the only veteran army sergeant in his company who had advised him that much more drill practice would prove of immense value keeping the men cohesively engaged if and when the shooting began.

The sergeant pointed over to a troop of cavalry practicing dressage maneuvers and compared the young volunteers in the company to the horses the riders were learning to control.

"De'll break, Son. Snap off like twigs in a haed win', they will," the tough Irishman veteran had said. "Yer hardness now'll keep 'em from witherin' 'n boltin' later. They need spunk as a unit, not as individual lads. Watchin' out for their mates, not just for themselves."

McEmeel, identifying with his non-commissioned comrades, many of whom just a few weeks ago were tavern chums, dismissed his frustrated drill sergeant's concerns, and told him that *he* believed his Dorchester troops would be better served by "the morale attained through a collegial camp atmosphere, than by doing senseless dispiriting exercises in this humid weather." Enough was enough. They had practiced shooting, maneuvers and marching. And, empathizing with them, he hated the Washington heat. Unfortunately for McEmeel and his company, the disgusted veteran sergeant transferred to another regiment, the Irish Brigade that later distinguished itself repeatedly during the coming conflicts.

◇◇◇◇

Jon Evan McEmeel was an elated, nervous twenty-eight year-old when, on July 16th, 1861 he marched with his regiment in Brigadier General Irwin McDowell's army onto Virginia's soil for the first time to attack rebel forces that had been gathering near Manassas, one of Virginia's most important railroad junctions.

The excitement of the anticipated battle brought out huge crowds to cheer the grand procession that smartly pranced the streets the day before the departure. The Dorchester company was right in the middle of it all, and McEmeel thumped his chest with pride as he thought about the drubbing he and his men would give to their rag-tag miscreant opponents.

The energy of the celebrations reminded him of the Wide Awake Movement's processions, but with the added flair of martial music to accompany them all along the route the next day. They marched well in formation. They seemed ready. He kept to himself his hopes that this massive show of overwhelming force would be enough to scare the rebels into submission, perhaps without a shot being fired.

In a plan of attack approved by Lincoln and General Winfield Scott, McDowell's army began moving out in three columns in a procession to march the twenty-five miles to the site of the expected confrontation. Two columns were aimed at the important Manassas Junction and one moved westward, circling around the Confederate positions to cut off their anticipated route of retreat from the large Union army's attack.

Unfortunately, McDowell's forces embarked much more slowly than he expected. It took over nine hours for the last of his army's columns to exit the Washington area, some crossing the river, others moving southwest from the periphery of the city.

Over the next two days, thousands of civilians followed to witness the spectacle. Like many other well-heeled citizens of Washington, unbeknownst to him, McEmeel's wife, Kathleen, and several of her friends travelled in carriages and armed themselves with parasols to shield them from the July sun. They carried opera glasses for better views of the contest. Kathleen and her entourage of Washington friends, all of them dressed in Sunday finery, also packed picnic baskets. She told McEmeel later that she had hoped to have the chance to share the food with him and introduce her friends to his handsome men if the opportunity presented itself.

Most of the thirty-five thousand Union troops, strung out over ten miles, were fatigued by mid-day because of the terrible delays and logistic poor planning. Command had ordered them to be mustered and ready for marching at four that morning. They then stood in formation for hours waiting for the order to move out.

When they finally did move, because the dirt roads were so narrow, no more than four men could walk abreast in each of the routes' several well-worn sections. Contributing to the confusion, the Union Army's intelligence staff had distributed to the regimental officers hastily copied versions from old, inaccurate originals. Many of the roads and thoroughfares depicted on them were incomplete, or had never existed in the first place. Rivers appeared where thoroughfares were supposed to be. If an axel broke when a wagon went over a deep rut in the old roads, or an officer stopped to read one of the confusing maps, the entire procession following behind stalled to a halt. Entire companies that veered away in an effort to bypass the slowly plodding main column simply got lost for hours. McEmeel later estimated that his own company had made hundreds of stops and starts over the course of the late, humid morning, so that it took his troops over three hours to creep less than a half mile.

He began to feel that standing and waiting was just as exhausting as the marching, more so perhaps, because of the boredom, anger and impatience that attended the enormous inefficiency of the procession. When he walked forward up the road on one of the many delays, he saw that the older soldiers and veterans in some of the other companies seemed to be calmer than his own men. Many of them sat by the side of the road playing cards and distracted themselves by their banter. When he returned to his own ranks, he realized that the men in his company — the younger, inexperienced men especially — wore tense impatient expressions. He wondered whether that would make any difference in the upcoming fight. Some of the men in his company spoke out-loud their agitated discontent. As he continued that morning, feeling the anxiety increasing amongst his men, he realized that he and his men would have been better served had he not provoked the transfer of his veteran sergeant.

But several other miscalculations and logistical mistakes by the planners of the campaign worsened the already frustrating situation. The quartermasters of the hastily assembled new army hadn't provisioned for adequate water supplies and most of the unseasoned soldiers up and down the line consumed the contents of their canteens, water or whiskey, within the first few hours. As the day's heat increased, all along the line men began discarding coats, then rain gear, then bedding, and then anything else they deemed too heavy to lug. Some men, especially those who were at the end of their 90-day term and had already drawn most of their final pay, laid their rifles and ammunition by the side of the road, dropped out of the formation altogether and turned back towards Washington. Seeing the discarded, expensive equipment along the road, McEmeel seriously considered leaving his heavy sword by the wayside as well but decided against that . . . he couldn't come home to Kathleen without it, after all, so instead, he ordered a private to carry it for him.

When the first units of the Union's exhausted forces finally reached the Centerville area almost two full days later, reconnaissance discovered Confederate units blocking further progress to Manassas Junction. On hearing this, McDowell, personally reconnoitering the situation with his staff, realized the rebels had ensconced themselves at every one of the eight crossable fords along an eight-mile meandering eight-foot wide stretch of the nearby Occoquan River, which the locals called the "Bull Run." Their positions were strong. An assault by one of the brigades the day before had been readily repulsed.

While he sat on his horse, attempting to stay out of range of Confederate marksmen shooting at them from across the river, McDowell vented his frustration that his army had lost every element of surprise. One of his officers commented to another that the Confederate cavalry had quietly tracked them ever since it crossed into Virginia soil. "We've moved like a fat, sloppy pig," the officer commented quietly. "What did he expect?"

And unbeknownst to them all, a reliable Confederate spy network had already conveyed McDowell's battle and route plans to P. T. Beauregard, the Confederate commander on the field.

CHAPTER SEVEN

⟨⟨⟨⟩⟩⟩

Kathleen

July 16th, 1862-Washington, District of Columbia

Even if the favor Emmy requested, to care for Jacob and Sarah, was only to be for a short time-a week or ten days at most, she said, it came at an inconvenient time and would obligate her to stay in Washington when she already had plans to be in New York. And Kathleen had too many other things on her mind right now. She had been brooding over her husband's abrupt departure back to New Orleans "on orders" from General Butler. It was the last thing she needed, she told herself — having to watch those two strange, disagreeable children, a selfish imposition from Emmy, a sister who, she had decided long ago, was simply spoiled, inconsiderate and no matter what anyone else thought about her, gallingly pietistic.

She argued vehemently with Emmy against the request, but in the end, had given up, and that made her especially cross. She felt anxious as well, for in her thirty-five years, she really had never taken care of children before. Perhaps it also was that her husband willingly and covertly had agreed to help Emmy travel into Virginia across rebel lines without consulting her beforehand. Was his act contributing to this unbecoming anger and resentment that roiled inside? She didn't know. But she felt left out and betrayed. And that was not an uncommon feeling for her, she conceded. It came over her as far back as she could remember.

◇◇◇◇

Kathleen Lorraine O'Malley's favorite game when she was a small child was "Traveling to Jerusalem," a nursery rhyme and sport also known as "Musical Chairs." She took an immense and disproportionate amount of pride in her skill and conduct in it. To the amusement of some who watched the fierce little red-haired girl play, she associated the family's parlor piano with the game rather than with music her mother occasionally played.

Beyond the age when most children have tired of such games, Kathleen insisted on playing the contest whenever the opportunity presented itself, particularly when her sister Emmy, younger by two years, would likely be a participant.

On one occasion, as her father later ruefully observed, she told a hapless six-year-old playmate who was circling the chairs behind her, "You know, I *always* win."

And indeed, she was correct, at least as it related to the game itself.

In many ways, the Jerusalem nursery school pastime stood as a metaphor that typified her way of seeing the world — a ferocious, competitive pride defined much of what she did. Everyone her age was a potential rival unless they were willing to submit to her square-faced aggression.

As she grew older, Kathleen found other ways to win, sometimes overt — with repeated domineering provocations of her cousins and playmates that not infrequently escalated to crying, hair-pulling, name-calling and then extended internecine disputes — and sometimes subtle, like hiding her sister's shoes so that the family would be late for Sunday morning church ceremonies. The behavior was so irksome to her father that when she was twelve, he had labeled her and her predictable competitiveness as "ridiculous, obnoxious, and obdurate."

She seemed to pay no attention to her father's insults, or to his punishments. She dismissed the criticisms of playmates, and found convoluted justification for her increasingly impudent actions.

By the time Kathleen was fifteen, she finally fell into a lassitude that frequently besets truculent teenagers who believe they somehow are disadvantaged.

"Why try? I am unloved. You know Father has hated me since the moment I was born, or at least since the day Emmy was born," she confided to her soft-hearted mother, Abby, one day.

Abby O'Malley, who knew that her husband's stubborn rejections of Kathleen's repeated overtures likely played a great part in the worsening of the alienation, watched with a sense of sad helplessness her older daughter's descent into self-pity. Despite her attempted intercessions on Kathleen's behalf, Abby's husband, Kern, who was fond of labeling others, had also applied to his oldest daughter another unenviable descriptor, calling her "willfully feckless."

As her sister Emmy, who, by observing the deleterious outcomes of her sister's willful behavior, learned to comport herself in a dignified and quiet, confident manner, Kathleen developed a sullen haughtiness that distanced her further from her father and most of her extended family.

Then Kathleen ran away.

She quietly returned four months later pregnant and had no reliable story that would help identify the likely father. Fortunately for her, her family, and the soul her father told her she "had erred into existence," she miscarried.

But then things changed dramatically. Within months after her sister Emmy accepted the marriage proposal of an older, very wealthy, enterprising wayfarer named John Tern, and moved away for adventures and bounty in the great Oregon Territory, Kathleen did a remarkable turnabout.

She devised ways to revise her image. She completed finishing school. She re-engaged in the Boston upper class Irish social circles. She applied charm, feigned graciousness, laughed frequently and used her still fresh beauty to lure young men to her favor. Demonstrating an almost cat-like alacrity, she practiced managing concomitant relationships with several beaux, often playing one off against the other.

Three years later, with the tepid approval of her father, she married a young man named Jon Evan McEmeel, a handsome, self-confident, garrulous young man who she realized knew clever ways of maneuvering his way up and into the graces of numerous wealthy social circles. This was a skill that Kathleen believed would be extremely useful to them both, and one that her father, again near bankruptcy, envied as well.

Kathleen and Jon McEmeel's marriage was overtly gay and seemed truly amiable to observers who worried about such things. Her father, although reserving his ultimate benediction, slowly and with stubborn reserve, reluctantly accepted them into his favor. Kathleen, sensing her father's holdback, was undeterred, however. As her father began showing his age, she rightly realized how important legacy had become to him, more so after news arrived from the Oregon territory of her sister Emmy's first pregnancy. So she and McEmeel began in earnest the intimacies necessary to start their own family.

Unfortunately, they failed, despite numerous consultations with a variety of local experts on such matters. Kathleen miscarried three times and thus remained childless during the ten years of their marriage. But, at least during Emmy's absence, she stood as her mother's only confidant and in her own mind at least, her father's only daughter.

When her sister Emmy and her two children returned to Boston from their ordeals of living in the Pacific Northwest and the tragedies that had befallen them while traveling across Panama, Kathleen experienced an awakened sense of displacement.

This was complicated further by the anger she experienced from the emotional distance that had grown between herself and her husband, one that presented itself shortly after their first attempts at intimacy, and severely worsened after her second miscarriage. Their mutual pride prevented them from closing the gap between themselves. They blamed each other for their lack of success in starting their family. McEmeel, the second son in a family of five brothers and three sisters, reminded Kathleen that, to his knowledge, no woman had ever miscarried in his large and fertile Catholic family. Kathleen in turn, knowing that she was being blamed, attempted to save face by confiding a bald lie to friends — that McEmeel had some "disabilities."

To compensate for her frustration, when her father, riding on the coattails of Benjamin Butler, was elected as a Massachusetts congressman, she threw herself into the widespread ebullience brought on by the dizzying array of political events that swept through the country in the 1860 elections. The secession of Confederate states increased the frenzied excitement within the Boston Irish parishes, both conservative Democrat and liberal Republican.

When Lincoln called for volunteers to put down the rebellion, Kathleen saw substantial fresh opportunity. She repeatedly lobbied her father to use his newfound influence to put her husband into a prominent position within the newly-formed militia in Dorchester. Her father, still lukewarm to McEmeel, reluctantly complied, and her husband stepped into a new role. Kathleen knew he was unprepared for this responsibility, but was confident nonetheless that he would find a way to succeed and open doors for prosperity and position.

On July 20th of 1861, in that first year of what was predicted to be a brief and limited conflict, in the mid-morning fresh, cool calm of a day destined to be sticky, tongue-hanging hot, one day after the last of the troops of the Army of the Potomac had finally departed from Washington, Kathleen followed. Accompanied by Assistant Ambassador Roland Ferdinand Escoffiere, a French diplomat and admirer, and a group of seven of her young women friends — all riding together in two open-aired carriages — Kathleen directed the entourage to head for Virginia's Centerville. There, she reassured them, she would find a picnic spot that would be far enough away from the river mosquitos but with sufficient high ground clearance that they might observe some of the confrontation of their great army with the Confederate rabble.

The grand army's destination, the Manassas Railroad Junction, had not been a well-kept secret, nor had Kathleen's husband kept what he knew about the campaign confidential. And thus in preparation for the adventure she was orchestrating for her friends whom she hoped to impress, Kathleen had purchased a map from one of the army engineers showing some of the terrain around the Manassas Junction.

The roads to Centerville were mostly unobstructed by the mid-day, because most of the Union army's regiments had finally made their way to their assigned staging points near the Bull Run creek. A few times, the bevy of eight excited, chattering women and their one greatly stimulated male companion, pulled aside to make way for the passing of caissons and cannon. No less than four separate times along the way, Kathleen's two carriages — each festooned with the young women's open gay parasols that made the lorries look like moving *jardiniéres* of pink and yellow flowers — were approached and then escorted for a short distance by groups of mounted Union dragoons.

In each circumstance, the young soldiers initiated their conversations on the pretense of concern for the safety of the women, but quickly showed by their conversations that they were more interested in flirtation and attention from the women. The lively banter between the women and the soldiers increased the overall excitement of the day, thus the twenty-five mile trip into Virginia passed quickly indeed.

Kathleen ably demonstrated to her companions her skills in play and coy repartee with the dashing young mounted soldiers, each troop dressed in distinctly different colors denoting their regimental origins. Most of the young women in her entourage had never heard the polite Wisconsin twang or the terse, plain pronunciation of the Maine men who had pranced about during the cantering at the side their carriages. After each escorting group's departure, the young women called out to each other from their carriages, comparing their impressions of the men and their mannerisms.

The lively chatter going back and forth between her carriages continued all the way to the outskirts of Centerville, Virginia where they were stopped by soldiers at a log barrier who told them the town was "already too full of gawking civilians" like themselves.

"Obliged t' turn y' back, Ladies," the weathered old sergeant directing the roadblock told them with a tip of his kepi. "Likely y' want see much in any case."

Kathleen tried to argue her way past the barriers, but ultimately understood she would not win this test. So she complied and instructed the drivers to turn about. When they were far enough away from the soldiers, she stopped the carriages, pulled out her map and looked southward where there appeared to be wooded high ground and bluffs in an area to the east named "Centerville Ridge."

A few minutes later, she recognized Signal Corps insignias on a large company of passing riders heading in that same direction and, on a hunch, she instructed the lorry drivers to follow them. They lost track of the riders, but within twenty minutes, slowly following the narrow road upwards, they found the soldiers again, moving about in an encampment on a small clearing that opened onto a high bluff looking westward across the marshes on each side of the confluent rivers several hundred feet below.

She saw soldiers pulling wires up the steep hill to a tent covering a telegraph station. They could hear intermittent cannon fire in the far off distance to the south of the camp. Kathleen saw that the signal corps soldiers were waving flags. Turning westward with her opera glasses, she could see relays of Union flagmen in the distance responding vigorously.

After discussing their predicament with the major in command, a pleasant gentleman named Philip Fagan, she returned to her group.

"I presented some papers and told them my husband was a captain down there in Henzelman's regiment, and my father was one of the new congressmen from Massachusetts. He said we looked harmless enough," she laughed. "We have permission to set down here, but we have to stay out of their way. We can go back and try to get into Centerville again in the morning to hear about what we've missed. The major said he expected that the rabble will have turned and fled by then and there should be a big celebration afterwards."

So they spread blankets, opened their baskets and, while passing chutney, sausages, crumbly cheese, crusty bread and sweet preserves, they listened to the rumble of heavy cannon coming from a few miles down-river. The cannonade continued for almost an hour. By the early evening the firing had all but stopped. For several hours it was quiet except for occasional distant musket fire. As darkness came on, they could see thousands of campfires of the massive Union army sprawled off in the distance north and south all the way to the Bull Run River.

They carried their excited conversations about the adventure of the day over into a picnic dinner, speculating about what the men they knew would do after their commissions ended and what likely would happen to the rebels when the Union Army swept them away. Would they all be hanged, or just their leaders?

Kathleen reminded them that Jefferson Davis had almost won the Democratic nomination for presidency, and her father's former law partner, General Benjamin Butler, had voted for Davis on fifty-seven straight ballots. Such a shame that this dispute couldn't be settled with more diplomacy and negotiation, they all agreed.

Although it was a very warm evening, the breeze push-ing over the bluff was enough to chill them a bit, so they built a small camp fire, and Kathleen persuaded them to play her favorite new board game "The Checkered Game of Life," which they continued until, with her accumula-tion of property and riches, she was sufficiently certain that she had come close enough to the 100 points neces-sary to win the contest and no one could catch up.

Assuring herself that she was simply playing a harm-less game that heightened the fun for the evening, unob-served in the darkness by her friends, she allowed Roland Escoffier to rub his elbow, and then his knee against hers. She could sense that it excited him and that added to the sport of the evening. She even pressed back slightly, feign-ing ignorance to his overture. At one point she gave him a sly glance, then when he brightened, shook her head slightly, declining his further attentions. But she raised her eyebrow at him during that glance, telling herself, and him if he noticed it, she hoped she could keep the door open to future escapades. With his connections, she might need him at some point in the future, she thought to herself.

They finally bedded down at ten o'clock, all resting close to one another near the fire. Kathleen wondered aloud whether the battle was over already, or whether they might see more events on the next day. She wanted to go to a party. She said she hoped that McEmeel — she had referred to him by his last name for over a year — had taken care of himself. Without children, she wasn't ready to be a widow, she said aloud, although to herself, she knew they were beyond that as a couple now.

The fire died down a bit, and although everyone, including Escoffier, had finally fallen asleep, the camp of the Signal Corp company was active and made a lot of noise. Kathleen ruminated about her marriage and her relationship with her husband. She was unhappy, she had to admit. But at least she *did* have a husband. That was one advantage she had over her sister, Emmy, who upon arriving home with her two children, had quickly won over — regained actually — the affections of her father.

It didn't matter to her father that her sister's children were odd, to say the least, Kathleen thought. The daughter, Sarah, just entering her teenage years, was impertinent and rude. The son, Jacob, was a crude little being, an unrefined, ill-mannered backwoods type, and impenetrable like his sister, she had decided. And he was disturbed. Broken by the Indians. He had awakened the household regularly with what Emmy described as his "night terrors." The boy kept to himself, talked to himself, and seldom spoke to anyone else except his brash older sister.

She had expressed opinions to Emmy, delicately of course, and had diplomatically suggested the boy be brought to a New York medical doctor whom she had heard was a leading expert in treatment of insanity and the disturbed. The doctor had done wonders with a high percentage of his patients. She had read the testimonials, published on the back pages of *The Tribune*. Kathleen even offered to help pay for the evaluation and treatment should the boy need — to be "kept." But Emmy had ignored her suggestions, as had Emmy and Kathleen's father and mother.

Her father truly seemed to dote on them, she thought. Of course her father would side with Emmy and favor his grandchildren. They were legacy. After Kathleen and Emmy's mother died shortly after Emmy returned from the Oregon Territory, the attention he showed to Emmy's children increased to the point of being an absolute irritation to her, she concluded. It scraped at her craw like a swallowed, stale crust of burnt bread.

She estimated she fell asleep at two o'clock A.M., shortly after brief conversation with the officer of the watch from the Signal Corps.

At six o'clock, she awakened to what she thought was the beginning of a thunderstorm, but then remembered where she was and realized she was hearing a barrage from what had to be very big cannon. The explosions continued for at least fifteen minutes. When it ceased, she could hear small arms fire emanating from the same area west and north of the bluff where they had picnicked. She couldn't tell how far away the gunfire was, but it didn't move any closer over the next hour before it, too, died down. During the night, so much mist had arisen from the rivers below the bluff that they could only see the tops of the trees. Although several riders came and went, carrying dispatches to the officers, the Signal Corps soldiers stood by idly until eight o'clock, when the fog cleared enough that they could see some of the movement of troops in the distance.

Kathleen watched as best she could with her opera glasses. She couldn't really tell one side from the other, but the soldiers off to her left were waving their small red flags again. Signals. Waving in patterns, back and forth. The men seemed agitated.

While the rest of the women in her party and Escoffier awakened, Kathleen walked over to the Union officer she had befriended the previous evening.

"It's all starting in a very short while," he said. "Can't see much from up here, Miss. But as I said last evening, I'm expectin' the field to be swept clear shortly. Then you all can return to your nice comfortable homes," with a tiny hint of derision in his voice, Kathleen thought.

When the cannon and rifle fire started up again at nine-thirty it was already hot. Kathleen estimated it must have been at least 80 degrees, and dense smoke from the encounters off to the northwest quickly obscured whatever visibility had previously been possible. From what she could deduce, the military maneuvers had gotten off way behind schedule.

By ten o'clock, it was obvious that the position that the Signal Corps had taken was useless for observation. Despite that, the soldiers did not decamp. For a short while horsemen brought news and dispatches from McDowell's headquarters, but, Kathleen concluded, likely because the message about the futility of their observation post had been conveyed, the riders stopped coming. The Signal Corps soldiers seemed ebullient, however. She heard several reports that the enemy was retreating.

The sounds of the distant battle continued all morning. By eleven-fifteen, because they could see nothing from their perch, Kathleen decided to make another attempt to enter Centerville with her entourage. Perhaps they could help some of the soldiers or celebrate their victory. They packed their baskets and, with the sounds of the gunfire unabated in the distance, they began their descent from the wooded ridge. By twelve-thirty they had found the turn-pike that coursed towards Centerville. This time, no one prevented their entry into the small town at one o'clock.

What they found surprised them. The dusty little town was filled with the carriages of other civilians, some of whom she recognized from the congressional parties her father had held. Three telegraph stations, surrounded by excited, happy people, reporters, and soldiers, busily received messages and conveyed others, apparently back to Washington.

Although the general atmosphere was jubilant — they heard that the rebels had retreated in disarray and McDowell was committing all of his forces to push them off the field — wagons with wounded men were passing through the streets onto the turnpike that led back to Washington. Many of the men were moaning and curs-ing. Each time a wagon passed over one particularly large pothole, the wailing and groaning intensified. Five lorries passed carrying mangled corpses only, partially covered with tarps. Another cart passed full of bloody bodies, all wearing the same regimental colors, all headless, as if a scimitar had swept across the lot.

Kathleen had never really seen dead bodies or wounded men before, and it was clear that none of the young women in the two carriages she had rented had seen this type of misery before, either. She looked at Escoffier, and as much as he chattered with the women and tried to ignore the bloody parade, she noticed that his face was almost white.

One of the wagons, awaiting the clearing of a queue up ahead, came to a halt directly in front of their two lor-ries. She saw the faces of the men in it who were wounded.

Their uniforms were gray, like the one her husband's unit wore. She looked for McEmeel, but didn't see him. It was hot. One of the young women called to her to open up one of the baskets to give the men some water. Kathleen nodded. They opened the trunk carrying their baskets. No water. Just jams and jellies.

◇◇◇◇

Thinking back on the events of that horrible day one year ago, all the thousands of men lost, she wondered how she herself had survived.

The day they spent in Centerville turned ugly by 3:00, when it was clear that the field was lost and the Union army was in full retreat. The soldiers came pouring into Centerville, a disordered array of terrified men. Some wore serious expressions, others had angst pressed deeply into their faces, so deeply that she wondered if the impression would be permanent. All moved swiftly with purpose, which she read as a desperate desire to escape. Many repeatedly looked back at where they had come from, trying to see if pursuit was close.

"It's a fookin' disaster, one grizzled sergeant said to her as he stopped briefly by their lorry. "Best be movin', lest you get yersef pinned by one of dem bastards, Lassie," then looking over the women in the carriages, "by bayonet or otherwise. Ha!"

He moved on.

She looked with her opera glasses down the road at a small bridge on the narrowest part of the turnpike, where a horse had reared and the wagon it pulled tipped over, blocking the entire panicked procession behind it. Men pulled out of the backlogged crowd at the bridge's far side, dropped their rifles onto the bank and threw themselves into the stream to cross. She could recognize no groups of soldiers with more than four or five wearing the same uniform, a sloppy hodgepodge of colors-dark blue, teal, crimson, gray, gold and green. As she watched the mob surge by and across the river in bolts and swells, it reminded her of the festoon of a wedding gone-wrong, wind-shaken into a torrent, its bloodied multi-colored petals rushing downstream and away.

She ordered her drivers to head back quickly to the Potomac. She remembered she hadn't really thought much about McEmeel on that day.

Her two carriages raced into the forefront of the disturbed, disorganized, fleeing, terrified mess of an army. At one bogged-down intersection, she grabbed the carriage whip and fought off a small mob of wounded and exhausted soldiers who begged them for a ride.

In the darkness, late that evening, they heard church bells ringing continuously and knew they had found the outskirts of Washington. Crossing back into the capital, torches sputtered on every street and in every building and house. When she reached her father's brownstone however, she found the house empty.

She closed the door behind her. The noise from the outside faded. She remembered listening to the three clocks in the house, ticking out of synch. They seemed louder than ever before. It was at that moment she thought again about McEmeel. Taking in a deep breath, she wondered if he was lost. Did it matter, she wondered? Weren't they both lost?

Her father had come in a short while later, she remembered, with her sister Emmy and her two children.

"I want you to pack up some travel clothing," he said to them. "If the rebels make it into this city, they'll torch it and likely lynch anyone they think might have supported our strange, gangly leader during the elections. One telegram I saw said they have been executing their prisoners at Manassas."

She remembered packing a suitcase, and for some reason had decided to include a pair of dance slippers.

What should she make of that, she wondered?

CHAPTER EIGHT

<XXXX>

McEmeel

One Year Earlier-July 19th, 1861-Manassas
Junction, Virginia

He did not know Kathleen had arranged for an excursion to follow the troops to Manassas. He thought he had left her in the safety of Washington.

The spent, dehydrated men of the Dorchester Company finally arrived and settled into the outskirts of Centerville, a few miles away from Bull Run stream at 10:30 in the evening of July 19th. Although he was bleary-eyed tired, McEmeel could not sleep, but found a man-sized rock and lay back against it. He took off his boots to relieve pressure on huge blisters that had formed on the first day of the march, and while he sat there gulping water and wondering about his own resolve, a corporal brought him orders that he and his exhausted men were to quietly muster in less than three hours to begin a looping, end-around six-mile march in the darkness. McDowell's new, hastily drawn up plan called for a surprise attack by two-thirds of the Union's regimental strength against the Confederate unprotected northeast flank.

After reading the orders, McEmeel called out to his lieutenants as he attempted to pull the boots back over his swollen feet.

"We have been ordered to get our men ready for another march in three hours," he said.

The blisters on his heels broke. He already had begun to feel that his commanders might not know what they were doing, but the sting of chafing bloody blisters on both heels reinforced that notion with every step.

The plan, dependent on a before dawn surprise flanking attack on the undefended Confederate left, was doomed because of significant miscalculations about the travel time necessary for the Union troops to reach their assembly points. Once again, moving the troops out of camp, this time in darkness, immediately became a logistical mess. Even with a full moon on the ascent, rapid travel without the benefit of torchlight in the dark through the tangled woods and along the hairpin turns of the Bull Run creek was impossible.

When the advanced contingents of Union troops finally found their bearings, crossed over an unguarded ford at Sudley's Springs, and began reorganizing their formations at an unfinished railroad moving westward towards their objective, it was already sun up. Their movement was now visible to the Confederate signal corps who relayed that information to the northernmost commanders about the approaching forces.

What should have been a coordinated rapid flanking action by a force of over 13,000 Union troops turned into a valiant but sputtered advance, moving slowly enough that the Confederates were able to divert 2,300 troops away from their positions guarding the easternmost river fords. Despite being greatly outnumbered, they moved quickly and aggressively, assaulting the bewildered larger force, retarding the onslaught of the Union's massive flanking action.

The majority of McEmeel's undisciplined company, spread out in the darkness, had gotten lost in the thickets. Two of his lieutenants and their men were commandeered away from him without his knowledge by an artillery battery commander who needed manpower to dislodge his field cannon, mired axel-deep in mud. McEmeel's sergeants were unable to locate dozens of their Dorchester men back into the formation for several hours and they did not cross Sudley's Spring, the destination where they had been ordered to assemble, until 11 o'clock in the morning, four hours later than had been planned. By that time, the battle was already well underway.

A few hours earlier, in the Union's advance from the north, the first shots from the Confederates, who had been rushed forward and were well concealed in the tall grass, surprised the Rhode Island soldiers who marched in the Union's first formation. As men and boys dropped, wounded and dead in the haze of the morning, a few of the green young men broke ranks and ran, but most continued forward, encouraged by the veterans who understood the importance of maintaining a careful, disciplined, cohesive line of fire.

"Hold. Hold. Hold." "Front line, DOWN!"

At that command, the Union front line stopped, knelt and the men immediately behind them braced themselves against their backs. On command, they raised their rifles.

"Pick your targets. Aim low!" their major yelled. "Cut their legs out! Now FIRE!"

The simultaneous explosion from 200 barrels deafened every soldier along the line. The exchange of gunfire immediately obscured the field with black and grey smoke. Dead grass caught fire in small patches. Field howitzers, Parrot and Napoleon guns, pushed forward by both sides, opened up, spraying grape shot into the lines. More men went down. Union brigades from New Hampshire and New York were moved forward.

Far in the rear, McEmeel listened to the hellfire, his only sense that a battle was raging because the thirty-foot tall veil of gray gun smoke obscured the field. Standing in formation in the morning sun, he felt faint. His gut ached and he forgot about his blisters as he tried not to envision what was waiting for them in the cloud a half mile up ahead.

Although outnumbered, the Confederates, companies from South Carolina, Alabama, Mississippi and Louisiana, held their ground and several times charged the Union lines. More Union troops were moved forward. Stubbornly and slowly the Confederates moved south, down the slope, down onto the turnpike and then, at their commander's order, rapidly up the hill past a house and held at the crest where they could watch the oncoming masses of Union infantry.

In the opening salvos and then all through the battle, men on both sides fired into the fog at figures they assumed were their enemies, simply because those figures seemed to be pointing weapons in their general direction. The wide array of colors and uniforms, the similarity of battle flags the foes had chosen to mark their regiments worsened the already disastrous confusion.

◇◇◇◇

At noon, his Dorchester "Gray Devils" company, regathered and positioned in the middle third of their regiment, was moved forward with the initial thrust of the Union's flanking action, but then was held again to a reserve station. Listening to the clash in the distance, men's agonizing and angry screams could now be heard mixed into the gunfire.

Unbeknownst to the Union command, by the early morning, 9,000 additional Confederate reinforcements from Joseph Johnston's army had arrived from the Shenandoah Valley. Because Johnston's troops, seasoned by their minor battles in the North Valley, had ridden railroad flatcars instead of marching the twenty-five miles to Manassas, they were fresh for the fray. J.E.B. Stuart's cavalry and Thomas Jackson's cannons poured into the fight.

At two o'clock the two Massachusetts regiments, the 11th Volunteers and the 5th "Minute Men" were moved forward to join the vicious battle on the hill to their left, from where word had come that a desperate, bloody back-and-forth struggle had erupted over the control of eleven Union cannon.

McEmeel, like most of the men in the company had never heard incoming explosions, the unnerving zip of bullets whizzing overhead, the sickening dull thud and snap of lead striking into flesh, the screams of agony as bones broke and bellies burst.

As McEmeel's company rushed forward up the slope to the hilltop, they passed red-shirted New York Fireman Zuaves hiding in the gully off to their right. The percussion of the cannon fire striking the ground two hundred yards in front of them shook the ground and splattered huge clouds of dust and debris into their advance. Sprinkles of smoking and burning hay floated to the ground with each strike.

"Oh, Hell and Merciful Jesus!" he heard one boy, a German kid he knew named Ulbrecht, cough out when a slug slammed into his chest. The boy fell and disappeared in the grass as the company moved forward. McEmeel never saw him again.

Captain Jon Evan McEmeel became a casualty in the first fifteen minutes of his company's full engagement in the battle, not from a bullet or shrapnel, but from a badly twisted knee and ankle, sustained when he caught his heel stepping over the body of what he assumed, but couldn't be certain, was a mangled Confederate soldier.

At first, feeling a sharp snapping pain in his knee that ran all the way up into his groin and into his foot, he thought he had been hit by a bullet. But he saw no blood. Unable to walk without severe pain, supported by the young soldier he previously had ordered to carry his sword, he lagged behind his men advancing up the slope. As his men moved forward into range of the Confederate guns, he tried to encourage them by cheering after them "Keep at 'em, Boys!" but was drowned out by the deafening gunfire. Then the impact of an explosion less than five yards away disintegrated two men in front of him and the concussion convulsed the ground, throwing him and his aide onto their backs. He lost consciousness for a few moments.

When he remembered where he was, he wiped dirt from his eyes and scrubbed pebbles from his face. He found gristle, bone and two teeth stuck to his cheek. They weren't his own. He looked over at the young soldier who had been supporting him and saw that his entire jaw had been blown away. Another explosion threw dirt over them both and the soil mixed into the pumping blood from the dying, gurgling boy. He reached over to the boy, tried to call out to him, then remembered he had never learned his name.

McEmeel, covered in the blood of the dead young man and surrounded by the corpses of other soldiers who had been cut down in the repeated and accurate Confederate volleys, watched the Union lines moving forward and past him. He didn't want to lay amongst the dead or wounded, so he forced himself to stand up and attempted to move forward, using the scabbard of his broken sword as a cane.

Bypassed by other advancing units, tracking his progress forward by the bodies of men he recognized, he crossed a ditch and then started up what appeared to be another gradually sloping hill. He couldn't tell how far it extended because the smoke restricted his view to less than fifty yards. As more explosions erupted all around him, he realized he couldn't tell whether they were from the enemy that had retreated into the smoke ahead, or from the Union batteries behind him.

He could no longer stand the pain shooting up his leg, so he stopped after another ten yards and sat down in a slight hollow, under what was left of a large-trunked maple, with several other men. Most were wounded. He tried to listen to the fight up ahead, although a high-pitched hum in his head that had begun after the first shots had been fired, muffled the hearing in both ears. The thunder of the batteries sounded close to each other but he really couldn't estimate how far apart they were.

Down below in the hollow, McEmeel watched the battle progress up the hill with more and more men under the Union flags moving forward past him towards what he assumed was another plateau. Explosions, small arms fire and screaming of wounded men all around him continued for almost three hours into the early afternoon. Intermittently he heard cheering in the distance and he hoped it was coming from the men he had watched move up the hill.

Then he heard a terrifying sound, something he had heard only in his imagination in the past, something he thought could only be the scream of the banshee his uncle had once described in a late night bedtime story. That green horrid screaming specter, an unwelcome visitor in nightmares he had endured repeatedly as a small child, came alive from up the hill. But the high-pitched, angry wailing he heard now came from what sounded like a thousand-headed Banshee up there in the smoke where his men had disappeared, and it kept up for almost fifteen minutes, a horrible screaming din that pierced through the buzzing in his ears.

And then he saw Union soldiers, more Fire Zuaves, each without his turban, and gray-clad comrades from the 11ᵗʰ Regiment surge past him out of the smoke, away from the fight, one after another down the hill. Several were without their rifles. Every one wore the desperate expression of men in a terrified panic. Dragoons and riderless horses thundered past, heading back north. They all had seen the banshee, he thought! Somehow, he picked himself up and followed them as did the men who could and those that were not already dead, all hiding near the splintered maple. The screaming rebel yells grew louder.

He didn't remember running, but he did — down the hill and then past a shell-ridden stone house and back up an incline to a plateau where he had first hurt his leg. He ran until he heard the banshee's screaming behind him fade away completely.

About one hundred yards up the hill he saw a buckboard with three men sitting upright. Then he remembered his torn leg. It screamed pain down into his ankle. He tried to reach the wagon but couldn't walk any more so he lay down.

The buckboard stopped and two men ran over.

"Let's help ye up, Cap'n. Ye tern up pretty bad."

They carried him to the dray. It was filled with wounded men. He looked over the other passengers. One young man's right leg was neatly filleted, almost all the way up into his groin where a tourniquet was tightly bound. The leg wasn't bleeding but the skin, flapped to each side of the exposed, comminuted femur and tibia was blue black. Two men, tucked unconscious in the corner, appeared to be dead.

They moved east to a dirt turnpike crowded with soldiers, horses and civilians in carriages clogging the narrow road, all rushing back east to Centerville and on to Fairfield. As confused as he was from the pain and the repeated concussions he had sustained, he tried to make sense of the conversations of the soldiers they passed. He tried to keep awake en route.

When he recognized a soldier from his own company, without revealing what had befallen him, he queried details of the battle up on the plateau after he had dropped out of the attack. He learned from another soldier, a lieutenant from another company, that all but two of the Dorchester officers had been killed in a rebel bayonet charge near a house that sat on top of the hill. The lieutenant said it appeared that they had fought desperately around several cannon but he had been told that almost half of the men in the Dorchester Company had been killed, wounded or taken prisoner.

From that and from other conversations he realized that no one knew he had dropped out of the attack early on. Because he was completely covered in dried blood and couldn't walk, the lieutenant with whom he spoke assumed he had been wounded and commended him for his valor. McEmeel kept quiet, tried to keep awake and pieced together details of the fight on the hill.

On arrival in Washington thirty hours later, he was transported with all the other men on the lorry to a small church, crowded with the men who had been wounded at Bull Run. There, a gray-faced nun in a gray habit began cutting off his uniform. She commented out loud to the surrounding staff about McEmeel's garments which were stiffened from dried blood and embedded bone chips. She called a staff physician to examine his knee and ankle swelling.

"Looks to be a severe internal derangement, perhaps a break of the plateau of the tibia," the physician said, moving the lower leg. "If he keeps it, likely'll never walk right again, he said to McEmeel's dismay.

It took a week to sort things out in the capital city. Lincoln replaced McDowell with "Little Mac" McClellan, whose prime directive was to make a disciplined army out of the chaotic mess that remained after Bull Run — and prepare for an extended war. McClellan's first order was to dismiss all of the 90-day volunteers, many of whom had been the first to flee when the tide had changed during the battle at Bull Run. Captain McEmeel received a promotion to Major, largely based on hearsay and the reports he himself submitted about the events that had occurred on the rolling hills outside of Manassas on July 21st.

His report, pieced together by talking with several of the survivors from his company, omitted a number of personal details, but was, in its prose and color, a masterful concoction. He wrote over one hundred letters to relatives about the fate of their sons, fathers and husbands. The calligraphy was ornate and worthy of framing, according to one bereaved recipient. In every letter, having personally dropped out of the fray early on, he made up the details and, convincing himself it was the right thing to do, in every letter he extolled the dead man's valor. For those men who were missing, he lied that the last time he had seen them, they "seemed filled with purpose."

Kathleen, whose sister Emmy had found him two days after he had reached the safety of Washington, commissioned his broken sword to be encased and placed over the parlor fireplace mantle of her father's leased brownstone mansion. Every time he looked at the memento his bitter contempt for fools increased.

On a Saturday morning, July 21st 1861, two weeks after Bull Run, while recovering in his father-in-law Kern O'Malley's house on Michigan Street, a carriage with a military escort arrived with a visitor. General Benjamin Butler, invited to visit him by Congressman O'Malley — Butler's ex-partner in a law practice in Boston — introduced himself. In their brief meeting, Butler said he wanted to pay his respects, but also make an offer to McEmeel, who had been declared one of the many heroes of the Battle of Bull Run, the bloodiest battle ever in the history of the United States.

"Ben Butler likes what he heard about your valor, Young Man," Butler said. "Ordered you be transferred to my command. Need the services of an accomplished, educated Massachusetts man with the credentials of a hero." Looking down at McEmeel's casted leg, and over at the tray of medicines and the near-empty bottle of laudanum next to his chair, sensing his hesitancy, Butler said quietly, "We have a long fight in front of us, don't we, Son?"

◇◇◇◇

Eleven months later, while sitting with his leg raised on the divan in his parlor, McEmeel read his sister-in-law,

Emmy's note asking him for his help. He tried to recall details about that very first meeting with Ben Butler a year ago, and how much had changed in his own life as a result of it since then. He remembered that on that same occasion, while looking out the window after Butler had departed, he had seen the General stop his carriage down the street to converse with Emmy who had been returning with her son and daughter from a visit to a doctor.

He had wondered how Butler knew Emmy, and what they had said to each other. Should he, could he play upon that relationship? he thought back then. And now, he wondered how much Emmy knew about his own activities that had begun on that day with his association with Butler. It *was* evident that she *did* know that he had been profiting handsomely as the result of his finding ways to smuggle embargoed goods across the lines. In both directions.

Should he help Emmy, his earnest, honest sister-in-law, someone he respected immensely? Perhaps give her an introduction to one or more of the agents who he contracted to work for the clever organization to which he belonged? Perhaps Pen Basetyr or Henri Lebo, agents who knew the Virginia peninsula well and could guide her to find her fiancé? And how might he profit from that favor to her if he did so? Given his high regard for Emmy, should he even be deliberating like that?

Indeed, would it benefit him, or would it pull him further into the General's private circle, which increasingly, he wondered, might be one of the bottomless morasses that Dante had written about?

With that thought, he paused, stood up and limped over to the encased broken-blade sword and looked at his reflection in the mirror behind it. He had aged. He felt his cheekbones and studied the cracks and crowfeet that hadn't been there just one year ago. He remembered when he had been a fresher man, and when he was a half-believer in the God-given meaning of life.

Somehow, thinking about that gave him pause for the first time in over four years. Was he getting soft?

CHAPTER NINE

◇◇◇◇◇

Basetyr and Lebo

1852 to 1862-Mason-Dixon Line

Their business together had begun long before the war. They were clever at it, those two unlikely partners, playing upon whichever needs came to the surface first and provided the greatest amount of profit in cash or barter. For Pen Basetyr, her own work started at the age of ten, in 1850, with the well-meaning, Quakers mostly, who used the pathways that she had provided for the successful transport of escaped slaves out of Virginia.

When she realized she was sought after for this ability, she decided that she could make a good living at it. So she began charging for her services. Ten years later, in early 1862, after her chance meeting with Henri Lebo, a forty-year-old enterprising privateer who knew how to move stolen goods up the Mississippi, Pen found a way to expand her gains, smuggling by mule-train shipments of contraband. "Contraband," as defined by their indirect patron, General Benjamin Butler, included slaves. On more than one occasion the two unlikely partners doubled their take on the same deal involving the very same victims. Lebo never told Basetyr that after she led the slaves out — he on occasion had returned the escapees to the slave owners who wanted their property back. His associate's contract to transport goods was with the Quakers, not with the slaves themselves, he reasoned, and likely no one would connect him to Basetyr's "exporting" contract.

Shortly after the war started and the Union embargoes heightened the need on one side for what the other could mostly supply, like raw cotton to supply the northern mills, or quinine to provide for the rebel armies, they found other routes and ways to smuggle the contraband. Basetyr knew some of the best ways *out* from the Confederate-held territories. Lebo knew the best ways *in*. Basetyr knew the unmapped roads and backwoods. Lebo and the numerous people who contracted with him were experts at navigating the Potomac and the southern waterways. They knew where there were unguarded, unwatched fields and water supplies. Both of them preferred to be in the thick of it.

Within few months of the implementation of Winfield Scott's "Anaconda Plan," with a strict embargo imposed along the coast, up the Mississippi and at every interface between the two combatants, Basetyr and Lebo were rich, by the standards within which they had been raised, although neither of them would admit much comfort for that. Both knew the war would last longer than most hoped, but it would end sometime, and within a peacetime economy, they would likely have to find additional ways to benefit from their form of business. Despite the gains each of them made, they kept it personal, saved their gains and never let loose of their tight control or personal participation in the processes. Unwarranted trust was not part of the game.

No one, except for those like some within Ben Butler's ambitious entourage that dealt with contraband on both sides of the border, would likely have connected the two, for they had been exceptionally careful to preserve their appearances of differing purpose and political mindset. But in a number of instances and in a number of designated destinations, shacks hidden in Virginia hollows mostly, they had shared intimacies.

Yet, if one of them were asked, while in a stupor or on the edge of slumber when the tendency to guard is lowest, neither would likely have admitted affection or even attraction for the other. They were in business together. The intimate moments were no more than brief exchanges, fair trades that fit the momentary needs of two successful business associates. After such encounters, each left a copy of a coded manifest for the other to supply. And a few dollars. In Confederate script, which both knew likely would be worthless at some point. It was part of their secret little joke.

Lebo had started it.

Basetyr, not to be outdone, had replied in kind on the next tryst. She left one dollar less.

CHAPTER TEN

✕✕✕✕

Sarah

July 16ᵗʰ, 1862-Washington, District of Columbia

She knew her mother would not change her mind. Her mother was always firm about her decisions and never made them carelessly, as far as Sarah could remember. But that didn't stop her from shaking her head angrily and pleading when her brother Jacob began crying while their mother told them she would be going away for a short while. What she hated more than her mother's departure was that it would be her aunt, Kathleen, who would be minding them.

She didn't like her aunt. She just didn't like her. And her aunt didn't like her or Jacob either, she knew. It wasn't difficult for her to see, by the way her aunt gave her so little opportunity to speak, by the way her aunt pursed her lips tightly when she did try to speak, and just glared at her at times. She was an angry woman for some reason, Sarah had concluded. So she kept quiet and stayed out of her aunt's way.

This time, Sarah knew she would have to stay put. She wouldn't be able to follow her mother the way she had in the Pacific Northwest Territory, because her mother would see to that. And she had her nine-year-old step-brother Jacob to take care of, even though he had been so much more difficult to reach lately.

Her mother expected that of her.

Jacob had warmed for a while, started talking again, after their mother had asked Jojo, the young native who had guided for them in the Northwest, to accompany them back to Boston. Jacob had taken to JoJo.

But no one had heard from JoJo since the incidents two years previously in Panama. If he was dead, they never found his body. That made her so very sad, not only because JoJo had been a protector, but also because he always made them laugh. He interpreted the world for them in a different way than did her mother. He was an outsider, looking in, gently and with a curiosity that was infectious, she realized. And he always shared his observations generously.

She missed him and hoped he hadn't perished like so many of the others on that trip. She missed him.

CHAPTER ELEVEN

◇◇◇◇

Jojo

July 14ᵗʰ, 1862,

To convince the ship's first mate that he too was an Irishman, on the first day out of port in New Orleans, Jojo had worked the well-rehearsed brogue he had learned from listening to the Gaelic of stevedores in San Francisco. It worked for almost a full day, even though his dark complexion and Pacific Coastal Indian features undermined his ruse. The first mate, a hearty giant named McClinton, who had emigrated from County Cork twelve years before, liked to laugh, fortunately.

"An' I suppose yer be tellin' me next that yer *Black* Irish," McClinton said, which confused Jojo by the reference. McClinton tolerated Jojo's prank and told him that his accent was so good that it almost made him homesick. After listening to Jojo's reasons for enlisting and watching him work industriously in every task he was assigned, McClinton decided to help him move on up through the ranks.

"We'll make you a bosun's mate over time, Son. Prepare to learn everything we throw at yer about how a ship runs," he said.

Thus began Jojo-the-polyglot's brief good fortune while a shipmate in the Union navy.

McClinton had been a river pilot for several years on several stretches of the Mississippi and thus, was an exceptionally valuable asset to the newly formed Union navy, as he would have been for the Confederates who had failed to recruit him in New Orleans. When the opportunity for reassignment north to a new ship presented itself to the ship's exceptionally able first mate, McClinton decided to bring along Jojo and two other equally dependable seamen.

In a small wooden, unmarked steamer, flying a Kentucky flag, the four men slipped past the guns of the rebel strongholds along the Mississippi, and made their way to the newly-won Fort Pillow, where they were assigned to the *U.S.S. Cairo*, a new 175-foot long, 550-ton ironclad.

Up to that point, Jojo had not really realized the full significance of war between the states, nor had he seen the degree of devastation that the cannon, next to which he birthed at night, could bring to other human beings. Had he understood what he was about to witness as a result of his rash enlistment decision in New Orleans, he never would have taken the oath, he told himself.

Certainly he had known about cannons. One of the warring Northwest clans, led by the notorious "Black Wind" Haida chieftain, Anah Nawitka, had used a small cannon, mounted on the prow of his longboat, to attack neighboring tribes. Jojo also had watched a few artillery exercises of British frigates moving through the waters of the Pacific Northwest.

But he had never witnessed the impact of a full broadside from one of the ships, nor had he seen the types of wounds that resulted from canister, shrapnel and wood splinters. Until he participated in the Memphis naval battle, he had been a virgin to it all, he realized in retrospect some time later. The war and its cannons had just snuck up on him.

During the months of April and May, all of it, the river, the people, the uniforms, the talk of commanding the waterways, was stimulating enough that he was swept along in it. Several mates told him that the reassignment to the *Cairo*, which he had been given for merit, was a great honor. But, after two months in the Union navy, Jojo was frustrated enough that he started to look for opportunities to leave as soon as the opportunity presented itself. For it wasn't what he had expected.

In New Orleans, he had enlisted simply and finally to learn first-hand all about *sailing*, something he had wanted to do since a young Bella Coola teen in the northern part of the British-held Pacific Northwest. But the only sails on the heavily armored *Cairo*, steaming down the Mississippi River to join the federal attack on Memphis, were from the shipmates' laundry drying on the beefy ironclad's short masts. The wind that their skivvies caught didn't do much to push the ship along.

In his depression over what he considered his mistaken, possibly ruinous enlistment, he quieted down and tried to keep himself safe so that he could survive the next year. Despite the fact that the Federal ironclads controlled all but the ports of Memphis and Vicksburg now, their formidable presence discouraging all but the frequent pot-shot takers who came out to plink at the passing iron behemoths, more than one of the rebel shoreline shooters found his mark during those early days. So Jojo decided to stay below, no matter how far away his ship was from the river's banks. Better to roast like a suckling pig down below than lose an arm or take a gut shot while trying to cool off, he told himself.

That caution seemed to make his misery worse. The big, black, hot machine on which he now rode just cooked the juice out of him and that of all the other crewmen who stayed inside for the same reasons. And it was always hot, even on overcast and rainy days, because of the poorly insulated boilers whose steam pushed the ship's huge paddlewheel. Sunny days worsened his feelings of woe. Rather than being reminded of the wonders of being alive on a clear, blue-sky day — the wind blowing through his hair as he had experienced riding a canoe as he had in the past — by being stuck inside, he felt oppressed instead.

It was stultifying down below. He saw that the swabs learned to wash the decks quickly, lest the water evaporate immediately in a dirty steam that left the deck's sandy grit in place and without evidence of their efforts. It had to be well over a hundred degrees on the second deck even at night, he thought. Then, the second week of their trip down river, he burned his hand on the three inch, sun-heated iron plate covering the *Cairo's* flanks! He wondered if this might be good practice should he ever be forced to visit the white man's hell.

But hell took another form almost immediately after the transfer up river to the *Cairo*. McClinton, the new first mate, was readily accepted by the crew he inherited. Jojo was not. His dark features turned heads. Even though he wore no distinctive tattoos that identified his Pacific Coast Indian heritage, his high cheekbones and promi-nent forehead set him apart from the rest of the crew who were entirely of white European stock.

In the few months he had served on the small gun-boat in New Orleans before being given the privilege of transferring North with McClinton, he had deflected any criticism easily with his wit. And, because at least a quar-ter of the crew on that ship had been of native descent and several others were negro, the prejudices expressed by the white sailors were spread out against many. On the *Cairo*, however, he alone, among 250 other men, was not white.

One of the men told him he had lost several relatives from Sioux raids up the northern Missouri and aimed to take a few red scalps before he finished his life.

"We jus' don't like savages here," a short wiry sailor with black teeth said to him on the first day. Jojo later thought that amusing, given what he had seen them do to Fort Pillow.

McClinton tried as best he could, but could not pro-tect him. The resentment was overtly expressed by several of the sailors when McClinton wasn't around to intercede, and was covertly exercised when he was. On two occasions, Jojo found human feces in his shoes.

He knew better than to complain, however.

Instead, to keep the peace, and reduce the tensions he felt, Jojo readily volunteered for the least desirable assignments, including working the coal tending in front of the boilers, washing the latrines and serving as the lowest man on the five-man gun crew. He learned to not inhale through his nose when cleaning the latrines, and stripped almost naked when working the coal on the boilers. He hoped that there would not be much battle action so that he would not lose his hearing from the cannon fire.

At 4:00 a.m. on June 6th, 1862, when they reached the other Union siege ships anchored off Memphis, the captain moved their vessel to line up in a row with the four other Union ironclads and in front of five rams, all positioned stern-first to the city, thereby presenting the smallest target should an attack be launched by the Confederate River Defense Fleet. Seeing this, Jojo thought they might at last be safe from the sniping and decided to risk getting out of the heat down below. After the captain left the ship before the impending battle to meet with the flotilla command, Jojo was invited up top by McClinton and was able to look through his telescope for a few minutes.

While watching two Union mortar barges tossing their 90-pound projectiles through the sky, arching towards the city almost a mile away, Jojo moved the scope across the Memphis early morning's landscape in the distance. It was a beautiful town, positioned high above the bluffs bordering the river, with the dawn's glint sparkling off the copper tops of several churches. What he could see through the river's morning mist, was a city not yet destroyed, the way he saw the Union ironclads and mortars had left Fort Pillow and its surrounding town. But the bombardment had only just started and all of the exploding mortar shots had, thus far, fallen short.

He couldn't imagine the brute consequence of so much mass striking the wooden and brick structures of the town and wondered again about the insanity of it all.

At 5:30 a.m, announced by the sound of a rebel cannon's *pop* over a mile away, the battle of Memphis began, just as Jojo was preparing for an early mess with all of the other shipmates on his shift. The alarm bells clanged all down the line of linked Union ships. Jojo could hear excited hollering and the rumble of footsteps throughout the *Cairo* and from the nearby ships, all moving stern-first, as men ran to their battle stations.

While running from his breakfast to the mid-deck station, unable to find the cotton plugs he always carried to protect his hearing, Jojo took a piece of chewed bread and stuffed it in each of his ears. Waiting for the powder tender to load powder charges into the bow's starboard 30-pounder Parrot gun, he jostled with the other swab mate to quickly peer through the cannon's fire portal at the unfolding battle.

The rising sun started to light the river below Memphis. He could make out seven or eight rebel ships, lined up bow to stern about seven or eight hundred yards away. The Confederate ships were huge, but had no iron plating covering their sides. "Cotton clads" he had heard someone refer to them. Their flanks were stacked from the waterline to the upper decks with huge bales of cotton! He could only make out a few cannon on each ship.

One by one, the Confederates began firing at the Union line. The U.S.S. *Carondelet*, moving slightly behind and to the left of the *Cairo*, fired a response from its starboard rear cannon, shaking Jojo with the deep thunderclap. The percussion shook the *Cairo*, and he noticed their ten-year-old "powder monkey," thrown off balance from the *Cairo*'s lateral movement to the explosion, drop the shell he was carrying. It rolled across the deck to the starboard side.

"Swab 'er, Mates," hollered the gunner, moving Jojo and the other gunnery swab aside to peer out of the portal. While Jojo swabbed the bore, the fuse-mate gunner placed the fuse into the conical iron shell, sealed it, and then moved the projectile to the front of the big gun. After the powder tender shoved the powder charge down the gun's bore, Jojo and the other gunnery swab hoisted their thirty-pound cone-shaped shell up to the cannon's muzzle, then watched as a fourth gunner shoved it in. Jojo wanted to cover his ears, waiting with some dread, for the order to be given to fire the beast, but knew he would have to wait until the gunner gave the order.

"Take the middle of the line!" the chief gunnery mate shouted.

The gunner mate began lining up the sight, ordering Jojo and two of the other crew to make slight adjustment with the cannon truncheons. While he did so, Jojo thought it was strange that neither the gunner mate nor the chief covered their ears. Both of them likely were already too deaf to care any more, he realized.

"That's good, Mates!" screamed the gunner mate. "Poke the bitch."

On that command, the fuse mate gunner pushed a sharp rod into the vent hole to pierce the powder bag inside, then placed a primer attached to a lanyard into it.

"At will!" screamed the gunner.

Jojo and the other men stepped away from the cannon.

The fuse mate gunner pulled the lanyard.

The explosion recoiled the two-ton Parrot gun almost four feet backwards.

"On point! One Hundred yards short!" screamed the chief gunner.

The crew pushed the cannon forward and began reloading.

The gunner peered along the sight. As the new charges and projectile were being rammed down the bore, he moved to the second cannon. He ordered the fuse mate gunner to pull the lanyard attached to the primer pin.

"Paste the bastards!" he screamed.

The *Cairo's* second stern cannon exploded.

"We're short by fifty and off to the right!" shouted the chief gunner.

To his right and left, Jojo heard the other Union ships discharging their two stern cannons as they moved into the fight.

"Turning about!" He thought he heard McClinton's booming voice from the upper deck.

As the ship rotated to the left, Jojo looked out of the port hole. One of the Confederate ship's tall stacks had been cut in two. Two of the other rebel ships were burning and it looked like one was aground. The line had broken and the remaining Confederate rams were steaming up river closing on the Union ships. Every ship on both sides was firing, although most of the firing from the *Cairo* was from the port side guns. Jojo ran over to that side to help carry ammunition to the batteries. He heard an explosion immediately to his right and through the port hole was able to see a rebel ship on fire, then explode and sink within what seemed like only a few seconds.

The battle lasted less than two hours. By 6:30 a.m., the few rebel ships remaining afloat had turned and fled and were being pursued by the Union Ironclads.

Jojo later learned that only one rebel ship had survived long enough to escape. Hundreds of rebel sailors perished. Only one Union soldier, Colonel Charles Ellet, the commander of the Union rams, was injured, shot through the knee by a sniper.

Memphis surrendered a few hours later.

The next day and continuing over the next three weeks, Jojo's routine returned to its boring, uncomfortable predictability-whistled reveille at 5:00 a.m., ship cleaning until breakfast at 8:00, painting and cleaning and watch until darkness.

On July 21st, he received a letter from a Mr. Patrick Dolan, who identified himself as an attorney from Boston. Dolan's letter, sent only one month earlier, explained that he had been looking for Jojo for almost two years at the behest of Mrs. Emmy O'Malley Evers, and was following a lead that came after the Union had taken New Orleans. He hoped that the letter reached him and that he was, indeed, the man they were looking for. Reading that, Jojo looked at the posting and wondered if there were any other men named Na'Pen'tjo in the world.

He read the brief letter over and over again. It gave the attorney's address in Boston, and instructions on how to make a draw in banks in either New Orleans or Cincinnati for a trip back to Washington, D.C., where Emmy and her family now resided. He was to respond by telegraph as soon as conveniently possible, and then notify Dolan of the details when he had been granted leave to travel back East to rejoin the Evers family.

Jojo showed the letter to McClinton, who petitioned the Washington Department to give his young friend an early discharge from service on the *Cairo*.

The petition was denied, as was a request for an extended leave. Jojo would have to survive somehow the term of his enlistment. He sealed the letter in a rubberized envelope and kept it on his person at all times.

Eight more months.

CHAPTER TWELVE

⟨⟨⟨⟩⟩⟩

Lebo and Emmy

1837-New Orleans and the Mississippi River

Henri Lebo considered himself to be decisive and fast as a thinker. He proved that to others whenever he felt it was necessary and disliked anyone who, in his typical, less-than-humble opinion, was not so equipped.

To his credit and reputation, he kept most of his promises. When a bargain was struck, he believed he honored it and let everyone know that was how he did business. When he thought someone was equivocating, or worse, breaking the accord that had been struck with him, Henri punished that person. His lean code, keeping promises to other white men, and his mean, retributive perspective, was uncommon among the New Orleans River Rats and smugglers with whom he had grown up, as well as the other thieves in his family. It differentiated him.

Lebo had come to understand that made him an anomaly in his chosen trade, and he was proud of it. He firmly believed that the best way to protect his backside was to serve unambiguous notice to all with whom he dealt the precepts by which he operated. And then, prominently enforce them.

To those who knew him in the various river ports along the Mississippi and Potomac, it was well known that he had killed more than one prevaricator, or *briseur*, as he liked to describe the victim afterwards. "A deal's a deal" he had been heard to say as he walked away from a freshly killed, ex-partner. He preferred to slit throats so that there would be no noise or further argument as the man or woman died.

Yet, with all the violence he had visited upon others over the years, he didn't consider himself to be a violent man. He was simply conducting his business as an honorable trader, employing an honorable synthesis of the traditional mores of the bayous and ports. A promise keeper, he was. He kept his promises — and promised to kill anyone who didn't do the same.

Abandoned at birth by his mother and then adopted into the protection of her half-brother, whom everyone called *Mon Oncle*, Henri learned the importance of finding opportunity wherever and whenever it presented itself. When he was a small boy, less than six, one of the assignments given to him by his uncle was to sit and beg at the docks where the international array of ships unloaded their cargo. There, he learned to recognize when the ship-hands gave special care to the crates and bundles they took from the holds, what was guarded and what was neglected. He listened to the ship and dock hands' gossip and reported back to his uncle everything he learned. His uncle always shared with him a bit of the spoils.

He traveled on the swamp routes with his older cousin as they transported a variety of pickings to landings up river, once as far north as Baton Rouge, eighty miles away. And on one cold rainy day, at the age of ten, he received a gift from his uncle as they were about to embark on a long canoe trip to Natchez. It was a thin stiletto with a sturdy eight-inch blade.

His uncle, Stefan Lebo, who tended to be garrulous when not doing business, loved to pontificate almost as much as he enjoyed boasting. All the way up the river he told Henri and his cousin about the things he had seen in his life, the number of women with whom he had consorted over the years all along the Mississippi, including details of several of the encounters, his preferences for the special tricks of Cajun women, the differences between the types of snakes one might find on the river banks, and his aid to the "Maricans" in the New Orleans battles in '14 who pushed the Brits out for good.

Henri's uncle said he hated the Brits, Spanish and all people who thought they were superior. He said that Vicksburg people were like that. They hanged their gamblers and "perfumed their own stink," although he said, it didn't really help. If they ever visited that northern city, with its *prétentieux merde,* he predicted they would find very few easy women there. But he promised they would try, nevertheless, if only to get something under the noses of the "stuck up shits."

That led to further long discourses about the qualities of different women and his love for them, in every shape, age and color, although he professed a distinct preference for fat ones with big bosoms.

"Every woman is a mystery and puzzle, you know. Puzzles one can figure out. But most mysteries, like why this moon we see tonight drives us crazy once a month, are never solved," he laughed. "When you try to unravel it, what makes a woman a woman, and why she is the way she is, you are left with a few pieces of string and a number of knots. If you have one long piece of string, and try to hold on to both ends, it is impossible to undo the knots. Yes?" He laughed again. "I, myself, I have tried to hold on to all kinds of string in my life. I am 'appy that, in a few cases, I have been lucky enough to hold on to one end for even a short time."

Henri noted that his uncle paused for a long time, then sighed. "You will need to grow up soon, Henri," he said. "The bes' way is weeth a patient woman," he laughed, "for your first sacrifice on the altar of Venus. I will arrange it." His cousin, older by a few years, laughed when he said that, as well, as if it were an old, frequently-told joke, and from that Henri knew that his cousin likely had previously been initiated.

At Bayou Sara, near Fort Adams and few miles south of the Louisiana-Mississippi border, they hitched a long tow from a steamer headed for Carondelet. They unhitched their tow of five canoes a few miles down-river from Natchez and camped in the shelter of a quiet cove. As they sat by the fire, Henri's uncle talked about emigrating from Corsica with a contingent of settlers who had been paroled by the Bonaparte-appointed governor in '01. When they arrived, his family had been given its own land up river, although the best land, vast fertile estates and miles of river front with natural ports had been controlled by Spanish and French aristocrats for several generations.

"Go out, find women and make new citizens, they told us. They gave us land and told us they would protect us from the tribes." He laughed. "They didn't. Then the little bastard, that Bonaparte, he sold it all to the 'Maricans, right from under us and then everything went to hell."

From his sleeve, he pulled his own stiletto out and flipped it into the log in front of them. By the smooth way he handled the long, thin weapon, Henri knew his uncle had experience.

"Thees is the little, slim friend of poor men like me, Henri," he said, referring to the stiletto. "Back in the days, thees thin blade was feared by the wealthy ones, even if they wore their fancy armor. You see? It slips right through the eye slits in their helmets. It cuts right through the leather and chainmail they thought protected them from poor ones like us. It works even better when they don't wear the armor, of course." Seeing that he had both Henri and his other nephew's attention, he lowered his voice to a quiet whisper .

"You steek it 'ere, Boys," his uncle continued, pointing to the soft space on the left side of Henri's neck, just above his collar-bone. "One quick push. Down to the heart. No mess. No blood on the outside that way." He laughed, "They jus' roll their eyes and keel over. Den, you walk away. Quietly."

They hid their other boats and paddled up to the outskirts of Natchez with a sample of each item they had transported-three different types of pistols, a small oak cask of Amontillado, a tiny mother cask of fine Italian vinegar, a crystal candelabra, a wind-up music box, a large polished clear, green peridot stone and a small ruby, and a bolt of delicate Spanish lace — all stolen from the docks and warehouses of New Orleans.

Henri's uncle knew where to go in Natches to find likely buyers. He was careful to not expose his wares to any one buyer, bringing to each meeting only one or two items. Henri, who had never witnessed trading negotiations before, carefully watched how the trading men behaved, and listened keenly to how they negotiated. He knew what the stolen items likely would have brought in New Orleans and was fascinated at how much more they were valued only 180 miles to the north of the port town. He thought he could tell when one of the traders bluffed.

When the skies started to get darker later in the day, his uncle was quick to terminate the meetings and quickly and quietly leave, maneuvering their small boat back to the place on the down-river bayou where they had hidden their goods.

By the end of the second day, his uncle had cut deals with three separate buyers and arranged for exchange in private meeting places where, Henri assumed, his uncle was quite familiar with the clientele. The first two exchanges transpired just as his uncle said they would. As part of the agreement arranged beforehand, the buyer and a small boy about Henri's age arrived in a boat. The buyer showed his coins, sent the boy to inspect the goods while Henri's cousin inspected the payment, always biting on the silver or gold coin to test its softness. When both of the boys nodded, the transaction was completed and the parties departed with their goods.

On the third encounter, scheduled to occur at 3:00 in the afternoon, they moored the canoes with the Amontillado and some of the pistols by the side of a dock at a place down river, at a landing called Avalange. When the Choctaw with whom he had negotiated didn't show after fifteen minutes, his uncle Stefan said, "We must go. Now!" But as they started to paddle away, a canoe with three men appeared, moving fast towards them.

His uncle landed their canoe on the shore and quietly said, "Run, Boys!" Henri saw anger and fear in his uncle's eyes. Henri ran towards the woods, but when he looked back he saw his cousin instead trying to push the boat out onto the downstream current.

"Run, Henri!" he heard his uncle call out again. Then he heard his uncle cursing loudly *"Fils de pute! Batârds!"* Then three gunshots and more screaming.

Henri waited, hidden in the woods, straining to hear for sounds of pursuit from the Choctaw men, or a call back from his uncle. Then, after silence for over a half hour, he circled back through the woods to the water's edge downstream. Both of his uncle's canoes were gone.

His uncle lay face down in the river.

Henri never found his cousin.

He searched for two days to find where his uncle had hidden the other boats, or find their encampment, but he was lost, he realized.

Henri had one of the silver coins in his pocket, given to him by his uncle after the first transaction. So he was able to buy some food. There wasn't enough left to buy a fare on a boat, so he walked and begged his way down river. It took him ten days to get back to New Orleans.

Making his way back down river, he thought about what he had witnessed. His uncle had always warned him to always trust his senses, to watch men's eyes when they bargained.

Didn't his uncle see that the Choctaw with whom he bargained didn't blink, even once? Henri had seen it. The man sat down, put both hands on the table, politely waited until his uncle had opened up the cloth covering the pistols or the pearls, didn't reach for them until his uncle nodded permission. Didn't argue. Offered a great price for both the whole lot of pistols and all the gems. He didn't fidget, glance around, tense up or give anything away from his face. His voice never changed.

But Henri had learned by watching men and women when he was working as a beggar that a person gave away a lot of information without knowing it. He always thought it was interesting that a person's face was different depending on which eye you looked at. Both sides said something about the person, he had realized. The left eye of a right-handed man told you if a man was listening carefully to your words. The right eye, only to his own. If either eye moved away from yours when you focused on it, it told you he either didn't believe you or himself. Henri could tell when a man was lying, and after begging on the docks and on the city streets for four years, he could predict who would be most likely to give him something for his efforts.

The easiest were the kind ones, the ones who actually looked at him, even for a second, when he appealed to them. Somewhere they had been told that turning away from those who were less fortunate was sinful. He bet they had heard that from soft-hearted mothers who believed the priests, contemptible fools really, because they were so easy and gullible. After a few years he had decided that it would be fun to try to persuade the ones who almost certainly would refuse his pleas. So during his final year working the docks and streets a beggar, after making his marks in the morning, he spent the rest of many days challenging himself to make "conversions" of the ones who put the most into their gruff demeanors. He got good at it. And he always went to the eyes first.

But his uncle hadn't seen it.

The Choctaw had dead eyes.

◇◇◇◇

July 22nd to July 24th, 1862
Potomac River and Countryside of East Virginia

Emmy had been warned by her brother-in-law, McEmeel, that Henri Lebo was dependable, but because he, like everyone in his trade, was known to play both sides, she should pay him handsomely up front and deposit the remainder with a sizable bonus into a Baltimore escrow agent's hands for the completion of his obligations to her.

To come up with Lebo's fee, over a thousand dollars in gold, she had to borrow money from Patrick Dolan, a former partner of her father. Dolan said that he was certain that an advance on the contents of a package — a huge diamond that had been gifted to her son two years previously by an insane murderer from Panama — would amply cover any expenses she might incur on this expensive quest. She had hoped it never would have to be redeemed for any reason. But she had no choice. She wondered whether there was a curse on that diamond.

Despite her repeated pleas, Lebo had insisted on delaying their journey for five days, waiting for McClellan to complete the evacuation of his troops by transports from the embarkation place at Harrison Landing on the Peninsula. The Union's beaten forces would be moving back down the James River to Yorktown and Norfolk, both recently abandoned by the rebels, and then subsequently would be redistributed north. Lebo said the rebels also were moving most of their forces away from the eastern part of the peninsula back towards Richmond.

He also said he hoped there would be fewer of the Virginia "Minute Men" or "Vigilance Committee" riders prowling about as well, as they would surely be busy mending their own after the way the area had been devastated by the fights everyone was now calling "the Seven Days" battles.

As she had been instructed by Lebo, Emmy carried little with her and dressed herself like a man, in britches, slouch hat and long coat. It would be a rapid, exhausting trip, he said, but would provide her the most direct, least discoverable means to achieve her stated objective of locating Brett. A few brief stops on the way, he said. Lebo figured they could cover twenty miles each day on fresh horses, but would need to ride with little rest for themselves.

Because she was paying so well, he told her he would accompany her all the way, ferrying her by night in a small skiff down the Potomac to a landing south of Alexandria, then guiding her by horse to the small town of Fredericksburg, which he said was half-way between Washington and Richmond. There they would be met by a business associate who would row them across the Rappahannock River. After that, another friend would guide them southeast onto the Peninsula and west towards the headwaters of the Chickahominy River. They would have to skirt the swamps, and that would take an extra day at least. Lebo said he had "eyes and ears" down there, looking and listening for information about Brett.

"If we ken move fast, we ken get you down there an' back here in a week. If'n you're lucky to find yer man," Lebo said. "Figgerin' three days to find him and take care of what you need to do. Ten days at most, total, if'n we move quickly."

He said another associate, an "occasional partner" named Pen Basetyr would bring her all the way back as far as Harper's Ferry along a different route. She would have to make her way back to Washington D.C. from Harper's Ferry on her own. If she made it *that* far.

Emmy noted that Lebo was an even more interesting man than she had assumed he might be. He reminded her of the new president, Abraham Lincoln, whom she had seen only once, observed during his inauguration, from a perch off to the left and in front of the podium provided to the families of congressmen.

Lebo, like Lincoln, was lanky and had eyes that had seen much, although they weren't deep set like those of the new president. But, unlike the man from Illinois, Lebo's movements were quick and agile. He had looked her up and down more than once, she noticed, and when not darting his eyes almost constantly, he returned his gaze to her, again looking her up and down. Somehow, however, that scrutiny did not bother Emmy, for McEmeel, attempting to give her some reassurances, had told her Lebo was the most cautious man he had ever met.

She watched him while he carried a few boxes to the boat. His actions were efficient. Could she trust him?

After Lebo helped her board the small boat, he strapped across his chest two ammunition belts, each carrying two big revolver-type pistols, then loaded and placed a short double-barrel shotgun and a new Spencer rimfire rifle at his feet.

"Ya know how to shoot, Lady?" he asked. When she nodded, he handed her a huge six-shot LeMatt pistol.

"You might need this at some point, if not for the Yanks, then for the Rebs — if'n we cain't avoid 'em or persuade 'em." His nostrils flared when he said that.

Seeing her hesitation, he said, "Got any objections to that?" When she hesitated again, he said, "Y'know they'll hang us. Yanks or Rebs. Don't matter who. Were steppin' into the places they both think they own." He reached over to take back the pistol, but Emmy pulled the heavy LeMatt back and placed it under her coat.

They moved quickly down the western shoreline southward, far enough away from the river's edge to avoid the reach of sentry bullets, stopping twice and lying down in the boat as Union steam-powered paddle wheelers moved up river in the opposite direction, headed for Washington. It was dark enough that the ships would likely not have noticed their small craft, but each time Lebo told her to be prepared.

Three hours after departing Washington they landed at a tiny inlet and hid their boat in the bushes. Lebo walked into the woods, leaving Emmy with her thoughts about the sanity of this mission. She was certain her children would be safe. She needed to find Brett she told herself. For a moment she thought about whether she might have enough time to learn about what happened to George Pickett as well. She wondered whether she should try to see him, but fought that thought. He might be dead after all. The thought of either of them injured or dead made her sick to her stomach. She felt the chill of the river edge and pulled hands up into the sleeves of her long coat and tucked her arms across her chest.

Thirty minutes later Lebo returned leading two saddled horses. It was almost pitch-black dark.

"We ride hard now," he said. "Need to get to Fredericksburg afore sunup."

They had no light but that of a small sliver of the early August moon which slipped in and out from the low rolling cloud cover, so the going was slow almost all the way, even when they found cleared fields between the woods. Even so, it was obvious to her that Lebo knew his way through these parts well, leading them onto the roads only when the paths they followed intersected with them.

When they stopped for their first rest in the cover of a dense thicket, Emmy estimated that they had ridden non-stop for over four hours. It was already almost 3:30. She peered through Lebo's blackened brass telescope at the woods in front of them, looking for any movement in the morning's darkness. After watching for fifteen minutes they moved out from the woods onto another barren field and after riding hard for another hour, they were at a river's edge on the outskirts of Fredericksburg. Lebo halted their heavily lathered horses.

"Presuming this is the Rappahannock?" Emmy asked quietly. Lebo was silent.

After ten minutes, he pulled out a cigar and lit it. A minute later, a rider leading two horses quietly moved out of the thickets downstream, paused and lit a match to a cigar. After waiting another minute, Lebo took the reins from Emmy and rode to the spot across the river from the rider, then kicked his horse into the stream and they forded over.

They dismounted and climbed onto the fresh horses. The rider accompanied them a few miles, and after Lebo tossed a small purse to him, he turned up into the brush and disappeared. No words were exchanged.

The yellow-brown rays of a cloud-filtered sunrise gradually revealed detail of the fields they had been crossing since leaving the Rappahannock. From the trampled ground beneath them, the beaten-down crops and piles of garbage strewn about in every direction, Emmy saw for the first time the result of what she realized must have been a huge army's sprawling encampment sites. Although it had rained heavily a few days before, the deep ruts in the roads and fields had not been smoothed away. As they traveled further south, she saw that wide expanses of ancient chestnut and oak woods had been freshly clear-cut. She saw houses with broken-down doors, shattered windows. She counted dozens of burned out barns. She realized she had seen little livestock in any of the fields since circumventing Fredericksburg three hours before.

Thirty minutes later they halted on the crest of a sparsely timbered spiny ridge and peered down into a low stretch of valley, barren of all but a few trees. It hadn't always been like this, Emmy thought, not from the descriptions that Rory Brett had given her about the lush valleys and hills of his Virginia.

Lebo dismounted and helped her down.

When Lebo returned from relieving himself, she asked "Mr. Lebo, how much longer before we reach the Chickahominy?"

He held up his hand, nodded over to her left and, when she turned, she was surprised to see a portly, short, black-clad man carrying a long ten-gauge shotgun riding towards them on a small black Morgan. He had come so quietly she hadn't even noticed him.

"Ma'am," said the man when he reached them, tipping his hat and nodding at Emmy. "Reverend Ardy Dabbs here. Pleased to meet you and be of assistance."

Emmy shook the preacher's hand. Unlike the hands of other preachers she had met in the past, his was that of a working man, with rough skin and swollen red knuckles, like the ones she had felt in handshakes with farmers and lumbermen. His nails were clean.

Dabbs' rolling, ample jowls coalesced together mid-line at a long, stiff wiry gray chin-beard that partially covered the bulging neck that strained his collar buttons. His intense, pudding-brown eyes carried an expression that reminded her of the worried looks her family's old yellow retriever sometimes had given her when she had lived in the Pacific Northwest a few years ago. The dog had always fretted and whined about what it should do to get her approval, she remembered. It seldom did the right thing, however. It was a terrible watchdog, she mused. "Not a dram of canine instinct," her late husband Isaac had once said about the creature. The Haida savages killed her dog in their attack on her home on Whidbey Island.

She wondered if there was any correlation between what she saw on this preacher's face and the gentle but relatively useless disposition of their family's old dog. Should have started barking long before it did that fatal night, she rued.

"Reverend Dabbs, we've come a long way — "

"Excuse me, Ma'am," Dabbs interrupted. "Got word from Henri about your quest . . . inquired about your fiancé. Hate to disappoint . . . cain't really say I learned much, other'n there was a passel of fighting, up river on the Chickahominy where you'd said his home was. They're gonna be recoverin' up there for a long time, I'm told."

The preacher's sad, weighty expression was genuine, Emmy decided. He was not lying. He was distracted, she surmised, and grieving over many things. But he was earnest.

He then tipped his hat at Lebo and said, "Henri. Didn't think you would be carrying her this far yourself. Glad y' made it through, though. Heard the damned Vigilance Committee's gettin' back on its feet. Otis Loller again. Figger you two might have a day or two at the most, to stay outta their reach." He then turned back to Emmy and said, "Henri's the careful one. Always. Pays t' be nowadays."

They rode eastward over more hilly beech and pine-covered terrain, so they could stay hidden, carefully avoiding any place that had more than one or two houses.

"Where have you been before now?" Dabbs asked.

Emmy thought about that. "I returned to Boston from the Oregon Territory with my family two years ago," she said. As they rode on, she told him what she had endured in the Pacific Northwest: how her husband had been murdered and beheaded by aborigines, how her young boy had been kidnapped and tortured. She told him about her own ordeals in Panama, when the train on which they had been traveling had been robbed and she and several others had been taken hostage. She found herself getting choked up again when she related the part about all the murders, and about captivity to the notorious killer called Bocamalo.

When the preacher asked why she had taken on this new challenge, she told him how Brett had saved her down in Panama, how her son and daughter had almost immediately taken to Brett, almost as if he was their own father reborn, and then later, how Brett had proposed to her in Boston.

"He's a young, idealistic man, like what most of the men fighting against each other down here are, I expect,"

Emmy said. "But I have never seen anyone quite as tender as this."

The preacher nodded as he listened silently. His sadness expanded. He sighed.

They rode quietly for a few minutes. "Well, I see why you are risking your hide on this," he finally said. "Most wouldn't, I reckon. But I see why you are doing this."

Emmy saw him studying her.

"I do believe, respectfully Ma'am, that you haven't decided whether you fully love this young man . . . but . . . you have your family to look out for and...an obligation, you feel. And you are a woman of honor, aren't you?" he said.

With that, Emmy slowed her horse down to a walk and lagged behind a bit, wondering whether what he had concluded fit her motives. She realized he was smarter than she had assumed from his basset-like looks.

They rode on for another half hour without speaking. Then he said to both of them, "Henri, Ma'am . . . if y'all'd be will'n' to oblige me, I think you might want to see a few things before moving on. It's just a little bit out of the way you're travelin' anyways. It'll set the tone, in a manner of speakin', of what you are ridin' into."

Without asking Emmy's assent, Lebo nodded and turned his horse after the preacher.

Within a half hour they jigged back and forth up and over another ridge. From the crest, looking in the distance to the southeast, they could see smoke emanating behind what appeared to be a long grove of trees in the narrow valley and a wide river below. Emmy estimated the smoke billows stretched at least a half mile. Thousands of birds, crows and white-winged blackbirds, mostly, swarmed and swooped over the area, diving into the grove and mixing almost indistinguishably with the black and gray smoke. Emmy covered her face to help block a putrid, sour smell that was blowing in their direction. It was a rotten, sulfurous stink.

"They call this river landing area down there behind those trees 'White House Landing,'" the preacher said, pointing from the far end of the grove over to the right to a knoll at the other end. This over here's where the Yanks stored and then dumped their supplies near the end, when they knew they had their asses whipped. That over there . . . that's where they blew up their munitions as they were pullin' out," he said, nodding at the most dense cloud of black and gray smoke."

We figger they stripped the fields and houses around here for a hundred square miles to add to what they brought with 'em down the Chesapeake and on up the James and Pamunkey Rivers. Twice the lot they needed to feed themselves. They coulda kept their big party goin' for months with what they all piled up. Then, when they lost their gall, they just set it all afire. Shot the horses and mules they couldn't bring with 'em. The heap's been burnin' for over ten days now, even with this danged drizzle."

They rode back west for a few miles, away from the dump and the stench of waste.

"We're figgerin' may be thirteen or fourteen thousand of our boys dead or badly wounded, just to get the Bluebellies to go back to their own homes, and just leave us alone," he went on as they were riding.

"Lot of the Yanks started lagging and deserting' after the third battle. Roved the area around here in gangs. Like a bunch of dogs in packs. What houses they found buttoned up, they unbuttoned, so to speak, and beggin' your pardon." He shook his head in disgust.

"At Malvern Hill, the bodies are laid out so thick on the field that you cain't walk a step without steppin' on one of them."

He looked squarely at Emmy. "So, Ma'am . . . respectfully acknowledging what is likely your most honest and earnest of intentions, I'd be very careful about talkin' in the Boston accent I heard when we conversed. Folks are savagely angered all around and there's been enough hangin' already of suspected Yankee sympathizers in this war of Northern aggression . . . without so much as anything that resembles even a bit of the fairness accorded to beasts even."

Emmy saw a mix of anger and grief in his eyes.

He didn't say very much after that. Indeed, the tone was "set," as he had put it, she realized, and it drifted over what was likely once a verdant valley, now a willfully turned wasteland.

They headed southwest, to avoid the first set of swamps of the northern shores of the Chickahominy, which were overflowing again from several days of rain. After another hour they stopped.

"I kin take you a few more miles up towards where Henri said you'd be headed. But I'm not known in these parts . . . and frankly, Ma'am," he said, nodding at Lebo, "as much as I have learned to respect this man's cold-hearted abilities over the past few years, I don't want to be anywhere near you two if you start turnin' heads wonderin'. Afraid this storm's far from over."

They rode a few more miles upstream.

The stout little preacher turned back to Lebo and Emmy, then looking at her with the same expression she had seen on the faces of the grieving in Washington, he said "Ma'am, from what you told me, you've had your deep sorra's aplenty. Given that there's more 'n one family in my own flock that have lost as many as three sons and a father in this last bloody mess . . . and most of their hopes . . . folks prayin that Ol' Jackson can keep the Yankees out of the Shenandoah long enough so that fewer people will starve out here when this next winter sets in . . . well, I'm hopin' you find yer young man, leave, and keep one more tragedy from adding to all this grieving goin' on. Never kin tell if one more sorra' might break the sad back of this arrogant stubborn land."

He turned to Lebo. "You don't need to pay me for this one, Henri. Horses and a few provisions are waitin' up near the village you're looking for. Credits for 'em's under my name if you need it. At the Methodist church. Only one along that side of the river near Richmond. Ask for Mrs. Celestine Barkus, but when you meet her, address her as Celee. Best of luck. Please bring some quinine next time."

Lebo watched the man depart into the woods, then turned back to Emmy. "Quiet ride now, Lady. More hills 'n woods. Figgerin' about six, maybe seven hours 'fore we get near to the area where you said your man's home is. Quiet ride. We'll see others on the roads we'll have to ride on. When we do, I will do the talkin'."

CHAPTER THIRTEEN

✕✕✕✕

Kathleen

July 23, 1862-Washington, District of Columbia

Inconsiderate. The message she received from her sister, Emmy, tersely noting that she might be detained a bit longer than she had anticipated just rubbed her the wrong way. A ridiculous rescue mission, so very typical of the way her sister always seemed to reason things out. Romantic risk taking, ever since she had watched Emmy's behavior when they were growing up. So very typical for her to have decided to move to the Pacific Northwest with a big-talking adventurer. So very typical for Emmy to have impulsively accepted the proposal from another adventurer while she was still supposedly mourning the passing of her first husband. So very typical for her to have gotten herself into a fix up in Vancouver and then in Panama, to have found a naive beau as a result of that misadventure who actually proposed to her. So very typical that her miscreant sibling would inconvenience everyone around her with some ridiculous notion that she might penetrate the wall separating the two warring communities, let alone find the man and get him home.

Kathleen had received a second letter from Escoffier, the French consulate in New York, imploring her to join him for a special week at his estate in the Westchester countryside for a celebration of the French participation in the American War of Independence from the Brits.

When she read between the lines, he was offering more, she realized.

They had talked about Paris and the Dordogne, the Loire and the countryside in Bourdeaux. He had volunteered to give her, and her husband, of course, should he opt to join them, a grand tour complete with the "grandest of accoutrements," as he put it.

She wondered if he would be a good lover. The day after that second letter, her nephew Jacob gave her the excuse she needed to pursue what Escoffier had intimated. Jacob set fire to the brownstone again.

CHAPTER FOURTEEN

✕✕✕✕

Emmy and Lebo

July 24ᵗʰ to July 26ᵗʰ, 1862-Virginia Countryside

Shortly after the departure of the preacher, they had stopped in the woods for two hours to eat and sleep, but then pushed on, this time westward, to stay on the schedule that Lebo had set. Her safe exit, he had said, would be with the one guide who he truly trusted, Pen Basetyr, and Pen knew better than to linger when someone was late.

Emmy was exhausted by mid-morning. Her low back, sides and neck ached from the ride over the uneven ground they traversed and she noticed that Lebo held his side when they moved uphill on the ridges. She kept alert as best she could. They were close to the middle tributary streams of the Chickahominy, he said, so she kept herself awake by thinking about Brett, and how he fit in with everything else she had experienced in her life thus far, and how, if Brett had survived, he would fit in with whatever Providence had in store for her and her family.

She thought about the preacher, Ardy Dabbs, whose keenness she had misjudged. The man had put his finger on something, her ambivalence, she realized. Even now she wondered whether this was the right thing to do, to leave her children, place herself in certain peril, compelled, this time, not by a ferocious parental instinct to protect her child, as she had when she had taken herself into the Tsimshian aboriginal camps in Vancouver, but by duty — and, she had to admit, the obligation that comes when someone expresses love for you.

How much of her determination to endure this test was driven by her need for the security found in a future relationship with someone who might be a good mate? How much of her resolve was simply due to her own innate stubbornness? Was that a family trait? She had always been praised for her tenacity, but wondered how much that characteristic was simply another manifestation of the O'Malley clan's stubbornness, which her sister and both of her children exhibited. She chastised herself when she admitted to herself that might be the case. But stubbornness kept one alive, she mused. Those who concede too early, die before their time. "The meek shall inherit the earth." There was a different meaning to that, she realized, and laughed to herself at the cynicism of that bitter, alternative interpretation.

They stopped to water their horses when they reached a large orchard bordering a stream that Lebo said was a part of the Chickahominy. Sitting upon her mount, she looked past hundreds of freshly-felled cherry and apple trees covering a gradual slope on a large estate. On the hill above she could see the burned out remains of what had been a grand house. Around the stumps of each tree and scattered all around the branches she saw cherry pits mixed in with hoof marks and human tracks. Whoever had eaten the cherries had cut down the trees to get at them, she realized. Rows of plum and pear trees in the orchard were untouched. Their fruit wasn't ripe yet. The stumps of the cherry trees were thick and gnarled. Had to be over fifty years old she thought.

She asked Lebo about the preacher. "He seemed distraught. Keeping something to himself," she said.

"Dabbs has two sons. One's in Fredrick and the other's in Williamsburg. One's wearing blue. Married hisself a mulatto. The other's wearing buttercup and gray and has his own blacks. Likely they were both down here scrabbling against each other. Last time we spoke before now, the preacher said he expected to lose both of 'em afore it's over."

Emmy thought about the implications of the extremely different choices that had been made by the preacher's two sons. Lincoln was getting more and more pressure, her father had told her, to force himself into the discomforts of finally doing something that abolished the laws permitting men to keep others as slaves. Beginning only a week after the firing on Fort Sumter, Washington had been overwhelmed by a huge number of negro refugees, all escapees coming from as far south as Texas and Louisiana. She had tried to help by volunteering her services and Sarah's at the Episcopal parish her family attended. The pathetic state of most of them, many debilitated with illness and starvation, demonstrated to her the cruelty of their plight. The legal and political wrangling that had perpetuated this condition was deplorable.

She chastised herself for not doing more, for not speaking up loudly enough, for not putting up a better fight with her sister Kathleen and her husband, who, despite benefiting from the privileges accorded to those on the Union's side, frequently made terrible comments about the people they called "the troublesome darkies." It was a prevalent prejudice, she knew — hypocritically, smugly and quietly spoken by those who thought of themselves as "progressive" within affluent Boston social circles. She would address that somehow when she returned, she decided.

Lebo kept them off the roads as much as possible, but the closer they moved towards Richmond, the more it became apparent to Emmy that he did not know this terrain as well as he had the backwoods and lesser roads they had traveled at the beginning of their journey. Several times they had to backtrack because they had come up to the edge of ridges that fell off too steeply for their horses to descend. Finally, he decided that they should just keep to the river's edge as best they could, even if it meant riding sometimes on the well-traveled road that moved north to south along the Chickahominy. Whenever they saw riders moving down the road they moved into the woods and let the riders pass. Most were uniformed cavalry.

Two hours after departing from the destroyed orchard they heard men's voices and sounds of construction. Moving into the woods parallel to the road, they saw a partially constructed bridge in the distance with barebacked men, mostly negroes, crawling all over it, hammering and sawing. The charred remains of broad timbers lay to the side. Emmy realized that the bridge must have been burned during the battles, by one side or the other. Enough of the bridge had repaired that carriages crossed it slowly, with a long line of vehicles on both sides of the river, each waiting its turn for the slow crossing.

"Have to move upstream. Find a ford," Lebo said, so they backtracked again and made their way up into the hills running parallel to the river, keeping the stream below and the roads that ran with it on both sides in sight as much as possible.

Slower going, but safer, she thought.

The Confederate military traffic on the roads down below increased on both sides of the river, with wagons moving slowly northward mostly, towards Richmond, Lebo told her. Not every rider or group of men was uniformed, but almost all carried rifles and muskets.

"There's our ford," Lebo said, pointing down at a large group of horsemen in plain clothes across the river. "That'd be Otis Loller down there. The fat one sitting on the blue Roan. He's sheriff of this here Henrico County. We don't like each other much."

Loller and his men, resting their horses, were watching two riders mid-stream, riding away from them. The second rider's hat blew off and drifted down the river.

They slowly emerged from the river, pushing their mounts up the bank, then crossed the road onto a patch of short grass and for a moment, Emmy thought they were headed straight up the hill into the woods directly towards where she and Lebo were concealed.

Lebo dismounted. "Get off yer mare. Quietly," he whispered.

He unholstered two of his pistols. She held her hands over the horses' muzzles, stroked their necks to keep them calm as the riders rapidly passed through the woods less than seventy-five yards in front of them.

They waited.

Five minutes later she heard a thumping sound and loud whooping shout as the hatless rider, a boy in his early teens, with long curly red hair, now with a drum slung around his neck, and carrying another hat, emerged from the woods further up ahead.

The second rider, an older teen followed, waving a tattered banner. Emmy recognized the flag he waved. It was festooned with the blue and white Massachusetts regimental colors.

The red-haired teen rode down the hill clumsily beating the drum with a single drumstick, *Rap, Rap, Tha-thump.*

The two whooped again loudly at their companions across the river, re-crossed the ford, and rejoined them, handing the regimental flag to one of the other riders. The red-haired boy put the hat he carried onto his head and the seven riders trotted away, with the drum sound receding northward in the direction that Lebo said was near their own destination.

"Let's just take ourselves a look over there," Lebo said, holstering his pistols and pointing with his chin at the woods ahead. They remounted and, continuing to stay hidden, rode in the underbrush until they picked up the trail where the rider had entered and then emerged from the woods. They followed the path until they came to a slight clearing.

At the far end they saw a line of bloated bodies face down in the grass, twelve blue-coated Union soldiers, all but a few with their arms tied behind their backs. None of their uniforms were similar, and each one was shoeless.

"Stragglers," Lebo said.

They had been executed while kneeling, each shot at the nape of the neck.

Lebo dismounted and inspected, turning each stiff body over onto its back, one at a time. The third corpse lay with its left arm outstretched. When Lebo turned it over, Emmy could see, even with the bloating of its features, that it had been a young boy, likely in his early teens. His right hand, hidden under his body, still clutched a drumstick like the one they had seen the redheaded rider using to beat his drum.

Lebo looked at the shoulder insignias of the bodies to the drummer's right and left, also young teens.

"Regimental fife and drum," he said to Emmy. "They must've got lost. Fell behind or ran. Got found, got themselves executed by Viriginie Vigilance Committee 'citizens'."

Emmy had seen brutal scenes like this before. As she covered her mouth and nose to avoid the sulfurous stench in the grove, she thought about what she had experienced in Panama when the train on which she and her family had been riding was held up by the notorious "Derienni" gold robbers of the Isthmus. The Panamanian bandits had murdered passengers indiscriminately and randomly during and after the robbery.

What she saw before her now was a sad, savage, vicious act, defying the conventions of fair treatment of prisoners. Many of the victims had been teens. But as she thought about it, the situations here and down in Panama were similar, likely the result of a self-righteous, retributive anger — the poor and disadvantaged against the privileged, "defenders" against "invaders."

"Cain't cross here, now." Lebo said, peering through his telescope into the fields beyond the ford where the red-headed drummer had rejoined his gang. So they continued northward in the woods, keeping out of sight, then down a slope into a valley where the river below forked southwest.

Three miles further the ground turned mushy soft, and from the mosquitos and flies, it was evident that flooding from constant summer rains had turned the ground into a boggy swamp. Fresh stumps from thousands of young, felled trees ran parallel to the remains of makeshift corduroy roads moving over the soft ground in the middle of the wide valley. Abandoned equipment, some of it obviously new and unused, empty, overturned caissons and wagons, smoldering piles of torched foodstuff, broken barrels and garbage lined both sides of the roads, mired in the black ooze of the surrounding swamp.

On both sides, the ground had been torn up by what appeared to be the movement of thousands of wagons, men and mules, all moving in the same direction as she and Lebo were traveling. A sixteen-pounder brass Parrot cannon lay on its side in its carriage, broken wheels up, discarded like a tossed toy that was no longer of any interest to the children who had been given it as a present. Here and there they saw people rummaging through the piles of boxes and barrels of spoiled food. Three dogs, undeterred by their approach, fought over the hind-quarter remains of a mule from the team that had pulled the cannon. Emmy realized the unlucky animal had been shot dead where it had struggled in the muck, likely after it slipped off the corduroy path, pulling the other mules with it and tipping the heavy cannon over.

Over and over again, all along the three-mile valley, they saw dead animals that had slipped off of the path and had smothered in the surrounding muck. In each instance, their bloated abdomens likely had burst, their heads and backs were already blending into the black muck in which they lay, half covered.

"Heard about this. Little Mac's little yellow belly," Lebo said, referring to the fiasco of McClellan's ignominious retreat from the Peninsula, something which was being cheered in the papers in Richmond and decried in the publications from Washington, New York, Chicago and Boston.

"Cain't imagine Bobby Lee woulda let the Yanks get away this easy. Has to have been a big fight around here. Somewhere up ahead," said Lebo.

Emmy had read accounts of the battles in the Washington papers and smuggled copies of the *Richmond Whig*. There had been seven or eight encounters in all. She wondered if they were traveling through the area the newspapers had called "White Oaks Swamp," which had mostly been an artillery duel between the retreating Union rearguard and the South's now famous "Stonewall Jackson" who Lee had sent to pursue them.

After traveling northwest another mile and a half, they emerged from the swamp and found the site of the battle Lebo had said he thought was up ahead — first by the thousands of birds and flies that swarmed above the field and then by the smell. A half dozen four-man work-gangs of negro workers, each party watched by armed white men on horseback, labored throughout a rolling half mile of what, from the traces left of manicured fields, previously had been a prosperous farm. The burned-out shell of a large farmhouse lay in the middle.

As Emmy and Lebo got closer, they saw that each work-gang of blacks surrounded a buckboard, onto which lay human corpses and body parts stacked on top of each other. The carcasses of hundreds of dead horses, some in large clusters, where the tethered animals likely had been caught in artillery barrages, lay in a bizarre, grotesque array of stiff postures. The bloated, stinking body of one animal lay directly on its back with all four legs pointing straight up. Work gangs were stacking wood and lighting fires around each one of the horse carcasses. The smell from the cremations was sulfurous and sweet.

Emmy again covered her face and breathed through her mouth as much as possible and tried to move away from the carcasses to avoid the swarms of flies and fleas that covered them.

Lebo rode up to one of the work-gang overseers, conversed for several minutes, then returned to Emmy.

"That man says they call this place 'Frayser's Farm.' Yanks moved thousands of supply wagons through last week, said he counted over four thousand of 'em, hightailin' their asses outa here by way of how we come here over that swamp back there. Says Longstreet tried to catch the Yanks right down there afore'n they got their supply trains to their boats waitin' for 'em down on the James. Didn't quite catch 'em, because some slaves told 'em about the fastest roads outta here. Bitch of a fight, though, he says."

They rode down closer to the destroyed farmhouse and over the torn ground, passing scores of people picking through the debris of the battle that had occurred almost ten days before. They were piling discarded items onto carts or into pull-alongs and haversacks.

Emmy noted that they didn't seem to mind the flies.

Lebo continued, "Man said Yanks left coupla thousand of their own wounded behind up at Savage Station. Just left 'em. Yella bastards." He spit. "Ya don't leave yer wounded behind like that."

They headed north for four miles before they again found what appeared to Lebo to be the swampy curves of the sinuous lower Chickahominy. Every farm and village they passed along the way had been ravaged by the movement of the two huge opposing armies churning up the ground they both claimed as their own.

◇◇◇◇◇

Twenty minutes later they found the Methodist church that the Reverend Dabbs had said would provide a contact for fresh horses and brief haven.

Lebo rode up to the small house to the rear of the church and knocked at the door. As Dabbs had told him to do, he told the person who came to the door, a dirty-faced boy who appeared to Emmy to be about Jacob's age of eight or nine, that he was looking for Mrs. Celestine "Celee" Barcus.

The child closed the door, leaving Lebo on the porch. They waited quietly for five minutes, then Lebo moved back to his horse, mounted and started to unsheathe his rifle, when a toothless, stubble bearded man, barefoot and dressed only in filthy gray long johns, emerged from the back of the small house. Emmy estimated he was about the age her father had been before he died, but much more nimble. He carried a double-barreled shotgun and pointed it directly at Lebo, moved his aim to Emmy, then back to Lebo.

"What's yer business?" the man asked.

"A good reverend we met back near the Rapahan-nock said we might find a bit of help here in our travels," said Lebo. "Lookin' for Missus Barcus. Celee Barcus. Is she about?"

Lebo moved his horse slightly in front of Emmy's, shielding her partly from the man's barrels.

"We mean no harm, and in any case, we'd be mighty relieved, Mister, if you'd put down that there scattergun," he said. The old man looked them over for what seemed to Emmy like an eternal minute, then lowered the shotgun and motioned for them to follow him.

"She ain't here no more," the man said, backing his way around to the back of the church next to the house.

Still carrying his rifle, Lebo dismounted and helped Emmy down, then led both horses to the rear of the church. A small shattered, leaning barn, not visible from the road, missing one door and part of the roof, stood immediately behind the dilapidated church.

The man walked into the barn.

They followed, but Lebo held Emmy back with his outstretched arm and kept them far enough away so that, she realized, the scattergun would be less likely to hurt them.

From the darkness, but still visible, the old man turned and said simply, "Cain't help ya now. Sorry."

Lebo seemed surprised and angry. "Mister, beggin' your pardon, but we already paid for the help that's supposed to be provided here."

"You did, I admit," the man said. "Missus Barcus done bought the horses and vittles. Had 'em ready. Sheriff and the Vigilance Committee came by and took it all yesterday. Both horses. 'Redistributing,' they called it. Left us enough to get by for a week, maybe."

"And where's Missus Barcus?" Lebo asked again. Emmy saw Lebo's eyes glance to the side door of the house. She saw what he saw, the young boy running away from the house down the lane to the road. Lebo raised his rifle and pointed it at the man's head. "Do I need to ask less politely?" The old man, surprised by Lebo's quickness, lay his shotgun on the ground.

"They took her too," he said. "Up to Richmond maybe, if'n they didn't hang her already. Please . . . I just worked for the lady. Me an' my boy."

Lebo handed the rifle to Emmy. "Watch this ol' fella, will ya?"

He mounted his horse and galloped off down the lane, returning a few minutes later with the boy suspended by the belt of his britches.

Emmy turned her head as he rode up, and when the old man saw the sudden opening, he ducked and reached for the shotgun resting on the ground.

Lebo reared and spun his horse, dropped the boy, and shot the man through the chest as he was fumbling for the hammers on the weapon.

The man's shotgun discharged, but the impact of Lebo's bullet threw him off and into a pile of straw and manure.

Emmy, struck by a few of the buckshot in her right leg, recovered. She then stooped down to see if she could help the dying man, who was still clutching the shotgun.

She pried the weapon, one hammer still cocked, from his hands.

"I'm sorry," she said to the man.

"Devil curse ya bastards!" the man sputtered, spitting up gobs of bright red blood. He took two small shallow breaths, then died.

Emmy felt the sting of the pellets in her leg as she wiped the man's blood from her hands.

"Ol' fool," Lebo said, glaring at Emmy as he dismounted. He kept his rifle pointed at the boy's head. Emmy understood that she should not have allowed herself to be distracted.

The boy looked down at the old man's body, spit and then shuffled calmly, pokerfaced.

Lebo pushed his rifle on the boy's shoulder and made him sit down.

"Tie him up," he told Emmy, walked to the back door of the house and kicked it in, two pistols drawn. He emerged a few minutes later from the front of the house, holstering his pistols, leading by the hand an almond-eyed, small mulatto girl who appeared to Emmy to be three or four years younger than the boy, perhaps three or four years old.

"Lookie what I found," he said as he handed the little girl over to Emmy. "Now . . . let's us have ourselves a nice quiet conversation, shall we?" he said, sitting down next to the boy. "Without any more stupidity or the risk of any of them Vigilance Committee folks' rude interruptions. Eh?"

The young boy, understanding his predicament, started talking rapidly and in a monotone.

Noting the dead old man, he said, "That man there, name's Bob Kitely. Came n' worked for Missus Barcus an' her husband, the preacher, like my Ma and her Ma did. They're all dead now. Typhus, they said. Missus Barcus tried carryin' on after her husband died 'bout six months ago. Hired Kitely to be a foreman afore the fightin' started up. He made me find the sheriff an' he tol' 'em she was a doing some smugglin."

The boy looked up at Emmy. His face was flushed. "Gettin' by that way, I guess."

He continued. "Sheriff's mixed in with the Vig'lance boys that's been watchin' over this area for folks with Northern leanin'. Hung some folks, lots of darkies too, all up and down this road out yonder."

He went on, speaking faster in an almost breathless hush, staring at the ground while he did so. "Never seen so many soldiers. Both sides. Talked to fellas from 'Bama, 'n

Macon, 'n Florida. Then, a few days later, ever'n I talked with was Yanks, blue coats from Maine, n' Chicago 'n Pittsburg, 'n a place called Minnysoda. Swedes 'n Irish, they said they were, mostly," the boy said.

He told them that thousands of soldiers, including cavalry and artillery, had passed down the same road over the preceding fortnight. He had watched the bluecoats marching north, then retreating south ten days later. The cannon fire had continued day and night for several days. The church next door had been used as headquarters by the Union, then briefly as a hospital by the rebels after a fight at Savage's Station, the main junction of the railroad up the road.

"Ya don't want to go in there now," he said indicating the chapel. "Ain't sanitary. Ain't sanctified any more either, ah guess."

After a few minutes, despite Lebo's previous admonition to let him do all of the talking, Emmy could restrain herself no longer after the boy prattled on and on about the fighting.

"Son, did you know or hear anything about a doctor named 'Brett'? Up further north on this river?" she said. The young boy nodded, tilted his head.

"Did."

Emmy held her breath and waited for him to go on.

"You ain't afar from his place. About three miles or so up the road. If'n ya'll let me go . . . untie me, I kin take ya there," he said. Looking back at Kitely's body again, he said, "Man twern't my father. Beat me 'n this lil' girl there, regular."

"I already figgered that," said Lebo. "Did the ol' bastard do anythin' else to either of you two?"

When the boy hesitated and looked down, Emmy, looking at the boy's welts and bruises and the filthy state of both children, seeing the shame in the boy's eyes and the glazed expression on the little girl's face, said, "That bastard."

Lebo's mouth stretched into a bitter grin. "Figured he was that kind. Figgerin' that ol' man turned over Missus Barcus. Tol' you to do the same to us. That right?" He said, scratching his chin.

The boy nodded again.

They heard the sound of a horse whinnying from the front of the house. Looking out from the barn, they saw a Dun-colored quarter horse with black hind stockings, tied to the hitching post in front.

A drum was tied to the horse's saddle.

A minute later, the redheaded teenager they had seen earlier in the day stepped into view. He mounted his horse and slowly rode off, looking back at the house a few times.

"Well, better we do a bit more ridin' now," Lebo said to Emmy. "'Spect Otis to be riding through this area agin pretty soon."

He dragged the old man's body into the outhouse in the back, closed the door, and started to mount his horse.

Emmy looked at the two children and called to Lebo "We can't just leave these children here!"

Lebo grimaced, spit, and paused, thinking about the circumstances. He dismounted and then untied the boy.

"'Spect your right," he said. "Boy'll tell 'em where were headed."

He walked to the back of the barn and returned with an old, emaciated swayback mare.

"An' leavin' 'em wouldn't be proper now, would it?" he said, scowling as he harnessed the animal. He lifted the boy then the little girl onto the tired old animal's slumped back. He looked at the little girl, sitting in front of the boy, shook his head, turned and walked back into the house, emerging with a small ragamuffin doll. He handed it to the little girl who eagerly pulled it to herself.

"Now let's go see 'bout findin' this man of yours so we can get this job done and git outta here, 'afore we git ourselves caught by those bastards."

Emmy cinched her belt, pulled herself up onto her lathered mare and took a deep breath. Watching Lebo, followed by the strange, pathetic sight of the two children riding up ahead, she felt her heart pounding into her neck. She reached down and felt the buckshot wounds that had cut through her boot into her leg. They weren't deep, because she could feel the pellets under her skin. She would squeeze them out later.

Lockjaw be damned.

CHAPTER FIFTEEN

◇◇◇◇

Kathleen and Penrose

July 26th to July 29th, 1862-Washington, District of Columbia and White Plains, New York

Kathleen hadn't heard from Emmy for five days, and from what she had learned by speaking with one of her husband's contacts, it sounded as if another offensive was already starting in Virginia where her sister had headed.

After Jacob set fire to the library in the brownstone, the smoke stink in her clothing was sufficient to convince her that she needed to move out sooner than she had originally planned. McEmeel had departed on orders for New Orleans a full two weeks previously, so she had no one else's counsel than her own.

Her niece, Sarah, the rude, precious, precocious little thing, had protested vehemently when she announced that they would leave for New York before her mother's return and that she intended to bring her brother, Jacob to a Manhattan naturopath who specialized in diseases of the mind and psychological disturbances.

Kathleen simply told Sarah that her mind was made up.

She sent a telegram to make arrangements for the visit. She sent a second to Escoffier. If all worked out, she would have an expert's opinion on the best therapies for her nephew, she would spend a lovely weekend as a private guest at Escoffier's estate, and be back in Washington well before her sister's return. Perhaps she might even find a cure for the boy!

The train ride to New York through Baltimore and then up to Philadelphia took a bit longer than she anticipated because Stonewall Jackson, Jubal Early or some other fearful rebel had, on the previous day, raided one of the trains and had burned a few trestles. She didn't understand why both of the children seemed so anxious as they rode on this modern convenience. Didn't they understand what a wondrous contrivance these railroad cars were, compared to the horse and buggy? Or the hazards of going out onto the Atlantic in a bucket of a boat — she certainly knew about that — or walking on foot, the way poor people had to get about?

The event they had experienced on the Panama railroad two years ago was an anomaly. But the trains were being accompanied along all of the routes now by the boys in blue, so she felt well protected.

The children were simply spoiled, Kate concluded.

Then, when they stopped in Philadelphia to switch from the B&O line to what everyone called the "Pensy" that would take them directly into New York, Jacob tried to run away. Her sister's little monster didn't get very far. She found him almost immediately, so her trip was inconvenienced only slightly.

To her great delight, Escoffier was waiting at the station when they arrived. He took Kathleen's arm, and in front of both of the children, kissed her hand, squeezed it hard and then whispered something in French to her. She did not speak a word of that languid language, but the way he said it absolutely melted her and sent a flush right down to her toes. She tried to commit the sound of the phrase he whispered in her ear to memory, so that she might have something to carry her forward over the next few days.

Roland Escoffier, the deputy ambassador to the United States, carried a certain flair, she thought. She had changed her mind about him over the past year, since they all traveled to the site of the first Mannassas debacle. He seemed taller and more elegant.

She wondered what the Loire Valley that he called home was like. What did a truffle taste like? Did the French really stuff their geese to swell their livers for their *fois gras*, that Escoffier had described? Was it like the chopped liver she had grown fond of in Boston? Should she purchase a new dress and shoes for this upcoming country dalliance? Was Escoffier a gentleman in intimate moments? Could she tolerate the necessary diplomacy of a quiet encounter when she felt the need to be so very direct in everything she did? Would he teach her anything that she did not already know?

She briefly thought of how stale everything had gotten in her estranged relationship with McEmeel and wondered whether she would ever go back to him when he finally settled down. She wondered if his demons would ever again make him a sane, tolerable man. She hated what this silly war had done to their plans for life, but also wondered if it made any difference. She wondered if their marriage had been doomed from the outset, pushed repeatedly to the brink of dissolution by the muddled interference of her well-meaning but unrealistic parents.

She wondered if taking Escoffier as a lover would save that marriage. She wondered if she could win Escoffier's heart, and then control him as easily as she had during their jaunt down to Bull Run a year earlier.

The next morning she woke early, dressed, then ordered a breakfast for herself. She remembered that the children liked plain food, so she ordered a new type of breakfast called Granula, which was offered by the hotel as a cold-milk breakfast alternative to the croissant, eggs and bacon she ordered for herself. The Granula was expensive, so she insisted that the children finish the concoction, although she didn't try it herself to see if it was as repugnant and tasteless as Sarah had insisted.

One hour later she and the children set out for the Westchester countryside, purportedly to see the splendid gardens about which many people form New York had boasted. However, her real destination was the sanitarium directed by the well-regarded physician, Doctor Hastings Penrose, who had been recommended by both Escoffier and a friend she knew in Washington, D.C.

The consultation with Penrose would be expensive. But Kathleen had also been assured by Escoffier that the institute Penrose directed had a reputation for thorough evaluations, as well as comfortable lodging available, complete with a responsible governess, which would allow her to briefly leave Sarah in their care while her brother Jacob was being assessed. Kathleen reasoned that it would be important that she not interfere with the evaluation, as her sister might have done were she in the same situation, so that Dr. Penrose could focus his entire attention on Jacob.

She would, however, be certain that the staff understood just how severe Jacob's condition was.

The bronze cast sign, "The Westchester Institute" at the gates of the asylum did not give away Kathleen's purpose to Sarah who was unusually quick and, at least in Kathleen's experience with her, almost always quite suspicious about most things.

A wide, graveled topiary-lined lane entering the Asylum's extensive grounds bordered manicured flowered gardens and quiet ponds, and led up to a large, tall flat-faced tudor-style mansion sprawling on both sides into several two-story, plain but well constructed buildings. Gardeners trimmed the edges of the clover grass and what she assumed were caretakers, all white-clad, walked arm in arm with well dressed people, women mostly. On one of the paved pathways, the attendants pushed people in modern conveniences-high backed cane-weave wheel chairs-along the broad, stone-edged pathway around one of the larger ponds. She saw one woman being pushed in a bath chair, similar to the one her father had purchased for her mother in the last year of her life. Everyone seemed peacefully occupied. Kathleen noted that Jacob simply stared ahead, showing little interest in the beautiful surroundings.

Several staff standing on the marble steps were waiting for them when their carriage pulled into the courtyard. A small man with a softly lined face and a long hook of a nose, introduced himself simply as "Mr. Tinder," the personal assistant to Dr. Penrose. Tinder helped Kathleen down from the lorry, leading her as he did so to a plainly dressed, red-faced woman, whom he introduced as "Governess Theodora Plum." Jacob stayed in the carriage, staring straight ahead, twirling his thumbs and talking in a whisper to himself. Tinder looked at Jacob for an extended moment, smiled sympathetically at Kathleen, and when Jacob and Sarah finally came down from the carriage, he led them all into the Mansion. Governess Plum, head held stiffly and straight, stared at Sarah, sideways glancing occasionally at Tinder as if waiting for some instructions.

Tinder and Plum conducted a brief tour, starting with the high ceilinged vestibule of the building with five arched hallways, each with highly polished wooden floors.

"To our immediate left," Tinder said, "is the hallway leading to the administrative offices, where you will meet our staff and Dr. Penrose. In front of us is the hallway that takes one to the gymnasium and spa and the meeting rooms for our guests. That door," he said with obvious pride, "leads to the treatment areas. Very advanced. To our immediate right are two hallways that lead to our guest rooms."

Tinder showed Kathleen and the children one of the rooms, a very clean and simple cubicle with a single bed, a writing desk, an armoire without mirror, and a rocking chair. A small painting of a garden with pink and blue flowers hung on the wall facing the bed. One small window opened to the outside gardens. Tinder turned to Kathleen and noted that Dr. Penrose was waiting for them.

"We are going to pay a visit to someone," Kathleen said to Jacob, "an important person I want you to meet."

She turned to Sarah. "Sarah, I believe Mrs. Plum is here to show you around. We will be staying here for a few days."

Kathleen and Jacob then followed Tinder, and Governess Plum told Sarah to follow her so she could see the other guest quarters. As they moved away towards the administrative hallway, Kathleen saw Jacob turn and say quietly over his shoulder to his sister Sarah, "I don't like this place."

◇◇◇◇◇

Doctor H. Hastings Penrose, a native of Pennsylvania, was an herbalist and naturopath, who, according to Escoffier, had complemented his naturopathic training with studies of the German and British theories on the treatment of disturbed individuals. Having established a successful naturopathic practice in Philadelphia, he built and operated for ten years a small asylum for the mentally disturbed in the affluent northern outskirts of the city.

In 1850, he moved to New York to take on the purportedly extremely lucrative position as the director of the new *Westchester Institute and Asylum for the Disturbed and Insane*.

"The Hotel," as the asylum was referred to by locals, advertised itself as a "quiet haven for those plagued by diseases of the mind," and distinguished itself from other asylums by offering inmates a pleasant countryside setting, complete with spa, mud baths, and sulfur springs. Penrose's influence brought to the asylum the latest in medicinals, herbal remedies, electro-magnetism, enemas and cathartics coupled with traditional and long advocated "Heroic Medicine" therapies, like purging, bleeding, centrifugal mechanics and near-drowning regimens that had been vigorously defended by venerable Philadelphia healers such as the famous Benjamin Rush.

Penrose lectured extensively to the lay public and to the medical professionals who would listen to him about the various causes of, and treatments prescribed for madness. Although ongoing debates had continued within medical and caretaker communities regarding the efficacy of many of the various treatment regimens then in practice, some of which had been utilized by healers since Hippocrates first taught them, Penrose was of the opinion that one should not disregard anything that might bring about a cure to the patient and thus, relief to the families who had the burden of caring.

Thus, although he disagreed with Benjamin Rush's theory that madness resulted from malfunctions of the brain's blood circulation, he often used Rush's "centrifugal chair" for certain cases of intractable madness. He concurred with Germanic medical theory that madness resided in the mind, and swore that he had created permanent cures by means of forced discipline and sturdy restraint processes.

In every public presentation, and especially the ones he gave to audiences of potential financial backers of the Westchester Institute, he boasted of the high rate of cures the institute had effected since his assumption of directorial responsibilities. On the back pages of two well-read newspapers, the *New York World* and the *Washington Daily National Intelligencer*, he had printed testimonials from satisfied patients and families.

Colleagues, both admirers and detractors, frequently commented about his ample persuasive abilities, and many envied the wealth he had created for himself during his thirty-four years of medical and psychiatric practice in Pennsylvania and New York.

In only one instance had any of the various accusations leveled against Penrose ever lingered in the public's eye. In that circumstance, involving the involuntary commitment of a woman in the Philadelphia asylum he had built, he was accused of accepting an "honorarium" from the woman's husband in return for his diagnosis of her as "hysterical" and "certifiably insane." The woman's elderly parents sued to have her released, and after a few years of wrangling in the local courts, the situation resolved itself after the woman hanged herself while in the custody of a temporary guardian appointed by the courts. Penrose vigorously protested as "preposterous poppycock" various and several allegations that his institute afterwards had quietly paid an undisclosed sum to the parents to end the matter.

In 1856, less than six years after Penrose's appointment as the physician-director of the *Westchester*, the institute's board of governors learned that the asylum's financial condition was solidly and, for the foreseeable future, intractably profitable. Its debts were negligible, and as a result of Penrose's prolific salesmanship, The *Westchester's* endowment was growing rapidly.

As a result, the board authorized Penrose's ambitious plan to greatly beautify the physical plant, purchase and expand its grounds to adjacent properties, and advertise its services widely to affluent communities all along the Atlantic seaboard. Those services included the treatment of disturbed children, rebellious adolescents, and patients afflicted with addictions to alcohol and opiate medicinals. *The Westchester* expanded further to house long-term and permanent inmates. Most of them were women, many of them involuntarily committed by concerned spouses.

Although Penrose concurred with Benjamin Rush's hypothesis that the black skin of the negro was a treatable disease "acquired by atmospheric conditions of origin," he subscribed to the theory that "negro lassitude" was an unfortunate and incurable hereditary trait. *The Westchester* exclusively treated white people, and no negroes were allowed on its campus, either as employees or patients.

Although he introduced himself to families in the anteroom adorned with the diplomas and certificates of distinction, and examined patients in their rooms or in the treatment facilities, Penrose always met his patients for their first visit alone in his own inner office. There, without distractions, he carefully observed how the new patient reacted to the sumptuous layout of the room, and the numerous curiosities with which he adorned his desk and shelves.

He had placed a large, distortion mirror behind his desk, and covered one wall with an array of masks from a variety of sources, including a long-nosed *Arlequino* of the *Comediae del Arte*, wooden animal carvings from New Zealand and Pacific Northwest aboriginal tribes, a voudou haunt mask from Haiti and straw-and-nail spirit weavings from the Belgian African Congo. Next to the low seat in which he always insisted the patient sit, he placed a huge spinning globe covered with a many-colored map that bore no resemblance to the known world.

In one corner, behind the tall, high-backed chair in which he himself sat, he had arranged on the credenza a human skeleton, grinning crosslegged in tall riding boots and dressed with a plumed hat. The windowless room and all of its decorations, he once had explained to an admirer, was purposefully designed to provoke the patient's psychosis — "a rapid incursion into their disturbance, with which I can determine my best intervention," he boasted. Each initial interview, whether with adult or child, began the same way, with the same list of questions, the answers to which he quietly recorded in a large, ostrich skin covered red journal.

After saying goodbye to Kathleen who was leaving for an engagement at an estate near Lyndenhurst, Penrose guided Jacob Evers into his office. He directed the boy to sit in the low chair, stood by his desk and stared at him for over a minute without speaking. He opened the red journal.

"Your name is Jacob. Who is Jacob and what at does Jacob do?" he asked.

Jacob did not answer. Penrose waited for almost a full minute for an answer, then repeated the question. "Little boy, who is Jacob and what does Jacob do?"

Jacob stared at the wall of masks and did not blink.

Penrose stared at Jacob, waiting, watching. He pulled a stool over to Jacob and leaned forward, staring at him at eye level. Waiting.

"Who is Jacob?"

He put his right hand on Jacob's knee, squeezing it, moving it slightly upwards onto his thigh.

"Your aunt and your mother have left you here. Did you know that? How do you feel about that?"

Jacob slowly turned away from the masks on the wall over, and looked into Penrose's eyes.

"How do you feel about that, Little Boy?" Penrose asked again, squeezing Jacob's thigh a little higher up.

The staff in the hallway burst into the room less than half a minute after all the yelling started. Penrose stood backed into a corner holding his bloody, mangled index finger with his handkerchief.

"Get the little bastard out of here!" he commanded quietly.

Jacob didn't stop screaming for two hours. Later, after he was tied down into the restraining crib, he screamed all night.

CHAPTER SIXTEEN

◇◇◇◇

Jacob

"Don't do that to me! Don't do that to me! Don't you do that to me!" Jacob screamed.

He was locked down into some contraption, a flat cage or trap like the ones his father used to catch raccoons. His wrists and legs cinched down, a steel strap pulled across his chest, he tried to move his hips and arch his back. But he couldn't move the cage.

"Don't! Don't! Don't! You don't understand! Let me go. Let me go!"

He heard murmurs outside in the hall, then the door opened. It was Mr. Tinder and the Governess Plum. Both of them looked angry. Their faces were bright red.

"Quiet, you little monster!" Tinder said, and punched the restraining cage. "You've done some damage."

"Let me out of this! You don't understand!"

"We understand very well, you Brat! Doctor Penrose will need to have his finger amputated thanks to you! Your aunt will pay for this!"

Tinder turned and stalked out. Governess Plum stared at Jacob for a few moments, then turned and left without a word, closing the door behind her. In the dark room, only a small beam of late afternoon light came through the tiny window opposite the crib.

"You don't understand. You don't understand!" Jacob began sobbing uncontrollably now.

"Please. Please!" He kept crying and crying. Each sob seemed to provoke another as, in the blur of the pain and outrage, he tried to put together what had happened, the insult of it all — his aunt leaving him there with that man, the doctor touching him like he did, his mother and Sarah leaving him.

When he finally was able to stop crying after what seemed a long, long time, he tried wriggling out of the straps but could not do so. His eyes burned, his shirt was soaked from perspiration and he had peed his pants. He took a deep breath and, feeling very tired, he closed his eyes. It helped make the burning in his eyes a bit better. He fell asleep.

He woke when he thought he heard some movement off to his left. Was it in the room? He couldn't tell.

"Hello?" he said hesitantly.

Nothing.

Was something in the room with him? he wondered. An animal?

The devil?

His heart started pounding hard again. The devil! He pushed that thought away. His mother and the preacher had told him there weren't devils. Just bad humans.

He listened for movement, breathing.

Nothing.

He closed his eyes again.

As the daylight had waned, the room grew completely dark, but his eyes had become accustomed to it and, turning his head to the left, he was able to see from the corner of his left eye a sliver of light beneath the door from the hallway.

He strained to hear anything that might indicate that someone was outside.

"Hello? Hello? Is anybody here?"

Nothing. No one was listening, he realized.

He turned his head to the right and tried to look up at where he thought the small window had been, but could see no light.

He turned back to the left and the light under the door was now gone.

Had he imagined it?

No light in the room now.

He listened to himself breathing.

Was something else outside the room?

Was something inside of the room with him?

He thought about devils.

He thought about the time, when he was a little boy, five years old, three years ago or so, his father, Isaac took him to a new church in nearby Anacortes for a Sunday service. A traveling Baptist preacher had been invited to conduct the services to the small congregation that day, and

Jacob remembered hearing for the first time the story from the Bible of how God had cast his favorite angel, Lucifer, down into the bottom of a place called Hell. Where there was no light.

Darkness.

Like this place here, he thought.

The preacher talked about Hell's fire that gave horrible heat, worse than the sun. It was a black heat, the preacher said. No light.

"And the Devil stayed there and hated God because he wasn't as powerful as God and he pulled creatures who hadn't been christened or who died while doing evil or who carried hatred in their chests or who stole or killed others or who coveted or who sinned without the forgiveness of Jesus," the preacher hollered down at the people in the church. Jacob remembered chills running up and down his back when he heard that sermon.

As he thought about it again now, Jacob tried but couldn't remember all the things that got you there, but the place, that Hell, was full of people who were damned by their actions. And there were beasts and snakes, like the ones he saw in Panama. And killers, like the ones who had taken him away from his home. Like the one who killed his father and took off his face and wore it and beat him when he was tied up in the Northerners' hut.

What had his father done, what had *he* done to be hurt like that? he wondered.

Jacob tried not to think about it, but he remembered that the devil was black and red. Black skin, not like the negroes, dull deep black like a piece of coal. Red eyes, like when the coal gets caught on fire. The preacher had described the black skin. He said it had scales on it like a snake and if you looked at the devil when his back was turned to you, he looked like a serpent because his tail was so thick and it whipped back and forth, but you could tell he wasn't a snake because he also had long legs with hooves that split, like the ones on a goat. And you didn't want the devil to look at you because once he got you in his sight he wouldn't give up trying to tempt you 'til he got you to come with him down to Hell with him and all the other beasts and men. The evil men who surrounded him. Their souls. Because their bodies had rotted away.

Jacob had his first nightmare that night after hearing that preacher. He didn't call out because he woke up immediately and found Sarah sleeping next to him and remembered that he was dreaming. He asked his father, Isaac, about the devils, but Isaac said he had come to believe that the devil looked more like a human than the preacher had said. And he thought they were all around.

"In and out of a lot of people," his father had said.

When he asked Sarah about it, she had just shaken her head.

"Mother said the devil was a made up thing, to keep people going to church," she laughed. "Sounds like that preacher gave it out and got to you!"

Where was Sarah now? Had she been wrong?

Was the Devil in the room with him now?

Waiting?

CHAPTER SEVENTEEN

◇◇◇◇

Emmy and Lebo

July 27th to July 28th, 1862-Virginia Countryside

L ess than a mile into their ride from the Methodist church, the swayback carrying the two children simply stopped moving. It bowed its head almost to the ground and stood trembling, breathing loudly.

Emmy watched the animal panting, the struggle of the poor beast loudly pronounced by the sound emanating from its wasted, emaciated rib cage. She knew that it would be hopeless to prod the old mare. It had given out.

She dismounted, plucked off the little girl and placed her on her own mount. Lebo did the same with the boy, then took off the harness from the dying animal. Looking back down the road a minute later, Emmy saw that the horse had not moved from the side of the road where they had left it.

Further up the road, off to the right, they saw five corpses hanging, four men and one woman. Tied onto the neck of one of the bodies, a sign said "Collaberators." Covering the little girl's eyes, Emmy asked the boy if the woman's body was that of Celee Barcus. He nodded his head.

As the boy had promised, he led them to what was left of the Brett estate, which was only a few miles further up north from the church. Emmy recognized it immediately from the pictures Brett had shown her when he proposed to her on his visit to Boston. A yellow flag, denoting that it had been used as a hospital, hung from the house's roof beam and flapped listlessly in a tepid wind. At first, the two-story house, built in the style of many of the columned mansions in that area, but constructed in sturdy brick rather than wood, appeared to be intact.

The closer they got to the deserted house, however, it became apparent that the damage from the Union's assault ten days ago had been extensive. Several gray bullet holes marked the yellow banner. The bricks on the south side of the building showed the pocked marks, top to bottom, from shell shot. The remnants of drapes hung on the windows, every one shattered and hanging in shards. All the remaining doors lay ajar, twisted off their hinges. The front porch and columns, scorched from a fire that for some reason had not completely destroyed the portico or consumed the rest of the house, lay covered with debris.

When they rode to the back of the house they found overturned, bullet riddled bloody tables in front of a half-destroyed barn. Hundreds of blackbirds and ravens picked at garbage all around the rear of the house and into the scorched fields beyond. A pile of single unmatched, shoes lay next to the waxen, stinking carcasses of what had been two pigs.

"Rebs wouldn't a wasted these animals. Must of bin fat Yanks comin' through last," said Lebo.

Inside the wrecked house, the stench almost overwhelmed them and they had to cover their faces and breathe through their mouths to move about. The parlor and kitchen floors were covered with the sticky filth of dried blood. The wainscoting and wallpaper was spattered with blood and sooty debris was pushed into every corner. The ceiling, dotted with long strings of blood speckles from arteries severed during the surgeries performed in that room, slumped in its center. A wide halo of blood, its rust colored core ringed by a pale pink, stained half of the dining room ceiling, likely from leakage through from the room above. The railings to the upstairs had been torn off and the master bedroom and side rooms were covered with empty litters, piles of bloody rags, bandages and fragments of uniforms.

Emmy looked for any sign that would give her a clue as to Brett's fate. On every wall, close to the floor, she found notes written in pencil and a few scratched in blood. They were names and dates mostly. One read "Sgt. Ralph Wayne Thomas, kilt slowly by a gut shot, July 19, 1862."

In the waning light, Emmy read nothing in the notes that indicated anything from Brett.

Lebo, who had gone outside to hide the horses, returned as Emmy finished inspecting the writing on the walls on the second floor.

"Better look at this," he said.

He took her to a long narrow ditch behind the barn. In it, partially covered with soil, lay a row of dead men, several dozen, all Confederate soldiers. Even though she again felt almost overwhelmed by the smell, Emmy forced herself to step into the ditch, swatting aside rats and birds as she moved along to each body. With Lebo's help, she uncovered and inspected every one of them, peering closely at the swollen, yellow-black faces.

Brett's body was not in the mass grave.

Climbing out of the ditch, Emmy didn't try to hold back the pain she felt, and started to weep. She had held some faint hope that he might have recovered and returned to his home, the one he had proposed would someday belong to them and their new family. The carnage she had witnessed here and at every stop along the way diminished her hopes that she might ever find Brett's whereabouts, but seeing that the men in the ditch had all been rebels confirmed Lebo's speculation that the last occupants of the Brett estate likely had been a Union force, rapidly moving through the area, taking their own dead with them.

There were no gravesites she could see in the surrounding fields. The Confederates, who she had been told, had asked Brett's permission to occupy his home for their hospital, would have respected his wishes. She knew he loved his home, and would not have wanted its fields desecrated.

"I need to go to Richmond," she said to Lebo. "I know you didn't bargain for that, but if he has survived, he'd likely be in one of their hospitals."

Lebo did not hide his displeasure. "You ain't prepared for Richmond, Lady. With all due respect. Ain't dressed for it, don't know anybody. Likely 'll get yourself arrested."

He heaved a sigh, looked her over, then spit.

"Well, dammit," he muttered.

He had no choice. She was resolute.

⬦⬦⬦⬦

With the late afternoon sun tipping over the western tree line, Lebo decided it was best that they move into the woods to rest for the evening. They would head west into Richmond before daybreak, staying off the main road as much as possible. They didn't build a fire.

Emmy asked the boy his name.

"Jedadiah," he said.

"Your name?" she asked the little girl. The girl didn't answer, opened her mouth as if to speak, but looked up at Emmy with a worried expression.

"Tongue tied," said the boy. "Deaf, too. Think her mother called her 'Claris' or 'Clarissa'."

"How'd you two end up with that ol' man? asked Lebo. The boy simply shrugged and turned away.

Emmy found a small stream and washed herself, relieved that she hadn't had to deal with the curse yet this month. She brought the little girl over to the stream and bathed her, using a few of the clean rags she would have used for containing menstrual blood. Then Emmy combed through Clarissa's knotted hair, remembering as she did so what it was like when her children were that age not so long ago.

Emmy was surprised at how willingly the girl allowed her to bathe her, and as the dirt washed away, she noted bruises on the girl's arms, back and legs. Emmy wondered who the little girl's mother and father might have been like — white man with blue eyes and a black slave, or black man with a white, blue-eyed woman? What were the circumstances of their union? Had it been love or had it been rape?

From the little girl's actions, watching Emmy closely and tagging after her, anticipating at times what Emmy was going to do, then helping her do it in her own way, it was clear to Emmy that she was intelligent and understood most of what Emmy tried to convey.

Emmy tried scrubbing the filth from the child's dress, hung it to dry in the early evening heat.

The boy, however, wouldn't allow her to wash his face or hands, and remained silent for the rest of the afternoon, leaning up against a tree, whittling the bark off of one stick with another.

They shared some salted pork and tack, then the four of them silently sat in the woods, waiting for the protection of full darkness. Emmy covered the children with her own blanket and moved close to them. It wasn't cold. Although she was bone tired and fell asleep immediately, she slept fitfully, waking when she found the little girl snuggled up to her chest.

In her half-sleep, she thought about her situation, how she might go about finding information about Brett, and wondered what she should do with the children when they arrived in Richmond. She thought about Jacob, comparing him to this little boy. She wondered about the big-eyed little girl sleeping in her arms.

What would become of her?

Who would take her in when this world was so very upside down and broken?

◇◇◇◇

Lebo shook her awake in the darkness.

"Get movin'," he said quietly. "We're gonna have visitors shortly."

As she rubbed her eyes, trying to bring herself awake to understand what he was talking about, she saw that Lebo had saddled both of the horses and was strapping on both pistol belts.

"Our little bastard's slipped away. Misjudged him, dammit," he said.

He walked to the edge of the trees overlooking the road below. When he returned he lifted the little girl onto the saddle of Emmy's mare.

"Expect they'll be comin' from the direction we came." Pointing to the left, he said "We'll head down this away toward Richmond. Expect we'll be there by about nine, or so."

As Emmy's eyes adjusted to the darkness, she could see Lebo's grim, angry, determined expression.

Less than five minutes after departing, moving through the woods running parallel to the road, they heard hoof beats in the distance coming from the east. Several horses. They could see the faint light of torches moving along the road towards them.

"Too late! You get on down to that road and move fast away from the sun up," he said to Emmy, pulling his Spencer out of its sheath. He dismounted and tied his horse to a small sapling.

"You're gonna look for a yella painted house on the east side, on a street called 'Cary.' Not far from the big ironworks on the river. Tredegar, it's called. Ask for where 'Noah's Ark' is, an' ask for Miss Janie Jones. Use my name," he said with a small laugh. "She'll know Pen Basetyr too . . . can help you find your man if he's in town in one of the hospitals . . . or prisons."

"What if your friend isn't there?" Emmy asked.

"If Janie ain't there, then work your way on up to Josie DeMeritt's place, up by the Chimborazo hospital. She knows me too. Better get out of these britches an' dress well if'n you find your way up there," Lebo said, smiling slightly.

When Emmy hesitated, sensing she was worried about him, Lebo shook his head, "Am expectin' to collect that bonus that's awaitin' for me up in Baltimore. Cain't, if either one of us is dead. Tell ol' Janie I miss her a lot. All right to tell the same to Josie if ya get the chance."

He stopped and turned back to Emmy.

"Gimme that big LeMatt."

Emmy handed over the heavy pistol she had been carrying.

"Take this." He handed her a small two-barreled derringer.

Judgin' by what we seen, if you get yerself caught by these bastards . . . " He pointed to Clarissa's temple, " . . .

one shot for the little one here, and the second for yerself. Same place."

He moved off into the woods. Emmy moved her horse as quietly as she could onto the road.

Less than a minute later, she heard a rifle shot. Then another.

She heard men hollering, far down the road, horses whinnying and more shots.

She kicked her heels into her mare's flanks and as she headed west, coming from the woods where she had last seen Lebo, mixed in with the intermittent sounds of gunshots, she heard a beating: *Rap Rap Rap*. It was the redheaded boy's drum.

CHAPTER EIGHTEEN

⟨⟨⟨⟩⟩⟩

Sarah

July 29ᵗʰ, 1862-White Plains, New York

S arah watched the Governess Plum as she toured her through the different amenities of the "rest hotel," the term the woman used to referred to the institute. Plum was mid-fifties, walked with a slight limp, and wore her gray-blonde hair tightly pulled into a braid and bun. Sarah wondered whether sun exposure, pumice scrubbing, or lots of whiskey drinking caused the woman to have such a red flushed face. The woman certainly didn't seem very happy. Sarah wondered why the woman seemed to be carrying anger all up and down her stiff back.

As the tour of the facility concluded, Mrs. Plum showed Sarah the room where she would be quartered, simple accommodations, but a private room, she said.

"Will my aunt and Jacob be in the rooms next to this one?" Sarah asked, as she started to test the firmness of the mattress.

Plum waited until Sarah sat on the bed in her room, then quickly backed to the door.

"Your aunt asked me to tell you that she would be away for a few days, but you would have many activities to keep you fully occupied." Closing the door behind her as she left the room, she then said, "Dinner later this evening will be delivered to your room, Young Lady." The governess had a strange, satisfied smile on her face as she said that, Sarah noted.

She didn't know what to say at the abruptness of the woman's unexpected departure. Following, she went to the door and tried opening the latch.

The door wouldn't open!

"Hello? Mrs. Plum? The door seems to be locked!" She tried shaking the door, pushing and then pulling at the latch, but it wouldn't move.

Why . . . how could her aunt have done that . . . left her and Jacob?

And why was she being locked in her room?

Then she thought of Jacob. Where was he and what was happening to him?

She pounded on the door, but heard nothing.

She pounded louder. *Bam, Bam, Bam, Bam!*

Nothing.

"Jacob?" she called out.

Bam, Bam, Bam, Bam!

Nothing!

The tiny window near the bed — constructed, as she thought about it later, so that "guests" couldn't possibly escape from it — opened only a few inches and was so small that, even if she had thrown her chair at it and broken the glass, the frame was so tight she couldn't have wiggled one leg outside. The longer window above it — she saw that it had no way to open it — was so high she couldn't reach it. The small writing desk and bed were bolted down!

What was her aunt Kathleen thinking?!!

It took Sarah almost a full day to get out of that room while the "good doctor Penrose," as her aunt referred to him earlier in the day, was "healing" her brother.

She wasn't certain she would have been able to escape, had she not, late in the afternoon, spoken to the lady who whispered.

The lady was a lot older than her mother, she believed, although she never really saw her at the beginning, so at that time, she couldn't be sure.

Sarah heard a knock on her door — a small rapping that she almost didn't hear because she had been crying — a few hours after Mrs. Plum had locked her in. Faint. But there it was.

Tic Tic Tic.

"Hello?"

"Are you all right, Sweetie?"

At first Sarah thought it was the ghost of her grandmother, Abby, talking to her. Same tender tone, but in a whisper.

She had liked her grandmother Abby, even though she hadn't much time to get to know her before she went and died shortly after they moved up to Boston. There had been something about the way Abby had spoken . . . the gentleness about everything she did . . . that made Sarah instantly know, from the moment she met her, that she was safe . . . protected . . . but in a different way than the way her own mother, Emmy, so steely and direct in every way, managed to watch over her.

But then Abby had died. Too brief a stay. Didn't really get to enjoy her, the way she had in knowing her doting grandfather, Kern.

And now he was gone too.

Tic tic tic.

"Hello?"

"There is a way out, Sweetie. Go to your window."

Sarah went to the tiny window in the room and opened it again, then heard the door to the room next door opening and closing, then the window in the room to the left, next to hers, opening up.

"Are you there?"

"Yes. I am," Sarah said. "Who are you?"

There was a long pause.

"I don't remember anymore," the lady replied. "I have been here so long." Another long pause. "It doesn't matter, now. But you are too young. Why are you here?"

Sarah explained that she had accompanied her brother, whom her aunt had proclaimed "disturbed," and then her aunt had just . . . left them! She didn't know what had happened to Jacob, she said.

"He is most certainly being 'kept'," the lady said, with some emphasis. "That's how it all starts."

Sarah asked her what that meant. The lady told her about Dr. Penrose and how he and some of the others on his staff — no matter how it had been described to others — really treated patients, how she and other women had been institutionalized . . . and how she had been abandoned by her own family and husband.

Over eight years ago.

"The other day, I couldn't remember my husband's name," the lady said. "Tried. Couldn't."

Sarah thought she heard a subtle change in the tone of the woman's whisper, from bewilderment . . . to resignation.

"Stopped hating him a long time ago. But I can't remember his name any more," she said. "The staff, Dr. Penrose, told some people that my forgetting things was the consequence of my deep disturbance. Funny . . . I can't forget Penrose's name." Sarah thought she heard bitterness in the lady's whisper.

As Sarah listened, she wondered if that would somehow also be her own fate. Abandoned, alone somehow. She had promised Jacob she would watch over him. She wondered if that would be his fate too. She was failing him.

The lady went on, telling her about when she had been a little girl, an only child, and how, after years caring for her father, she had been invited to come to New York from Savannah to marry with her large dowry to a younger man and how, after her father died, there was no one left "on her side." The lady explained that she had gone into a long period of "grief," as she called it, because her husband just had lost interest in her and then the world just had slipped away, it seemed.

And then one day she was taken here . . . for a rest, she was told, and that rest had lasted for so very long, and it wasn't a rest any more. Hadn't been for several years, no matter how much she cried about it. She had walks in the garden with a man named Jonathan and, after he left, with a man named Thomas, and then with Robert, who reminded her of her husband somehow — perhaps she said, because he didn't pay her much attention, either.

"I am lost now," she said.

The lady stopped talking and closed the window for a minute, then opened it again.

The easiest way to get out of the room, she went on, was by pushing a bit of paper in the latch plate so that the latch of the lock was blocked and then it could only partially close. It worked all of the time because the attendants who delivered food in the evening were sloppy, she said. She had learned how to do that a few years ago, and had found a way to leave the dormitory and walk about the grounds at night after dark, sometimes placing little pieces of ribbon on the trees so she could be reminded of her secret escapes when she was taken out on Wednesdays and Saturdays. She had even gone to the rail station once at two in the morning, but it was closed and she didn't have any money to buy a ticket and even if she did, didn't know where she would go. She didn't remember her name anymore. Thought it was 'Mary,' but wasn't sure.

"Penrose is a monster," she said. "He has . . . contraptions."

The lady paused for a bit.

She whispered quieter now, even more faintly, but angrily, "He has drowned a few of us." She closed her window.

Sarah sat down on the bed and waited, but the woman did not come back.

How to put it together? Why did her aunt leave them? Why would she? Didn't she understand what Jacob had been through already?

When was her aunt coming back? Would she ever? And what was this place?

Would her mother find out?

Was her mother all right?

What would make anyone give power to a man like Penrose who, from the lady's description, sounded like he was a monster? Were people afraid of him, like what she had seen with Anah, the aborigine "tyee" chief in the Oregon territory?

Had people given Penrose power because he appeared to be very smart, or had wonderful credentials, as her aunt had told her?

Or was Penrose a "seducer" — "a charismatic," as her mother had described Rafael Bocamalo, the man who had killed so many people when their train was robbed in Panama?

Why did this Doctor Penrose have the power to get away with so much? Who would stop someone like this? Wasn't that adult society's responsibility?

She decided what the lady had described would not happen to her or to Jacob. She could figure a way out, get to the rail station somehow. She had a silver coin in her shoe so she could get tickets. Maybe find Jonny and Falco, the children of Scarpello, the man who had saved them during the train robbery in Panama. Didn't they live in New York now, in the city someplace? What was name of that place?

She found a piece of stationery in the desk drawer and folded a piece to try jamming the lock when the opportunity arose. The lady, "Mary," said to wait to leave until late, four hours after midnight, when it would be safe to walk the halls, usually when no attendants were around. A chime clock would toll on the hour.

Four bongs.

She wondered if she would ever see that lady, Mary, the one with the kind voice like her grandmother's.

CHAPTER NINETEEN

◇◇◇◇

Emmy

July 29ᵗʰ, 1862-Richmond, Virginia

B y sun up, Emmy could see she was back on what had to be the main western road from the Chickahominy into Richmond. Heavy military and civilian traffic moved in both directions, with wagons carrying wounded soldiers, she surmised, from across the peninsula's seven battlefields. Four times she was stopped by overworked sentries, each time passing through by telling the truth to the young men who stopped her.

"Going to Richmond to see if I can find my fiancé," she said. When one soldier realized she was a young woman riding with a child peeping out of her long coat, he asked no further questions, but simply shook his head and waved her on.

She was fortunate, she realized, because both Lebo and Dabbs had predicted that it would only be a matter of days before Jeff Davis imposed even stricter regulations for martial law on the city. Other than an identification letter of passage Lebo had given her, forged likely, from one of the Maryland Congressmen Lebo said was friendly to the Confederacy, she had no official papers, and nothing signed from the provost marshall's office.

On reaching Richmond, she was surprised how much it resembled Washington. Like its Union counterpart, the Confederate capital was overflowing with soldiers, workers and vagrants, white and black. Wagons blocked streets, horses and horse teams were hitched on every corner. Barkers, streetwalkers and vendors moved up and down the thoroughfares that had had been built for a much smaller population. She passed saloons and hospitals, prisons and graveyards cut into vacant lots. Slaves pushed wagons filled with possessions of their dispossessed owners. Funeral processions moved slowly along several streets, and bells rang intermittently from every church. Long lines of disheveled civilians waited for soup and bread all along Main Street and Cary. Wounded men in bandages convalesced in yards and parks. From the barred windows of a squat building, blue uniformed prisoners waved at her and other passersby on the street below.

As she rode up the hill to St. John Episcopal Parish, she was relieved to escape for a brief time from the pungent miasma of charnel from the broken flesh that stank every street in the main part of town.

Before reaching the church that she had reason to believe would most likely give her some help in her quest, she rehearsed the plea she would use to convince the minister that he should assist her.

But when she introduced herself at the rectory, she received a cold, curt answer.

"You have a Yankee voice, you look like a tramp, and make for an impossible task to fill, Young Lady," the cleric said with a dour sneer, moving his eyes to Clarissa. His lip curled in a frown as he looked at the small mulatto child, then up at Emmy.

"We can't help you. And shame on you." He closed the door on her face.

With the minister's presumptuous rebuke, despite her reluctance to follow Lebo's advice, she remounted and rode down the hill toward the area one person told her was called "Jackson Ward." She wondered what she would find when she reached the places Lebo had told her to find, almost certainly "leisure houses," given the way he had laughed before he moved away into the woods to cover her escape.

And what if she failed there too? She was a mess, she admitted to herself. Given her state, how would she be allowed to inquire about Brett at any of the hospitals in the area? When she had volunteered to nurse soldiers in the Washington hospitals, she had been advised to clothe herself and Sarah in simple but respectable Sunday dress so that they would not be judged to be opportunists like the thieves or prostitutes who plied their trades in some of the shabbier institutions that cared for vulnerable, wounded men. Now she was grubby dirty, and despite the rough appearance of the populace she passed in the crowded streets, she turned heads riding down the street with the small child in her lap.

How would the hospitals ever receive her?

It wasn't difficult for her to find "Noah's Ark." When she approached the two story yellow house on Cary in the Jackson Ward of the city, she had her answer. A very tired looking woman stood on the stoop, smoking a thick black cigar. She looked at Emmy and, admitting through the door a young Confederate officer shouldering past her, the woman turned and said to Emmy, "Honey, all our beds are taken."

"I'm looking for Miss Jane Jones" Emmy tried to explain, as the door was being closed on her.

The woman, a slim, pan-faced brunette with the stiff posture of a primary school teacher, laughed. "I'm Janie Jones and I'm about to be detained." She snorted, then spit without taking the cigar from her mouth.

"Henri Lebo sent me," Emmy said. The woman hesitated, sniffed, then put down her cigar on the counter inside. She tilted her head and looked at Emmy again, wondering. "You're too skinny to make me any money . . . even if you like to dress as a man, like you do, Darlin'. Henri would know that."

"Please . . . it's not like that . . . I just need to buy a bath and a change of clothing, to go to the hospitals to find someone . . . and find a place for this little one," Emmy said, referring to the little girl.

Taking the black cigar from her mouth, the woman bit the corner of her lower lip, looked down at the girl and then again at Emmy.

In a different voice, now coquettish and gay, she called out over her shoulder, to the soldier standing in the parlor "You go sit yourself down now, Lieutenant Sweetie. One of the girls'll be down in a minute," then turned back to Emmy standing outside on the porch. "Caint do anything about this one," noting Clarissa. She opened the door, spit onto the porch, stubbed out her cigar and let Emmy and the child in.

CHAPTER TWENTY

<XXXX>

Kathleen

August 1ˢᵗ, 1862-New York City

When Kathleen returned to the Westchester Institute from Roland Escoffier's soiree at his estate near Lyndenhurst, her presence extended at his request for an extra night, she expected to find Sarah mildly but manageably upset.

Kathleen was not concerned, however. After all, the progress Dr. Penrose had promised in the treatment of Sarah's disturbed brother, Jacob, would be worth the minor inconvenience of dealing with her insolent niece's petulant demonstrations.

And Kathleen expected that ultimately — if not immediately, then later — she would be congratulated and thanked by all concerned for her clever, tidy intervention on her nephew's behalf.

Instead of an upset, spoiled niece waiting for her, however, she found chaos. Somehow, according to Tinder and Mrs. Plum, the children had gone missing!

To her dismay, the local police showed no interest in providing assistance. It took Kathleen almost two days to determine where Sarah and Jacob had gone.

"Disappeared? What do you mean they disappeared?" Kathleen hollered at Tinder when she first was given the news.

"And where is Doctor Penrose?" she shouted.

"He isn't available," Tinder responded. "He is indisposed. And frankly, I believe he will not be willing to speak with you, Mrs. McEmeel."

Tinder then angrily explained that during Penrose's "intake" session with Jacob, the boy had become violent and then had bitten off the tip of the director's little finger! Damages, both for the director's medical treatment and emotional distress, were being assessed. Tinder implied that those costs would be added to the expenses already incurred by Kathleen for her nephew's detainment and her niece's lodging!

At that, Kathleen began screaming, cursing loudly and slapping at Tinder. Escoffier had to pull her off of the man, who then retreated back into his office and bolted the door behind him. He refused to come out.

When Kathleen finally calmed down, Escoffier convinced her that she should enlist the help of a private investigator. They found a reliable Westchester man named Doyle "Church" Grimes, to look for the children.

Doyle Grimes was a well-known detective, having settled in Westchester County to establish private investigatory service after several years of military police duty in Virginia and Manhattan municipal police work. In the military he tracked down deserters. In New York he hunted murderers. He had made a name for himself in the upper echelons of Westchester by tracking runaway children and kidnap victims. The *Police Gazette* mentioned him in numerous accounts, included a drawing of his handsome profile in a front-page story about a recent spate of child abductions, and in the lurid article reported several instances in which he had located the victims. In more than half of the cases, he returned them alive to their parents. His services were considered expensive, but reliably competent.

Two days later, after succeeding in interviewing both Tinder and Governess Plum, then sleuthing at known embarkation points, Grimes reported to Kathleen and Escoffier that the children had made their way to the White Plains train station, and from there had boarded the Harlem train.

The vendor at the White Plains station, Grimes said, remembered the two children, because it was odd, the man related, to see unaccompanied minors purchasing tickets. The young teenaged girl, matching Sarah's description, he said, seemed anxious and very determined. The little boy, eight or nine years old, who accompanied the girl seemed preoccupied and clung tightly to her. The station vendor remembered selling the girl two one-way tickets that would have given them passage all the way to the terminal on Boone Street in Manhattan. But he noted that they could have disembarked at any of the several stations along the way.

"Didn't have enough in change to go much farther than that, though," the vendor commented. "Certainly not transfer to another rail."

So, Grimes deduced, the children were someplace between White Plains and lower Manhattan Island. Unless Kathleen knew that Sarah and Jacob had a destination that would cause them to disembark earlier than the end terminal, Grimes suggested they start at Boone Street.

Although Kathleen and Escoffier had parted ways two days previously a bit estranged after their weekend together, due in part to his casual comment that Kathleen was "terribly restrained by her mixed-up Catholic and Episcopal inhibitions" — there were just some things she *wouldn't* do, after all — he agreed to accompany Kathleen with Grimes into Manhattan to help find the children.

Kathleen noted that the Harlem and New York Railroad, which she learned had been purchased and progressively improved by Cornelius Vanderbilt several years previously, provided a much more comfortable ride compared to what she had experienced while traveling up from Washington and through the filthy station in Union-held Baltimore.

The trip into Manhattan took almost three hours, so while she rode, she thought about what she would tell her sister, Emmy, when she returned, assuming she hadn't gotten herself killed traipsing around in rebel-held territory on her "rescue mission."

"I thought Jacob was deteriorating and was at my wits end with him," she said to Escoffier rehearsing what she would say to Emmy. "I thought poor Jacob would bene-fit greatly by the rest that this luxurious institute was to provide."

Escoffier nodded in agreement.

"It has a wonderful reputation, you know," Kath-leen said to Grimes, who was sitting across the aisle, and seemed to be casually watching all of the other passengers.

Grimes smiled politely at her remark.

"Let's hope we can locate the children quickly," said Grimes, which to Kathleen seemed quite obvious.

By the expression she gave to him, he felt the need to elaborate.

"Ma'am, what I mean by that is . . . well they are going into some pretty rough territory down there, if they rode all the way to the end. That's *Five Points* territory. Little ones disappear. Forever."

"Surely, the Metropolitan police and authorities will guide us," Kathleen said.

Grimes gave a half smile and glanced at Escoffier to see if he understood the naiveté of his lady friend's asser-tion. Kathleen didn't miss the look.

"I will double the fee if you can help us regain them by tomorrow," she said. Grimes nodded and glanced at Escof-fier again, but Escoffier was simply nodding as well.

Neither one of them understood.

CHAPTER TWENTY-ONE

◇◇◇◇

Sarah

July 29th-31st, 1862-Westchester and New York City

In the late evening or early morning of that day — she didn't know at the time because she didn't have a timepiece — she had found Jacob locked down inside a narrow contraption constructed of iron and wicker. She later learned the device was called a "restraining crib," used by asylums to keep uncooperative or violent patients immobile at night. The instrument really looked more like a flat, slatted coffin, she thought.

It hadn't been that difficult to find Jacob that night they escaped, she reflected. After the experiment finding the way to get out from her own locked room, she had just listened then followed the sounds of his crying, down the second of the two unattended hallways that Mr. Tinder earlier had said was for "long-term guests."

Jacob had just been left unattended in a locked crib in that dark room!

Poor Jacob, flush-faced and drenched in perspiration, was hoarse from hollering when she found him. She pried the latch open on the crib, pulled him out, and held him in her arms until he calmed down. Then she filled a wash basin with water and gently sponged him off. The bruises on his wrists and ankles from the leather straps and abrasions on his arms and legs from where he had rubbed against the wooden slats on the crib weren't deep, but she was careful when she dressed him. He was so drained of energy!

"Come on, Sweetheart. I'm here. I'm here," she said softly. She rocked him a bit, but then when she thought she heard a noise outside, hurried to redress him.

She was relieved that no one was in the hallway outside that room. But when they walked out to the lobby, a woman stood there waiting. Sarah was frightened at first, thinking they had been discovered, but when the woman spoke and she heard her voice, Sarah realized, it was the lady from the room next to hers, the one who told her how to get out! She had wispy, thin hair, was balding on the left side of her scalp almost, but her face was not much older than her mother's.

She didn't look at all like Sarah had imagined. Her expression was sad and vacant. But then, when she looked directly at her, the lady seemed to come alive.

"Come, Little Ones," the lady had whispered. "Follow me."

The cold air outside chilled Sarah, but the lady had a blanket for them. She wrapped it around them. She said she knew the way to the train station.

They walked for a few hours and during the entire time no one spoke, the lady walking several steps ahead of them in a fast, determined pace. Finally, in the early morning light, Sarah saw a sign along the gravel road. They were arriving at the township of White Plains, population 321.

One mile later, they entered a small hamlet. A man walking behind a horse-drawn cart stacked with trunks and suitcases crossed the road ahead of them onto a graveled path. They followed him for a short distance down a tree-lined lane to a small building, standing next to a large locomotive, sulking on the tracks before the morning run. Nine or ten people stood in line waiting for the gate to open to the passenger cars trailing behind the big machine.

The lady stopped and pointed to the ticket office, then spoke for the second time since they had left the asylum.

"Do you have any money?" she asked.

Sarah nodded, and took off her shoe to show her the silver coin she hidden there.

"Good," the lady said. "I have none." Then she took her blanket from their shoulders and pointed again to the ticket office and the man behind the till who was watching them, his head tilted quizzically.

"Take this." She gave Sarah a small sack.

When Sarah turned to talk to the lady after purchasing the tickets for herself and Jacob, she was gone. She opened the sack the lady had given them. It contained several pieces of dried, stale bread.

They crossed into Manhattan at eight o'clock in the morning. Jacob slept nestled up to her. The trip had taken a few hours, and she didn't have much energy to watch the people the way she usually liked to do, although she did find one woman across the aisle quite interesting. The woman, dressed entirely in pink, and sweating heavily, had fastened her blouse's collar all the way up to her chin, which didn't hide a huge bulging mass on her neck that strained the buttons. The woman's eyes bulged, reminding Sarah of fat, sick oysters trying to escape from the confinement of their shells. For the first time Sarah could ever remember, she found herself turning away every time the woman returned a look in her direction. The conductor, a dour man with an asymmetrical face, didn't return Sarah's greeting to him when he took her tickets.

The view outside quickly changed from pastures to towns and then into a big sprawling city that went on and on. So many buildings! She saw many tall ones, some at least five floors high! She tried waking Jacob to show him, but he was fast asleep. "Poor baby," she remembered thinking. A light rain started, streaking the windows and blurring the view.

Riding into the city, Sarah rehearsed how she would find the Manhattan home of Jonny and Falco Scarpello, with whom they had shared an adventure in the Panama isthmus two years previously when they all had run away and hidden in the jungle during a train heist. They had been discovered by Embera aborigines and kept in their village until they had been, for some unexplained reason, escorted by them back into "civilization." The next year, her mother, Emmy, had received a few letters from Jonny and Falco's father, Ari, who had returned to Panama to attempt to find his wife, kidnapped during the heist. The Scarpellos could help them find their way back to Washington, D.C., Sarah thought, or contact their mother who had promised she would be back there by this time.

Sarah had no intention of reaching out to her aunt, Kathleen.

When the train stopped, Sarah had to follow the conductor down the aisle and ask her question repeatedly before he stopped and reluctantly gave her any information. He said walking "west" in the direction towards the Hudson River should lead to the cross streets, "Broadway" and "Moore," of the neighborhood where she remembered her mother had once said Ari Scarpello had left his two children in the care of a relative named Carlucci.

She and Jacob headed out through the first door from the station, and the first thing she noted was that the mud-covered streets carried the heavy stink of garbage mixed with animal dung. She became confused. She didn't know which way was west, and because the sky was overcast, she couldn't really tell which way the sun was moving.

Two streets from the station, she saw a woman who seemed to be drunk, skirts up, defecating right in the street next to a man who stood unsteadily, watching her, one arm propped against a brick building while he urinated on it. Men and women, seemingly taking no notice, walked right by the couple.

After walking for a short distance, Sarah decided she needed to seek help finding the Scarpellos. She approached a leather-faced, tub-bellied man, wearing a tall hat and blue uniform, a policeman, swearing in a low growl at a swarthy street vendor. She noticed that the policeman's left thumb was missing. The vendor, his cart loaded with scrap metal and tipped precariously forward, seemed to be protesting loudly about something in a language she didn't understand. She waited for a few minutes listening to their argument, then interrupted them and tried to ask the policeman for directions.

"Beat it, Vermin" the policeman said, continuing his animated dialogue with the vendor.

Undeterred by his rudeness, Sarah spoke to him again. "Sir, we truly need your official assistance." The policeman glared down at her, sneered, then turned his back to her, continuing his heated exchange. Sarah, pulling Jacob with her, walked around to face the policeman again, and as she did so, he reached down and rapped the shin of her right leg with the long black club he carried. The vendor, seeing this, shook his head, reached into his vest, retrieving some coins which he handed over to the policeman. At this, the policeman smiled, pocketed the coins, and walked away. Sarah, tears filling her eyes while she rubbed her stinging shin, watched the policeman whistling and twirling the stick as he moved down the street. She pulled Jacob closer to her.

"Please, which way is the Hudson River?" she called out to the departing vendor. Ignoring her, the man threw up his arm and pushed his cart away.

"Sir, which way is the river?" she asked a short tweed-coated man, walking hurriedly back in the direction of the train station. He jerked his thumb off to the right. Sarah thanked him and she and Jacob crossed the street and headed to where she hoped they would find Jonny and Falco Scarpello.

No street signs marked the way, however. Within a few blocks, Sarah realized they were truly lost now. They walked past two and three story dilapidated houses and buildings and empty lots filled with garbage. It started to rain hard and within a few minutes, the street flooded turning the dirt walkway into sloppy stinking mud. There was no place hide in the downpour. Huge rats scurried into holes above the water line. The rain stopped as suddenly as it had come on. She heard hollering emanating from several of the houses. Not far away she heard a gunshot, then another, their sounds muffled by the thickness of the air. People fighting in the summer's humid heat.

They walked a bit further and then she realized that she and Jacob were being watched. Several boys and a few girls, all of them filthy, moved into the street from covered areas and followed behind them. She increased her pace, passing a man and a woman fighting on the stoop of one of the houses. The woman was crying, punching and pushing on his chest with balled fists.

"You son of a bitch. You son of a bitch, bastard," the woman shrieked at the man. He held her at arms length, laughing and slapping at her.

The toughs following Sarah and Jacob increased their pace as well. A few steps further, and one of the smaller girls broke from the rest and rushed ahead to Sarah, grabbing and pulling at her coat. Sarah whipped around and screamed "Back off!" The girl grabbed Sarah's hair, pulling her off balance. Two other children rushed forward and began slapping and punching Sarah. At this, Jacob, who had been holding on to Sarah, kicked the first girl in the thigh and then tackled one of the boys who had jumped into the muddy fray.

She heard a piercing whistle and then a loud voice scream with so much authority that she, Jacob and the four children fighting them immediately stopped.

"Hey! You heard the girl. Back off!" the voice said.

The street toughs shrank back. It wasn't an adult's voice. It was a young boy's tenor, spoken with a strange, confident command.

He wasn't bigger than the rest of kids on the street, Sarah remembered. In fact, he was a pretty boy almost, she recalled thinking about Robby when he ran up beside her and interceded — a pretty boy with broad shoulders wearing dirty, patched-together clothing. But his red-cheeked face was scrubbed and his young face shone from under the tattered old army kepi he wore cocked to the side of a bushel of thick coal black hair. He seemed about the same age as her and was just a bit taller than her, she estimated.

Their followers had started to regather. He turned and stared at them. Sarah remembered how ferocious he seemed.

He spoke again without raising his voice, "I said 'scram', Chums. I mean it."

Puffing up his chest while speaking. He opened his coat with his left hand and showed them all his right hand resting on the handle of a big, mean looking, holstered pistol, its long barrel protruding beneath his belt.

Seeing the weapon, the toughs backed away, then disbursed.

"You two pups better follow me," he said to her and Jacob, then turned and walked across the street.

Sarah remembered feeling immediately calmed.

"Name's Robby. Robby Hoyt. Yours?"

"Jacob!" her brother had said almost immediately.

Amazing, she remembered thinking, because those were the first words Jacob had really said since she had helped him escape from the Westchester asylum. She almost forgot to respond to Robby's question.

"Sarah. Sarah Evers. He's my brother," she then said.

They walked a block further, crossing another busy street then turned onto a vacant alleyway. Repeatedly looking over his shoulder as they walked, the boy made for a plain, heavy wooden door thirty feet away from the alley's entrance. He pulled a key from his pocket and opened the door. An unlit stairway descended into the darkness.

When Sarah and Jacob hesitated, the boy, Robby, said, "They'll be back, ya know."

They followed him in. Before doing so, she noticed that it had started raining again as she looked down the street. She didn't see anyone coming in either direction. But she went in.

That decision had changed her life, she later realized.

CHAPTER TWENTY-TWO

◇◇◇◇

Jacob

July 29th-31st, 1862-Westchester and New York City

When Sarah found him in the room, he was awake again, crying. Tied down as he was, he had begun thinking he was back in the hut where he had been kept prisoner almost four years ago. Except it was warm here. No rain. No chanting by captors. He didn't feel drugged like he had been then, he reasoned. This time he had been put into restraints by white people like him.

He heard the latch and the door creep open. He gasped, held his breath — who was coming? To hurt him?

Then he heard her voice.

"Jacob?"

It was Sarah! He exhaled and started crying again quietly.

She opened the cage, unbuckled the leather restraints, and pulled him out.

She took off his wet shirt and pants and sponged him off with cool water. It felt so good.

A lady was waiting for them in the hall.

They followed her outside, then they walked and walked and he was so tired, but Sarah kept propping him up.

"We're getting us far away from here, Jacob."

Then they got on a train and he fell asleep.

He didn't remember anything about the trip into the big city, New York. But it was bigger than Washington and dirtier, he could tell, as soon as they exited the train station. More people. Lots of kids, but none of them were dressed like him or Sarah. They tried talking to a policeman but he hit Sarah and took a swipe at him as well.

"We're not going to get any help from the police," his sister said. "Got to find where Jonny and Falco Scarpello live."

So they walked and walked.

And then those kids chased them and grabbed him and threw Sarah down.

And that's when they met Robby Hoyt. He scared the kids away.

He took them to his place.

Underground.

"Come on. Ain't Hell, Pup," he remembered Robby saying to him, just as he was starting to worry that Robby might be the Devil trying to fool them.

"An I ain't the Devil," Robby said, as if reading Jacob's mind. "Least not to some people."

CHAPTER TWENTY-THREE

◇◇◇◇

Robby

July 31ˢᵗ, 1862-New York City

A quarter of the way down the long flight of stairs leading from the street, Robby stopped, lit a lantern and guided Sarah and Jacob the rest of the way to a small anteroom. Three metal doors, two on the right and one on the left, each padlocked shut, stood a few feet from the bottom of the steps. Robby pulled a keychain from his jacket and unlocked the one to the left.

"You'll get used to the smell," Robby said, seeing both Sarah and Jacob covering their mouths and noses as they followed him into the huge cellar of an abandoned tanning factory. "Ain't a bit as bad as it used to be when this place was operating last year."

"I know this odor!" Sarah said. "It's what our barn smelled like whenever my step-father rendered lard and tanned cattle hides."

Jacob nodded, then shook his head in disgust, Robby noted.

"Did he use sulfur-acid, like this place?" Robby asked, pointing past a stack of stretching rigs to the huge vats in the center of the room.

"He used cattle brains to soften the hides," Sarah said. "The old-fashioned way, like the aborigines do it."

"Can we leave this room now?" Jacob asked, looking back at the door through which they had entered.

At that, Robby laughed, selected another key, then led them to a door at the far end of the low-ceilinged factory.

◇◇◇◇

Robby Allen Hoyt knew the buried pathways of New York better than most people knew the streets high above the city's vast labyrinth of dark underground passageways.

He learned his subterranean navigation from his father, Adam "Thin-Stick" Hoyt, a tall, gangly New York City employee and volunteer fireman who, after the disastrous 1835 Lower Manhattan fire that destroyed 700 houses over a seventeen-block area, took on the official assignment of locating, mapping and then planning access to island's many aquifers.

For eleven years, Thin-Stick explored the waterways and gas tunnels, and helped plan the famous Croton Aqueduct that fed the city with fresh water. Because of the expertise he had gained, after another great fire broke out in 1845, he was invited to join an elite reserve unit called the "Exempt Fireman's Company," made up of firemen who, in return for their service, were paid and also officially excused from militia and jury duty. Continuing his municipal duties, by mid-century, he had left his sign-off initials on every water-feed plan of the city. One of his associates, noting the compulsive, possessive pride Thin-Stick took in his work, teased that he also likely had left his mark on every hydrant from mid-Manhattan to the Battery.

In 1854, after the death of his wife during a devastating cholera epidemic that hit the Five Points area, the elder Hoyt began bringing his young son with him on his official forays into New York's numerous caverns, aqueducts and abandoned tunnels, many all-but-forgotten over the years as the seventeenth century town had expanded and transformed itself from a Dutch-controlled country village into a nineteenth century metropolis.

When Thin-Stick died from a Yellow Fever outbreak in 1858, his sister took in her ten-year-old nephew. But then she died within a few months from the same disease that killed her brother.

Robby, placed into a Catholic orphanage, ran away from it within four days of being placed there. Determined to make it on his own at the age when many children faced with homelessness would have perished, he survived because he knew where to find safety, food, clean water and shelter. All was available to him because he had memorized the maps his father had created for the city, as well as the many places and pathways that his father knew, but never committed to paper.

He, like his father, detested the politicians and the corrupt police force that worked for them.

"Thugs in blue," is what his father often said, referring to the Municipal Police who patrolled the city's streets. "Bastard's are fat on bribes and beat the honest blokes. Stay out of their way, Son."

Robby did, using his knowledge of the underworld to avoid them, as well as the denizens who inhabited the interconnecting hovels dug into the basements of almost every house in lower Manhattan.

But he stayed a loner, interacting, on occasion, with former colleagues of his father, and working intermittently as a newsboy to make spare change. He didn't need the help of adults, he told himself, and practiced a disciplined routine to avoid the temporal needs that might make him dependent on anyone else.

On July 31st, Robby Hoyt had ventured out from his haunts near Mulberry to scout the Bloom Street market stalls for the appearance of fresh citrus, the only sweet indulgence he allowed himself. Because the market was so close to the railroad terminal, its vendors were first to receive countryside produce brought into lower Manhattan. Because the cargoes from New York's wharves fed into to the Bloom Street terminal spurs for eventual distribution northward to the rest of New York, the Bloom Street market vendors also had first pick from shipments from warmer climates, whereas by the time street vendors and local stores received the produce, it was close to spoiling.

Robby had already bagged a plump orange when he looked up and saw Sarah and Jacob wandering down the street past the market. By the way they were attired — she wearing a pretty pale blue dress with frills, and he, wearing a well-tailored, albeit wrinkled jerkin and long pants — Robby knew the pair was lost and was heading in a direction — towards Five Points and its numerous gangs — that would cause the two of them great harm.

Curious for what might transpire, and because he found the girl strangely attractive, he decided to follow them.

His observation was correct. They were lost.

He watched the girl, who appeared to be about his same age, attempt to get help from a cop named Mulally, a carry-over from the corrupt Municipal police force. Mullaly was shaking down a little Sicilian fruit peddler when the girl in the blue dress approached. Robby knew the cop, had observed the mean bastard for the past three years using his beat prowl to pad his own pockets with chump change.

It didn't surprise him when Mulally hit the girl with his baton. Robby didn't like that, but waited to see how the girl would react.

She didn't cry, but instead, rubbed her bruised shin, then said to Mulally, "You, Sir, are a disgrace to your uniform." She then backed away and repeated her queries to numerous passersby. She and the boy with her then headed off west, in the direction of the Hudson River.

When he saw the twosome wander into territory dominated by the Pug-Uglies, a vicious gang of murderers, he knew that it wouldn't be long before the kids would be mugged.

Less than five minutes later, it happened.

He intervened quickly, before any of the older gangsters in the area decided to help out the street waifs who were attempting to roll the girl and boy. He could have left them after guiding them away in a different direction. To safety.

But for reasons he didn't really understand, he decided to also do something he had never done before.

He brought them, other people, two hapless strangers at that, into his secure, private world.

Fifteen minutes later, in the abandoned underground tanning factory, far below the alleyways from which they had escaped, he observed their confused reactions.

"Stick with me," he reassured them quietly.

Then, after he saw the effect his intervention had upon them, he went a step further.

"I'm gonna show you pups some things I bet you never seen," he heard himself boasting to them that day, watching the uncertainty betrayed by their expressions. "Unless you two have someplace else to go — and wanna go back outside with the gang that was following you." He touched the hem of Sarah's torn dress, where she had been grabbed by two of the urchins.

He watched Sarah and Jacob look back at the way they had come, then at each other.

They silently followed him through the next door to his domain.

CHAPTER TWENTY-FOUR

◇◇◇◇

Emmy

July 30th to August 4th, 1862-Richmond, Virginia

She knew that Janie Jones likely wasn't marking it up all that much. Emmy paid twenty-five dollars in gold for some plain clean clothing, which was five times more than what she would have paid for similar items in Washington.

Because of the Union embargo and Virginia's disrupted internal supply lines, everything had become expensive in Richmond, she quickly learned. People were making do with the materials that were available, buttons from pomegranate seeds, hats woven out of corn husks, shoes with wooden soles and shoe lasts cut from increasingly scarce leather. Coffee and tea were no longer available except at exorbitant prices.

She had no choice but to pay the cost Janie had asked. She couldn't present herself to local hospitals dressed as a man, as she had been.

After sponging herself off and resting for an hour in the one upstairs room that wasn't in constant use, she purchased some food for herself and Clarissa and spoke with some of the women, straggling one by one after their upstairs bedroom trysts, through the Ark's small kitchen and onto the back porch for a smoke, waiting on the hot August day until the next customer asked to review them.

Emmy suspended judgement as she always had done. Although the walls were thin upstairs, letting in every grunt, moan and bed squeak from both of the rooms next to the one in which she had rested, she had heard nothing she hadn't before. The sounds of rowdy intercourse she had heard when she stayed in the small quarters in British Columbia and in the hotel in Panama had been just as loud or louder. And in those circumstances she had to insist that her children cover their ears all night. At least she didn't have to do that with Clarissa, deaf as she was, who slept comfortably in her arms.

In the kitchen, she listened carefully, hoping in her conversations to learn as much as she could about the layout of the city's many hospitals and prisons, so that she could determine where best to focus her time in locating Brett if he had been taken here.

As exhausted as she was, she noted that every one of the women, ranging in age from early teens to mid thirties, appeared haggard. Each had a story that did not sound all that dissimilar to what she had perceived was unique to her own circumstance. At least three were widows supporting young families. Each had experienced tragedies that forced them into selling themselves. Two of the women, one black and the other white, told her they had no choice but to work for Janie because they needed money for their medicine and really couldn't live without it. Emmy knew what the "medicine" was. She suspected her own brother-in-law, Jon McEmeel, was also addicted to Laudanum. He had the means to keep himself in supply. These women were trapped in their excuse.

She learned that two of the older women, about her own age, both of whom insisted on distinguishing themselves from those who had to "walk the streets," had worked as a "house" prostitute for over four years.

"We are high priced whores!" the fatter of the two laughed. "Clean, ya know. Don' have to be liftin' our skirts for a quarter or pull of tabac'"

Together, she said, they had moved their trade from Alexandria when the Union occupied that town and disrupted their customer base. They, like several hundred other prostitutes, had come to Richmond after the Confederacy moved its capital to the city from Mobile and headquartered the army of Virginia there. Richmond's population, like that of Washington, D.C., had quadrupled within a few months, and with it came thousands of potential customers, including soldiers and traders using its railroad junctions and convenient rivers.

The city's pleasure trade had increased proportionally, and within a month, its two most influential newspapers, the *Whig* and the *Examiner*, bemoaned in repeated editorials the failure of Christian and governmental regulation.

Another paper, The *Richmond Enquirer*, estimated that over 1,500 women, not a few men, and a few men pretending to be women, now plied their tricks in over fifty different "ill-governed" houses and saloons. The Jackson Ward, from Second Street and all the way down Cary Avenue, had over twenty such houses, with its scantily dressed women blatantly beckoning to potential customers passing by. Six of the established houses were within three blocks of the capitol building. Two were only a block away from the three-story mansion the government had leased for Jefferson Davis and his family.

The prevalent ambience of social decay, combined with the charnel house stink of death emanating from the many hospitals and embalming stations on every street, led Emmy to wonder how the town could survive for long. But D.C. was little better off, Emmy realized. After the war, the economies of one or both cities would shift away from the profession of undertaking, but likely keep most of trade as infrastructure.

At 10:00, a diminutive woman a few years younger than her stepped into the kitchen from the porch, pulled out a pack of playing cards and laid out the start of a game of solitaire. She said her name was Alice and she had moved up from Mobile with the troops that had volunteered after the monumental Manassas victory.

Through Alice's sheer blouse, Emmy saw that she was covered with blue, swirling tattoos from her shoulders down to the small of her back. As if talking to the cards, Alice said she added decorations over the course of four years as a way of memorializing her sorrows after the loss of more than one soldier-lover.

"Thay've bin done by one of *the* foremost artists in the region," Alice said proudly, referring to the tattoos. "Exhibited, he was, in some fine galrees up in Charleston. He said I am a livin' breathin' canvas fer him."

At that, another young woman, no more than fifteen or sixteen, by Emmy's estimate, turned and demurely showed off her own decoration, a small red-tinted rose with blue paisley leaves on the right cheek of her bottom.

"I show this to them last," the girl said, laughing, "to give 'em something to remember me by."

Janie Jones, listening to the women parading their stories, told Emmy she had been a school teacher before she discovered this much more profitable trade.

"I was good at it. But there's more security in this, than trying to teach anyone anything lately," she said, lighting another cigar then stepping out and again spitting off the porch through the space of a missing front tooth.

She came back in, poured herself a drink from a small flask, and sat down next to Emmy. After listening to Emmy recount her own story, and then about Brett, she downed the glass of whisky, put her arm around Emmy's shoulder and said, "Forget about that man, Sweetie. He's not here. He's probably run off putting his head into a grinder like the rest of 'em."

She stuck out her tongue and moved it back and forth across her upper teeth. "You know, you really need the company of a good woman who can take care of you." The women at the table all laughed in agreement.

Disregarding the madame's overture, Emmy pressed the women for advice about where she might start looking to find Brett.

"Chimborazo," said the tattooed woman, "up on the hill. 'Ceptin won't let you in the door to see any of em if'n ya don' have a letter or sumpin', ah bin tol. You best be takin' yourself up to Josie DeMerritt's to get a swipe at that."

"*The Dispatch*," said Janie, "or the *Herald'l* have names. Best place to read, if he's in one of the hospitals . . . or his body's been identified."

◇◇◇◇

Like the trade of Janie Jones, her crass, sometimes drunken counterpart in the Jackson Ward, Josie DeMerrit's upscale business was dictated by its location and choice of women. In contrast to Jones, however, as the proprietor of Richmond's most luxurious pleasure house, DeMerrit never had been accused of the various crimes involving prostitution. So well-connected was she by the clientele she serviced that Josie, a quiet, modest-appearing honey-blonde with widely spaced blue eyes, had never paid a fine or even spent a day in court.

Prudently, DeMerritt kept records, all well hidden, and although she would have never admitted it, it was easy to deduce that she did so, because of the calm, matter of fact, silken-voiced ease with which she recounted enough personal details about themselves to the officers, physicians and politicians who visited her establishment's beautiful women. From memory, she addressed by his first name, each customer, whom she insisted wear formal attire before entry. She kept her three-story house and its plush furniture immaculately clean, its entrances and exits perfectly disguised, and its women entertainers accoutered in elegant dresses with subtly colored wide bows, fine laces and clean, white silken undergarments. The enormously expensive fabrics the women wore had been smuggled in from England and France by blockade runners and smugglers like Henri Lebo. Josie insisted on weekly examinations for the women from well-paid physician-customers, and she moved her women out at the first sign of any illness or pregnancy. Her customers kept coming back to her well-kept secret.

Normally, Emmy, plain dressed as she was, would have been turned away by DeMerrit, who once had been shot at by a similarly dressed woman, who was convinced, correctly so, that her husband was inside visiting the establishment.

But Emmy was undeterred by DeMerrit's initial rejection.

As she had done with Jane Jones, by invoking Henri Lebo's name, she was able to persuade the proprietress to speak with her. Emmy was not let into the house beyond the atrium, however, until she said to DeMerrit, "I can pay you for this information."

What she saw inside the house rivaled the expensive decor of the wealthy homes of Boston and Washington, D.C., except that the alabaster and marble statues, as well as the huge paintings, all depicted naked women in a variety of lewd acts with men as well as with animals.

"Not subtle at all," she said quietly to herself, looking at what she recognized as a bust of Leda swooning spread-legged beneath a spread-winged giant swan.

"I believe I need to visit Chimborazo and any of the other hospitals where someone might have been taken for malaria."

"My Dear," said DeMerrit, "you must know there are over fifty hospitals in Richmond alone? Is your young man a soldier? That would narrow it down, but only by half."

Emmy explained that Brett was not in the military, but believed he had cared for wounded soldiers after the Gaines Mill fight. DeMerrit told her that only military were being treated at the massive Chimborazo facility, but he might be there. Emmy explained that Brett had resigned from the Union's army but, as far as she knew from his letters, he also had refused to join the Confederate army.

"Well, that'd make him a traitor in many peoples' eyes," DeMerrit said, "on both sides, wouldn't it, Dear?"

Emmy understood the logic in that and took a deep breath, nodding.

"You might also want to visit where they're keeping the scoundrels who are spying for the Yankees. It's on Broad Street, right across from Libby Prison where they're keeping the Yankee officers. We in Richmond call it 'Castle Thunder.'"

Despite her apparent lack of sympathy for Emmy, DeMerrit wrote the name of two physicians, a list of the twenty-four private hospitals in town, and the name of the commandant of Castle Thunder. "Another customer," she said.

"Tell them I insisted on the help that only they could give. And please let them know that I hope their lovely wives are doing well in all this wretched sticky heat. Tell them that, exactly as I have said it."

◇◇◇◇

The first physician, Surgeon Stephan Holtz, M.D., recently named the deputy adjutant for the twenty-five military hospitals in Richmond's city limits, held the rank of major. Holtz took her to Chimborazo first, the massive seventy-five ward facility on Richmond's second hill. He explained that each ward housed forty men, convalescing from wounds and diseases.

"If your man has malaria and isn't dead," he said, "he'll be in one of the wards we keep separate from the others."

Holtz said that he expected that they would be seeing many others coming in, mostly from companies of soldiers from rural areas who had never been exposed to such diseases. Almost one quarter of the Alabama regiments had come down with measles, he said.

"You'll find intractable dysentery cases over in Wards 16 to 26, amputations and amputees down by the surgery units on Wards 55 to 75, near the incinerator, so we don't have to bury the parts," he said with a hint of pride. The dead rooms are close to the road so we can ship them off down the hill to Oakwood and Hollywood quickly."

He changed tone, becoming more somber.

"Too many inevitably soon-to-be morbid ones after the Malvern Hill fight. Couldn't bring them here to die. Had to let them deteriorate there, then put them under on the field," he said. "Regretful. Deserved being identified and buried properly," he said, shaking his head in disgust.

Emmy learned from Holtz that although all of the hospitals in the city had registration processes, only a few had followed Chimborazo's system.

"Against regulations for you to go into any of the wards unless you locate his name for me," he said, "but you are free to examine the registry, Young Lady."

Emmy spent four hours sifting through the Chimborazo registration books. Date of entry, Name, Diagnosis-listed simply as "Wound" or "Illness"-location by ward, and disposition-listed as "Discharged", or "Died." If nothing was listed next to the name in the Disposition column, it meant that the patient was still there.

She found no record of anyone by the last name of Brett, in the thousands of entries scribed in just over few weeks since the peninsula battles. Men moving in and out, one way or another.

After Chimborazo, over the course of the next two days, Emmy rode to each of the fifteen other army hospitals where malaria and infection cases would have been sent. At one, General Hospital number 4, she became excited when she found a "P. Brett" in the log, but when she reached the bedside, she found an emaciated young man in his late teens, delirious and dying of dysentery. He couldn't speak to her, so she was unable to determine if there was any relation to Rory Brett.

That sultry evening, because all of the hotels were full, she again had to rent a room in Janie James brothel, paying full price to Janie and one of the girls for what would have amounted to sixteen "sessions."

Odd name, "Noah's Ark," she thought with some amusement. Given the brevity of the coupling going on, perhaps the participants didn't appreciate the widespread signs of an impending flood, she thought. Or perhaps they did, but just hadn't found the right mate yet for a long journey. That made her smile a bit.

Plugging her ears with wads of cotton to block out the sounds next door, she stayed awake to read a copy of the *Richmond Enquirer*. On the front page she found a story about the actions of her father's former law partner, Senator Benjamin Butler, titled "More Insults to Women in New Orleans by General Butler." The article, accompanied by a series of letters and an opinion editorial denouncing Butler, described his "Order Number 28" in which he commanded that any woman found "insulting" Union military personnel, either by action or attitude, would be arrested and treated as a "woman of the town plying her trade."

He had imprisoned women in New Orleans, and hung a prominent citizen for taking down the Union flag.

She recalled the controversy that had been created when the first news of that order had been published in Washington, D.C.'s papers in late May, and the calls from various factions for Lincoln to dismiss Butler. The *Enquirer* article included quotes from a speech by a British politician, delivered in the House of Commons, condemning Butler's treatment of women.

Emmy thought about her own interactions with Butler, in Boston when she was sixteen — he had attempted to fondle her — and then his advances last year in Washington, D.C. She understood why the women of New Orleans were calling him "The Beast." But she had a different reason.

She found no news in the *Enquirer* about further actions on the Chickahominy, but read several reports predicting that the Union army would again be moving towards the Manassas railroad junction, this time under the command of General John Pope, purportedly to counter the northward movement of General Stonewall Jackson's army.

Hadn't the combatants had enough of Manassas and the Bull Run Creek by now, she wondered?

Rory Brett's name did not appear on any of the casualty lists. There was no news of George Pickett either.

Emmy fell into a deep slumber, waking a few times to the sounds of men and women laughing loudly, pounding on the walls, clomping of boots in the hallway outside her door. Clarissa turned and started to wake. Emmy looked at the girl's soft curls and tender face, which, unlike her arms and legs, were unscarred.

"Sleep, Little One," she said quietly.

Early the next day, she accompanied another of Josie's DeMerrit's physician associates, Doctor Joseph Gruber, to the private hospitals they thought most likely to have ill refugees from the Peninsula battles. She visited four hospitals accompanied by Gruber, and the rest by herself.

On her tenth hospital visit, at *General Baptist Hospital*, she was informed that a patient named Brett had passed away two days previously. The attending physician told her she could inspect the body if it was still there. When she recovered from the wrenching faintness that overwhelmed her at that news, she clenched her jaw and followed the attending physician to the Dead Room. The body was still there.

It wasn't Rory.

En route to still more hospitals, the private ones, she met with the commandant of the infamous "Castle Thunder," Captain George Alexander. Castle Thunder, three warehouses hastily converted to a prison for the incarceration of civilians and deserters, housed over a thousand men and women prisoners. Josie DeMerrit had warned her that Alexander, who had escaped from a Union prison the year before, had been accused of horrific crimes in his treatment of the political prisoners incarcerated in the three-story block house building, but thus far, he had not even been reprimanded by the Confederate command.

Alexander's punishments and the privations he imposed were purportedly so harsh, that several "despondent" prisoners had supposedly hung themselves. Josie advised her to be honest with Alexander about her purpose, be brief with her visit and keep her questions to a minimum. Her Boston accent would irritate him, and he had a short temper. Josie said he once had vented his anger on her girls. She did not elaborate, but told Emmy that she had a lifetime of favors due from him as a result.

Alexander, short and dark in complexion and demeanor, did not accompany her in her tour, but waited in his office for her to complete her inspection of the three buildings as well as the solitary confinement "booths" in the cellar of one of the warehouses. Emmy wretched up bile each time she entered one of the buildings. The smell, worse than anything she had encountered at any of the hospitals, north or south, stuck to her clothing. The walls, covered with scurrying vermin, held chained men and women in tight spaces built for half of the number of the prisoners they housed. Large, overflowing buckets of excrement stood in the corner of each space. Huge, brazen rats, one the size of a cat, crawled across her feet as she stepped from cell to cell. The "solitary confinement cells" each held two men.

Her visit was brief, but sufficient. No Brett. The air outside almost seemed fresh when she moved to her next destination.

On her thirteenth hospital visit, at Chisolm Memorial, she saw George Pickett.

Pickett, whom she had known when she lived in the Pacific Northwest, emerged from the front door of the hospital, just as Emmy turned the corner on Broad Street. His left arm was in a sling, but he was standing upright and looked healthy. He seemed taller, his face was bright, but he seemed much older. He had gained weight. Dressed in a Confederate Brigadier General's uniform, he had adorned himself in a red cape, long, elegantly cut and highly polished cavalry boots, a dress sword, and wore his hair longer, with shiny ringlets slicked over his shoulders. His walk, too, was different from what she remembered from three years ago — bold and proud as before, but now his hips as well as shoulders were thrust forward.

Emmy, stunned at this transformation from the reserved, shy man she had known back then, held back and watched.

It wasn't her George Pickett.

She compared what she saw with the impression of him she had kept with her over the past three and a half years, from their long moments together and the sleepless, wide-awake, deeply memorable night they had spent talking and walking on the beach on San Juan Island.

A few moments later, a young woman emerged from the same door, moved up to Pickett and snuggled into his free arm, looking up at him adoringly. She was very young, no more than seventeen or eighteen, Emmy surmised, at least twenty-five years younger than him. The girl was at most a few years older than she herself had been when she married her first husband fourteen years ago.

Pickett turned to the young woman and kissed her on the forehead. It was tender. He seemed happy, but also hesitant, almost, Emmy thought.

A carriage pulled up with four mounted dragoons in escort, and after the couple seated themselves, it pulled away, passing Emmy on the street. She held her breath as his carriage passed, hesitating, wondering whether to reach out to him for help? She wondered whether that was what she might need from him. Pickett turned briefly and looked at Emmy for a moment, but she could not tell whether he recognized her. If he did, she realized, he showed no signs of it.

She felt her heart pounding, but pushed the experience down, trying to not dwell on it, then moved down the street in the opposite direction, visiting one more hospital before retiring back to the Ark.

The Franciscan nuns managing the facility allowed her to walk through one of the crowded wards, because most of the men in it had no identification, were confused or moribund. She saw blind men and weeping men and bandaged men and broken men. A few reached out to her as she passed. One touched her hand and looked up at her when she stopped. His look to her was beyond imploring. Resigned, she realized.

"I'm sorry," was all she could say, knowing she had no way of helping.

She passed seventy beds and then was taken to the Dead room. She sucked in her breath again, musing as she did so that holding her breath protected her from both the stench and the sorrow.

No Brett.

She exhaled fully again only when she was back outside.

The walk from the last hospital to the Ark took her forty minutes, mostly downhill fortunately, because she had no energy left and felt especially depleted now.

She tried to put together the events of the day — the dying and wounded, her failure to locate anything that might help her find Brett, and then the happenstance of seeing Pickett.

As she walked, she allowed herself to think about Pickett again and how he had changed and what it meant to her. He seemed energized by this conflict, the grand adventure of it all, she realized. A few years before, he had been a Union captain, stuck in Bellingham of the Washington Territory, likely the most remote of outposts of the new country. He had seemed a depressed, restrained and stoic man then.

On Whidbey, she had shared private thoughts with him and sensed as he did so, in turn, his loneliness and isolation. A few weeks later when, newly widowed as she was after the massacre at her home, she went to him in Port Townsend to seek assistance in finding her kidnapped son, Pickett had been gallant and kind, but could not help her when she needed it desperately.

She had forgiven him for that. He had been duty bound, after all, she understood.

So, she had taken on the risk of traveling into a hostile countryside inhabited by aborigines and had succeeded in finding her kidnapped son.

By herself.

Without the help of governments, or men with power.

Then, after all the trauma, a few months later, she had again reached out to Pickett on San Juan, but this time, not for help, but rather, it was because she knew there had been a mutual attraction between them. Unfinished business. She had sought him out again to see if there was anything — some little, mutual spark that would give hope for a kindling of sorts — to light them beyond what she knew were mutually felt painful inhibitions — to find some proper way to overcome the overwhelming sense of propriety and duty she knew they *both* felt — to perhaps attempt some way to touch each other's souls in a personal, perhaps even eventual intimate relationship.

It had struck her as ironic that each of them, she and Pickett, had faced terrible privation and danger in their younger lives. Each had been previously married twice and had lost their spouses early in their marriages. Both she and Pickett had killed, she the amateur in that. From those experiences, early on they had become seasoned adults. Both she and Pickett had a yearning.

Yet neither of them had been able to break out of propriety on that eventful day. After hours of talking, his cape over her shoulders, as they watched the tide come, then go, their relationship remained a platonic one. She and Pickett had parted respecting one another, but both were alone again inside, she knew.

Today, after seeing him again, she was happy for him, she told herself, all the while as she reasoned that, fighting back a deep nausea she didn't understand.

From what she had read, George Pickett again was a decorated hero, ascended in rank, a leader of men engaged in a struggle of warriors, likely buoyed and certainly burdened with the adulation that comes with the prominence of such approbations. Carried upwards, albeit frequently cursed down by the weight of that awesome responsibility, in the public's eye as he was, Emmy surmised that he would be perhaps somewhat more cautious, despite what she believed was his innate pluckiness. For he was even more duty-bound now.

And who was the young woman? Emmy wondered.

Perhaps she herself had looked like that when she knew him a few years back.

Emmy was happy for him, she told herself again. But, remembering that nightlong walk on the beach with him, she also suspected he was still a lonely man somehow.

"Am I hoping for that?" she asked herself.

Was the younger woman cleaving through all that propriety for him, cutting the Gordian Knot imposed by societal norms, in a way that she, herself, had been unable?

And what of Brett? she thought, attempting to shake off her thoughts of Pickett. Rory Brett had, with *great* risk to himself, renounced the pomp and swagger of the military life and had settled into the respectful, busy routine of practicing as a plain country doctor, and like all the citizens living of both sides, was truly unprotected now. Brett, unlike what she had just seen in George Pickett, was lost in the swamp of it all.

She thought that strange and ironic. Both Brett and Pickett had been in the military. They both had arduous professions, with years of training that would harden anyone, she thought. But despite that, Rory Brett was so naive, so much more tender, she surmised, and so much more vulnerable than Pickett allowed himself to be.

Why was that? Was it related to their "specializations" of their duties within the military, Pickett the warrior who wounded others, Brett the healer who had once patched those wounds?

Or was the difference she saw between the two of them caused by something more profound, perhaps an issue of will? she wondered — allowing or not allowing oneself to remain open to the pain of others, to maintain empathy? Or closing oneself off, to protect oneself as a first responsibility, *before* administering the duty to protect others?

Rory Brett had talked about that dilemma once. As a physician, he struggled with his desire to be a compassionate healer while at the same time growing to be a pragmatic and effective physician who could manage horrific morbidities and death. He had feared he would not be able to balance the two, apply both his head *and* his heart to his profession.

As sensitive as he was, how would Rory Brett, young Rory, Rory the poet, survive all of this?

Pickett, the warrior, could handle himself, she knew.

How would Rory Brett survive without her, she wondered?

She stopped when she heard herself thinking those thoughts. Such arrogance! Yet, she sensed that she alone could save him now. Was *that* why she was on this quest? Because she had a duty? Or was it for something far more important and so much less circumscribed?

Love?

Love — especially the essence of connection between two people — had always been the great ambiguity, she knew, its magnificence encompassing all of the virtues she believed one should live for — responsibility, charity, "doing the right thing" — all of it driven, in herself at least, by a powerful compulsion that she did not understand.

Yet, as she attempted to understand it, to release it, to employ it, that *love* — her reactions and behavior with it had varied terribly and unpredictably. It wavered. At times she knew she handled her appetites strictly and borne from the depths of restraint, as if her needs were an animal that needed to be tethered inside, looking out from inside of her entire being, then steered by and into a societal dull-edged pen of expectations.

Alternatively, at times, she knew she acted as if she had been given license to roam, with a permissiveness that gave her *wild* pleasure. But that behavior also frightened her because she knew she could become addicted to that pleasure.

In either case, whether she accepted the limits she imposed on herself, or ignored them, she knew that her own actions, especially as it related to the word "love," would ultimately define who she really was.

Was she a girl, or a woman, at love? she wondered.

She stopped walking for a moment on the corner of Broad Street and Cary Avenue and scanned the James River below.

Thinking now about both Pickett, Brett, and even her deceased husband Isaac, she knew she had been indecisive about giving in to love and the terrifying joy that accompanied it.

She regretted that, she knew. Why the indecision? What had she been protecting? Ignoring the blisters that had formed on both of her feet, she started walking again.

As was her habit during times like this, she reaffirmed her resolve to accommodate to the vicissitudes of all that came her way.

"Take it in. Sort it all out later," she said out loud to herself. Irrespective of whether that meant for joy or pain, she would assimilate what she experienced, then observe and incorporate into her self-understanding the consequences of her decisions and her actions. *That,* perhaps, especially would create a permanency to her understanding of the word, "love" and how she needed to make it be part of her, once and for all.

And in all of that, with whatever lay ahead, she would be on the lookout for the makings of joy, she told herself.

"Neither the pain nor the joy, suppress," she heard herself say, repeating an old adage, the origins of which she didn't remember.

She felt the blister on her right foot break.

The summer sun had baked her hard, and by now, Emmy's perspiration had drenched her blouse. Her hair fell out of its braids. Each step chafed, worsened somehow by walking down hill. The raw rub reminded her that she she still was almost a half hour away from resting.

As she neared the Noah's Ark, the area turned rougher, with toughs and trampy women loitering on the streets. The sweltering, humid heat of Richmond's early evening seemed to increase, with no relief from the faint river breeze that wafted the oil-yard smells of the Tradegar Steel Works and railroad up to Cary Avenue, mingling with the stench of the town.

She realized she had visited twenty-nine hospitals and one prison in her three days here, all within a nine-mile radius. Although most of her visits had been brief, with reviews of long lists of patients, the few times she had been allowed to walk the wards looking for Brett, the five visits to hospital Dead Rooms had been draining enough. Her feet and legs ached and the numbness she sometimes felt in her right, clumsy arm, wounded two years ago in Panama, had returned and wouldn't go away. She hadn't eaten since last evening. She was almost out of the gold coins she had belted to herself when she began. There were at least fifteen other hospitals in Richmond she hadn't visited, and she had visited no cemeteries yet.

She would have to save that for last.

With that thought, she stopped for a moment, sat down on a brown patch of grass, took a deep breath, then burst out crying. For a few moments only. As was her habit, she pushed it all back in. She stood up, wiped her tears and walked up to the porch and into the Ark.

Janie Jones was waiting for her, Clarissa in hand.

"Better see this, Honey," showing Emmy the evening edition of the *Richmond Dispatch*.

On the second page, in the left hand column before the testimonials about the efficacy of mesmerism and the legal proceedings of the county, was an article titled: "Posse Ambushed on Macon Road."

The sub-title read "Sheriff Otis Loller's two sons murdered. Large reward offered." Reading further, Emmy saw a fair description of Lebo, Clarissa and herself, most certainly provided by the little boy, Jedediah. She was being described as a Yankee spy and kidnapper. Lebo's whereabouts were unknown. Speculation was that she and Clarissa were hiding somewhere in Richmond.

"Coupla the girls already came upon this," Janie said. If they can read well enough, they'll put it together, right off. An' I don't want to hang with you, Honey."

Emmy understood. She would have no choice. Her search for Brett was over.

"An I *ain't* keeping this one," Janie said, handing Clarissa over to Emmy.

Emmy nodded.

"Pen Basetyr's on the way. You be gone as soon as she gets here."

CHAPTER TWENTY-FIVE

⋄⋄⋄⋄

Cross

July 14ᵗʰ to July 28ᵗʰ 1862 — Virginia

His duty done by delivering the deserter Rory Brett, Major Jonah Cross found orders waiting for when he arrived at his brigade's headquarters in Williamsburg. He was to immediately rejoin his regiment, assigned to General Fitz John Porter's Fifth Corps, assembling in Washington.

By the time he reached the capital two days later, however, his regiment had already departed across the Potomac, headed for Manassas to counter what appeared to be a concerted move northward by Lee and Jackson. Rumors were that Lee planned to advance from there onto Washington.

Cross headed out immediately and while ferrying across the Potomac, he carefully felt his swollen lower jaw, aching constantly from the broken tooth he had sustained three weeks ago while biting down on a stale, hard-as-stone army biscuit. He hadn't taken the time to soak it in coffee. Now he didn't have time to attend to it properly, pain or not. He wasn't going to miss out on a good fight.

Normally, when he thought about going up against any foe, he thrust his jaw forward. That hurt too much now. He would use the pain to keep himself alert and properly angry. His saliva tasted sour and putrid and that made him think about how much he hated the rebel traitors.

Riding down to Centerville where Porter's Corps had encamped gave him the opportunity to reflect a bit on what he had accomplished thus far. He had comported himself honorably and admirably in three vicious peninsula campaign fights, the last one at Malvern Hill especially. His personal actions had resulted in the capture of an entire rebel battery, and his company had taken over one hundred fifty rebel prisoners and killed five times that number. Risking his own life, he had re-crossed into enemy territory to capture a deserter, Rory Brett, and successfully delivered him to the provost marshall's representative.

He hoped that these accomplishments would somehow reach the ears of General Scott, the man he respected most in his life. Whether they merited a decoration or another promotion mattered far less than to be regarded highly by the old hero. He had always felt that way. Scott, speaking a military language Cross understood and demanding a disciplined protocol that was straightforward and relatively easy to follow, was much more of a father to him than his own, dour and disapproving father ever had been.

That made him think of Brett again, who, while part of Winfield Scott's entourage, had abandoned his commission, then showed up on the Virginia Peninsula taking care of Confederates. Traitor bastard!

The recapture of Brett had been interesting. Finding Brett again wasn't difficult, for he was wandering not that far from where he had cut him loose the day before. Finding Brett's mule that had trotted off proved much more difficult, not because of the animal's location, but because of its ornery disposition, the complete opposite of how his prisoner behaved, which seemed to be resigned and depressed. Brett just came along! They had traveled with enough caution, staying off of open stretches and keeping to the woods, that they evaded more than one full company of rebel troops and a few cavalry units.

Hiding in the shade to watch a passing Confederate battery of howitzers moving in the direction of Harrison's Landing, likely to continue harassing the retreat of the Union army, Cross had studied Brett for a few moments.

The man was beaten down.

"What made you desert, Brett?" Cross asked.

"Didn't." Brett answered. "But you've already made up your explanations."

"Just curious. Expect you'd be at least a Colonel by now if you'd not run away in Panama like you did, with all that you had going for you, being in Scott's circle, like you was."

"Submitted my resignation months before, Soldier."

Brett then had explained about how his requests for leave had been ignored by Scott's administrative staff for months. He told how his father had died while he had waited, and how he had decided to take it into his own hands when the Panama train, carrying scores of passengers as well as his future fiancée, had derailed. The "accident" had proven to be a hijacking. Brett's request to bring medical aide to the disaster site had been denied.

"There's protocol and procedure," said Cross.

Brett shook his head, looking at Cross. "There's more to life than ribbons and epaulettes, Soldier,"

"There's honor and duty," Cross shot back. "You helped the godforsaken rebs."

"Had no choice. One can't stand by watching wounded men dying."

"You are a traitor," said Cross.

"I am a doctor," Brett replied to that.

"There's common sense and decency," Brett said after a long pause. "May you understand that someday, Young Man."

Cross quieted, mulling the exchange while watching the Confederate caissons rolling by. He touched his face.

"You might want to let me look at that swollen jaw of yours," said Brett.

Cross chose to not respond.

That was the extent of their exchange. After the Confederates had passed, he and Brett, still cinched to the mule, stayed north of the cannon fire and swung southward when they reached the large creek that Cross remembered had fed into the James River. One mile further east, they encountered the picket lines of the Union's rearguard and found a camp in severe disarray, with over a thousand wagons awaiting evacuation sprawled across forty acres facing the riverfront.

One of the picket cavalrymen recognized Cross and rode up to them.

"Beggin' yer pardon, Sir. You be Jonah Cross, ain't ya? Third Pennsylvania. Heard 'bout ya at Malvern Hill, Sir."

Cross had returned the salute with a big smile, he remembered, and caught Brett looking at him and shaking his head.

Brett just didn't understand, he remembered thinking.

But the man had allowed himself to be handed over to the Provost Marshall without protest.

Cross's written report had been terse:

> Delivered on this 4th day of July, 1862, Lieutenant Rory Brett, M.D., Assistant Surgeon, whom I arrested on July 3rd, 1862, on orders issued in Panama City, New Grenada, during the first week of February 1860, by Lt. Col. George Persons, general staff of Major General Winfield Scott. Surgeon Brett was to be apprehended and delivered to provost marshall's office to be tried on the basis of desertion of duty.
>
> Respectfully submitted,
>
> Brevet Major Jonah Cross
>
> Third Pennsylvania, US Army.

Cross told the provost officer he would be available to testify in the case of courts martial, depending upon how they decided on Brett's case, whether he was a deserter or a rebel — or, as what Brett seemed to be saying, simply a civilian doctor helping whichever side came to him with its wounded.

He would let the courts martial process decide Brett's fate.

He wondered whether they would hang him, set him free, or let him rot.

◇◇◇◇

One week later, closing in on Centerville and the site of the Bull Run battle one year previously, Cross thought about avenging the shame of that ignominious defeat by the ragtag rebels. Given the chance again, he would cut them down as he had at Malvern and Frayser Farm.

By the time he reached camp however, his head and jaw were throbbing, every muscle ached, and he knew he had a fever. The clanking of his saber in its scabbard was so damned loud, even when his horse was at a full stop.

When he found his tent, he would take off his sword and just lie down for a bit to rest, let the dizziness pass, he told himself.

"Should have let the doc look at this forsaken tooth," he said to himself, just before he fell asleep.

CHAPTER TWENTY-SIX

◇◇◇◇◇

Brett

July 5ᵗʰ to September 5ᵗʰ, 1862-Eastern Virginia

Beyond his or her personal focus, every person directly or indirectly involved with the Union's assault on the peninsula of Virginia in 1862's Mid Summer, as well as the Confederacy's defense of it, would have complained about the same thing — the confusion and enormous waste that resulted from it. Dragged from one prison to another, handed from one provost's area of responsibility into another's set of "tasks," Rory Brett was no exception to that.

He was the shell of what he had been just six weeks before. He had lost thirty or more pounds, by his own rough estimate, and his confusion had increased. He suffered repeated bouts of watery diarrhea likely from the gruel served to him and the other prisoners. It tasted like watered chalk. He had no appetite. He hadn't heard from Emmy for over three months and most of his letters before his capture had been returned unopened. His spirits, usually buoyed by a self-reinforced sense of purpose, had descended into what he hoped was the nadir of his misery.

He had never felt so close to giving up in his entire life. The disarray into which he had been placed worsened what might have otherwise been a more easily navigated defense from the accusations that had been thrown at him by Cross.

Why was he imprisoned? What were the charges? Where was he?

Who was he?

He was no longer Dr. Rory Brett, a physician from Henrico County, Virginia. He had been given a number, written in permanent ink onto the tunic he wore, and onto his left wrist. When he looked at the numbers, he realized that someone had transcribed them sloppily, his wrist identifying him as "790170", his tunic as "790270." Which number was he, he wondered?

In the brief interview he was granted after being transferred from the James River prison ship, escaping from the Peninsula like all the rest, he told his captors his name but was not given the opportunity to elaborate on the circumstances of his arrest or send notification of his circumstance to Emmy or anyone else. He invoked the name of Emmy's deceased father, the Congressman Kern O'Malley from Massachusetts, and mentioned that he himself was a former associate of Dr. John Letterman, who, he had learned, now reported to General McClellan.

But as far as he could tell, no one paid attention to any of those associations.

Manacled into the confinement of another small, cold cell, Brett tried conversing in the dark with the two other men he had seen chained to the wall as he was. The man on his left, however, hung his head, chin to chest, and snored as if he were in a deep sleep. The other, on the right, labored with deep stertorous respirations and was unresponsive to Brett's attempts to awake him. The guard who delivered the ration of hard bread and water in the evening ignored his request to send a message.

"I don't do favors fer anybody, Reb. You ain't conning me," was all he said to Brett as he locked the door and left.

The next morning they unchained the prisoner to the right and dragged his dead body away. The other man continued to snore. By that evening he was dead also, and Brett was alone in his cell.

The courts martial process in 1861 had been a mess, like most of everything else in the hastily assembled Union Army. By this time, one year later, it was not much improved. The infrastructure of the army had been repeatedly reorganized, generals and officers had been replaced, either because of failures or politics, and entire regimental command structures had been moved, reassembled with different leaders. Competent and incompetent officers alike had been killed or wounded or mustered out.

Unbeknownst to him, there was little in the way of written material to detain him. Lincoln's suspension of the *Writ of Habeas Corpus* had ensured that. Furthermore, in the aftermath of the disorderly retreat from the Peninsula, the official arrest paperwork that Jonah Cross had submitted, like Brett himself, had been shuttled from one location to another. Within a week, it was no longer in the same place as Brett. Filed in boxes sandwiched in with other official and irrelevant paperwork, it ultimately was sent to a holding area for army reports in Alexandria.

Complicating the due process, Captain David Bretlow, the first provost officer who had received the report, had been baffled over how to submit it further, causing him to procrastinate its forwarding. Since Brett wasn't a current officer of any Federal regiment, the matter would not likely be appropriately submitted to *regimental* courts martial, which was something Bretlow understood. Because the allegation of desertion was a *capital* crime and related to an incident that was almost three years old, and involved the former commander-in-chief, Winfield Scott, Bretlow reasoned that the matter should be handled by a *general* courts martial process, which entailed an entirely different set of rules and a much higher level of review.

But Winfield Scott, replaced by McClellan, was no longer in active service and, after the death of his wife, had all but disappeared from public view. To further complicate things, McClellan had then been replaced by John Pope as commander-in-chief. Assistant Provost Bretlow, a conscientious but duly cautious man, decided he would refer the matter to Command as soon as he could find the time, for a decision as to the best way to proceed. The paperwork was moved to Alexandria before he had the chance to complete that task

Four days later, Rory Brett was moved to another prison and five days later to another, a squat concrete building with a large basement that had been converted into individual solitary cells. Although not technically a dungeon cell, this one, measuring less than three or four feet in each direction, was smaller than the last two in which he had been kept. In each move, the basis of his imprisonment became less clear to his captors, and the official registry simply listed his number, and the allegation of "treason."

On the seventh day of that imprisonment, the prisoners in the basement were allowed to come outside to exercise for a half hour. While walking in a small circle in the courtyard with other prisoners from the building, Brett was able to see what appeared to be dozens of wind swept acres, rolling down hill to a wide, ugly gray river. The grounds were covered with tents, all enclosed by a tall grate fence and guarded by men in watchtowers set at 100-yard intervals. A thin wire, bristling with sharp spikes, rimmed the fence. Another prisoner, a young man with busy unkempt wiry sideburns who, like him, had nothing that identified him as a Confederate soldier, told him the name of the facility.

"This is Point Lookout," he said quietly.

"Them's prisoners' tents over there," said a bald man walking in front of them. "Yer in Maryland, Boys." The corporal assigned to oversee the exercise, took notice and hollered for the men to keep their mouths shut.

Brett realized that he had never been to Maryland before. He had heard it was beautiful, but couldn't see anything that affirmed that.

"Why are you here?" he whispered to the young man with the sideburns.

"I write poetry," was all the young man said back. His response was too loud. The guard walked over to the young poet and clubbed him.

"Exercise's over, Rebs." He clubbed the man again and again on the arms and legs then ordered the men to go back inside.

That evening, alone in his cell, Brett couldn't sleep. His legs and arms ached and his neck felt stiff. He had no fever and felt lucid, but he was restless and felt a melancholia like he had never before experienced. His attempts at communicating with the commander, with anybody, had been repeatedly ignored.

"Hey," he heard someone say down the row. For the first time he realized that there was another prisoner in this dark cold section. It was the voice of the young man with the frizzy sideburns. Brett, in the languor of his doldrums, debated whether to answer back.

"Hey, back," he responded finally.

"You a Yank or a Reb?"

"Neither, thank you."

"Then why have they incarcerated you?" the man asked. It was a young voice, cracking slightly, Brett thought, the timbre barely beyond the point of adolescent maturity.

"Gods and Generals," he responded. "And you?"

"Muses and my musings," the young man said. "Published finally. But in the wrong place at the wrong time, right before the Yanks arrested the entire Maryland legislature, he laughed. "Saying my mind and speaking out about tyranny. Likely different generals than yours, but the same old gods, I expect."

Brett laughed at that, but it hurt to do so.

"We need to win," the young voice said.

"And why is that?" Brett asked.

"So we can be the ones that write the history. Everybody knows that."

Brett didn't respond.

"Will you die here, too?" asked the young man.

Brett hadn't given that consequence a lot of thought, because he knew he was not a traitor. But he knew that the penalty for treason, should it be substantiated for some unfathomable reason, would be his execution. Likely by hanging.

That wasn't always the case. He recalled the penalty for desertion that Winfield Scott had approved after the battle of Churobusco in Mexico.

Although both Scott and Zachary Taylor had prominently proclaimed their largesse by the generous way they treated *Mexican* military captives, particularly the officer class, they hadn't treated their own in the same way. Seventy men from the predominantly Catholic San Patricio Brigade, who had deserted to fight on the side of the Mexicans who shared their religion, were sentenced by court martial to be executed. Scott pardoned five, hanged fifty and ordered the remaining to be given fifty lashes by hand-picked mule skinners.

Brett, who had witnessed the executions and subsequently treated the victims of the whippings, had heard that Scott himself had promised the floggers large bonuses if their whippings killed any of them while on the block.

Four bonuses were paid out. Scott then ordered that all of the whipping survivors be branded on their cheeks with the letter "D."

When Brett cared for the whipping victims afterwards, he remarked to himself that the lash wounds had been so severe that very few islands of dermis remained for healing the exposed, bloody pulp. Several of those whipped died afterwards from fulminant suppuration.

His loathing for Winfield Scott had begun on that day.

After that detestable affair, Brett had studied the conventions and codes of conduct outlining the treatment of prisoners of war, and had previously assumed both sides of this conflict were observing. Both the Union and the Confederate States had proclaimed their humane treatment of captured combatants. Those conventions, codified during the war against Britain in 1812, forbade the physical punishment of prisoners. No beatings or floggings. Prisoners were to be provided with adequate food and shelter.

So was this a different situation, somehow, akin to the inhuman way he had seen Confederate forces treating negro soldier prisoners who wore Union uniforms? Other than what he had seen during the Churobusco incident, his Union captors were demonstrating a brutality that he had not seen before. From what he could tell, the Union was housing thousands of prisoners in tents outside. Inside, as cold as it was during these summer months, he believed he fared no better. Would he be branded? Was he in a queue to be hung?

He didn't answer the young man's question about whether he would die here.

He couldn't. He had moved back inside. Retreating away from allowing himself to plunge into a bleak despair, he thought again about Emmy Evers. He began composing to himself what he would tell her when and if he got the chance to send a message out.

He decided it would be a long letter, composed in elegant style, on clean crisp paper, and envisioned it would be couriered to her by a young, well-paid messenger boy who would interrupt Emmy on the street where she lived in Boston as she walked with her children from a Sunday worship.

She would receive the letter in the way he had watched her do — quietly, with dignified composure, thanking the young boy and reaching into her purse for a modest tip.

She would walk on for a few minutes, containing herself while Jacob and Sarah watched her with growing anticipation.

She would glance at the envelope only once, feel its smooth surface and trace in her mind the swirl of the calligraphed address. Knowing Emmy, she would walk up the steps, send the children to their rooms, carry the letter to her office and close the door. Then, with quiet composure, she would open the envelope, lay out the pages, and read them carefully. Once, twice, three times. She would smile finally and swell with joy at the words she had read. *His* words! A soaring prosaic proclamation, intermixed with subtle poetry, finely crafted, whose ambiguities worked on every line and at every level of nuance, reinforcing the only conclusion at which she could arrive. He loved her so deeply, so thoroughly, so unabashedly, so . . . .

Had she forgotten about him? Could she? Would she? She had not a dram of cruelty in her. It wasn't in her voice or movement, in anything he had ever seen in her. He had watched her in Colon, recovering from a terrible concussion and shoulder wound, comatose for days. He had bathed her, sponged her when she was in the worst of a fever, dared cradle her for a bit when he thought she might not survive. Even then, unconscious, with all guards down, she was the epitome of grace. He knew he was in love then. It hadn't gone away.

But where was she? Was he counting too much on her refined sense of responsibility, rather than a true love for him, that kept him in her thoughts?

How could he reach her? Somehow, he had to send his spirit through the bleakness and find her. With a shard of stone he scratched a small poem in large letters onto the stone wall behind him and leaned up against it:

Time now has been.
You are here, away.
In and out and in,
You are there, close.

He finally slept.

They exercised in a warm summer downpour two days later. The same bald man who had told Brett they were at Point Lookout, quietly said the news was that Lee had just "most definitely whipped" the Yankees, again at Manassas Junction. The Confederates would move on Washington soon, he predicted.

"Bobby Lee and Jackson are unstoppable," the man behind them shouted out, too loudly.

With that outburst, a private and the corporal over-seeing the exercise walked over and clubbed Brett and the other two men hard on their backs, necks and heads with the butts of their rifles. Repeatedly. Brutally. Each blow harder, the meanness and anger jolting through the club and into his ribs and neck, from one angry mind into another's back and spirit.

He had covered his head. Although he knew some of his ribs were broken, he did not faint. He heard himself screaming out at the guards to stop beating the other prisoners. The other two men were unconscious when the guards carried them away.

Later, in the cell, while trying to delicately rub out the sharp soreness from his ribs where the soldier had struck him, Brett ruminated about the Confederate's jubilant outburst that had provoked the vicious beating. Brett knew that who won really didn't matter to him. It really never had. The indefensibility of slavery could not persist in the long run. But he knew that politics and viciousness would continue on, practiced by both sides, as they had before the hooting and shooting had started.

The killing and maiming settled nothing. It just made the combatants dig in more deeply. Their resentments, firmly rooted along the ruts they had carved out for them-selves, would be sustained, nourished for generations by the blood they spilled into this ground, ultimately bearing malignant fruit, poisoning all who willed to bite into it. He wondered how widespread the anger would be, and for how long the bitterness would persist.

Each day it went on made it worse. The war just had to be over with. The beating he and his companions had just endured, as well as the words that had released the emotion behind it, were manifestations of a human failing — being repeated all across this land, a million fold. Condoned violence. Every sad sin, dismissing the rights of man, given free rein "for cause," justified by perceptions of who drew the first blood.

He knew he had to find Emmy and get her and her family away from it before it was too late for them as well.

One week later, after the second battle loss at Bull Run, the rumor was that Lincoln finally listened to John Pope's critics, and again gave command to "Little Mac" McClellan. With Pope's departure, many of the military cronies he had brought into administrative command with him were replaced, including the provost marshal in Alexandria. New papers with details about other prisoners were stacked onto the cartons containing Cross's report about Brett.

In the morning exercise, again in a downpour, he saw that neither of the other two men who had been beaten were there. If the young man was in his cell in the darkness, he did not respond when Brett called out that evening.

The next morning, in the pencil beams of light that peeked in through a low, grated window for a few minutes each sunrise, Brett saw that the dampness of the cell had washed away the poem he had scratched into the wall.

CHAPTER TWENTY SEVEN

◇◇◇◇◇

Kathleen

August 2ⁿᵈ to August 4th, 1862-New York City

By the time Kathleen, Escoffier and Investigator Grimes reached mid-Manhattan on the Harlem train, almost two and a half days had passed since the children had disappeared.

Reasoning that the children would not have known where to get off and would have been told to do so at the end of the line, Grimes advised Kathleen and Escoffier that they ride the train all the way down to the Broome Street terminal. Closing on their destination, Kathleen observed that houses, tenements and shacks and in some places, piles of garbage twenty feet high, pushed up close to the tracks. Having bypassed the city in her trip from Baltimore to Westchester, she hadn't realized how densely packed it was with buildings, all along the way down south.

"Filthy, filthy, filthy!" she said to Escoffier and Grimes.

"City's busting at its seams," Grimes said. "Population's tripled over the past twelve years. Almost a million, they think. A thousand a day, comin' in by boat. Spudniggers mostly" he laughed, referring to the hoards of Irish immigrating into ports that weren't being stoppered by the Union blockade. "Good fodder for your Mr. Lincoln."

Kathleen ignored his crassness. Her Irish family had been called that and worse, she recalled, before they found their wealth and status in Boston. Her father had told her of his own struggles as a young immigrant. She carried faint memories of prejudicial comments from some children who said they were "native born", but she had been able to skirt it all. It had surprised her how much her family's emerging wealth and power cut through those barriers. One had simply to look the part, she discovered. No one looked the part down here.

"How will we find them?" she asked, as the train slowed nearing the terminal.

"We may not," replied Grimes. Noting that she dismissed that comment, he said, "We'll start with the peelers . . . the constables."

On Broome Street, Grimes found the stationmaster and conducted an interview that, although brief, seemed thorough enough to Kathleen. The man had not noticed any children matching Sarah's and Jacob's description, wearing the clothing that would have made them stand out amongst the dozens of urchins who stood begging on the corners and exits of the building. He said that almost four thousand passengers passed through the terminal every day. Lots of children all over, he said. "Little gutter rats," he called them.

As they walked a half block to the Metropolitan Police station, Grimes explained that only a few years ago there had been two competing police forces in the city. One, the Municipal Police, supported the former notoriously corrupt mayor. The other, named the Metropolitan Police, had been formed and ordered to replace "The Municipals" by the governor. Armed troops enforced the take-over, but not without a terrific fight. Several of the men from the Municipals had retained their jobs as "Metropolitans," so much of the corruption, briefly suppressed and with good-intention, had quickly re-emerged.

"It's still a mess," Grimes said. "Likely always will be. Just have to know who your you're working with."

At the station, they spoke to the watch captain who told them that no children had presented themselves in the previous two days, nor had there been any incidents, other than the usual victim complaints about "guttersnipe" pickpocketing and mugging. She noticed that Grimes spent much more time talking to two policemen who apparently walked this local beat and would have been patrolling in the perimeter when Sarah and Jacob might have disembarked from the train.

"Pug Uglies be devlin' round Mulberry. So best bypass it through Johnny-town to Bleeker. Be trying' Broad, too. Missions be there and do-gooders that yer low-tide 'squeekers coulda kinned to — wee marks, by their description. If their small snow didn't bring in the ponces by Five Points n' they ain't already been made part of the trade," the taller of the two cops said, through a thick Irish accent. The other cop nodded in agreement, pointing down the street to his right.

Grimes turned to Kathleen and Escoffier who obviously were bewildered by the slang.

"He's sayin' we should start at Bleeker Street by way of where the Chinamen have lots of shops, and then make our way to Broad. Best to avoid getting there by Mulberry because there are some dangerous thugs in the area. The children could be at one of the missions. If they haven't wandered in the wrong direction, been taken, dressed as they were," he paused, attempting to let it sink in, "for other purposes."

For the first time, by the tone in Grimes' voice and the flatness of his expression, the firm, cold reality of the situation settled on Kathleen. If the children hadn't found a safe haven, they might never be found.

By two o'clock the next afternoon, they had visited four missions and spoken with multiple people, including ministers, church volunteers, street people and other policemen walking their beats. No one had seen children who matched Sarah and Jacob's description. Escoffier suggested to Kathleen that she consider creating circulars that could be pasted on lampposts and the many announcement boards.

Kathleen told Grimes she would give an ample reward for information that led to the children's recovery. She increased her bonus offer to Grimes.

When they reached the lower part of the street called Broadway, Grimes informed them he estimated there would be at least a dozen other places that they needed to visit that afternoon, before it got too dark to safely travel, even in a carriage.

Kathleen, as tired as she was, suggested that they split up. She knew the questions to ask and Escoffier was keeping notes with leads. Grimes would take half of them, and she and Escoffier would explore the other half. They would meet that evening at the Astor House hotel on Vesey, with or without the children, at seven o'clock. If his search had been unsuccessful, Grimes was to bring other investigators for her to interview. If she and Escoffier had found the children, she would celebrate by treating them all to a sumptuous dinner. The children would likely be very hungry, she reasoned.

Grimes reluctantly agreed. He turned north, Kathleen and Escoffier turned south, walking along Broadway then moving in the direction they assumed from Grimes' instructions, would lead them to a row of missions and churches. But on an impulse, one of the first places she decided to examine was on the street she remembered the children mentioning when they all were on their way to Westchester — where there lived some Dago fellow and his children who her sister, Emmy had met two years ago in Panama.

Grimes had said he knew the area and had urged her to wait for him to accompany her and Escoffier, because she didn't really know her way around the city, she reasoned. But she could read street signs as well as anyone else. So she disregarded his admonition and she and Escoffier headed west instead of south.

Less than a block from the Broadway, the buildings changed in character to what they had seen in the immediate area on Broome Street, with cheap wood construction rather than with stone exteriors of the affluent Broadway Street. Garbage and clutter stood on the stoops of several of the houses. Hundreds of people milled about, vendors sold vegetables and housewares amidst a cacophonous din. A man wearing a bloody, fly-covered apron, butchered meat from an open cart, tossing bits of the gristle to dogs and children standing by. Next to the butcher, a swarthy man sang a song that seemed to match the grinding noises of his spinning grindstone on which he sharpened a long black blade.

Neither Kathleen nor Escoffier heard the crow-whistle by the lookout on the corner as they passed him when they turned onto Carter Street. The loud call, "Fresh Fish!" hollered out by the same tough blended in to the background noise of the busy street. Had they paid attention, they might have noticed several men and a few women turn their heads in their direction. One of them, a spindly-legged boy in his early teens, immediately crossed the street from a half block away, and walked directly towards Kathleen and Escoffier. Two others, a grinning man with black teeth and a grim-faced, determined girl briskly walked up to within a few feet of their new marks, trailing behind them at the same pace as they walked.

When Kathleen and Escoffier came to an alleyway crossing Carter Street, the spindly legged boy facing them pulled from his knickers a long stiletto with a wavy curved blade. Escoffier saw the knife, stopped, put his arm in front of Kathleen, and reached for a two shot Derringer in his vest. But the pair behind them moved right up to them, easily disarming Escoffier, then sticking the tips of their short blades far enough into the small of their backs that Kathleen and Escoffier had no choice but to turn into the alley. The noise in the street was so loud that it drowned out Kathleen's cries of alarm. Three other young men and another woman moved into the alley joining in on the mugging. In less than a minute both Kathleen and Escoffier, clubbed repeatedly with brickbats, their clothing pulled and torn, lay helpless on the ground behind a tall garbage pile.

Kathleen awoke with Doyle Grimes kneeling down next her. She turned her head and saw two Metropolitan police covering the stripped, bloodied corpse of Escoffier.

"I told you to allow me to accompany you here, Madame." Grimes said.

CHAPTER TWENTY-EIGHT

◇◇◇◇

Emmy and Basetyr

*August 5th to August 8th, 1862-Richmond
and the Virginia Countryside*

When Pen Basetyr, Henri Lebo's smuggling partner, walked into the parlor at the Noah's Ark, Emmy thought she was seeing yet another of Richmond's businessmen seeking the pleasure of one of Janie Jones' whores. Basetyr, dressed head to toe like a man, from her gray derby down to black riding boots, swaggered into the room like a bantam rooster. When she sat down on a hard-backed chair, the large pistol in the front pocket of her britches bulged forward in her groin. Her speech was confident and brash and although she spoke in a voice that matched her small-boned frame, its tone was more tenor-like than alto, and thus did not betray her gender. Her short-cut hair was tucked neatly upwards into the bowler. She wore a faint, wispy moustache.

Janie Jones ran over to Basetyr, put her arm around her neck, sat on her lap, and introduced her to Emmy.

"This here's Pen," Janie said. "Great on the road an' great in the sack!" she laughed.

Basetyr blushed slightly — not the way a young man might, Emmy noted — then brushed Janie off her lap. She stood up and looked over her client. Emmy was still wearing the skirt and blouse she had purchased from Janie.

Cocking her head at Emmy, she said to Janie: "Pretty, ain't she?"

"She's a straight one, Pen!" Janie laughed. "Gonna get herself hanged! Maybe you too!"

Emmy declined a reaction to Janie's comments, but watched Basetyr's face.

Basetyr paused for a moment, looked over Emmy again, then down at Clarissa who was holding Emmy's hand, then said, "Well, let's move" and strutted to the back door and on to the porch outside.

So who was this strange person, Pen Basetyr? Could she be trusted, Emmy wondered?

◇◇◇◇

Penelope Basetyr defined herself at the age of ten, when she abandoned the name she had been given by her father and the clothing worn by women. Small framed as she was, and almost always dressed in hand-me-down trousers and loose calico shirts, she easily was mistaken for an undernourished adolescent boy, which gave her an advantage in the smuggling business she had chosen to pursue. She knew Quakers and Quaker ways, having grown up in the heavily wooded outskirts of a German-speaking community of Friends on the Mason-Dixon line, where Virginia bordered both Maryland and Pennsylvania at the Potomac River. That became especially important as she increased her participation in what was being called up North by the abolitionists an "underground railroad."

In 1847, the year she turned ten, her stepmother, Tess Ulman-Basetyr finally summoned the courage to leave her husband, a mercurially tempered man, who fouled by frequent expletives what little charm he might otherwise have possessed. His violent outbursts terrorized the family and frequently left Tess or her children bruised and bleeding. He had never broken her bones, but she knew that he was capable of murder.

"Has it in him," Tess said, knowing he would sob and beg forgiveness afterwards, then later, rationalize it away with some form of blame for anyone but himself. Taking the three young children she had given him during their four years of marriage, ostensively to care for an ailing sister a day's trip away on a farm near the Potomac, Tess left her stepchildren, Penelope and her older brother, to care for their father who had been debilitated the year before from a stroke.

"Y'ar my surragits" Penelope heard her stepmother say. "Yer brother cain work the fields and you cain work . . . the cabin . . . so the Lord cain't hold my leavin' my obligation to a husbin' whose down. Em not coming beck to that dog. Don' a come a lookin' for us."

Seeing her stepdaughter's surprise and looking her and her older brother up and down she said, "I've watched yeh. Ye'll be a woman soon enough. Expect you know how to fend for yourself b'now."

When Penelope started to protest she was told "Best be nimble, girl. An good luck with the curse when it starts itself." Those were the last words she ever heard from her stepmother, who Penelope later learned had taken up with a more evenly dispositioned man she met in Sharpsville.

It wasn't a good arrangement for Penelope, who long before had developed a hatred for her life in that household, and in particular, for her father, Benjamin Basetyr. The man, despite trying earnestly, had been a meager provider for over five years. He was a failure as a farmer, and had twice allowed himself to be swindled from most of his earnings as a woodsman. Five years previously he had been dismissed from his position as a part time teacher at the small school in the township, purportedly for reasons of incompetence and abuse.

Making Penelope's embarrassment worse, the other small children ridiculed her father because of the thick glasses he wore which seemed to amplify the appearance of an owl with cross-eyed strabismus. She watched her father completely give up after repetitive disappointments.

In the month before he suffered his stroke, in desperation he had walked sixty miles north and applied for a teaching position that had come open at the only other school in the county. Unfortunately, his reputation, tied to his nickname of "Lazy-eyed Ben," had preceded him in his interview. The school master at that institution had been informed that it referred less to Benjamin Basetyr's strabismus than to his violent, mercurial temper — he was known for the inaccurate aim of the slaps he bestowed on any pupil he deemed lazy or impertinent. Sometimes, it was said, he actually had struck the wrong child during his fits.

The rejection from the only work in which he had ever made a fair, albeit modest living amplified Basetyr's frustration and anger. He took it out on his family. Then he was knocked down with a debilitating stroke. Then his wife left him.

The resulting infirmity, a lame left arm, clumsy gait and garbled speech, weakened him, but he retained ample energy, and after he realized that his wife really wasn't coming back he began to beat Penelope regularly for what he slurred out as "infractions and complicity with your whore of a step-mother. Less than a fortnight later, Basetyr tried to pull her into his bed. Her thirteen-year-old brother, with whom she had bunked on occasion in the past few years, stood by and laughed. She managed to wriggle free and, while her father lurched about the barnyard screaming into the darkness for her to return, she hid behind a tall chestnut woodpile. Her brother found her and called for Basetyr, but Penelope outran both their grasps, disappeared into the woods, then doubled back and quietly crawled into the chicken coup.

"Get back here, ya little bitch. You need a good whippin!" she heard her father screaming out at the thickets where he thought she had hidden.

Early the next morning, she immersed and washed herself in the cold chill of the water trough, then pulled a few scraps of clothing hanging on the line outside, her brother's, retrieved a bundle of salt pork and rusk from the larder, and headed off through the woods. Fearing the village's people would side with her father, no matter what she said, she didn't even try to go there. For the rest of her life she remembered that day with the sun coming up. She didn't feel sorry for herself as she walked east. The cool air waving through the early wheat found and ran over her face and through her wet hair. She would always relate that to the elation of leaving pain behind.

She had no particular direction in mind when she first had set off. The warm nights during the first several weeks she wandered about in the early summer of West Virginia allowed her to sleep without much discomfort. She knew she wasn't afraid of the woods. The soft beds that she found for herself, when the light faded the green to black, provided far more comfort during those summer months than what was left back at the filthy place where she had grown up. Uncommonly seasoned for her age, when the bark on one's shell should have been more tender, she realized she really didn't have fears in the night sleeping outside by herself and understood that she preferred it actually, when she thought back on the tight quarters in which she had shared with a strange, strained family and the imposition of such order.

The woods were hers. From the age of six she had worked in the forest with her father and brother and accompanied them on trips hauling lumber through it to sawmills along the river where they camped and hunted. She knew how to trap and fish, skin and cook squirrel and small birds. Within a few days after leaving she had learned to forage by theft from the several prosperous farms that dotted the river. They seldom had enough farmhands to watch over what she might steal, she knew. And she was a silent, clever thief. She kept away from the townships and stayed close to the woods where she had always felt comfortable, following the Potomac along its slow moving course but far enough away from the bustle of towns near the capital. She knew the splendid privacy of the woods. She never had much use for talking. She learned the easiest fords, swam all the way across the river at its slowest and narrowest places, and at the wider necks hitched rides back and forth into Virginia and Pennsylvania holding onto the sides of barges pulled across by long ropes.

Her favorite thing, next to waking in the morning to the dew and hazy sparkle of light filtering through the canopy, was nestling into the secure covering of a makeshift lean-to and hearing the patter of a warm summer rain's cleaning the dust off the leaves.

Six weeks into what she considered the great freeing adventure of her life, while sitting in the bent fork of a wild cherry tree, eating dried corn from one of the farm bins she had visited the previous night, she observed a neat but modestly dressed man and woman making their way tentatively along a deer trail. Quakers, likely, she thought. It had just rained and she had shed her clothing to let the warm downpour cleanse her as she liked to do. So when she saw the couple, her first thought was to cover herself. But she had learned by watching different animals moving in the woods that the best way to remain undiscovered was to be still. So she sat there motionless, naked in the crook of the tree, watching them. By their hesitation and posture they likely were lost, she surmised. She waited until they passed.

After several minutes she saw them come right back to the same place. They began to argue with each other. The man fell silent as the woman continued to berate him.

"Foolish!" she heard the woman say to the man in a cross tone that reminded her of the way her stepmother had often spoken to her father. The couple turned and disappeared back in the direction from which they had come, making a lot of noise as they did so. She smiled at that while she quietly slipped to the ground, quickly redressed and put the unfinished cobs in her pocket. The couple returned as she knew they likely would. After a few minutes the man whistled two notes that didn't sound anything like she knew would be part of the forest. She heard a second whistle. Two notes. A few minutes later, five negroes, a tall, sturdy young man, two women and two small girls, all of them shoeless, looking bewildered and frightened, joined the couple. They carried no baggage. They were lean and seemed worn down.

Penelope knew what she was witnessing. Runners. She continued to watch. The seven people began moving off in what she figured was the wrong direction, unless they had decided to go back into Virginia and be recaptured. She followed and watched them reach a wall of brambles. They stopped. They sat down. Both of the little girls started to cry.

She knew they likely were running from something they didn't like, being slaves and all. She knew what if felt like to escape from something you hated. But they were lost in a way she had never felt, because she knew the woods. It'd been natural for her. She thought about that. They looked pathetic, she thought.

After a few minutes she spoke up.

"Best ye be movin' in the other direction lest yer fixin' to get yersef caught 'n whipped hard."

No one in group reacted at first, but one by one, they all turned to stare at her. She smiled knowing that she must have been a strange spectacle. Did they think she was some small, ten-year-old angel? Or a little devil?

She moved closer, then reached into her pocket and tossed a cob to the smallest child. "Y'all might want to faller me."

She turned and walked away in the direction that she knew would take them on a path skirting a thick briar patch, over a hill and down to the river and an easy ford.

They followed. No words were spoken until they reached the river.

"What be thy name, little brother?" the white Quaker man asked after her.

For the first time he realized it felt good to be a boy.

"Pen," she had said.

◇◇◇◇

"Passel of rawness you and Henri Lebo scratched up here, Lady" Basetyr said dryly to Emmy, as they rowed across a narrowing of the James, up river from Richmond.

"Almost didn't come, after hearing' 'bout its complications, the shoot out an' all."

Emmy didn't respond.

"Ya think Henri survived?" Basetyr asked, after a pause.

292

"I don't know," Emmy responded. "The newspaper didn't say anything about that."

"If'n he didn't . . . well, that'd make me real sad,' she said after a minute of quiet rowing. "Real sad."

They rowed another few minutes without speaking.

"Expectin' you'll pay me good 'n more if we get you home with yore pretty white neck still unstretched," said Basetyr.

"I will, indeed, Miss Basetyr," said Emmy.

"Friends call me 'Pen'," Basetyr said, aiming the boat towards a landing hidden by tall reeds.

After a pause, she continued. "You didn't react the way most do when they first meet me, Lady. Still, I expect you have some questions. Most do, if'n they don't write me off soon as they think they got me figured out.

. . . I'm 'other,' after all."

"I'm not disturbed, Pen," Emmy responded, "and I don't have any questions." She looked at Pen Basetyr's sturdy, small frame and strong hands as she easily managed the large flat-bottomed boat against the current.

"I admit that I was expecting a man. Because no one said anything to make me think otherwise. But then," Emmy continued, "Seeing what I saw in Henry Lebo, I don't think he would have spoken as highly of you if you weren't competent at what you do."

Emmy noticed that Basetyr smiled briefly when she said that.

Clarissa slept as Emmy rowed alongside Basetyr. Emmy looked at the little girl, bundled into a ball of blankets. At least the women at Noah's Ark had given her clean clothing for the girl and Jamie Jones hadn't charged her for it. She was out of gold anyway and had tossed her belt. Basetyr, like Henri Lebo, had been paid half in advance, with the balance and same large bonus, almost a thousand dollars in gold, waiting in Baltimore on the same terms she had promised Lebo — that she make it back to Washington, D.C. alive.

On the other side, two horses were tied, hidden in the thickets. From the river, Emmy and Pen moved north for several minutes into a long stretch of scrub pines and from there stopped and looked back in the direction of where they had landed their boat. Emmy saw it first and Basetyr confirmed what she saw, several torches at the river's edge. The torches were on both sides of the river.

"They'll figure it out pretty quick. Track when there's enough light. One of the gals at Noah's Ark musta talked," Basetyr said.

They rode non-stop for two hours before resting for a few minutes, standing in a small stream, one of the many tributaries of the Chickahominy swamps and river. Basetyr insisted Emmy relieve herself in the running water.

"They'll be trackin' us hard," Basetyr said. "Let the river carry our piss scent away." Clarissa, watching this, did the same as the two women.

From there, they headed west for a few more miles before turning north again crossing and recrossing, running long lengths of every stream they found to confuse the trackers. Basetyr found a few large fields where the Union army had camped and foraged, with the ground churned up and covered with hoof marks. She looked for rocky exits to the fields, and when she found one she led Emmy as far up the rock-covered draws as she could.

"If'n they got hounds...." She didn't have to finish. Emmy knew what that meant — the odds of surviving the posse would be poor.

By early morning as the mist cleared, Emmy could see several more fields in the distance. Tatters of fences separated them.

"By my calculations, we have a coupla hours on them at most. Keep plowin', Lady."

Basetyr rode ahead mostly, alternating carrying Clarissa. Emmy hadn't slept for over a day, but for some reason, perhaps because she knew they couldn't stop during the long ride, she found herself lucid and bitter about her failure.

She wondered . . . should she have stayed in Richmond? Should she have tried to hide there and persist looking for Brett? Should she have taken on all of this when the predictable odds against her success were as great as they likely were and had proven to be?

She remembered when she had previously defied the advice of others like Pickett and her brother-in-law, when she had embarked on the journey to recover her kidnapped son.

She had succeeded in that. Perhaps that was why she had taken on this challenge, to follow her instinctive need to do something bigger and more important than herself.

Or was that really the reason?

Should she have stayed and risked reaching out to Pickett? she asked herself. She hadn't expected to see him. Why hadn't she called out to him when she saw him? Was it because he was with another woman? Did she still have unresolved feelings for him that she didn't understand yet — that were, in some way, contributing to her failure to commit to Rory Brett?" She didn't know, and knew she would have to figure that out — if she survived.

She shifted away from that question and thought about why she was here in the first place and what she had and had not accomplished. Unfinished business. She felt for the last letter he had sent her, carried next to her heart. Poor Rory. She hoped some angel might whisper to him that she had been at his doorstep, had been up and down the scale of hopefulness with each moment of her ride into and away from this troubled, ravaged land.

One hour later, turning onto a high road that Basetyr said was a few miles south of the town of Po River, they stopped again to rest their mounts. Emmy scanned the horizon in all four directions. Looking back in the direction they had come, she watched for any signs, birds flying, colors, dust that would have given a hint of pursuers closing on them. But she saw none. When she looked northwest, in the opposite, she saw a few smoke stacks in the distance, faintly active as indicated by gray wisps. No wind. The smoke rose in lazy curls straight up. But no movement on the horizon. Then she saw the crows, hundreds of them, much closer, flying low in a circle, directly over a cleared field less than a quarter of a mile away, and in the direction Basetyr said they were headed.

Emmy covered Clarissa's eyes when they reached the field and saw what was there. She counted nine people, all negroes, three women and six children lay slaughtered, laying along side a narrow irrigation ditch. By the state of the corpses, the bodies had laid unburied for days. They rode further across the field and found the dismembered bodies of three negro men. A little further lay the headless body of a fourth.

"Runners," Basetyr said, shaking her head. "Seen this same scene over 'n over agin — twiced this many, not five miles from here." Basetyr sighed, looked over at Clarissa and Emmy. "Just ain't gonna let'm get away, the Rebs, even if they know in their hearts its all over. Been so, over that is, fer a long time, I reckon."

Emmy kept her hands over Clarrisa's eyes until they had passed the grisly scene and pulled a handkerchief over the little girl's nose to mask the stench. Riding on, she closed her own eyes and shuddered. She stopped her horse. Some of the children had been Clarissa and Jacob's ages. The people hadn't just been murdered. They had been mutilated, as well. It reminded her of what her husband Isaac found on Camano Island back in Washington four years before. The aborigines there had done the same thing to some free negro settlers.

"Cain't stop to be decent," said Basetyr. "Say yer prayer an let's keep movin."

Emmy stopped her horse again. Basetyr, seeing her pondering what she had just seen, rode back to her.

"Two an a half more days, Lady. Plow on." Basetyr's voice didn't waver, but Emmy heard the sadness at the bottom of it.

By nightfall, Basetyr said she thought they had covered at least twenty-five miles. She pointed to a row of poles along the road off to their left. "Union army cut all the telegraph wires in these parts. That's to our advantage, else'n we'd have the Vigilance folks waitin' fer us, no matter."

They rode for another quarter mile. "A dog don't care none 'bout telegraphs, though. Dogs 'll track you and yer horse fer a hundred miles, an' won't stop till they get ya treed. Hate them dogs," she said.

Basetyr explained that she thought Otis Loller, the sheriff of Henrico County and self appointed leader of the regional Virginia Vigilance Committee, thus hampered from getting word out in the direction they were headed, would bring as many men and dogs as he could muster into this hunt. They would pursue aggressively, spread out in two or more groups, dogs and riders running as far and as fast as they could. But they would likely pause at darkness to rest themselves, she thought. The dogs would need to be fed and then sleep. The only advantage Emmy, Clarissa and she had would be to keep moving fast.

Emmy looked at their horses. They were both heavily lathered.

Seeing Emmy's hesitation, Basetyr said "I got fresh un's, awaiting not far from the Rapidan. Plow on, Lady."

A few hours later, they stopped by another small stream and let their horses rest again. Emmy brushed the horses down, while Basetyr inspected the hooves of both of the mounts. They had been fortunate, Emmy knew. The horses had been sturdy during the entire run.

She watched Basetyr, talking softly to her horse, almost as if it were a child, while she tacked a nail into its front shoe. This was an extraordinary woman, she realized, just as Lebo had been an extraordinary man. Just as it had been with Lebo, it was clear to Emmy that Basetyr knew this countryside well and was comfortable moving through it in slim light. Both of them, Lebo and Basetyr, hardy and hard on the outside, betrayed a bit of tenderness on their inside by the way each of them had dealt with Clarissa. How would Pen Basetyr do in a fight if it came to that, she wondered?

Emmy spoke to Basetyr, "I was thinking about what you said . . . I get written off too, all the time. We all do, don't we? Women, that is. I am wondering when we will abandon the stubborn habit of pre-judging, branding really, someone as 'other' the way we do, by their cover. Like those ones back there."

Basetyr responded, "Well, I feel pretty comfortable in my own skin, and I don't give a damn what anybody else thinks about me. Personally, I like some women and I like some men. I do what I do because it makes me money and I'm pretty good at it. From what I can tell, you do what you think is right. That's the way I cut it, too."

They pushed on without further discussion.

A few hours after sun up, they stopped to calm Clarissa who had begun to cry for the first time during the entire ride. Basetyr picked up the girl, and to Emmy's surprise, started rocking her, again softening her voice as she did so. Clarissa fell asleep again.

"We gotta push on," Basetyr said, still holding the little girl. "Figure we've traveled about forty-five miles, or so. Almost half way."

At a small junction near an unfinished rail line, they stopped again, this time at a shed leaning up against an old gnarled chestnut tree whose limbs had pushed off part of the roof. Two horses were tied inside. A sack of oats and a bundle with four hard-boiled eggs, a loaf of bread and two small green apples. The bread was stale and the apples were sour, but Emmy thought it was the best meal she had ever eaten. Basetyr peeled her apple and gave half of it in bits to Clarissa.

"Guessin' you didn't find what you was lookin' for," she said to Emmy.

Emmy, who had tried not to mull over the events of the past week, turned to her and nodded abjectly. Her lucidity had passed. She was too tired to entertain sadness and immediately fell asleep against a large burl of the tree.

She dreamed she was with a man . . . Isaac, then Rory Brett, then someone else she didn't know. She was pregnant again, and the man acted like he was the father. He was pushing at her back, behind her, but she was holding him up. She desperately needed this sleep, but his knee was stuck in between her shoulder blades.

Basetyr awoke her after what seemed like only a few minutes. But Emmy's pocket watch indicated that Basetyr had let her and Clarissa sleep for over an hour. It was already noon. The horses were saddled.

"We'll be crossing the Rapidan then heading up into a leg of the Blue Ridge foothills in a bit," Basetyr said, pointing to the west. "Then we turn back west by Snickerville, cross the Shenandoah River and head up further east towards Sharpsburg. Cross the Potomac there. Too much going on down river at Harper's Ferry. Another full day, day and a half. If we make it that far, I figure I'm due my bonus."

By sunset, Emmy estimated that they had traveled another twenty miles or more, over rolling low hills and down into a wide valley that seemed untouched compared to what she had seen farther south. Basetyr told her that

McClellan had concentrated his forces closer to Richmond, and word was that he had purposely avoided foraging here or provoking the farmers who lived in this part of Virginia, hoping this part of the state, like the western counties, would eventually peacefully swing to Union control. It was pretty well known, she said, that the Union general, John Pope, who had been waging a vicious hard war further down in the southern part of the Shenandoah, had aggravated folks in that part of the state mightily. But the secession voting early on a year ago had shown the federals that they wouldn't lose much by despoiling the population in that region.

"I expect they'll do whatever they need to do to win this one," she said.

Because the ground hadn't been macerated as it had been by the thousands of wagons, troops and livestock involved further south in the Union's Peninsula campaign, Basetyr told Emmy she was concerned that their tracks would be that much easier to follow.

It was then that she noticed that they were intersecting frequently with the tracks of a large party, thirty or more, mostly on foot, with a few mules and one wagon. The tracks were moving in the same direction as she and Emmy, along the route she had used several times smuggling contraband, human and otherwise, out of the rebel held territory.

"More runners, I expect," Basetyr said. By the time darkness closed off most of the light, they had them sighted not far up ahead. Ten men, two white and eight negroes, the rest women and children walking alongside a cart filled with baggage. All of the men carried rifles. They weren't moving very fast.

"Well, we're in for a bit of a fur flying'," Basetyr said, pointing Emmy in the opposite direction behind them. Through her eyepiece Emmy saw oncoming torches, about a mile back, two groups of them in the distance. She couldn't hear dogs yet, but knew they were running ahead. Otis Loller's posse. For a fleeting moment, she thought about the small pistol Lebo had given her and shuddered.

"Move fast!" Basetyr commanded.

Emmy understood. They rode directly towards the negroes ahead, hollering and waving and whistling.

"We's friends! Don't shoot, dammit! Don't shoot! Sheriff's posse oncoming! Movin' up from the south."

Emmy and Basetyr, holding Clarissa tightly, didn't stop but rode on past the runners who had lowered their weapons and were looking southward past them in the direction of the oncoming converging two posses. When Emmy looked back, she saw that the band of runners were heading for a covering of high brush, hiding their wagon and spreading out in two lines, forming a funnel between the grove of trees through which the pursuers would have to ride. From what she could tell in the dim light, it looked like they were preparing to fight it out with Otis Loller.

She heard the first sounds of onrushing hounds, faint at first, then louder and louder. The dogs, about five of them, diverted off from the draw where Loller's posse would have to ride, and moved up the path where she and Basetyr had ridden.

"Damn! Damned dogs is hard on our tail," Basetyr hollered over to Emmy. "Dig it hard, Lady!"

Emmy spurred her horse attempting to keep up with Basetyr who galloped full tilt up to a narrow ridge and into a thicket of yellow pines. She could hear the dogs yelping, growling, howling, gaining on her fast. As she reached the thicket she saw Basetyr's horse, its rein thrown across a black berry patch. Had they been thrown?

The dogs, Blue Tic hounds all of them, were less than thirty yards away now. She tried to drive her horse through the brambles but it shied, stopped and reared.

The lead hound reached her mare just as its front legs were coming down and as the dog tried to jump up onto it, the horse turned, reared and kicked it in the side with its left hind hoof.

The dog yelped and flew off whining into the brambles.

Two other dogs were on them now, snapping. One jumped up and caught her mare's lip with its teeth and as the mare spun in a circle trying to dislodge it, the hound suspended off the ground, swung with it and off the horse's lip.

As Emmy reached into her pocket and pulled the derringer to get off a shot, her mare stopped spinning. Emmy was thrown off before she could cock the pistol. She hit the ground hard still holding the reins in one hand and the pistol in her other.

Two hounds came at her and went for her throat, grabbing at her arm, tearing her coat sleeve.

She didn't hear the blasts from Pen Basetyr's shotgun that sent the two dogs flying off her.

The last two hounds came at her, one biting her leg and the other going for her throat. Holding the dog away with her left arm, she cocked the derringer and fired both barrels into the animal.

The hound at her leg turned and ran off.

"You all right?" she heard Basetyr ask.

Emmy nodded, pulling herself up, calming her horse. Its lip was torn and bleeding, but she knew they would have to move away quickly before Loller unleashed more dogs. She knew the blood from the mare's cut would leave an easy trail for them.

"Git movin'," Basetyr hollered again as she remounted her horse. She handed Clarissa to Emmy and started to reload her double barrel.

"Damn! Looky down there!" said Basetyr looking up, pointing her shotgun down the ridge to where the runners had set up their positions to meet oncoming posse.

Less than three hundred yards away now, it was heading right into the runners' gauntlet.

A few seconds later the shooting started. From their vantage point in the hill's thickets Emmy could see that in less than a minute, many of the posse riders with torches, perfectly silhouetted targets in the blackness of the night, had been shot off of their horses.

A fitting dessert, she thought.

"Guess Ol' Loller weren't expectin' a reception like this," Basetyr said. "That'd be two ambushes the boy's stumbled under in less than a week."

Emmy nodded.

◇◇◇◇

They crossed the Shenandoah River at sunup and reached the Sharpsburg crossing by nine o'clock that morning.

Sitting at the Potomac's edge, watching river traffic moving southeast in the direction of Harpers's Ferry and Washington, Emmy looked down at Clarissa, again sleeping comfortably. What would she do with this little one, she wondered? She would have to find a way to help the girl learn to communicate when she got to Washington. She seemed malleable and smart enough to learn. She hoped she had enough personal reserve to address her needs.

She saw that Basetyr was studying her and Clarissa who had wakened and was looking about. Basetyr put out her hands and Clarissa immediately stood up and walked over to her, sat in her lap, nestled in under her coat, then closed her eyes and went back to sleep. Basetyr closed her own eyes, quietly smiled, and rocked slightly back and forth. "I think this little one likes me, Lady," she said pensively.

"I know you got means, and maybe you got a lot of time on yer hands too, but...well, I'd be willin' to keep her, if you' be willin'," Basetyr said.

Emmy looked at the two of them, then nodded. She was right. With the infirmities with which she had been saddled in life, Clarissa needed both a mother and a protector. She saw that Basetyr had a solid competency that went beyond what society believed most single women could provide, and a ferocious independence from a need for the approval of others. It was admirable, and she expected that Clarissa would do well by it. Little else mattered, she realized.

She nodded again.

She wondered about what it meant and how it felt to be "other." How did one survive as "other" in a hostile environment created not by the elements, but by the human tribe's instinctive need for security via conformity to rules and expectations? That made her think about her experience in Panama almost two years before, when she and several others had been taken hostage in a train heist by the bandit they called "Bocamalo." The man had surrounded himself with a loyal following of *descapacitados*, people, who like him, had been born with significant infirmities. *They* had survived by creating their own culture, it seemed, disregarding and disrespecting norms and "normal."

That made her think about her son, Jacob. He was no longer normal, she knew, and his suffering had changed him forever, she feared. Would he survive in this "normal" world, surrounded by "normal" people? Would his young rambunctious spirit, which she had sensed from the time he had been a small boy, bordering on the ferocious, ever re-emerge? Or would he be cowed and broken irreparably?

She could hardly wait to see him and Sarah.

She looked again at the two souls sitting across from her.

"Clarissa will need constant love and care, Pen. She will always be 'other.' I believe you will take good care of her," she said, knowing that would be the case.

CHAPTER TWENTY-NINE

◇◇◇◇

Emmy, McEmeel and Butler

August 9th, 1862 — on a train from Washington to New York City

B ecause of the news awaiting Emmy when she arrived — that Sarah and Jacob were missing — her harried stay in Washington lasted less than a few hours. She gave herself just enough time to gather some clean clothing, give herself the brief respite of soaking in a hot tub for a half-hour to clean the embedded grime of her long mounted ride back from Richmond, and then arrange for another advance on Jacob's diamond from her attorney, Mr. Dolan.

She sent a telegram to New Orleans to her brother-in-law, Jonathan McEmeel that she would be attending to

Kathleen in the New York Hospital, and another to Mr. Doyle Grimes, the private investigator who had sent word to her about the disappearance of her children. Then she boarded a northbound train.

How did the children get lost in New York, of all places? Why had Kathleen taken them there? Emmy tried to calm herself down. It would do no good to make assumptions. She decided to not speculate until she could confront Kathleen and talk to Grimes.

On the first long stop, she disembarked for a few minutes and wired Inspector Grimes again, instructing him to hire additional help and, at the highest level he could negotiate, arrange for police assistance. Then she re-boarded. Other than that, her only recourse, given that she was still hundreds of miles away from New York and could do little to impact their recovery yet, was to control her emotions and rest as much as she could.

She allowed herself to sleep on the New York-bound train's hard wooden seats. It wasn't difficult, as tired as she was. She slept all the way to Baltimore, stopped there briefly to check on the account where she had left completion deposits for Henri Lebo and Pen Basetyr. Lebo had drawn on the account. So he had survived, she realized. He was a rough man, but he had saved her life. She wondered about the relationship between Lebo and Basetyr. She didn't have enough information to go any further than conclude they were fond of each other.

From Baltimore, the trip to New York would take only one day — as long as Jubal Early's or Nathan Bedford Forrest's rebels hadn't been raiding the lines again.

On that leg of her journey, her worries crept in again. To keep herself from breaking apart thinking about Jacob and Sarah, she tried to read anything that was available.

She found a stale issue of *The Tribune*, and tried to concentrate on a published letter from Abraham Lincoln to the editor, Horace Greeley, who, in private and in print, had been repeatedly criticizing the Union's president for not making war more aggressively. Greeley, an opinionated Republican, demanded in an editorial that Lincoln declare that the war aims of the Union should be centered around the abolition of slavery.

Emmy read out loud to herself Lincoln's public response to Greeley's latest criticism:

> *My paramount object in this struggle is to save the Union, and is not either to save or destroy slavery. If I could save the Union without freeing any slave I would do it, and if I could save it by freeing all the slaves I would do it; and if I could save it by freeing some and leaving others alone I would also do that. What I do about slavery, and the colored race, I do because I believe it helps to save the Union; and what I forbear, I forbear because I do not believe it would help to save the Union. . . .*

An article, also on the first page, mentioned that Abraham Lincoln, through intermediaries, was rumored to have offered a commission of major general to Giuseppe Garibaldi, who she remembered, had been the revered leader of Antonio "Ari" Scarpello, the man who had saved her children in Panama. As she read further, she saw that

Garibaldi, the internationally famous Italian hero, had *declined* the invitation because Lincoln hadn't made the abolition of slavery the primary purpose of the war.

That seemed to corroborate what Greeley and others had been saying, she thought. Why was Lincoln taking his time? Did he and his cabinet really believe that by waiting to make such a stand they might change people's minds about which sides they would support?

Lincoln said that *his* war aim was to preserve the Union, in the quickest way possible. She thought about the morality of such a stance and she saw the direct pragmatism of the man's approach. Irrespective of his well-known beliefs about the abomination of enslavement of *any* person, Lincoln would do *whatever* was necessary to win the war and preserve the Union. Whatever was necessary.

She also understood what that meant in relation to what she had just witnessed on the fields of the Peninsula. It meant a war on civilians as well as the military.

This would continue to be a hard war for both sides, she realized, confused as it was because the moral purpose was still indistinctly stated. At least that was the way it seemed to her.

In many ways, the Union, by repeatedly invading "homeland" in Virginia as it had, had allowed a provocative "cause" to be built, around which white people of the South might rally, irrespective of whether they were for or against the enslavement of other human beings. Except for the people living in the large cities, most of the Northerners and Southerners with whom she had discussed issues over the past two years, clearly gave their local homeland primacy over the distant federal government's declared eminent domain.

She remembered the conversations she had with George Pickett, who detested slavery, but loved his Virginia. She had heard General Lee carried the same sentiment. People, even those considered "noble," put their own interests before those of others. It was no different in the North, where the war and the affairs in Washington, D.C. were an abstraction, especially to those who were not city folk. Certainly if the rebels took their war into Pennsylvania or even Maryland, the power standing behind both sides' sense of higher moral purpose might change.

But for now, it seemed that the people of the South felt grievously and repeatedly stung and abused in a much greater way than did the people of the North who, unlike the negroes who were directly affected by the injustice, were remote to the passions involved. Unless the northern populations were directly impacted by the tragedies, it would remain so.

Confirming that conclusion, when she arrived in New York, it seemed that the war was thousands of miles away and not at all on the minds of the common folk, as she had witnessed it was in Richmond and Washington. The New Yorkers busily went about their own business. There, the war was a story about others. No one wore black in the way it was donned in the capitals. She suspected it was the same in Boston and back on Whidbey Island in the Pacific Northwest.

She didn't have much time to ruminate about that and it didn't matter right now.

Her children were missing.

◇◇◇◇

August 10th-September 6th, 1862, New York City

Kathleen was a mess of apologies. In an uncharacteristic way, she also restrained herself from making excuses that would have manipulated anyone listening — at least those who did not know her well — into believing she was a blameless victim. Her right and left arms were casted and her face was deformed.

Emmy found her sitting in a wheeled-chair in the hospital's solarium that overlooked the East River. Kathleen was weeping. Emmy wasn't sure if the tears were from grief or from the irritation of two eyes horribly swollen shut and blackened.

"I tried to observe my reflection in the window before you came. I believe I am much prettier now than I was a few days ago," Kathleen tried to joke through her bleeding gums and broken jaw. Then she started to cry again.

Emmy had interviewed Grimes on her way to the hospital. She knew all of the sordid details already.

"Is there anything else you wish to tell me?" Emmy said.

"I thought I was doing the right thing."

"Oh, Kathleen. We all have a way of looking at things that way, at times, don't we?" Emmy said quietly holding down the rage she was feeling at the moment. She hadn't authorized Kathleen taking her children to New York, or Jacob to be "treated" by a quack doctor.

Emmy understood that her own decisions had precipitated serious consequences in her own lifetime, some beneficial, some not so. The challenge, in attempting, as she had disciplined herself over the years, to not be judgmental about *anyone* other than herself, was to not assume that in this case, her sister was rationalizing again.

Her older sister had always been prone to that behavior, using a very special looking glass indeed. When Emmy had been in Central America, she had heard that the ancient ones, Incas perhaps, drilled small holes in the center of their hand-held highly polished silver mirrors. She had speculated then that the old ones had done so to avoid tripping while they admired themselves as they walked. Had that also been a way of reminding themselves about the selfishness of narcissism? She wondered. Or did it help preserve their selfishness from the calamities associated with it? In any case, Kathleen had never looked ahead while looking at herself, she realized.

Emmy wondered if she, herself, might have also benefited by such a device.

"I trust that you will recover, Kathleen," with as much compassion as she could muster at the moment. "Your husband sent a message by wire that he is making his way back from New Orleans. Apparently, General Butler has been re-assigned and will govern eastern Virginia. So Jon was coming back in this direction, anyway. I expect he will be here in less than a week."

Kathleen took in a deep breath when she said that, Emmy noticed.

"Now I must find my children." She kissed Kathleen on the forehead, and turned away.

"He wasn't a bad man," Kathleen said after her. "Roland Escoffier, that is."

Her rage again seething inside, Emmy did not respond but left, wondering if Kathleen would ever be able to escape from herself.

She saw Doyle Grimes waiting for her in the foyer of the hospital talking with four hires, who, at her request, were reliable, street-wise men who knew the city well. As she walked up behind him, she overheard Grimes explain the situation to his group.

"The moxie belle upstairs took on two blinkers, a broken bone box and two snapped wings. An' she was the lucky one . . . just got a bunch of fives. The bully trap she was with got the eternity box."

The men all stood up and took off their hats when they realized she had arrived.

Grimes apologized, "Begging your pardon, Ma'am. I was just telling these men about your poor sister and Mr. Escoffier. I have a plan to find the children, if you will bear with me."

Grimes was well organized and efficient, Emmy realized. She listened to his proposed strategy to find Sarah and Jacob. They would quickly canvas the city, following the course of the Harlem-Manahattan rail, fanning out and interviewing police, welfare workers, missions and clergy within a four to six block radius of each stop. Two men would work the upper section, from Harlem moving south, two would start at 89th and move south down to 49th, and he and another man, would start at Broome Street where Kathleen had begun, and work their way to mid-town.

"Are you assigning enough men to the task, Mr. Grimes?" Emmy asked anxiously.

"These are good men, Ma'am. With many contacts. But if we don't find the kids by tomorrow, I've got others queued to go," he responded.

He went on. On every corner and on every bulletin board in every church, they would post the circulars that Emmy had commissioned which included drawings from photogravures of both children. They would talk to the newsboys who hawked the papers in which she had purchased ads, the *Daily Post, The Tribune,* and *The Police Gazette.* They would talk to the hundreds of young flower-selling girls, many of whom he added, were also selling themselves.

As she listened to the plan, Emmy was glad that she had the foresight to bring the pictures, considering how she had hurried to leave Washington, but regretted that the pictures had been taken over two years ago, when they were back in the Oregon Territory. Sarah was already becoming a young lady and her facial features were thinner now. Jacob's hair had been longer then. Both were taller now, although Jacob was short for his age.

"This is a good plan and I agree to this, Mr. Grimes. However I need to be looking as well," Emmy responded. Grimes objected, considering what had happened to Kathleen, but relented when Emmy agreed to pay for two Metropolitan police to accompany her.

The search began immediately.

On that first day, Emmy spoke with several people and quickly realized how difficult this task was going to be. As much as she had already spent to hire so many men — over two thousand dollars — the city was immense and the numbers of inhabitants seemed countless. Thousands of children roamed the streets at all hours of the day.

"Homeless. All of 'em ," Grimes noted, seeing Emmy's reaction to the many waifs who lined the sidewalks.

When she rode her carriage to the hotel in the evening, many of the same children she had seen early in the morning were still sitting in the same places.

"Spoke to a nun at the Dominican orphanage this afternoon," Grimes said, as he escorted Emmy in her carriage to her hotel late that evening. "Said she estimates the number of homeless kids is well over 20,000 now. Even more in Chicago and Philadelphia."

The war had worsened the homeless children problem, Emmy knew, because many families were shattered by the deaths and injuries to so many men who had been enlisted to fight it. Because of the Union's blockade of Confederate ports, all of the immigrants, called "Lincoln's Fodder," flooded into the northern cities. The Irish continued to arrive in droves, over a thousand a day, impoverished by the 1845 potato famine that had almost destroyed the economy of that country. The devastating effects of the blight had not truly abated since it had been declared "ended" by the British in 1849.

The Union army's enlistment process promised $300 bonuses to the new arrivals and a sure way to be fed three square meals a day by a well-provisioned army. Many men joined the Union army right off the boat, leaving their women and children behind to fend for themselves. Diseases like cholera, yellow fever and smallpox repeatedly swept through the crowded rookeries of the city.

The healthier of the children survived when their siblings and parents did not, leaving them with no means of support, food, clothing or shelter. They moved into the streets. Many then perished there. Most who survived were broken beings within a year. Some joined gangs, some became tied into the prostitution game, and only a fraction of them found relief with the help of agencies and religious institutions already overwhelmed by the influx of hundreds of thousands of immigrants.

Emmy quickly realized that the further she moved south and west in the city, the worse the living conditions were for those who inhabited it. In the "Five Points" area, close to where Kathleen had been beaten, she saw multiple windowless cellar doors beneath the stoops and under every building she passed. Grimes and the police who accompanied her said that the cellars intersected in a dangerous, impenetrable complex of passageways and coveys. Thousands and thousands of people dwelled in the cellar catacombs.

"It's an ants' nest of killers, whores and thieves, begging your pardon Ma'am," said Grimes. "No decent person goes underground. Before their time, that is."

The rookeries she visited over the next three weeks resembled what she had seen in both Boston and Washington, with multiple families packed into wooden houses built for single families, sometimes thirty people living on each dimly-lit floor of two and three story buildings, one bathroom per building. It was worse than what she had seen in the ghetto she had passed through in Panama City. Behind many of these buildings stood other makeshift structures, shacks and lean-tos, with no out-houses. Shantytowns composed of every sort of shelter, teeming with squatters who had fenced off small patches of land, spread in multiple places. Many grew potatoes, she noticed.

By contrast, the upper east side of the city from 59th Street on up to 90th was posh, with mansions and brownstones, surrounded by ornate, wrought-iron fences topped with pointed, sharpened spikes to keep out unwanted visitors. Several hotels with ornate alabaster statuary and crafted marble trim, every establishment protected by security guards and uniformed doormen, catered to the wealthy visitors. She noticed that many of the charities kept their offices there, side by side with banks and well-off churches. There, police in pairs, patrolled every avenue.

After a full week, Emmy felt she was no closer to finding Sarah or Jacob.

Emmy worked the search tirelessly, sixteen to eighteen hours a day, speaking with whomever might lend perspective or advice, learning what she could about the city's complex and overburdened infrastructure, and following each and every lead which she recorded in a ledger.

Throwing herself at this huge task kept her mind off of the realities she faced, as well as her grieving after her failure to find Rory Brett. Day by day, her hope for *his* well being diminished. At least, she told herself with little comfort, she had dozens of leads as to the whereabouts of Jacob and Sarah, with more coming in every day.

One of the first places she had visited, accompanied by Grimes and two policemen, was in the area where Kathleen and Escoffier had been assaulted, not far from the incomplete address on a cross street of Broadway she had for the man who had written to her about Scarpello's whereabouts.

Scarpello, that brave man who had saved his and her children in Panama, according to the letter, had returned to Panama to look for his wife after she disappeared in the train robbery. He had left his two children, ten-year-old Jonny and six-year-old Falco, in the protection of a cousin, a man named Carluccio. But she did not know the man's surname, and the man Grimes had assigned to the task said he could find no one in the vicinity of that address by that name. No one remembered the two boys.

Ten days into their search, with Grimes, and accompanied by two policemen wearing plain clothes, she interviewed a rough tough named Googy Cohen, who she was told, was a procurer for prostitutes, "a pimp," Grimes said. On the police's written assurance preserving his anonymity, and payment to him in advance for a quarter of the advertised $1,000 reward, Cohen gave them the address of an "establishment" where he said children were being kept, two of whom he thought exactly matched the description of Sarah and Jacob. The designated house, called *Flowers,* stood on the corner of Pearl and Chatham Streets. Cohen said he and other procurers knew the house as one of the many brothels catering to men with particular tastes.

While Emmy, with Grimes and two other police, stood outside waiting and hoping, two squads of policemen broke down the front and back doors of the house. When they emerged they led out in cuffs three scantily clad women, three partially dressed men-one of whom was a Tammany alderman from the district, and six children wrapped in blankets. Neither Sarah nor Jacob were in the mix of the frightened children, all of whom were under the age of twelve.

The police captain, a huge, big knuckled man known widely as "Clubber Williams'," said, "Ya wouldn't believe what we seen in there. What be this world comin' to?" he said, shaking his head angrily.

◇◇◇◇

Fourteen days after she started her search for her children, Emmy received two telegrams from her brother-in-law, Major Jon McEmeel, who was now in Newport, working in the advance party for General Butler who would arrive there within a few months.

The first telegram read: "Arriving Manhattan, Thursday from Newport."

The second read: "Rory Brett located."

◇◇◇◇

August 24th[th]-August 31st, 1862-New York City

Emmy was startled at his appearance. McEmeel seemed to have aged twenty years since the last time she saw him, only a few months ago. He had gained a lot of weight, was disheveled and slumped while he walked. His limp seemed more pronounced. Intermittently he winced when taking a step. His visit with Kathleen clearly had disturbed him. He seemed distracted.

"It is much more complicated than that, Emmy," McEmeel said, while he was leaving Kathleen's hospital ward. "If it *is* the same man, I am certain that in due course, his case can be examined. In due course. But at the same time, if it is your Dr. Brett," he went on, "I am afraid he has gotten himself into

320

a terrible fix. I am told he has purportedly struck out at his guards, he has been refusing to eat or exercise, and, McEmeel shook his head, "he has attempted to lodge complaints about conditions at Point Lookout-to the embarrassment and dismay of the superintendents. Not wise! To top it off, this man is accused variously of treason and desertion by none other than one of Winfield Scott's officers — for reasons that no one seems to understand, or for that matter, because he has been so disagreeable, no one cares to."

"Certainly you can intervene, Jon," Emmy said. "You have influence. You have connections. You work for Butler. Your contacts helped me cross the lines and return safely. I still have a sizable amount available from the advance on the future sale of Jacob's diamond. I can pay well."

"It's not the same, Emmy," McEmeel said. "There are no back channels here. I can't use the office of General Butler to challenge protocol in another general's courts martial, certainly not without his permission, particularly going up against Scott or Grant or Halleck, every one of whom hates our dear General. And Lincoln won't get involved or do anything to upset Grant, his 'general de jour.' He won't antagonize Butler either because he will need Massachusetts in the next election. He needs both of them."

"Can I go see Rory at least?" Emmy asked.

"The man is not allowed legal representation or visitors because of the charges that have been brought against him. Treason. You should know that."

Emmy discussed what might happen if the accusations against Brett were modified, by her explaining the circumstances of his purported desertion from Scott's service in

Panama. Perhaps she might be able to shed some light on a situation that had occurred over three years before.

McEmeel conceded that might provide some way of changing the situation.

One day later, McEmeel sent her a note informing her that the charges had been brought by a cavalry officer named Jonah Cross. Major Cross served in a Pennsylvania regiment that had fought in the recent second battle at Manassas. Another disaster for the Union. After the battle, the major's regiment had moved up to Antietam.

When the telegraph office opened the next morning, before she started investigating several more leads for the children's whereabouts, Emmy sent a telegram to the dragoon unit's regimental headquarters.

Two days later she received a telegram from the assistant surgeon assigned to the regiment. It said that on the eve of the Second Battle of Bull Run, Major Jonah Cross, Brett's accuser, had died in his sleep, "from an overwhelming suppuration of the jaw."

◇◇◇◇

September 1st to September 14thth, 1862-New York City

Emmy knew she had no choice now. She would have to appeal directly to Butler, despite the repulsiveness of having to request any favor from him.

She thought back about her last encounter with the man. It had been one year ago, on the occasion of Butler's visit to Jon McEmeel, who, with Kathleen, had also been staying with her father in Washington, D.C. Butler had offered McEmeel, recovering from his injury at the first Battle of Bull Run, a position on his staff. She, Jacob and Sarah had been returning from a walk, in which they had viewed the progress of construction on the capitol building's dome. Butler had stopped his carriage and called out to her. She remembered the conversation vividly, unfortunately.

"I was hoping I would see you here, Emmy!" Butler had called out from his carriage. "We had heard that you had finally come back from the wilds of the Pacific. Wondered whether you had changed any since you left Boston . . . thirteen years ago now isn't it?"

Jacob had run on ahead down the street, and Sarah, although intrigued with the conversation between the adults, dutifully had chased after him to retrieve him.

"You are as lovely as I remember you," Butler had said, looking at her in a way that made her uncomfortable.

Emmy remembered she had thanked him, then looked for Sarah and Jacob, hoping to bring them back to her side to protect her from what she feared Butler might say next.

"I've secured a great French cook for my guests. Great cook! I suppose, as you might surmise by how much my middle section has expanded lately," he laughed. "We would be delighted if you came to my home for dinner sometime soon," he went on.

She nodded, but didn't reply.

He paused for a moment.

"Wife's away, you know, back in Boston now. Poor dear. This miserable heat." He paused again, waiting. Finally he said in a lowered voice, "It would be quiet and discrete."

She remembered that he had watched closely for her reaction to his last comment. His head was tilted sideways, his eyelids were narrowed and his mouth was twisted into a half-smile, lips parted enough that she could see the dull yellow of his teeth.

Sarah returned with Jacob. Emmy remembered she had pulled them close to herself, without responding to Butler. She didn't know how to respond.

"Hello, Children!" he gave a quick smile at Jacob and Sarah. "Please think about it, Dear," he said, then tipped his hat and ordered the carriage to move on, his escort riding ahead and behind.

That afternoon, she received a letter in a plain envelope marked "To Mrs. Emmy Evers. Personal." It was from Major Clinton Ives, U.S. Army, Butler's personal Aide de Camp. The letter invited her to dine with the General the following week at one of his residences, this one across the river, in Alexandria.

In response, she composed a letter marked "Personal and Confidential," addressed directly to Butler, and sent it off in the morning post. It said:

> *General Butler, your invitation to join you for dinner at your residence in your wife's absence is not only inappropriate but insulting to me and disrespectful to her.*
>
> *Sincerely, Mrs. Emmy Evers.*

She had meant to say more, much more, but hoped that would be enough. He was an intelligent man.

She hadn't heard from Butler since then.

Given that history, how should she approach Butler? she wondered. The thought of dealing with him depressed her.

The next morning, she and Grimes met briefly with a woman named Frederica "Maud" Mandelbaum, known by the police as the "Queen of Fences," to determine whether the well-connected, notorious operator could provide information about Sarah and Jacob.

Mandelbaum, like all the others — officials as well as the thugs Emmy had met during her search — expected an up-front commission. As Emmy handed over two hundred dollars in gold, Mandelbaum smiled and promised she would spread the word through her extensive "network."

As Emmy watched the huge woman tuck away the pouch of gold coins into her deep cleavage, she wondered about the greed that stuck to every transaction in this city. There was a stated price and an unstated one, she now knew. The thugs asked for it outright, the officials expected it to be passed under the table. It hadn't been like that in the Pacific Northwest, she recalled.

She wondered about her own naiveté in this world and the rules of the game. It had all been so simple once upon a time. What would be next in her "education" about the way it all worked?

After the encounter with Mandelbaum, Emmy sent a letter marked "Personal and Confidential" to General Butler, who was scheduled to arrive in Washington that week. Without mentioning she had gotten the information from McEmeel, she explained that she had learned that her fiancé, Rory Brett, was apparently being kept as a prisoner at Point Look Out in Maryland. She asked if he, General

Butler, would be willing to intervene on her behalf in order to secure his release.

Four days later, she received a telegram from Lieutenant Colonel Clinton Ives, requesting that Emmy come to Washington in a week to meet with the General in his office. The meeting was schedule for a Friday at 6:00 p.m.

She spoke with Detective Grimes, who reassured her that he would conduct the search aggressively in her brief absence and notify her immediately by dispatch if anything new turned up from Mandelbaum's network.

In preparation, she read as much as she could in several newspapers about General Benjamin Butler's exploits, and searched her memory for recollections about him from her adolescent years when her father had been a law partner with him in Boston. In one of the copies of the *Olympia Intelligencer* sent to her by the brother of her deceased husband, Isaac, she found a transcript of a speech Butler had given right after the outbreak of the war. In that speech, Butler, newly appointed by Lincoln as a Major General, had implied that he *personally* would end the war.

When she returned to Washington a few days before her appointed meeting with Butler, she went to storage and read all the correspondence that had transpired between Ben Butler and her father, including some interesting notes her father had left in a personal diary. And she arranged to speak at length with Jon McEmeel who said, on the assurance of confidentiality, he would share with her several details about Butler's activities in New Orleans.

She knew that Butler, like her father Kern O'Malley, grew up in Massachusetts, in a poor family, without a father. Ambitious from the time he was a small boy, Butler's entrepreneurial activities started in Lowell, which was an always simmering pot of discontent over labor practices in the mills.

She thought it interesting that after failing in repeated attempts to win an appointment to West Point, Butler had decided to study for the ministry. A year later, he started studying law. He was good at it, apparently. By the time he took on Kern O'Malley as one of his partners, he had developed a prosperous legal business specializing in worker's compensation cases, mostly from mill workers who had claims against their employers.

Emmy heard her father mutter more than once that his senior partner had a bevy of young, penniless female plaintiff clients and wondered just how he was being compensated for his services, since no revenue was coming into the practice from those activities.

In the third year of their practice together, in 1838, when Emmy was eight years old, Butler successfully ran for office and suggested that Kern O'Malley do the same. Her father, however, was content with his practice and preferred to use much of his spare time to sail and explore the Northeast coastal regions and participate in political activities that were more liberal than those of Butler, a staunch defender of state's rights and slavery.

Emmy vaguely remembered that her father's differences with Butler's politics ultimately created enough friction that O'Malley left the arrangement. They remained cordial associates, nevertheless, for quite a while.

However, in the year before his death, Kern O'Malley distanced himself from Butler. He never explained why.

It was one entry in her father's diary, dated a few months before he died, that helped her understand the depth of his distaste for Butler, his older brother, Andrew Jackson Butler, as well as the reasons her father had become disdainful of her sister's Kathleen's husband, Jon McEmeel. Kern O'Malley had evidence that the entire Butler clan was involved in massive smuggling and profiteering activities. Jon McEmeel was caught up in it all, her father suspected.

Emmy knew that was true. It was McEmeel, after all, who had arranged for her journey into and out of Richmond to search for Brett. He also had quickly acquired a great amount of wealth in less than fourteen months of working with Butler.

◇◇◇◇

On the afternoon of September 11th, Emmy sat down for two hours with McEmeel who had just returned from an assignment in Maryland.

He looked even worse than before, she thought. His hands were shaking. He had the stubble of a poor shave on the left side of his neck and multiple razor nicks on his right face. The tone of his voice was far less firm than it had been her previous conversation with him. What was going on with him? she wondered.

McEmeel tried explaining his reasons for having joined Butler's command — his injury sustained at Bull Run would hobble him for the rest of his life, the doctors had told him. The army had no provisions for pensions for their wounded, and he knew he would be drummed out soon unless he could provide something in the service of the cause. He didn't want to be dependent on the influence or unpredictable beneficence of his father-in-law. McEmeel said he had been virtually penniless, his past work no longer available. And Butler was a rising, albeit constantly controversial bright star in a confusing constellation of political and military up-and-comers.

So, McEmeel explained, quite apologetically Emmy thought, he took the job Butler offered, immediately received another promotion and substantial increase in pay, and quickly found himself deep into the machinery of an organization as complex and opportunistic as its driven dynamo of a leader.

Butler was everywhere on stage, McEmeel said. The general spoke at rallies, carried along his own press writers who fed stories to any newspaper or periodical hungry for copy, and put himself in the center of any story he could, wherein his participation might generate opposing viewpoints. He commissioned a biographer to begin writing his story.

"Before I began working on Butler's staff," McEmeel went on, "The General was already widespread famous. He seized Baltimore, you might remember. That really pissed off Winfield Scott. Hadn't given him orders to do that! Oh you should have seen how Butler's staff bragged about that."

"Two weeks later, Butler dispatched his troops from Fort Monroe to disrupt elections and the Virginia statewide referendum on secession. No orders on that one either," McEmeel laughed, shaking his head. "Three weeks after that, he marched onto the Virginia Peninsula to take

Richmond. Told everyone he was going to end the war. Got his ass kicked."

Hearing that, Emmy remembered reading in several accounts that Butler was easily defeated by the Confederates at the battle of Big Bethel, thereby establishing within circles on both sides the perception that he was inept as a military leader.

To Butler's credit, McEmeel went on, Butler refused to return fugitive slaves into bondage, calling them "contraband of war," subject to seizure. The Congress, in its "First Confiscation Act," sustained Butler's "contraband" order. Fugitive slaves thereafter became referred to in the north by that term.

"You know the impact of all that," McEmeel said, referring to the fact that thousands of "contraband" negro souls fled to the new safety of Union lines, knowing that they would no longer have to worry about being returned to their former "owners" as had been the practice before that act.

Emmy remembered that Butler's action had surprised her when it happened because of his prior views on property rights, states' rights and slavery. She remembered hearing from her father that Butler was pro-slavery and had repeatedly supported Senator Jefferson Davis as a presidential candidate before the war. O'Malley commented that such a convenient turnabout by his former partner was entirely predictable, given his opportunistic proclivities.

"Ben Butler would sell his dear mother if it advanced his own fame and causes," her father had commented.

"But, you know," McEmeel continued, "it was after Bull Run, when I traveled with General Butler to New Orleans, that I really understood the broader implications of the term '*contraband*'," he laughed, shaking his head. "That's when everybody really began bringing in the dough."

Hearing that, Emmy recalled the newspaper article she had read in a Richmond paper, in which Butler's harsh martial law, incarceration and other actions against the women of New Orleans, had been decried in the British House of Commons. She found a cartoon of him in *Punch*, depicting him as the "Bluebeard of New Orleans," and read that a black market now existed in the town for ceramic reproductions of chamber pots with his image baked into the bottom. Neither image did his homeliness justice, she heard one wag say.

It was there, in New Orleans, McEmeel explained, Butler's brother Andrew, brought him into his own inner circle. Under the influence and authority of his brother's office, and using the Union military to conduct the process, Andrew began confiscating whatever he and his brother deemed worthy of taking from any Louisiana citizen who could be conveniently characterized as being "disloyal" to the Union. They appropriated personal effects of incarcerated southerners, shipments of miscellaneous goods, rigged seizure and auctions of hundreds of tons of cotton, now an extremely valuable commodity, which somehow conveniently ended up being re-shipped to Massachusetts mills owned by Butler, to Dover and Lowell cronies, or to British associates.

Butler's "side offices" became the trading sites of favors and influence. Understanding that the war might not go on forever, the atmosphere of activities took on a fevered pace.

"I am right in the middle of it all," McEmeel said with a half-smile that disappeared quickly.

He paused and stared off, as if thinking of something painful. He glanced at Emmy, watching for her reactions.

"It's pretty clever, you know," he said. "And Lincoln sent us there."

Emmy heard pride tinged with guilt in his voice when McEmeel said that. She remembered hearing rumors that Lincoln *had* to get Butler out of the eastern command, but couldn't fire him.

Her father had been right, Emmy realized. Without having to ask, she understood that her brother-in-law had benefitted mightily from his position. From what she could tell, he recorded transactions, facilitated trading and smuggling operations along the coast and into the North and South's river waterways.

"I hope, Emmy," McEmeel said, "that this bit of elaboration on what we do within our office, will help you understand the best way to approach the General. He is a *very* intelligent man. He may not be a good field general, but he takes care of his friends. Everything is business and he always personally benefits in every exchange. Consider approaching it that way."

Emmy had listened carefully to her brother-in-law's story. He was swept up into it all, she realized.

"Jon, I love you because you are my sister's husband, and because I knew you when you were younger, before all of this befell . . . all of us. I know that you are a better man than this." She paused before saying more, then, "I understand the reasons — for your rationalizations about your association with this — enterprise. But that's what they all are, Jon."

She saw McEmeel's face when she used the word "rationalizations." It fell, she thought.

She stood, paused for a few moments before leaving, and looked at him squarely. There was something else she detected in the way he had talked about New Orleans. Something in his tone and the pauses in his delivery. Was it embarrassment? Or was it remorse?

"Thank you for helping me with this important task in my life. It is very important to me."

She left the hospital and made her way back to her hotel. She would need to rest, somehow, before traveling to Washington to face Butler.

◇◇◇◇

September 14th, 1862-Washington, District of Columbia

When Emmy arrived at the outside door of Butler's office, off Pennsylvania Avenue, she stopped and looked for a few moments at the Capitol Dome revision that had been under construction for several years. The twenty-foot tall Statue of Freedom, recently completed, sat in a large crate near the cranes that would hoist it up the scaffolding to the top when the dome was completed. She wondered what would happen to the statue if the rebels ever succeeded in entering the city. She had heard that invading armies always despoiled monuments of defeated countries. What would happen to the Statue of Freedom's nose and breasts?

She took a deep breath, then pulled on the bell for the door of the locked building. This would not be pleasant. She hoped she could control it, however.

A guard let her into the building and escorted her down a deserted hallway to Butler's office, where she was admitted by Major Clinton Ives.

The interior of the office, including the anteroom, was unlike other offices she had seen in Washington when she had visited with her father. Ornate ivory carvings from six-foot long elephant tusks, bronze and gold statues, and expensive memorabilia covered the desk. Huge European oil paintings hung on the walls. Thick oriental carpets sprawled over the expensive marble floors.

Ives knocked on Butler's door, opened it, and, after admitting Emmy, asked Butler if he might need anything else before he left for the day.

Butler waved him off.

Ives saluted and closed the door behind him, leaving Emmy, files in hand, standing in front of Butler's desk.

The general, writing a letter with a gold quill pen, didn't look up as Ives departed.

Emmy studied him for a moment. He had gained a lot of weight since the last time she saw him a year before, which made his weak chin almost disappear into the folds of his neck. He still wore a droopy mustache that someone had said, with his sloped forehead and bald pate, made him look like a tuskless walrus.

After what seemed like a minute, Butler signed the letter with a flourish, stood up, walked around his huge desk, and looked over Emmy. His mouth was turned into a half smile.

"Sit down, my Dear," he said, indicating the plush bro-caded divan in the corner of the room.

He saw Emmy looking at the walls, desk and credenza, covered with beautiful, precious hammered silver and gold goblets and a bejeweled ivory chalice wrapped in gold.

"A few mementos . . . gifts from some Southern admir-ers," he said. "May I?" Without waiting for her reply, he placed himself opposite her on the other end of the short couch.

Emmy watched his eyes as he did so. Butler, mocked in caricatures for his congenitally droopy eyelids that made him always appear half awake, stared at Emmy's hands as he sat down. His small feet barely touched the ground as he positioned himself on the divan, his small shoulders and large head turned, directly facing Emmy. He tilted his head, again in the same manner, Emmy recalled, as he had done when he had propositioned her one year ago. His teeth seemed brighter now, however. She wondered if they had been professionally bleached and polished since then.

"Emmy, we were surprised to hear from you."

"I debated . . . whether to bother you, General."

Butler tilted his head to the other side, looking at her hands, and then down at her knees, then at her neck. He flicked his tongue against the corner of his mouth, then glanced up at her face and eyes.

"We heard about the trouble up in New York. Your sister and the children and all. Bit of a problem with the Frenchy getting himself killed. Major McEmeel hasn't said much about it. Is your sister doing better?"

Emmy nodded and thanked him for his concern.

"Could you explain a bit more what it is you think you might need from me?" he said.

She paused for a moment. As well connected as he was, she knew that Butler would already have looked into the situation. She knew this was his negotiating ploy, to determine her sense of urgency and distress. She decided to explain Brett's dilemma but avoid being direct with Butler straight out, to see how he might play with her in the exchange, and to position herself in a way that would either divert him towards an easily granted favor, or if that didn't work, force him to be overt in whatever she feared he believed would be a fair exchange.

"General, I mentioned in my letter that my . . . fiancé, Dr. Rory Brett, previously an assistant surgeon in General Scott's entourage, has been incarcerated at a prison in Maryland. Point Lookout. I understand that he has been charged with treason and desertion. I believe these charges are unfair and unfounded," she said, speaking slowly and carefully. "Unfortunately, because the writ of Habeus Corpus has been suspended by Mr. Lincoln, and also because of the nature of the charges, Rory...Dr. Brett... has not been allowed visitors or legal counsel. No one seems to be paying attention to the matter. I am also told that the conditions at Point Lookout are deplorable."

Butler continued looking at her neck as she spoke, darting his eyes occasionally up to her ears and hair. He did not look at her eyes.

"And . . . ?" he said.

Emmy was caught surprised by this response, which told her he intended to make her elaborate. If his generosity wasn't immediately forthcoming, he likely would make her beg, she realized. From what she could tell, he likely had no sense of loyalty to her father, his former business partner. She had no political contacts from her father's district that Butler would need in the future.

She decided to be direct in her request, get affirmation or refusal from him, and also perhaps, if there was more to this, flush out his intentions. She continued.

"I need you to intervene, Sir . . . to allow Dr. Brett to be represented, and to be certain he can have visitors, and can be evaluated for his well being."

"That's all?" he asked.

Emmy nodded.

Butler lifted his chin, glancing at her eyes again as he did so.

"I'm afraid that may be beyond my reach," he said.

"You are the most influential man in Washington, General."

He smirked at the compliment.

"I am not inclined to intervene, my Dear."

"All right . . . " she took a deep breath, "I beg of you, General."

Butler reached over and patted Emmy's knee, lingering there just a bit, then stood up abruptly, walked to his desk and turned his back to Emmy while he fished through some papers on his desk.

"This is very important to you. Isn't it?"

"Yes, of course it is," she responded.

"You realize, I am certain, that an intervention by my office in a general courts martial of another command would be inappropriate," he said, looking at her over his shoulder.

Emmy nodded. "Yes. I understand that."

"I suppose I *could* ask to look into the affairs and conditions at Point Lookout, to get at your beaux in that way, perhaps 'stumble', as it were, into enough information that I might confront the commander there to open up this case. A fishing expedition, as it were. With only one fish to catch," he laughed.

Emmy brightened. He was being reasonable.

"I would be so *very* grateful, General."

"Of course you would be, my Dear." Butler turned back to Emmy.

He had unbuttoned his trousers and had exposed himself. Semi-erect, he was fondling himself.

Looking directly into her eyes now, watching for her reaction, his half smile, half smirk had returned.

Emmy, stunned and nauseated by something she hadn't expected, turned her eyes away from Butler. Avoiding his eyes, she stood up and, as she turned to walk out of the office, overcoming the full flush she felt as well as the anger that urged her to slap him, she controlled the pace of her words to him. Raising her chin, she looked him squarely in the eyes.

"You, Sir, with the personal, self-made...king's mantle you seem to have claimed for yourself, hiding behind your feigned concern for the common people, are an embarrassment. I believe you are confirmation of the worst fears decent women and honorable men alike have about people who have taken power. Good evening."

She closed the door without slamming it as she left.

"It's just protocol, my Dear," she heard him say, laughing after her.

338

Rather than hiring a carriage, she walked the ten blocks to her hotel.

"Damn that little bastard!" she heard herself swear. By the time she reached the hotel, her anger had halved. She was getting back in control of herself.

In the Washington Hotel that evening, after calming herself more, Emmy wrote three letters, one to McEmeel, another one to General Scott, and the third, another appeal to the President, Abraham Lincoln. Her anger still boiled up and worsened the clumsiness in her right hand as she wrote, but her words were precise.

She said nothing in her letter to either Scott or Lincoln about her meeting with Butler, but recounted again, as she had in previous letters to them, the details of Rory Brett's resignation from the military, and his medical work aiding the wounded on both sides after the battle of Gaines' Mill.

Emmy's previous letters appealing to Scott and Lincoln had not been answered, but she would try again and again, if necessary. Because of what she perceived was Lincoln's kind nature, he might be approachable, she hoped, despite her late father's often strong, strident opposition to his presidency and the methods of his war efforts. She heard Lincoln was not traveling as she had been told the previous time she had brought her petition to the executive mansion.

If Lincoln was avoiding her or was obliged to do so, as she feared he might because of the rancor her father had created with the Republicans while he was alive, she would stand outside Lincoln's privy door night and day and wait the poor, noble man out if necessary. She would not give up.

In her telegram to McEmeel who had returned to Manhattan, she simply said that she would not elaborate on the meeting with Butler other than that his behavior had greatly embarrassed her and she would have nothing more to do with him. She would continue as best she could under the circumstances, she said, and again thanked him for whatever help he might continue to provide.

The next day, she again stood in line at the White House, hoping to find Lincoln. But after waiting for four hours she was told he was away, traveling.

Frustrated, the next morning she left to get back to New York to resume her search for her children.

◇◇◇◇

On September 17th, when she arrived back in Manhattan, waiting for her at the Astor Hotel was a telegram from James London, one of her late father's congressional colleagues. London was a "Copperhead Democrat" from Ohio with whom her father had sometimes forged voting alliances. In every circumstance, their collaboration had been critical of the way Lincoln and the Republicans had conducted the war.

London wrote that she was to return to Washington, D.C. the week of September 24th.

Because Lincoln needed broad-based support to overcome the outcry against his recent proclamation of Emancipation for the negroes, London believed this would be a good time for her to again try to present her petition about Brett to the President.

She was relieved. Lincoln would understand. She knew it in her heart.

CHAPTER THIRTY

⟨⟨⟨⟩⟩

McEmeel

September 19th, 1862-New York City

McEmeel was sweating again and wondered if the rain would cause steam to rise as the drops pattered his forehead. The up and down nausea and burning pangs in his belly that started up five days before this awful day had now worsened.

It was time to come home. Too much had happened in this dark week. Kathleen, still in the hospital, had refused to see him. Because her arms were still casted, she had dictated to him a brief note instead. She said she wasn't certain she could, or ever *would*, return to their marriage.

That had stunned him because he had always assumed that they would be together, irrespective of their personal actions and the estrangement that had increased during his absence. There had always been time, he thought, to get back to whatever was left that had held them together.

He declined to take a carriage and, with her note crumpled in his hand, he walked back to the apartment he had rented. He had forgotten his cane. It didn't matter. He needed to grind, bone-on-bone, as it were, step-by-step, on everything that had befallen him.

He was broken now, he knew. Was it from his dependence on Laudanum, worsened over the past four months, despite repeated, failed attempts to withdraw from it? It had been almost a week since his last dose but he didn't know if he could hold out any longer.

Was it guilt from all the privilege, unearned, he now believed, that he had been given in return for the image of respectability his medals gave to him and to the schemes in which he was involved?

Was it from his obvious complicity in the cleverness of the Butler entourage's New Orleans' swindles in which he had willingly participated?

Was it the remorse he felt over the self-promotion he had practiced?

Was it the women and what he knew most people would consider debauchery?

Or was it *all* of that, and his irresponsibility in everything in which he had conducted himself over the past several years?

Which of his sins, venial and mortal, most of which he had yet to confess, were bringing him to this dark place now, from which he felt he could not escape, irrespective of the brilliance of his rationalizations?

Was the withdrawal from the morphine contributing to his depression?

Much of the self-loathing he felt was externally driven, he understood, fostered by the chastisements he had endured in the confessional and by discussions with some of the few people he truly admired, like his sister-in-law, Emmy. She, unlike others he had met along the way during this war, had a calm, nonjudgmental directness about herself, and went about her life without a need for advantage, or so it seemed. So many others he knew were profiteering mightily by the national conflagration, like firemen who pilfered while they should have been simply dousing the flames. Emmy, he observed, simply took the onslaught of misfortune head on, never wavering.

But it was seeing his wife, Kathleen, beaten and shaken, that precipitated his gravest self-doubt, he knew. She would never be the same after that disabling experience. How much of her greed and how many of her shortsighted impulsive actions had been prompted and reinforced by his own selfish behaviors?

Did that mean he really loved her, after all?

He didn't know.

But now that was over, too.

The remorse and depression he felt had crept up on him slowly over the months, cooking him in the stew he had concocted, until the flesh fell off his bones and soul, its sour juice spilling over his sense of self-worth, sputtering into the fire beneath.

It had really started on one horrible night in New Orleans, during another screaming, drunken all night orgy at one of Andrew Butler's residences in the French Quarter, when McEmeel found himself wandering naked outside in the darkness. A red silk scarf was tied around his cock. As the Creole thumping beat faded behind him, he stepped away from himself for a moment, and catching his reflection in a darkened store-front window, marveled at the staggering bloat he saw. That wasn't him, was it? Was he now the devil? Couldn't be, he remembered thinking. The devil was a handsome thing, wasn't he? That's what he had been promised, after all, he thought.

He turned around, trying to change his perspective to something less disagreeable, and when he looked down the empty dark street back towards the music, his vision seemed to bisect. In his blurry right eye he saw the door leading back to the oily warmth and noise he had just left, the comfort of it all, pulling at him, from his shoulders all the way down into his groin. He had gone back there so many times. He knew the sirens and the snakes. Some even had names.

"Come on back in, Sweetie!" he heard them taunting from up the stairs. "We'll get it right for you."

In his left eye he saw his own white spindly legs struggling to hold up the snarling bedlam of it all, the shaking, larded, white-rice and garbage-eating traveler who had settled in a foreign land — a seductive place where he felt superior, but didn't really know the language or understand its currency, and had spent everything he had while lurching about its uneven soil. He had killed and then pissed on everything dear to him within reach while there. As disgusting as it was, who and what he saw in his left eye that night was clear enough.

He woke up the next morning from a painful, erotic dream that had gone on and on. He had been chasing a slithering big-bottomed mulatto woman, but just couldn't catch her. Lying next to the bed in his own apartment, he was uncovered, still naked and aching from a piss hard-on. The scarf was gone. He tried to get up, but felt like he was nailed to the floor. It took him hours to get himself back together to go to his work. Pulling his boots on, he looked up from the bed to the mirror on his bureau. The bloat, now in uniform, stared back at him.

Jon McEmeel sighed. He knew it was time to go home. Wherever that was.

When he finally arrived in his office that afternoon, in his locked desk drawer, he found an envelope containing $10,000 — his bimonthly cash share of auction spoils from the "contraband" he had helped confiscate from Southern citizens he had deemed to be disloyal to the Union. He didn't count the money as he had in the past. It would all be there, he knew. This time, instead of the rush — he felt a dull ache from his stomach down to his groin. And the red scarf was tied around the envelope.

A few months later, when he heard that Emmy had decided to directly appeal to Benjamin Butler, he knew he had to make a huge choice. Helping Emmy over the objections, or the orders of Butler or his minions certainly would ruin his own career. Going in the other direction, however — holding the line against Emmy's request or abetting Butler's predictable self-serving actions in response to the favors Emmy sought — would forever ruin his soul.

A week later, on a day when the heat in Manhattan had reached almost 100 degrees, he talked to a few friends about it, but they had offered no suggestions. None of them understood the crossroad he believed he had reached. That night, he took a few short drinks and snorted just a pinch of opium mixed with snuff. The swirling muddle immediately started again, and when he awoke in the early hours of the next morning, he remembered the bisection of his vision from that night in the French Quarter.

Then, later that week, after Emmy returned to Manhattan and confided in him about what had just transpired with Butler, he had his answer.

And he made his decision and knew what to do.

While in New Orleans in the Union general's entourage, he had been given an important responsibility by Benjamin Butler's brother, Andrew. Starting shortly after his arrival there, he, McEmeel became the recorder of all the business accounts that transpired in Butler's "side" office.

Over the past six months, in addition to his other responsibilities, McEmeel kept a ledger of account, the "Special Permit Memorandum Book" as mandated by military regulation. The transactions were worth millions. McEmeel knew he had directly benefitted the General and his brother. When Andrew Butler learned that his brother's command would be transferred to Norfolk, Virginia in a few months, with the ledger of account legally to be handed over to whomever replaced the General, Andrew Butler took the ledger and told McEmeel to begin a new one, with entries post-dated to the time they began governing New Orleans. In the new record, he ordered McEmeel to omit a significant number of transactions.

But McEmeel, anticipating that something like this might happen, had already made a duplicate copy of the

Special Permit book, sequestering it in his own apartment. The duplicate records could protect him from being framed or blackmailed. As far as he knew, no one had seen him with the duplicate ledger.

He knew if he turned his copy over to the Provost Marshall's office, he would certainly go to prison. But so would the General, his brother, and most of his staff.

With that copy, he knew how to help Emmy now. He would persuade Butler to intervene, and turn the bastard over at the same time. Maybe he would re-find his soul in doing so, he told himself.

He had his answer.

◇◇◇◇

When he returned to his quarters he found a telegram, sent by the only good friend he had in New Orleans and the only associate he trusted. The telegram said that his apartment in New Orleans had been broken into two nights before.

Ransacked. Turned upside down.

No person or persons knew about the ledger duplicate he kept, did they?

Because his friend didn't know of his activities in Butler's employ or know about the ledger, he couldn't risk asking him to look for it.

McEmeel didn't know if the duplicate ledger he secretly kept had been stolen. He wouldn't, until he returned to New Orleans in three weeks.

But there was no time for that. He knew he needed to get to the Provost General's office immediately. They would have to believe him.

As he left his quarters, he did not see the waiting, watching men — one on the right, two on the left — leaning against the columns of his hotel's portal.

CHAPTER THIRTY-ONE

◇◇◇◇◇

Brett

September 21st and 22nd, 1862-Point Lookout
Prison, Maryland

It was scurvy. Several of the other prisoners had it too. He knew the signs and symptoms well, the bruising and generalized rash, the muscle aching and lethargy, his bleeding gums. One of his canines had loosened a week ago and when he bit into a piece of stale bread, the tooth fell out. He accidentally swallowed it with the bread. The cavity left behind bled continuously, leaving a salty taste in his mouth. Now several other teeth were loose.

He again tried to appeal to the commandant through a plea reluctantly conveyed by one of the guards. This time he asked for limes for the other prisoners and now for himself. But he received no response.

It hurt too much and the cold fall days amplified his misery, so he had refused to exercise for over three weeks now. His captors didn't want to fight him, so they left him to himself. Then he had stopped eating for four days. Unlike when he tried fasting as protest, now he just had no appetite, and was afraid to lose any more teeth. Feeling his ribs, he recited to himself his skeletal anatomy again. He remembered he was a physician. It was a strange way to refresh his memory.

That morning the key keeper rattled the bars on all of the cages in the basement.

"Y'll be up today 'n outside if were havin' to drag yer sorry asses out. New commandant. He don't wanna come down inter this stinkin' hole and hef to smell yer stinkin' mess."

A few hours later, Brett and the other prisoners were dragged from the cellar. In the full light of an overcast day and in front of the other prisoners, his pants started to fall down over his hips to his mid thigh and he had to hold the waistband to keep them up. He had lost much more weight.

He forced himself to walk in the circle and lagged as the healthier prisoners lapped him. He didn't care. When he saw the new commander, he would figure a way to appeal to him-make some demonstration. Perhaps this one would attend to his duties, unlike the man who was being replaced in command of Point Look Out.

Fifteen minutes later, he heard brass and drums announcing what he thought was the new commander's arrival, but when Brett came around and was able to look through the gate onto the parade grounds outside the courtyard, he saw that the change of leadership ceremony already had occurred. The officers were retiring from the area.

Brett pulled himself out of line and walked in the direction of the gate, intending to call out to the departing company. The same private and corporal who had beaten him a month ago moved in his direction. Brett, seeing their approach, reached down and picked up a stone the size of his fist. It took all of his strength to throw it at them. The private ducked and the rock hit the corporal squarely in the forehead, knocking off his kepi, drawing a gush of blood. The other guard who had ducked turned on Brett and walked towards him. Brett bent down and picked up a stick and another stone, threatening the approaching guard.

"Go ahead and shoot me, you foul bastard son-of-a-bitch," he heard himself say, as he raised his stick.

The soldier raised his rifle and shot him.

Brett went down, holding his left thigh. Because they were fussing about the corporal's injury, it took almost a minute in the commotion that ensued for anyone to come to him as he lay there. As he looked up at the rolling clouds opening briefly and showing some blue, he knew his femur had been broken by the bullet. By the degree of swelling, he knew it had lacerated his femoral artery, as well.

He had a choice, he knew. He could ask the soldiers who finally came over to him to apply a tourniquet above the wound, possibly saving his life, at least long enough allow an amputation, and then wait to see if gangrene would later develop.

Or he could say nothing and simply ease out of this life.

With Emmy on his mind, he kept his thoughts to himself.

CHAPTER THIRTY-TWO

⬦⬦⬦⬦

Robby and Sarah

July 31ˢᵗ to September 26ᵗʰ, 1862

For fifty days, thirteen-year-old Robby Hoyt had his own gang.

Unlike those New York hard-lots who banded together at ground level, their crews and tribes developed from family relationships, neighborhood boundaries, shared ethnicities and religious beliefs, his gang was built around the need of his followers for safe movement — almost all of it which he provided in a generous, unrestricted, unbridled and secret way — underground far below a city bustling with many wonders.

Sarah and Jacob Evers were his first recruits. Both of them quickly became swept up in the adventure of it all.

"You pups look hungry," he told them shortly after he brought them down into his world.

As he opened a cupboard in a cache behind one of the many doors they went through that day, he saw that he was right. They ate every morsel of cheese, fruit and bread he put in front of them.

After feeding them, he took them down along another long, winding passageway, intermittently surfacing in the evening of that humid, hot summer day and then down again to a dry, warm, clean cubby hole with cots and straw bedding, located beneath the home on 17th Street where his aunt had previously kept a root cellar.

Jacob fell asleep immediately. Robby could tell that Sarah was exhausted too.

"Sleep, Miss Pup," he commanded.

"Is it safe down here?" Sarah responded.

"Safer than up above, unless you've got a better place to go," Robby mocked.

Sarah leaned back on the cot, warily watching him.

"We've got to find the Scarpellos and get a message to someone — to see if my mother has returned yet to Washington."

"We can do that when it is safe," Robby said, tossing her a wool blanket. He covered Jacob with another.

"Use this for a pillow," he said, handing Sarah a five-pound sack of beans. "Best I got."

When she didn't respond, he walked over to a locker and opened the latch.

"Got these from my aunt's house," he said, throwing several pieces of clothing over to Sarah. "Might fit ya. Might not. If they don't, I know where to get some other duds."

"Not a 'pup,' Mister. I'm older than you, most likely," Sarah said finally, trying to keep her eyes open.

Then she nodded off, too.

In the cool quiet of the root cellar, both she and Jacob slept until Robby woke them twelve hours later.

While his guests had slept that evening, and then for the next few days, he studied them.

The boy, Jacob, was small-boned and shorter than his stated age of nine. His demeanor, initially hesitant and somewhat shy, changed when he had slept for a few nights, however. Following Robby around the corridors, up into the streets and then back into passageways seemed to invigorate Jacob, and after three days of exploration, Robby noted that he started demonstrating an energetic inquisitiveness. It was because he felt safe, Robby realized.

The girl, Sarah, looked younger than she claimed to be, his own age of thirteen, but there was something about her that made him think she was, as she insisted, much older than him in some ways.

Why was that? he wondered. No girl, a pretty, fancy-dressed filly like this one especially, could be more experienced than a kid like him. Could she?

One week into it, when she opened up a bit and told him the story of her dramatic experiences in the Pacific Northwest, then again in Panama, he had a better understanding of this sturdy, attractive girl.

He had always been aware of girls. Tolerated them. But *she* intrigued and fascinated him in a way he had never known before with anyone else. Girl or boy. Ever. Sarah was different. That delighted him.

He found himself watching for her reactions constantly. He started showing off for her.

When he caught himself doing that, he told himself that he couldn't afford to do that. And she really was beyond his reach, anyway. She was a rich dame, or would be someday, he assumed. She ignored him. *He* was just a ferrel boy — one who had done quite well for himself, by himself, without anybody else's help, but far below her in station.

So he kept his attention on the things that he felt mattered the most right now. Surviving. He *couldn't* afford to be distracted, he told himself. And now he had taken on a responsibilty, because he had *disciples* for the first time in his life, following him and seeing the world as he did, reminding him a bit of how he had followed his own father. He was Jacob's guardian, after all. He was *her* guardian, too, even if she thought she could take care of herself.

So he kept to himself, except when he was showing them around. Teaching them the ropes and the tunnels. Teaching them how to survive in a tough world.

As if affirming his assumptions about how she might feel about him, he noted that Sarah resisted swinging fully into trusting him the way Jacob did. She kept to herself, as well.

Perhaps that was the reason, he told himself, that he made every effort to convince her that neither the police nor the churches would be of help in her efforts to get into contact with her relatives. To protect her and make certain she understood that.

She didn't like him, Robby was certain. *That* was the big challenge.

He needed time with her before she was taken away.

◇◇◇◇

Within a week of guiding them as tourists to the marvels of an unmapped metropolis, he acquired two more followers — the brothers who Sarah and Jacob had been searching for — ten-year-old Jonny Scarpello and his precocious six-and-a-half-year-old brother, Falco.

Finding the Scarpello boys had been easy for Robby. He knew the streets much better than did the men Detective Grimes had hired and who also had tried finding the Scarpello children as a way of possibly locating Sarah and Jacob.

"You must mean *West* Broadway," Robby said, when Sarah insisted that the boys lived somewhere near the corner of Moore and Broadway Avenue. "Moore don't cross the big Broadway."

"I don't remember anything about 'West' Broadway," Sarah protested. "I have a very good memory."

"Sure. But you're wrong, anyway," Robby teased her.

Robby also knew the right people to ask. In this case it was the newsboys who, like him, sold papers on the corners of the busiest avenues.

After a few hours of searching in the right neighborhoods, they learned that Jonny and Falco had been placed in a Sisters of Charity orphanage immediately after the cousin in whose care they had been left died during a typhus outbreak.

"Dey's half-orphans," a newsboy told them, meaning that Jonny and Falco had been given the mixed privilege of working during the day and getting one meal and a bed in the orphanage at night.

They found both of the boys working for a cobbler in a shoe repair shop on Mulberry.

Persuading them to leave their job and the orphanage wasn't difficult at all for Robby. Although he doubted that either of the boys had been abused in the Catholic asylum, he knew that they, as "half-orphans" had been obligated to hand over all of their earnings to the sisters in return for their upkeep. In addition, by looking at their hands, callused and stained from the hard work of bending and dying leather sixteen hours a day, both boys likely were exhausted.

They also were desperate.

"We stopped getting letters from Papa a few months after he left to find our Mama in Panama," Falco said.

"Both 'r dead, I bet," Jonny said grimly.

From what Sarah and Jacob had told him about their own ordeal in the hazardous Panama jungle, Robby understood that Jonny likely was correct. The brothers had no real hope. Like him and so many other children living on the streets of New York, the two boys were orphans of the storm.

"Well, we're *all* on our own, Pups," Robby said. "But it ain't so bad once you've figured it all out. Like me."

He promised them an alternative.

"I can teach ya the ropes, Pups," he said. "An' we can make some dough, have lots of fun, and grand — really grand — adventures," he added, glancing at Sarah for her reaction to what he expected she thought was a boast.

But it wasn't a boast. No one else in all of Manhattan could have fulfilled a promise like that in the ways Robby Hoyt was able. He knew the city in a way others did not.

His approach to survival had always been methodical and well planned, and he began teaching the other children to do as he did.

"First," he said, "there are the entrances and the exits." He explained that when traveling back from the "upper world," as he referred to the street level thoroughfares, he always checked to be certain he was not being observed. He used one of four separate, hidden entryways into the labyrinths below. From the entryway he selected, he then traversed a variety of passageways, intersecting with layer upon layer of narrow tunnels, all carved out over the years by the city for, gas, sewage and fresh water pipes.

He showed them a ring of keys and explained that, with self-taught locksmithing skills, he also had manufactured keys to numerous subterranean doors, some leading into storage vaults and church catacombs, others leading into private passageways such as the oak wood-lined cattle tunnels that several slaughter houses had cut underground to bring their New Jersey-bred cattle directly from the east-side Hudson docks to their butcheries.

In the catacombs he had found a way to discretely relieve corpses of gold rings and jewelry.

The big pistol that he sported had been holstered to the remains of a former police captain.

Because Robby was careful to avoid leaving any trace of these visits, and also because he stole only when necessary, he had been able to secure a modest, steady income, with miscellaneous booty exchanged for enough coin to feed himself with purchased, rather than pilfered, food and supplies.

He sternly commanded them to avoid stealing in the open, up on the streets, knowing all too well that doing so would eventually lead to a "pinch," by the likes of Mulally, the corrupt cop. A pinch would likely lead to an involuntary commitment, placement in another orphanage, or worse — "deportation" on one of the trains that shipped homeless children to farm communities throughout the northern states.

"Heard stories about them trains — they call 'em 'orphanages on wheels' — and where they send the kids to," he said. "It's like the end of the earth where ya fall off the edge," he said.

But the addition of four new mouths to feed required a reconsideration of his survival strategy that had worked so well for him over four years.

A week after he found Jonny and Falco Scarpello for Sarah and Jacob, he brought his little crew to one of his finds — an unused kitchen beneath a rectory that was being renovated on Greenwich. There, he prepared for them a large meal with figs, salami, fresh bread and pickles, jam and apples from supplies he had purchased earlier in the day.

"The last of great meals, this'll be," he said quietly when they finished, "unless we figure a way to resupply ourselves. I got ideas. Any you got suggestions?"

He waited for a response.

"I won't steal," Sarah said firmly. Jacob hesitated, then nodded in agreement.

"An' where do you think the dough comes from that feeds us? Robby asked.

"I aint 'fraid o' gettin' stuff" Jonny Scarpello said. "They don't miss it. Goes to waste otherwise. Us against them. An' its fun," he laughed.

His brother, Falco was silent and seemed embarrassed when Jonny said that, Robby noted.

"Well, Pups, we better get this little disagreement fixed," Robby said, looking back and forth between Jonny Scarpello and Sarah. "Otherwise — we're in for a short, hungry ride together."

Sarah shook her head. He could tell she wouldn't give.

With that discussion, still divided on whether to embark on more perilous adventures that involved a more significant amount of theft, they began their brief run as a clever, fast little pack. Robby acted as the mentor and mastermind. Jonny, and then Jacob took on the band's greater risks. Falco stood watch and learned during their escapades.

And Sarah, as best she could — given the reality of their situation — provided the conscience for their little gang of five.

◇◇◇◇◇

The survival tactics they initiated that night, far underground and in the coolest place of a city beset by a scorching mid-August draught, ultimately led to how the four boys finally got caught. The riskiness of their adventures thrilled them. They began to take greater challenges.

Three and a half weeks later, Robby convinced them that they should break in and attempt a modest, but possibly profitable heist at the fabulous P.T. Barnum American Museum located on Broadway and Anne Street.

"We get in quick, make our catch, and get out. They'll never know we were there. If we do it smart, we can make this a regular deal," he told them.

The first visit worked perfectly, and as he had planned. At two a.m. they entered through a vent grating into the huge museum's basement and moved directly up to the zoo exhibits located on the third floor. Robby picked the lock to the aviary and instructed the boys to pick up and pluck feathers from several of the exotic birds in four of the cages. They left within thirty minutes. The next day, Robby sold the colorful array of feathers for ten dollars to a hat designer catering to socialites on the Upper East Side of Manhattan.

Two days later, he treated Sarah and the boys to a visit to the museum during its regular hours. Jostling with the throngs of other paying customers, they spent hours on each floor, examining the oddities and exhibits.

Falco was fascinated by the two Beluga whales in the huge fish tank on the fourth floor. Jonny and Jacob pushed themselves to the front row during the presentation of the bearded lady and the Ape Man. Sarah wanted to see the small wonder, General Tom Thumb, but the line was too long.

Two weeks later, they entered the museum, again at 2 a.m., again with the straightforward intention of collecting the valuable feathers, as well as a few other items that Robby thought would not be missed, like the long feather boa worn by the Bearded Lady.

On this caper, however, Falco slipped away, forgetting his assignment to act as lookout.

The two security guards found Falco on the fifth floor aquarium where he had returned. He was sitting, staring wide-eyed at the two Beluga whales in the giant seawater tank. They picked up Jonny and Jacob in the menagerie, then Robby, but not before he had hidden Sarah.

"Wait for us at whichever hideout you can get to!" he said, as he pushed her into an open closet door. "Wait for me."

Afterwards, Sarah made her way back to the gang's hideout in a never-used boiler room built for an unfinished hotel on 36th Street. She waited for them for two days.

But they didn't come.

She then surfaced above ground briefly and made her way to another secret entrance leading to a cattle tunnel to the abandoned tanning factory where Robby had first taken her and Jacob several weeks previously. They weren't there either.

It was there, while foraging for food, that Sarah found sequestered in Robby's locker, a tall pile of torn reward posters with her and Jacob's pictures on them.

And on that same day, on September 26th, 1862, four days after they were caught in the Fabulous Barnum American Museum, Robby, Jacob, Jonny and Falco were placed on one of the west-bound "orphan trains" and shipped out of New York City with 112 other street children.

CHAPTER THIRTY-THREE

✧✧✧

Emmy

September 24th, 1862-Point Lookout Union Prison, Maryland

They had already buried Rory by the time she arrived. "The remains of the prisoner you seek are buried in Field number 6, the largest plot. Outbreak of cholera over the past four months. Afraid you'll have to do a bit of searching. Markers adorning it aren't placed in any particular order," the chaplain explained.

Field 6 was a plain, sopping tract, ankle-deep muddy, marked with several rows of unevenly placed, unpainted wooden sticks, each four inches wide and eighteen inches tall. The markers carried no names, but rather, penciled in faintly, numbers of the men who had died in the prison. Many of the markers had fallen over into their muddy berth.

After searching for over an hour, Emmy found the number, 790170, she had been given for Rory. On the same stick was another number — 790270.

What did that mean?

Couldn't they even get that right? Emmy said to herself.

She knelt down in the mud and held the marker.

Was that all she had of him?

She let herself go, weeping angrily because she realized that *was* all she had of him. She had no picture of him, no way of touching his cold body, no way of making even a simple feeble helpless gesture in front of his corpse — that she had been there. That she had loved him. Even if not enough.

Her request to the commandant to have Rory's body exhumed and moved to Boston was refused because of his "status."

As she was leaving the prison grounds, the chaplain handed her a large envelope. Inside were the letters she had sent to Point Lookout after she had learned Brett was being kept there. They were unopened. They had never been given to him.

There would be no closure for her.

CHAPTER THIRTY-FOUR

◇◇◇◇

Sarah

October 21st 1862-New York City Train Station

In a letter responding to a complaint from her mother asking the New York Medical Society to investigate the asylum, Mr. Tinder, writing on behalf of the Asylum, tried explaining that the "restraint crib" in which her brother had been locked before she found and extricated him were originally developed by reputable and esteemed German physician-experts. They had proven beneficial, if not curative, for patients with "conditions like Jacob's," Tinder had said. That was an odd theory, Sarah thought. The practice seemed more like a punishment of sorts for disturbed people who irritated their caretakers.

She turned her thoughts to her mother.

Sarah watched her staring out of the train window. Emmy had been very quiet this morning. That was so unlike her, Sarah realized.

In the past, Emmy would have organized everything, checked and rechecked her lists, hurried along Jacob, the predictably persistent dawdler.

As Sarah reflected on it, the dawdling they *both* did, she and Jacob, acting as co-conspirators when they had been younger, had always worked to test their mother's patience and endurance. Some of her own behavior in that regard had abated, she knew, now that she was almost an adult, with her having taken on some motherly responsibilities for Jacob. A year ago, she remembered, she would have intervened on her mother's behalf when he was pushing back as he so frequently did, especially when he was in one of his stubborn moods. Three years ago, Jojo would have stepped in. To discipline her, as well.

But everything was changed now, she knew.

Jacob was lost again.

They had learned from a telegram sent several months before, that Jojo had enlisted in the navy for a full year and was somewhere on an Ironclad ship on the Mississippi.

Her Aunt Kathleen was pregnant!

Kathleen's husband, Jon McEmeel, had gone missing. No one had heard from him for weeks.

And Dr. Brett had been killed.

Murdered by the guards, actually.

How had *she* survived herself, she wondered?

And how had she contributed to all of this?

She had failed Jacob, she knew. That was one very significant way in which she felt responsibility for all of these calamities.

How would they find Jacob, her perpetually lost, little boy brother?

It seemed impossible. According to Mr. Grimes, boys and girls, aged four to thirteen, picked up in a determined month-long police sweep that pulled almost three thousand homeless children off of the city streets, had been distributed for disposition to scores of private social service agencies throughout the city. In the bold social experiment, bypassing the normal procedures of orphanages that usually interred children for at least six months before out-placing them, the agencies then quickly transferred the children by train to communities across the northern states.

Beginning in late September and for several weeks afterwards, carload after carload of bewildered, excited children ages four to fourteen, scrubbed clean and, for the first time in most cases, clothed in donated but unsoiled garments, were sent out to over seventy small farm towns in Ohio, Pennsylvania, Indiana, Illinois, Iowa and Wisconsin, upper New York and then by other means of transportation, to hundreds more places. Some children had been sent as far as the Nebraska Territory!

"Better to get these children into Christian communities where they can possibly be adopted by hard-working, God-fearing Protestant families, than let them face the absolute certainty of freezing or starving to death on our streets during the upcoming winter," one well-respected minister had said. His earnest and eloquent plea had convinced enough participants in the city's extensive but disorganized welfare and social services community, that every group, including Catholics, Presbyterians, Baptists, Jewish and even a few non-denominational agencies contributed to the experiment.

By the time Sarah had found Mr. Grimes on October 2nd, Jacob, Robby and the Scarpello boys likely had been shipped out. But her mother was in Maryland, at the gravesite of Rory Brett, and when she returned from that sad trip, she and Inspector Grimes didn't figure that out for over a week afterwards. The police had no record of which one of over ninety westbound trainloads of children Jacob and the others might have been placed.

Knowing how paper and the writing on it could be lost or ruined in a sudden downpour, her mother had recorded three copies of the list they would follow in trying to find him. Sarah had helped record them. Each entry, culled and transcribed from seven of the ledgers of over forty-five of them that had shipped children within the last two weeks to towns in eight northern states, initial entries scribed by well-meaning, likely sweet, but harried volunteers of one beneficent society after another, gave minimal information that her mother or Mr. Grimes could use to find Jacob. Several agencies kept no records at all.

One entry she read had said simply : "Boy. Not teen. Deposited in Symerton, Illinois." No date.

Another said: "Male child, 8 or 9, Clam Falls, Wisconsin."

The first names of eighteen of the male children placed on recent west-bound trains had been recorded as "Jacob" "Jake" or simply the initial "J." Telegraphs sent to many locations had eliminated a good number of possibilities, but all of the ones on their list they would be following had sent no telegraph response. The most thorough records had been kept by the Children's Home Society, which also noted the surname of several of the receiving families and a brief description of the child. From that agency, however, of the ten children that were of Jacob's age and had at least the same first initial, none of the boys seemed to be a probable match.

Where was Clam Falls, Wisconsin, Sarah wondered?

Because the weather would be better in more southern climes during this time of year, the route they had chosen would take them to small townships across southern Pennsylvania and into Ohio and Indiana first. Mr. Grimes had volunteered to search in colder winter locations like upstate New York and western Massachusetts. But as each day passed, the possibility of recovering Jacob seemed to diminish. It was if Jacob again had become one little wind-tossed feather shaken out from a broken pillow onto the vicissitudes of an overcast, blustery day, Sarah thought.

She knew, as did her mother, that they had a terribly difficult search ahead of them, arduous, but so very different from what they had endured when trying to find Jacob in the Pacific Northwest's wilderness, four years ago. The great number of possible destinations would take months, maybe years to explore.

The orphan trains were a different form of kidnapping than that had been, Sarah reflected.

◇◇◇◇◇

She noticed as they headed to the train station this morning that her mother had sewn several strips of pretty colored silk material, a robin's egg blue, into the liner of the black petticoat's liner. She had asked her mother about that.

"It was from a dress I used to love, Sarah. I choose to see it as black with the color," Emmy had responded. "When accepting the black, we can see the color better, I've decided. Even if it's just for ourselves. At least that's what I'm trying to believe right now."

Their train slowly pulled out of the station, groaning and screeching as it overcame the inertia of its heavy load. Sarah put her fingers in her ears to block the shrieking, scraping metal-on-metal sounds and glanced over at her mother. Emmy had fallen asleep.

She watched her mother sleeping. It occurred to her that the way she slept, upright and straight like that, preserved her stateliness. She knew her mother didn't do that for any reason, however. That was just the way she was.

Sarah leaned across and looked at the papers Emmy held on her lap. It was Brett's last letter, she knew. She had seen her mother read and re-read the letter several times over the past few days. Emmy seldom showed very many emotions, especially grief, but Sarah knew that was the way her mother dealt with such things. Processing. Calmly. Her mother never burdened others with her feelings.

In a way, with her mother asleep, it made Sarah feel that she could go back to the private sorting she herself liked to do as well, in which she recollected all that she had experienced and tried to think about what it all meant.

She would think about Robby Hoyt again now, mull over all of the events again, hear his words, try to see his face again, from the time he had rescued them when she and Jacob were lost in the city, to the point at which both he and Jacob and the two Scarpello boys had been caught and sent off somewhere.

Why had she believed in Robby Hoyt, the way that she did? she asked herself.

That was how she survived, perhaps, she said to herself. By believing in him.

She thought about his words, the funny way he pontificated, the assertiveness with which he pronounced his philosophical observations, and the things he had said to her quietly in private.

She had never had the word "love" given to her in that way — the way she expected it might have meant when given to her mother by, God rest their souls, dear Rory Brett and her step father, dear Isaac.

What did Robby Hoyt really mean by that word when he used it that day, the last day she had seen him?

He had lain down next to her when Jacob, Jonny and Falco were asleep, all resting for a repeat of their biggest adventure — breaking in again during the night and following him around as he conducted another private tour for them of the wondrous Barnum American Museum building on Ann Street.

She had been awake, unable to sleep, anticipating seeing in the morning what he had promised to show her there — a real mermaid! It surprised her when Robby lay down next to her, because he had always slept alone in a room to the side of where they all slept.

In the darkness, he had reached over and gently touched her hand.

When he did that she was startled, remembering for a second that when she was a small girl, before she lived on their farm and saw animals mating, she thought that was how a woman got pregnant! Recollecting those thoughts, her reaction to his touch made her smile.

She had feelings for him, she knew and, as impudent as he always seemed to be, had wondered often how he felt about her. Then she thought about what it might mean to be pregnant. As much as she wanted Robby to touch her again, she became frightened.

"Not the right time in our lives, Young Sir," she said.

Robby looked over at her, surprised.

He nodded.

"You don't know what I was thinking," he said.

He kissed her on the cheek. Then he kissed the palm of her hand, and sat up.

She turned to him, wide-eyed, partly astonished partly pleased.

"Saw some guy do that to a dame once," he murmured.

She hadn't responded.

His back was to her.

"Guess I love you, Miss Pup," he said, sitting up. "Get some sleep."

He got up and left.

That had stunned her. She was left alone. She waited for him to come back, but he didn't.

Did he really love her? She wondered.

She had thought about all of that over and over again since that day.

She would put that on her long list of things she needed to understand, and in that way, control it better than how she had responded when he applied it to her — if and when it ever came along again — that "love." A wondrous thing it was, even in that form, and she wanted it to remain so, she thought. But because it had frightened her, she would not let it sneak up on her that way again. If and when it came — and if and when she accepted it — she would not let it wilt or wither away either.

Was that the way it — love that is — was supposed to be? Did he really love her? She wondered.

If so, why had he taken down the posters that would have let her and Jacob know that their aunt and then their mother had been looking for them for weeks?

Had he thought he was protecting her? Was that his way of showing "love?" Protecting her by keeping her?

Why had she believed Robby Hoyt, the way that she did? Had she made him into the gallant hero he so much wanted to be?

Was he one? A hero? Or was he a sick liar?

How much can one learn in just a few weeks, she wondered?

A lot, she realized.

Was that the way to acquire wisdom?

Her mother had told her once that one could control very little in one's life. What one *could* control, however, Emmy had said, was how one reacted to it all.

But would her mother really know about *these* things?

When would she tell her mother everything?

Would she?

Should she?

Could she ever?

CHAPTER THIRTY-FIVE

◇◇◇◇

Emmy

October 22nd, 1862 — New York to Baltimore

S he woke as the conductor passed through punching their tickets, but by the time the train pulled out of the station on its way to Baltimore, she started to drop away again.

It wasn't becoming, she knew. She wasn't setting a good example for Sarah, but she couldn't help it and wondered whether she should forgive herself a bit, stop fighting it and just let go, knowing that this could be a practice of sorts. Death wearing so many disguises, also could present itself this way, when it finally came some day, she knew-not that she was ready now-but she was determined to be dignified about it when the moment arrived. Then, she would withdraw with dignity, if she was fortunate. So controlling herself, fighting sleep, then drifting out, withdrawing quietly was a proper convenance.

She wondered . . . did the human species need death for the same purposes that its members needed sleep?

Did the collective of souls, the "mystical body," that Catholics talked about, the one that supposedly bound all sentient beings, need the death of its spent and worn-out members as an opportunity to refresh itself, as she had heard one preacher profess, in like manner as the body's cells rejuvenated themselves with sleep, predictably, in the cycle of each day?

Was that what war was really all about? Was the purging truly a Malthusian cleansing?

Or were death and sleep just inconvenient interruptions to one's living a fully conscious existence?

And how about love? She wondered.

Love, like Death came in many disguises as well, she mused. She always believed that one could not be human unless one had a *need* for Love.

In like manner, was Love, the "falling in" of it, also a similar inconvenience? And should it be controlled in the way she had tried so often to manage it — the way she was fighting sleep right now?

"The inconveniences of Love, Death and Sleep" . . . she smiled at the thought, as if it were the title of some abstract professorial thesis. She wondered if others felt that way. In what ways were they similar or dissimilar? Did one *have* to experience Love, the way one was forced to experience Death and Sleep? If one did not sleep one would certainly die, she believed. If one did not love, fully give of oneself to others, did one die, but in a different, slower way than if one refused to sleep?

Did one give to those whom one loved? Or was it the other way around? Rather, did we love those to whom we *give* — to those in whom we have invested ourselves?

And did one's soul perish if one did not fully give oneself to God? Investing oneself in God? That was certainly what she had been taught as a young girl.

She drifted off for a bit, but didn't dream, she realized when she woke when the train whistle sounded. She looked out the window at the white winter landscape passing quickly. They were heading into Pennsylvania. It was cold out there, she knew. She had seen white covered fields like this before, she knew, but didn't remember ever being on a train like this with that view.

Had it been in her dreams?

She wondered about dreams. If sleep was an inconvenience, she wondered, why was one given the opportunity to dream?

And what *were* dreams?

Were dreams the mind's way of escaping the inconvenient wasteful interruptions that sleep presented to her thinking life?

Or were dreams a delightful and terrifying vehicle of entertainment, given to humankind by God as compensation for the body's imperfect need to sleep?

Or, did God give humankind dreams to provide the mind's eye a new lens through which it might perceive all that it had experienced?

- To find an address for the things it couldn't ordinarily face?

- Repackage events in new, less trapping accouterments?
- Give symbolic handles to weighty, unresolved and unmanageable issues?
- Finish the cooking of raw victuals?
- Tie a name or face or color to imponderables, to help one replace the fearful amorphousness of one's feelings?
- Put categories and taxonomy to the things one sometimes imprecisely dropped into the soft hideaway bundles, like the pottage called "Love" by so many?

She didn't know. She had read many theories and had concluded none of the "experts" knew either.

Long ago, however, she had resolved to try to remember her dreams, record them occasionally, understanding that while she might never understand the dream-stories in themselves, doing so might help her understand that which she experienced during the preceding waking hours. She even had, on a few occasions, realized that she had used her dreams to understand things that had not *yet* occurred, but then did, so that when the event *did* in fact happen, she had been able to assuage herself and put into context things that might have been otherwise disconcerting or imponderable. She remembered that she had taught Sarah a word — "Prescience" — to describe a gift of foretelling. Perhaps remembering dreams made it easier to achieve that useful gift.

So, as much as she felt it was impolite to sleep in public, she welcomed dreams when they came and hoped that if she couldn't prevent herself from falling asleep on the first part of this next journey, at least she could dream a bit. Sort it all out *that* way, somehow . . . what had happened over the past several months. And what was to come.

◇◇◇◇◇

The melodious *Clack-Clack, Clack-Clack* of the train's passage over the steel rails blended into her waking moments, calming her, she realized. Rested now, she glanced over at Sarah on the bench across from her. As was her daughter's proclivity, she was watching every passenger who entered and exited.

She was almost fourteen now! Smart young woman already, precocious in so many ways, but so very tender and naive still, despite all she had seen.

Had she prepared Sarah the way she knew she must? Had she given her the right codes, the right questions to ask, so she could find the truth in what she would encounter, the problems she would have to confront in her own life? Would Sarah be a decisive and critical thinker when she was an adult? Had she taken enough time with Sarah?

She knew she hadn't done so for Jacob.

But somehow, perhaps because she had dreamed a good ending, she knew she would find him.

She had so very much to catch up on, with, and for him. For both of them.

Who was this Robby Hoyt? Sarah spoke about him very little, but with a sort of reverence, she noted. The little she had learned about him told her he was a complex young man who, at least the way Sarah described it, had watched over both her, Jacob and the two Scarpello boys.

She needed some time for Sarah to open up about what had occurred during the two months she and her brother were missing. When Sarah suddenly showed up a few weeks ago, Grimes had pounced on her. Where was Jacob?

Why hadn't she come forth before now? Sarah had just shut down and stopped talking altogether. When Emmy, carrying the grief of Brett's death, returned to New York and tried talking with her, Sarah was unusually non-communicative. It took repeated frustrating coaxing attempts to get enough information from her to figure out just what likely had happened to Jacob.

Emmy regretted that. She had run over Sarah with the anger she herself felt over so much that had happened. And that had made things much worse. Sarah was very confused now, she knew — with a lot bottled up inside.

Emmy had regained her composure and decided she needed to get Sarah's trust again. Patience worked off the top of a stubborn jar better than force ever could. Old wisdom. Less of a chance of breaking the bottle or churning its contents and ruining it completely.

She started to read Brett's last letter again and tried to think about him, but every time she had done this over the past four weeks, the swell of anger and remorse simply ruined her attempts to find a worthy explanation for all that had transpired, for all the misfortune and malice that had intervened since the time he had held her hand while lying in the grass, looking up at the sky on that blustery day in Boston. When he had proposed a future life together for them.

She regretted so much.

Had she accepted his handclasp too . . . lightly? His kisses too...respectfully? Even if she hadn't been ready to commit to him just then, might she have given him more . . . let go of his hand a second after, rather than before he did so? Let him kiss her fully? Would that have been honest? Would that have been a selfish act on her part, preserving his endearment, reserving her full affections for him until she had shaken free the memory of her own tragedies and the subsequent burdens she had taken on as a result? Or would have doing so been an act of kindness, a responsible gift to his heart, understanding that love changes and grows over time with the unfolding of one's understanding of another's soul? If one is patient.

Would her acceptance of his proposal have been misunderstood by him — as her acquiescence to the need for a more secure future for herself and her children?

Had she been presumptuous — assuming that Brett would wait for her — in this life or the next? Had she been arrogant?

And could she have done better by him when he was lost, by ramping up her assertiveness on his behalf when she learned he was in danger?

◇◇◇◇

The train moved into a tunnel and for thirty seconds she held her breath waiting for the light.

When it emerged, she sighed and felt anger swelling again.

It was interesting to her that Benjamin Butler, after the incident she had experienced in his office, took on the inspection of the Point Lookout prison where Brett had been kept, just as Butler had suggested he might do in his repulsive quid-pro-quo offer to her. But that vile opportunist's much ballyhooed inspection of Point Lookout had occurred six weeks too late. Brett was gone.

Had Butler done that as a way of atoning for his behavior, or as a clever way of covering himself from possible accusations? Or perhaps, she mused, was it Butler's cynical way of twisting her heart in a time of grief?

She wondered if the sudden disappearance of Jon McEmeel was in any way related to his promise to intervene on her behalf with Butler and his brother? Was Butler *that* vile?

Her sister Kathleen, now pregnant by her deceased lover, Escoffier, had interpreted and attributed McEmeel's disappearance as a consequence to her own misfortunes.

Poor Kathleen! Would she ever be able to escape from the traps she created for herself? Would they ever know what happened to McEmeel?

She thought about Butler again. He had once been a child...like Jacob. What had bent him and his brother into the persons they now were? she wondered. Evil, especially well-practiced as it seemed to be with that pair, was an acquired condition, she had always believed. Purposeful, pre-meditated murder, passion-induced killing, manslaughter and condoned violence — like what was happening all around this country now — all resulted from a loss of control and the failure of one's conscience to intercede...to effectively compete with one's baser instincts, didn't it? She had always taught her children that controlling passions, the exercise of discernment and the disciplining of temper was what separated a person's behavior from that of beasts.

She didn't believe — never had — that one was born "evil," or "sinful." Rather, each soul was inclined to be selfish and manipulative for its own survival. Her Jacob was a survivor, she knew. How would the events that he had to endure shape the rest of his life? Would he be "bent" or dysfunctional for the rest of his life? Would he someday be looked upon by others as an "evil" being? Would that be fair?

Given that consideration, did she have the fortitude to forgive the actions of evil beings like the aborigine Anah Nawitka, or the isthmus bandit Rafael Bocamalo, or the opportunist "Beast" Butler? Each had hurt her greatly. Each of them represented a test for her, she knew.

The shudder of the train as it braked entering the junction in New Rochelle distracted her from those thoughts.

From her cabin, she watched passengers boarding in the station and focused for a few moments on a couple walking arm in arm. The younger woman smiled up adoringly at the soldier, an officer in blue, who accompanied her. She thought about George Pickett. He had once worn blue like that. She was sad for the loss of the "Pickett George" she had known.

She would let that go. George Pickett was fixed for the duration of his life, she suspected, whether he survived this war, or not. Perhaps he was in love. She realized that she wished that she could have given herself permission to do that with him, put herself "in love." But it never would have worked out between the two of them, she knew.

She wished she could have given herself permission for many things.

To have been so much more *giving*.

She looked down at Brett's letter again and the poem she'd been able to expose by rubbing carbon pencil shavings onto the scratched impressions on the page, making the writing readable, albeit in negative:

"——- *t not, My Love*
Time now has been.
You are here, away.
In and out and in,
You are there, close."

Was the first word in the poem "Forget" or was it "Desert"?

She couldn't tell because it was too faint.
It made a difference, she knew.

She fell asleep again.

The rain's percussion on the roof of the car blended into a sweet but bitter reassurance, now mixing with the train's more predictable patter over the tracks.

She saw Jacob now.

She saw Brett.

CHAPTER THIRTY-SIX

◇◇◇◇

Jojo

December 12, 1862

Because of the many sandbars and submerged obstacles, the *U.S.S. Cairo* seldom traveled at night on any of the rivers, particularly the Yazoo, on which it had been assigned to patrol. Over the past two weeks, the ship had destroyed every rebel battery as far up as fifteen miles from the Yazoo's entry into the Mississippi.

The Western command had assigned the *Cairo* one final, additional mission, to batter a reputed stronghold of Confederate infantry sixteen miles upriver, before returning to its base in Memphis. The captain, thinking it would be best to surprise the rebel camp with an early morning

385

raid, decided to risk moving his big black ship in complete darkness through that snag and sandbar-laden stretch of the river — a hazardous task, even during daylight.

Jojo was fitfully asleep in a dreamless part of his slumber, when the first torpedo-mine exploded. His hammock swung towards the starboard bulkhead as the ship started to lean. The second mine's detonation tore a huge gash in the boiler. The ship began flooding rapidly. Men scurried up from the lower decks through the steam billowing upwards to escape drowning in the sinking iron coffin.

"Abandon ship! God damnit," he heard someone, possibly McClinton, bellowing through a megaphone.

Jojo looked over the rail and could make out three butternut-clad men, silhouetted by the torch one of them carried, whooping and cheering on the banks of the river. On the other side of the river a crowd of cheering men and women hooted and hollered as the big ship foundered.

The *Cairo* had only two shore boats. One had been moored right next to where the remotely detonated mine had exploded. The second boat, near the stern, was already full of men.

He jumped into the water and began swimming. He had never been afraid of what men called "cold" here on the Mississippi. He had swum in the Pacific Northwest's rivers. *That* was cold, he told himself.

All 187 men escaped the sinking of the *Cairo* that night. Jojo and twenty-two other men suffered broken bones or near drowning and were taken to the U.S.S. *Stanton*, a hospital ship, for recovery. When the *Stanton* docked in Cincinnati later that week, Jojo, holding the smeared but still-legible letter from attorney Patrick Dolan, walked away and headed for the rail station.

It was time to get back east and see Mrs. Evers.

He had had enough of this navy business and the fight of these passionate, methodical, crazy white men.

EPILOGUE

◇◇◇◇

Sarah

December 14th, 1862-Another small town, Wisconsin

The train slowed a mile or so before finally lugging to a stop at the shack that served as a station for the town of Paddock, Wisconsin. This small town was like the others Sarah and her mother had visited over the past four weeks. Hard-working, poor farm people in hard lives, had been given what was considered the chaff of society — big-city street waifs who, by the time they were shipped out to towns like this, had a survivor's fix on it all. A poor mix it was — an "immiscible recipe," as she heard her mother describe it, all of it created by well-intentioned do-gooders.

Could the chaff take roots when cast onto hard soil like this, she wondered?

It was cold outside and she wondered how it would bite when she and her mother descended into it again. Best to get into it fast. She was used to that now.

Fast immersions — shocking plunges, actually — was what she decided she had lived through these past few, fast years.

Fast immersions. Yes, that's what they really had been, Sarah realized the more she thought about it, as she buttoned her coat up to her neck. She had been born in some warmth on a Oregon Territory summer day, then bathed in the comfortable, lapping waters of her Northwest island home, slowly heated into her awkward, awakened life by a never-scalding, seldom-scolding sun.

And then something, some crow of God or some god-crow, took her outside and dipped her into one icy river after another.

The trips she took, away from her island home with her mother and brother, expanded what she knew about herself in relationship to everyone else, her place in the small part of the world she felt she owned, and her purpose in it, this bigger "adult" world, and where she herself might end up.

Her spirit had almost burst from those immersions, she felt, they had come on so fast, so cold that they slowed her pulse while she was in the plunge.

Fast immersions, then the bitter rewarming that quickened her heartbeat again. It was the out-coming, the reawakening that she hated the most about those experiences. Waiting for the bone chill to subside.

And each one, each deep dip into the realities of how adults saw and shaped it all, instilled a different memory of pain: San Francisco had scared her, more than the Isthmus did, even though Panama's jungle had been so different from the cold forests of the Oregon Territory, where *nothing* stuck to you — so unlike the way everything behaved in the jungle, where *everything* seemed to melt or decay on, and into you.

San Francisco had almost overwhelmed her, and she realized it was because of all of the souls passing in front and behind her, not stopping long enough for her proper discernment. At least on the Isthmus train, before the robbery, before she had gotten lost again, she had time to watch them for a while, some of those other souls.

And then on came Boston, with all its confused, confident people.

And then on came the east coast's Washington, the capital of confusion, where everyone seemed to be abiding and cleaving to conundrums, with senior people trying to pass their deductions from the grand mess, on to her and everyone else.

But it was the underworld in the caverns of New York that had impressed and scared her the most.

With old Robby Hoyt. Sarah smiled thinking about how she had come to thinking about him.

◇◇◇◇

She and her mother waited for a half hour for the preacher who was supposed to pick them up. Snow started falling, and its fine shimmering dust covered her hat and shoulders by the time the man arrived, muttering a passel of apologies for his tardiness.

Looking up at the vast prairie's gray horizon from the buckboard, she wondered about where she stood now under the big sky of this bigger world that she didn't know, but now understood *did* exist, and she compared her stance to how the adults she knew placed *themselves* in it. They had told her stories about even *bigger* places than this, with buildings and edifices made of stone-not-wood — granite, marble, sandstone — each durable, but with different life expectancies, each giving a different, false sense of permanency.

So the world was even bigger than she had ever imagined.

The adults told her about *millions* of souls walking about — so many, that one couldn't possibly study them the way she liked to do — to hold them in front of her — to see their destinies and predict how they might end up. She had once thought that doing so — practicing it constantly, would make her old soul's wisdom complete. But perhaps that never could be. Life-long, incomplete learning, then?

In any case, she, herself felt much smaller now in this world, whatever its dimensions, at the beginning of her fourteenth year. She wondered whether her ancient wisdom would wilt before she could get home again, wherever that turned out to be. It couldn't wither, because wilting was different than withering, wasn't it? She tried to remember.

Wilting, as she understood it from the lessons given to her by her mother, and applied to what she was now pondering, happened to young souls, young budding blooms like her, who hadn't experienced love yet, and were confronted, unprepared, by the heat of passion, ruining them before their time. *Withering* happened to old souls, long on the vine, who had *lost* love and then had dried up. But at least those souls *had* experienced it at least once, hadn't they? she hoped.

Would she need to accept love to prevent a wilting, she wondered?

Would she need to accept love and risk a withering some day?

Couldn't she avoid that withering...keep it, love that is, in its full, intense colorful array forever? How would she need to exercise love to prevent its withering, once accepted? How did one do that?

Or was withering an inevitability and what one needed to become a complete, old soul — experience the loss to fully appreciate the beauty of a loving in life — then fade away into dust? And if so, did that precious dust, what remained of old, complete souls, then become the soil God gave to new souls to germinate their love?

Was it possible to avoid both "wilting" and "withering"? Was she caught in fear between the two extremes?

Need she be?

Old Robby, she thought again, as she and her mother climbed down from the preacher's buckboard to the town's boarding house.

Where had Old Robby gone?

They hadn't found Jacob yet. They felt no closer to finding him.

Would Jacob survive this time, in this next chapter of his young life?

Would Robby be there to protect him this time, she wondered, as she thought about how he had tried doing so with her?

Author's Notes

NON-FICTION CHARACTERS:

General Benjamin "Beast" Butler (1818-1893) — Massachusetts Senator Benjamin Butler prominently established himself as an influential national politician and after forming two state regiments responding to Lincoln's call for a volunteer army, was named one of many "political generals" of the US Army during the American Civil War. Always controversial and aggressive, accused of corruption and opportunistic enrichment, widely considered inept as a military leader, he achieved the epithet "Beast Butler" as the result of his actions as the commander of New Orleans during its occupation. ***Butler's General Order Number 28***, infuriated southern citizens and received widespread criticism from critics in the north as well as abroad. Known as "the Woman's Order," it decreed that any woman *"showing contempt or insulting"* any U.S. Army officer or soldier should be treated as a *"woman of the town, plying her avocation"* (meaning solicitation of prostitution). The order authorized harsh measures including imprisonment for any woman so accused. Southern women decried the order as a legalization of abuse and rape. Because of this criticism as well as repeated accusations of Butler's corruption, Lincoln moved his political ally away from New Orleans and into the position of military governor of the Virginia peninsula. Butler, along with his brother Andrew Jackson Butler, amassed a huge fortune during the brief time they controlled New Orleans. He was accused of war crimes and profiteering, but after the assassination of President Lincoln, those investigations ceased. In 1863, to substantial fanfare, he did inspect Point Lookout Prison. Ref: *Butler, Benjamin E., Autobiography and Personal Reminiscences of Major General Butler, Benjamin E., 1892*; Hearn, Chester G., When the Devil Came Down to Dixie — Ben Butler in New Orleans. Baton Rouge: University of Louisiana Press, 1997.

George Pickett (1825-1875) and Sallie Anne Corbel (1843-1931) — George Pickett left San Juan Island, Washington after the Fort Sumter attack, resigning his commission as a U.S. Army Captain. By way of the Isthmus railroad, he traveled back to Virginia where he was given the rank of Lieutenant Colonel in James Longstreet's division of the newly formed Army of Northern Virginia. Pickett distinguished himself admirably in several battles and quickly ascended in rank. In the July 27, 1862 during an Confederate advance at the Battle of Gaines Mill (sometimes known as the Battle of the Chickahominy River), newly promoted Brigadier General Pickett sustained a serious shoulder wound. He met 18 year old Corbel "Sally"

Corbell shortly after that and married her in 1863 in Richmond, Virginia. Ref: Cordon, Lesley J., Pickett — *General George E. Pickett in Life & Legend*, Chapel Hill: The University of North Carolina Press, 1998.

General Winfield Scott (1786-1866), who achieved fame for his leadership in both the War of 1812 and the Mexican-American War of 1846, was the commander of U.S. Military at the outbreak of the war. With Lincoln, he devised the "Anaconda Plan" — a blockade of southern ports, control of New Orleans and the Mississippi, and destruction of southern rail lines — which severely restricted the Confederacy's economy. Scott was asked to command a newly formed 75,000 man army composed mostly of inexperienced volunteers. Almost half of the trained officers had resigned their commissions, including Robert E. Lee, Thomas "Stonewall" Jackson, Albert Sydney Johnston, Joseph Johnston, and George Pickett, to join the Confederate Army.

Despite his extensive battle experience and repeated diplomatic successes, Scott was criticized and ridiculed as being a dysfunctional and useless relic of the past. In June of 1862, Lincoln and Scott approved General Irwin McDowell's plan to take the Confederate capital with an inexperienced army. After the disastrous US military's defeat at the battle of Bull Run, during which he was accused of napping at the telegraph in his Washington D.C. Headquarters, Scott, then seventy-three years old, was replaced and retired by Lincoln. Ref: Johnson, Timothy D., *Winfield Scott — the Quest for Military Glory*, Kansas: The Press for the University of Kansas, 1998

Colonel Lafayette Guild, M.D., (1825-1870) directed the medical corps of the Army of Northern Virginia. In his pre-war years he distinguished himself by his studies of Yellow Fever. During the war, after Robert E. Lee's emergence as the commander of the Confederate forces, Guild became his personal physician. Ref: Freemon, Frank R., *Gangrene and Glory* — Medical Care during the American Civil War, Urbana: University of Illinois Press, 2001.

Janie James (birth and death dates unknown), the proprietor of the infamous "Noah's Ark" house of ill-fame in Richmond, began her career shortly after the Union Army occupied Alexandria, Virginia, thereby displacing hundreds of professional "pleasure workers." When the Confederacy moved its capital from Montgomery Alabama to Richmond, it stationed thousands of soldiers on the peninsula to defend it, providing an ample supply of customers for the prostitution business. Arrested and jailed several times, James had been a school teacher before the hardships of war prompted her to take up a profession that she described as being much more profitable.

Josephine DeMeritt (birth and death dates unknown), cleverly managed her discrete business for the wealthy upper class of Richmond until the city fell in 1865. In contrast to Janie James Noah's Ark, Demerritt's plush(establishment, located less than two blocks away from the Confederacy's Presidential mansion, was never raided, nor was DeMeritt ever arrested. Ref: Lowry, M.D., Thomas P., *The Story the Soldiers Wouldn't Tell — Sex in the Civil War*, Mechanicsville: Stackpole Books; 1994

PLACES AND EVENTS:

The Memphis Battle

The Union's navy, consisting of mainly ironclad steam-powered ships, easily crushed the make-shift, motley assortment of poorly armed river boats that had hastily been assembled by the Confederates. Called "Cotton-clads" by observers, so named because of the cotton bales stacked on their decks, the rebel "fleet" initiated the shooting, determinately charging into the anchored line of Union boats. Within minutes, the first rebel ship was sunk. The entire battle lasted less than an hour, and only one Confederate ship escaped from the fray. The mayor and city council of Memphis immediately surrendered the town after the defeat, thus avoiding the fate of Vicksburg which was devastated after a year-long Union siege. Ref: Bryan, Tony, *Mississippi River Gunboats of the American Civil War*, 1861-65, Long Island: Osprey Books, 2002

First Battle of Manassas (Bull Run)

As described by many historians, the first Manassas (Bull Run) battle, up to that point the bloodiest in the history of the young country, represented for many the end of innocence as well as naive assumptions about the romance of war. It also signaled to both sides that the war would be a long and hard-fought conflict. The battlefield itself is well preserved by the National Park Service. For those who cannot visit, this animated map from the Civil War Trust (https://www. civilwar.org/learn/maps/first-manassas-animated-map) nicely depicts the events during the battle's evolution. Ref: Hines,

Blaikie, *The Battle of First Bull Run — Manassas Campaign — July 16-22*, Thomasen: American Patriot Press, 2011

Chimborazo Hospital

By the time the Peninsula War began in the summer of 1862, almost fifty different hospitals had opened in and around Richmond to deal with the thousands of injured and ill men. Chimborazo's 71 wards, located atop the city's highest hill, housed 3500 casualties, more than half of all of the other Richmond hospitals combined. As Richmonds largest facility, it provided care for over 70,000 patients between the initial stages of the conflict until 1865. Ref: Calcutt, Rebecca Barbour, Richmond's Wartime Hospitals, Grema: Pelican Publishing Company, 2004. Green, Carol C. Chimborazo, Knoxville: University of Tennessee, 2004;

Wartime Military Medical Care

During the American Civil War, far more casualties in both armies resulted from diseases than from bullets. Measles, Smallpox, Yellow Fever, Malaria, chronic diarrhea and — for the Confederate army — malnutrition incapacitated thousands. **Jonathan Letterman, M.D. (1824 – 1872)**, appointed Surgeon General during the re-structuring of the U.S. Army by General McClellan, is credited with developing a well-organized battlefield evacuation system that saved thousands of lives on the Union side. By contrast, the letters of his counterpart, **Lafayette Guild, M.D.**, indicate that the Confederate army medical corps, beset by constant supply and personnel shortages, was much less successful. The National Civil War Medical

Museum in Fredrick, Maryland (http://www.civilwarmed. org) provides excellent exhibits depicting the state of medical care in the mid-19th century. Ref: Cunningham, H.H., *Doctors in Gray — The Confederate Medical Service*, Baton Rouge: Louisiana State University Press, 1958; Faust, Drew Gilpin, *This Republic of Suffering — Death and the American Civil War*, New York: Vintage Books, 2009; McGaugh, Scott. Surgeon in Blue — *Jonathan Letterman, the Civil War Doctor Who Pioneered Battlefield Care*, New York: Arcade Publishing, 2013;

GENERAL REFERENCES:

Asbury, Herbert, *The Gangs of New York*, New York, Vintage Books, 2008 (reprint from 1927 original); Brasher, Glenn David, *The Peninsula Campaign & the Necessity of Emancipation*, Chapel Hill: The University of North Carolina Press, 2012; Cisco, Walter Brian, *War Crimes Against Southern Civilians*, Gretna: Pelican Publishing Company, 2013; Gamwel, Lynn and Tomes, Nancy, *Madness in America — Cultural and Medical Perceptions of Mental Illness before 1914*, Ithica: Cornell University Press, 1995; Goodheart, Adam, *1861 — The Civil War Awakening*, New York: Vintage Books, 2011; Goodwin, Doris Kearns, *Team of Rivals — The Political Genius of Lincoln*, New York: Simon & Schuster, 2005; Grimsley, Mark, *The Hard Hand of War — Union Military Policy Toward Southern Civilians, 1861-1865*, Cambridge: Cambridge University Press, 1995; Newcomer, Elsie Renalds and Ramsey, Janet Renalds, *1861 — Life in the Shenandoah Valley*, Mechanicsville: Hills and Mills, 2011; Newcomer, Elsie Renalds and Ramsey, Janet Renalds, *1862*

— Life in the Shenandoah Valley, Mechanicsville: Hills and Mills, 2012; Reis, Jacob, *How the Other Half Lives*, New York: Charles Scribner & Sons, 1890; Sanders, Jr., Charles W., *While in the Hands of the Enemy — Military Prisons of the Civil War*, Baton Rouge: Louisiana State University Press, 2005; Whitaker, Robert, *Mad in America*, New York: Basic Books; 2002;

THE FAIRNESS OF BEASTS

Acknowledgments

To:
Allen Hurt and Barbara LaSalle,
for their consistent, constructive inspiration

To:
John DeDakis, Archana Murthy, Randy Mott,
Neil Gonzalez, Rose Ambrosio Bradley, Mike Green,
James Ferrari, Alex Head, Scott James, Francesca LaSalle,
Angela LaSalle, Patti Campbell McKillop, Brian McK-
illop, David McClinton, James Polley, Geoff Robinson,
Tom Skerritt,
Maureen Matthiesen Weber and Terry Wilkinson
for their production assistance, encouragement
and comments

THE FAIRNESS OF BEASTS

Reader's Guide Questions

1. What was General Winfield Scott's "Anaconda Plan?" Was it effective?

2. What was a "Political General" as employed by President Abraham Lincoln?

3. Why were escaped slaves called "Contraband" and what was the origin of that term?

4. Who were the "Wide Awakes" and what was their platform?

5. Discuss the reasons for the Union's surprising defeat at the First Battle of Bull Run (Manassas) in the summer of 1861.

6. What was the main cause of morbidity and mortality during the American Civil War?

7. What was "Hard War" as practiced by General John Pope in the Shenandoah Valley? Why was it not conducted in similar manner in other parts of Virginia, especially the western part of the state?

8. Discuss the military prison conditions in both the Confederacy and Union?

9. Why did Abraham Lincoln and Jefferson Davis suspend the rights of Habeus Corpus?

10. Discuss the impact of the Irish "Potato Famine" on the outcome of the American Civil War.

11. What was the prevalence of child homelessness during the mid-Nineteenth century in major eastern U.S. cities, especially New York, Philadelphia, Boston and Chicago?

About the Author

A physician, sculptor, award-winning filmmaker, and author, Gar LaSalle has been honored widely in the medical and fine arts communities for his leadership and creativity.

LaSalle's 1976 award winning feature length documentary, *Diary of a Moonlighter* premiered nationally on PBS and was the first-ever film about the new specialty of Emergency Medicine.

His two award-winning historical fiction novels. *Widow Walk*, published in 2014 by Greenleaf won multiple awards including the Eric Hoffer Award for Literature, the eLit Silver Medal, the IndieReaders Award for Best Novel, and the San Francisco Book Festival Grand Jury Prize for General Fiction.

Isthmus, published in 2015 by Avasta Press, the first sequel in the saga, was a finalist for the PNWWA Nancy Pearl award for literature.

Widow Walk has been optioned by Heyou Media Inc. for a feature film.

http://www.garlasalle.com/about/bio/

WIDOW WALK

THE FIRST BOOK IN THE AWARD-WINNING WIDOW WALK SAGA

I t is 1859 in the verdant, unexplored territory of the Pacific Northwest. While the American and British military square off over a boundary dispute, ambitious pioneers clash in a violent cultural war with indigenous "aboriginal" populations over control of this vast, fertile land.

Widow Walk is the compelling story of a courageous, young pioneer woman's perilous attempt to find her kidnapped son after her family home is attacked and her husband is murdered in a revenge massacre by a sociopathic predator. Built around the journey of the main character, Emmy Evers, this is a is a rich, deep story about love, greed, loneliness and revenge.

This new edition of *Widow Walk* (now optioned for a feature film), first published in 2015, won the Eric Hoffer New Horizon Award for best fiction, the USA Best Book Award, the Indie Readers Award for best fiction, the the eLit Silver Medal, the Grand Jury Prize for best fiction in the San Francisco Book Festival, and was a finalist for the International Book Awards.

"*Widow Walk* is American historical fiction in the finest tradition, a direct descendent of *Last of the Mohicans* and *Cold Mountain*. LaSalle recounts the brutal, poignant clash between Native American Indian tribes and white settlers in the Pacific Northwest with economy and beauty, writing clean, devastating prose that clutches at your heart. This lean, unsparing narrative will make you look away in sorrow—before raising your fist in triumph. A quintessential rendering of the American Experience."

—Richard Barager, author of *Altamont Augie*
Silver Medal winner 2011 Book of the Year Awards

Available at Amazon, Solipsispublishing.com, and
GarLaSalle.com

ISTHMUS

THE SECOND BOOK IN THE AWARD-WINNING WIDOW WALK SAGA

It is 1860 and revolution is erupting throughout the world over universal emancipation. Civil war looms in the Unites States. In the midst of it all, a young woman is moving back to Boston with what is left of her family, devastated and bankrupted by savage, tragic events that occurred less than a year ago in the Pacific Northwest.

They traverse a hostile terrain on the new Panama isthmus railroad, the most modern transportation in the world. From inside their coach they watch the humid forest, a different type of green from what they knew up north, slipping fast past, a warm verdant blur. Looking down the aisle they see an uncomfortable array of fellow travelers, an international mix of characters whom they will get to know all too well . . . each with hidden hopes and dreams . . . predators and victims, desperadoes and hangmen, widows and widow makers. A convenient ride through the jungle. An inconvenient assault. A run for their lives.

This new edition of *Isthmus*, first published in 2016, was a finalist for the Pacific Northwest Writers Association Nancy Pearl Award for excellence in fiction.

Available at Amazon, Solipsispublishing.com, and GarLaSalle.com

CPSIA information can be obtained
at www.ICGtesting.com
Printed in the USA
FSHW011018030219
55450FS

9 780997 8436